Love Returns
Through The
Portal Of
Time

KS. MICHAELS

Outskirts Press, Inc.
Denver, Colorado

Outskirts Press, Inc.
http://www.outskirtspress.com

ISBN: 978-1-4327-1760-5

Library of Congress Control Number: 2007940718

Outskirts Press and the "OP" logo are trademarks belonging to Outskirts Press, Inc.

PRINTED IN THE UNITED STATES OF AMERICA

This book is dedicated to my children, whose sweet souls have taught me more than I could ever have imagined.

Cover Story

The title, Love Returns Through the Portal of Time, is, in itself, a mouthful of mystery. The suspense takes hold from the turn of the very first pages as Gayle; the witch from Jason's incessant childhood nightmares is burned at the stake in a time where witchcraft was something from the forgotten past. Unbeknownst to Jason's parents, was a gift of healing that developed from the trauma of his childhood, the burns he received from his dreams. Shifting through time as the story unfolds, the soul of two people find how difficult, and yet, how easy, it was to remain together through the toils of eternity.

Once you establish the similarities of characters that take place through the time warp, the suspense intensifies. Jason lived out his life with his beloved wife in a time where science of the psyche was an untouched world.

In the present, Mike was a young, precocious soul who tried to survive tragedy and the loss of his identity that took place after dropping out of school and leaving the home of his abusive mother.

Dreams, visions, and an awareness of latent powers taunted him throughout his strife. The mystery behind the lady in white became a common occurrence at every turn. Pieces of the puzzle of life slowly came to view with every new relationship.

He befriended a beautiful diva named Crystal and soon became her lover. As her career took root with a rock and roll band, they found themselves growing more distant by the driving wedge of her alcoholism. Again, Mike found himself alone and lost from love. And again, the lady in white visits him. Another tragedy follows when Mike's brother chose to take his own life when the challenge of accepting his homosexuality had become too great a task.

By this time, Mike's powers intensified in salvoes. Sadness, destitution, anguish and hunger would normally force a person to a criminal life, but not Mike. The driving negative forces only make him and his psyche more powerful, hungrier for success and love.

Visions of his past-lives unfolded with less mystery. Faces of lost friends appeared in new ones. Events came to pass as foretold in his visions. And the lady in white was visiting his dreams more often, her face becoming more familiar. Destiny, instead of in fragments of puzzle pieces, come to pass in full-length, film-like daydreams.

The story culminates with the totally unexpected. The past came to meet the present with only visions to guide the way clear. A time capsule was discovered. Its contents were, both shocking and yet expected and confirming. One could only wonder what he might leave for himself in a time capsule to be found by him in a future incarnation. And what of the lady in white? Was she from the past, future or both, now that they finally found each other?

Chapter One
The Dream

Awakened by her own screams, Gayle opened her eyes. The small, dank dungeon cell offered no amenities. Her bloody wrists and ankles were shackled with heavy, rusted irons. She wiped the tears from her swollen eyes and cheeks with the apron of her dress. The dream was real and vivid to her as it had been many times before. With dawn upon her, Gayle had been accused by the people of the village, led by the Reverend Parris, of being a witch and consorting with the devil. In the past five years, there had been more than a dozen such trials, all of which culminated in the horrid sentencing of death.

As the encroaching flames grew greater, Gayle's braving face swelled red with ashen blisters. Her waist length hair ignited, as did her blood stained dress. The pain more immense by every passing moment, Gayle wrestled with the ropes that

1

bound her. The villagers, now with less anger in their eyes, read only of grotesque curiosity, curious of death and its nature of arrival. Gayle burned before their very eyes and yet no one of the phlegmatic crowd would hide from the sight. A painful, spine chilling, scream exuded through the air. With her body limp against the stake, she died.

One man, her neighbor, was boiled alive in a caldron for his conviction of witchcraft. Later, that same year his wife and three children followed, but by different means of pillory and torture.

The women accused of witchcraft were to be burned. Another heinous torture that many men fell fated to was that of the crushing beneath heavy stones. Their death is inevitable, but the stones are applied slowly to assure a confession of guilt, although, no man had lived long enough to give his confession. No one really knows how the conjecture and accusations of witchcraft and sorcery had begun, but many believe that it was originally a dispute over land and the proprietors. Many were accused and many died horrible deaths.

Gayle's father, Samuel Harris, possessed a belief similar to that of a physiocrat, he believed that land and the products are the only true sources of wealth and prosperity. At the time of Gayle's incarceration, Samuel was the owner of the most land throughout Salem. The previous owners of the most land had already been tried and put to death for crimes of witchcraft.

From the time of her premature birth, Gayle had

turned many heads and lifted as many brows with her clever and perceptive idiosyncrasies. Many of the townspeople defined her as "unnatural." She had an uncanny learning ability. When she was a young child, her mother, Sara never needed to train her twice in any of her schooling. By the time Gayle was ten years of age, she had learned all that her mother was capable of teaching. As Gayle grew older, her learning abilities had accelerated. As a result, her mother tried feverishly to protect and shroud her from influencing any of the neighboring villagers. The people of Salem were very superstitious. If any of the villagers had learned of Gayle's abilities, they most certainly would have feared her and would have had her put to death. One evening, when Gayle was just nine years old, her parents had invited friends over for supper and to talk of future plans for the church. As the meal was nearly over, Gayle fell tranced and abruptly stood up beside the table. With table settings crashing to the floor, Gayle just stood, still and quiet at first. Then, after several seconds, while everyone sat in question, she stepped back away from the table and proceeded to amble her way around the table. As she reached the chair that seated the woman who befriended her mother, Gayle began to speak in a low, gruff voice, very different from her own.

"Why art thou here?" she asked. "I see thou art sick with the stomach plague. Before the twentieth moon of the coming month, thou will be encountered by the grieving. And by mornin', your ashes will meet with the fertile soil." She collapsed to the floor. The trance had ended leaving Gayle tired and weak.

Sara quickly jumped to her feet, collected Gayle and shuffled her off to bed. At first the dinner guests showed slow reaction. Then, their anger was roused by fear. Ultimately, passing it off as a daft prank, they left that evening shortly after the episode. Sara had apologized for Gayle's behavior, explaining that she enjoyed playing games of that kind and that she meant no harm by them. But of course, the guests were not impressed in the least and showing their appalled dislike for the performance, they warned Samuel and Sara to keep Gayle from the public eye if she so feels fit to continue with playing her childish games.

To Gayle the truth was certain and obvious, to others, merely frightening. Twice before, Gayle had saved her father's life through the mystery of her waking premonitions. Once he was saved from the fever, from which many people of the village had died. Second, Samuel was saved from being crushed inside a barn that had collapsed beneath a tree after it had been struck by lightening, just as Gayle had predicted.

Gayle had also discovered cures by way of roots and herbs for various illnesses. The Harris' knew this power of magic could only be a gift from God. For if it were not, the power would no doubt be used for the favors of evil. This was clearly not the case. Only the power of God could be so kind to help those who suffer. But even still, these powers had to be harbored from all others because others saw this gift as only evil, the artifice of the devil through witchcraft. On the twentieth moon of the following month, the woman who was seated at the table died of a stomach disease. At the time, no one made mention of the prediction.

One warm summer afternoon, when Gayle was sixteen, she had taken a stroll down by the stream to fetch some water for the evening supper. The cooling water was refreshing to the touch. She paused from her chore and set to rest beside a tree.

Gayle was an enchanted looking young girl with long, brown, waist-length hair that resembled waves of soft, shiny silk. Her skin was white as smooth, virgin snow. But her finest quality was not of her beauty. Her calming, hypnotic quality of mannerism and innocent charm were superior to her physical. At first glimpse of her, one becomes lured to her as the sailors did to the songs of Sirens. With her ebony eyes her lure was of a halcyon splendor.

Gayle stood beside the stream gazing into the reflection of the dancing sun across the top of the water. She reached for the ties at the back of her bonnet, slowly pulling one lace free from the knot, allowing the bonnet to fall free to the ground. Her hair cascaded down her slender shoulders to its length. With her one hand propped against the tree, Gayle unlocked her boot buckles. After slipping out of her boots, she stepped slowly into the shallow waters of the streambed.

Not a single animal of the forest feared her

presence. The steady fish merely kissed away the bubbles from her ankles. The habitants of the forest gathered at the water's edge beside Gayle, as she stood sylph-like and knee deep in the cooling and refreshing water. Not far in the distance, in a sylvan glade, a stag of righteous majesty watched. At first he kept his distance, then cautiously approached. His powerful features grew more immense as he drew closer to Gayle. He ate berries from her hand that she had instinctively picked from the bush beside the streambed moments before the stag had appeared. The animals soon resumed the tasks of their own daily activities.

Gayle suddenly felt eerie, feeling of dread and pain accompanied by the taste of salt on her tongue. The pain was not her own, but of a stranger. She jerked on her boots as the remaining squirrels scampered off. Her premonition called her to a weakened bridge, just a few hundred yards away. Her first notion was unclear. She ran as fast as she could. The closer she got to the bridge the stronger the feeling of dread became. Upon arrival at the bridge, out of breath and with blistered feet from not taking the time to buckle her boots, Gayle encountered Reverend Parris with three women from his congregation. She hurriedly urged them to step off the bridge.

"What is thou concern child?" the Reverend asked.

"There's no time to explain, Reverend Sir," Gayle answered, still gasping for breath, "Thou must leave the bridge at once, 'tis going to fall. A young man will fall from his horse, break both his legs and bleed to death."

The three women who were in the company of the Reverend began to whisper amongst themselves. Gayle was ignored and scoffed at by the ladies. The Reverend stood upon the bridge with the ladies and his hands were cradled out in the direction of Gayle, who was standing just off to the side of the bridge.

"This be a fine bridge as 'tis been for many years child. And certainly thou can see, I ride no horse. I cannot fathom the game thou plays, but if 'tis what thou wish, so be it, Little One." The Reverend turned to the ladies and put forth an outstretched arm, gesturing the ladies' formal passage before him. As the ladies proceeded, a laugh broke out between them and the Reverend.

"I warn thee, please hurry! Thou must be quick!" Gayle said with a panic in her voice. But obviously, they did not take heed. Before they were halfway across the bridge, they had resumed their conversation, ignoring Gayle and her plea.

From a narrow passage behind the thickened brush came an out-of-control horse with its rider unable to control its charge. The approaching horse had startled a rattlesnake that had been resting in the shade beside the road. As the snake displayed his brash by sounding his rattles, the horse became feral and crazed. With a startling bray, its canter pace immediately drew upon salvoes of adrenalin and commenced an uncontrolled race through the forest brier.

The pompous and ignorant ladies, still upon the

bridge, suddenly turned. A curious, thunderous sound permeated the air and even the noble Reverend Parris ceased his boastful sermon to listen. The steed now closer and in open view, Gayle could see her premonition coming to reality. The froth about the mouth and the sweat from the large animal's powerful body had formed white foam. Droplets of the foam had sprayed from the horse and shot through the air in Gayle's direction, the sour and salty sweat landed upon her face and mouth.

The three frightened ladies scurried over to the bridge's end and dove over the side, just shy of the water's edge. But the proud and foolish Reverend stood palsied, unable to move his trembling legs. Now less than ten meters between them and what was to be a horrible collision, the horse reared up onto his hind legs, displaying grandeur of size, strength and beauty, but to the Reverend, the downfall meant a trampling death. Suddenly, a loud crack pierced the air and the ground began to shake beneath Gayle's feet. As the weary rider clutched firmly at the snaffle and the mighty steed rolled his hooves to the sky, the bridge came apart beneath the mighty animal. The trestles came through the decking planks with a tumultuous explosion. In an instant, the horse and rider vanished beneath the remaining pier.

As the cloud of dust settled, Gayle, the Reverend and the ladies saw the young man lying in the water. Both his legs had compound fractures. The horse was gone. Evidently, he was unharmed and had run off into the forest. But unfortunately, the rider was not blessed with such luck. The protruding bone from his right leg had severed an artery. The young man was immobile, his head still whirring and he was unaware of his fate. Broken boards and listing trestles were strewn upon the streambed. As Gayle approached the young man, she knew that even her healing powers of roots and herbs could do nothing for this poor, unfortunate man. His face grew pale as Gayle swabbed his forehead and cheeks with a torn cloth off her dress. Preoccupied with their bruises, the three ladies hadn't even taken notice of the young man and his fate. Gayle applied her belt to the man's leg as a tourniquet. She didn't possess enough strength to tighten the belt effectively. When she looked above to summon help from the Reverend, who was still standing upon the pier's end, she detected fear and apprehension in his face.

"Please Reverend, we can talk of it later. But for now, thou must help this man or he will surely die." Gayle pleaded.

The Reverend did not reply, nor did he so much as make an attempt to move. He just stood watching. Soon the ladies had joined the vigil at the side of the Reverend. With his trembling hand before him, he pointed in the direction of the bleeding man.

"'Tis the work of the devil himself," he said.

"'Twas the weight of the horse that caused the bridge to collapse. 'Tis not the work of the devil," she retorted, with defiance. "Thee must help at once, I have not the strength to stop the bleeding."

The Reverend shook his head and then turned to speak to the ladies. A moment later, two of the women turned and vanished down the road, heading toward the village. Gayle knew their departure was not to fetch help for the dying man. She continued to beg for help from the Reverend, but to no avail. He merely cast his jeering stare.

As Gayle worked futilely at saving the young man, her dress had absorbed the bloody waters of the stream, staining it red up to her waist. The muscles in her arms and shoulders grew weak and sore as the tourniquet slowly loosened due to her exhaustion. The young rider's face became pale and showed little life. Soon, he fell unconscious allowing his eyes to close and his head to sink below the water. Gayle reached behind his neck and lifted his head with one hand while the other pulled at the tourniquet. The pulsating artery increased its flow as she feverishly tried to maneuver his body. With his head propped by her lap, Gayle could hear that his breathing was becoming shallow. There was nothing more she could do for him but pray for God's mercy. She held him firmly against her body, making every attempt at keeping him from death's grasp. She never even heard the sound of the man's voice.

"Help...somebody, please help me." Her voice echoed through the forest. An answer came swiftly from the bridge's end.

"There's no need for that, child. Death will be gathering him soon. There's nothing you or I can do for him now. And 'tis for the better. The devil can take him back from where he came and put an end to any further torment." The Reverend responded.

"He is not with the devil, he be a man just as thee. He be a man deserving of life and should not be made to suffer."

"'Tis his own weakness against the church that kills him. The power of the church is impervious to such witchcraft. And thou shall pay for the attacks made upon the church and myself, his trial cometh now with death upon him." The Reverend announced with a pointing finger. "And a trial cometh for thee for consorting with this devil."

Appearing at the bridge's end came the two ladies who had gathered help from the village. Two men made their way to the water toward Gayle. Both of them were carrying heavy chains with shackles. The concerning help was not for Gayle or the dying young man, but for the safety of the church and its people. The shackles were meant for Gayle.

"Come away from him child," one of the men said to Gayle, "you must leave him and come with us."

"I will not, I cannot leave him." As Gayle replied, the young rider gasped for his last breath. His body stiffened for a moment and then simply relaxed. Without a word or another sound, the man died in Gayle's dutiful arms. Without delay the two men pulled Gayle from the corpse. They fitted the shackles to her wrists and ankles. Her body already exhausted, she was made to walk to the village while supporting the heavy chains. When Gayle arrived in the village, she was imprisoned in a small cell. She was informed that she would face the charges of witchcraft and her trial would convene that same evening. It was explained to her by the Reverend that to delay the proceedings of the trail by even one day, could result in the destruction of more innocent people, just as the young rider was destroyed.

Shortly after nightfall the trial had begun. Gayle was taken from her cell and brought to the pillory of the open court. It is required that all the people of the village appear and participate in the final judgment of all trials. The parochial church operated the court; therefore Reverend Parris was not only the found witness to the crimes of charge, but also the acting judge. The testimonials of the three women were also included with the proceedings. The first of the proceedings was an opening statement made by the Reverend Parris. He announced to the people that Gayle, formally known as "Abigayle" Harris, was accused of being a witch and had thus proven so by her acts of assault upon the Reverend and the three ladies. He claimed that it was the power of the church and its faithful followers that superseded her plans to assassinate him. He continued his speech with influential beliefs of the church. His deceptive ways were both cunning and strategically encouraged. The Reverend used the church to his own means and the people of the village knew that he had a great and devoted congregation. Any act in protest against the church would surely jeopardize one's own life and family as well. As a show of faith, the people of the village would never question the word of the church or the Reverend Parris. As he boasted his prowess over the evils of blasphemy, Gayle stood quiet and still with her eyes trained on the floor. Her bulwark of strength stood adamant against the Reverend. She kept her face veiled with her hair. At the closing of his speech to the people of the village and the seven judges of the bench, the Reverend conceded that the only way to abolish evil and its makings is to destroy its maker and advocates. Therefore, he concluded that Gayle must die by way of burning. He added that the execution must be conducted by morning. His deliberation of belief and opinion was delivered to the court. But more to the fact, Gayle had been sentenced without remorse or provocation. The court proceedings followed with a vote among the seven bench members and the objections. If none oppose, the Reverend's verdict of punishment is then carried out. Never in the past has anyone ever questioned the word of the noble Reverend Parris. The members of the court conducted their vote. The decision was made and by no surprise to anyone of the village, including Gayle. The Reverend Parris took pride in pronouncing judgment.

"'Tis my duty and obligation to the people of our community and its safety and well being that I do my best towards the protection of such. The said person of question, Abigayle Harris has been tried by a fair court of this community for the act of witchcraft and consorting with the Devil, resulting in the murder of one man who as yet not been identified by any member of this community. The decision of this court has been made without objection," the Reverend continued with righteous habitual conviction in his voice. "On the twelfth day of our month of May, sixteen hundred and ninety-two, Abigayle Harris shall die by burning until her soul is cleansed of evil and any works of the Devil."

"No," Sara Harris cried out. "She's just a baby. She hurt no man. Thou said the man had fallen from his horse. There's no evil in that. She's just a baby. She must not die. Please don't take my baby. She's not a witch.

Samuel firmly clutched at Sara's shoulders and pulled her to his chest as she crumpled and nearly fell crippled by the horror. Throughout the pleading of her mother and the pronouncing of the judgment, Gayle never lifted her head or revealed her eyes to any of the committee. Gayle possessed a mysterious inner strength of self-control and undaunted perseverance. This, no doubt, was a trait learned through her father, Samuel. He was indeed a strong-minded man, but as he comforted his wife, all the forces of the universe could not hold back his tears that he shed for the loss of his little girl that he loved so very much. Sara and Samuel held each other amid the people of the village as the arbitrary laws of Salem butchered their lives.

Suddenly, a hush fell upon the crowd. Gayle slowly began to move, methodically and robotic. She lifted her head allowing her hair to unveil her mysticism. As the light shone on her face, Gayle looked upon the crowd. She knew that she could not possibly change the decision of the court. More so, she knew what the verdict would be long before she entered the courtroom. It would be futile to even consider a plea of forgiveness or a change of heart. But that was not her intent. Due to Sara's sheltering of Gayle's mysticism, none of the people of Salem really knew much about her or even what she looked like. It was quite ironic how the people of Salem had just convicted Gayle of practicing witch-craft and yet none of them had a true notion of her abilities. At first glance, Gayle projected a powerful cognizance of bitter dread over the people who con-victed her. One woman fainted as she looked at Gayle's hypnotic eyes. All others experienced utter dread and fear. A shudder of fear infiltrated into the bones of every person who stood before the court-room. Some of the people tried shielding their eyes from her lure. Once Gayle had their undivided in-terest for just the moment, they could not look or draw away from her. Her abilities of domination were far beyond the comprehension of the com-moners, especially by those who don't understand. Her eyes loomed feral and bedeviling as she stood before the palsied crowd. She filled the room with a gripping rank of brimstone.

"Now—thee shall look upon me," she said, calmly with her soft tranquil voice as she pointed to the people. "I blame thee not. No, I blame thee not for the crime thou hast committed upon me. Thou flocking sheep are not to blame. The blame in its entirety should be unfurled upon the demagogue Reverend Parris, himself. Thou has made the claim of witchcraft and hold myself responsible. Well, if 'tis what thou wish, thou shall fester with it. And if any shall attempt to debase the immortality of my soul, the seeds of all hellion and evil within my being shall rise and destroy them with pestilence of such immensity thou has only heard stories of from the old slaved ones. Why should I tell unjustified lies, only to appease the ears of Reverend Parris? Yes, I am a witch," As she spoke, her powers of dread intensified.

The Reverend stared in shock, just as he did before when he stood over her on the crumpled bridge.

"And thou shall fear me for all thee years," she said. "Thou has desired the likes of a witch and now thou has attained such, and with all the evil the devil himself can dole." As the last of the words passed her pink supple lips, the simple-minded crowd began to gain back their confidence and showed anger towards her. As only a stolid crowd of fools could lack fear for such a small girl, they started to approach her.

Gayle, with her slight build and narrow-boned frame, was able to slip her small hands back through the opening of the shackles. And as they did, the chains and shackles that followed with their heaviness, fell to the hard wood floor with a loud crashing succession. Again, a fear-filled hush stifled the people. Just as the Reverend Parris had corralled his people into the beliefs of his church, Gayle had momentarily governed the insipid into her false facade of magic.

Gayle's dark eyes panned them with conspicuous fury. Then slowly, she turned to the Reverend and mocked her gruff voice. "Beware Reverend Parris. Hell is close on your heels and all those who follow you."

Keeping cadence with her performance, and with projecting a look of trance, Gayle walked toward the back door. The crowd backed from her path, clearing an aisle. No one dare come too close. The two guardsmen followed her from a fair distance back to her small cell adjacent to the courthouse. Once locked back in her cell and re-shackled at the wrists, Gayle's knees buckled, landing her on the dirt floor. Gayle's weary eyes released a flow of tears that she had been holding back with her pride throughout the whole ordeal. She bowed her head into her hands. The whispering sounds of the departing crowd were still audible. Her indignation and pride tried to muffle the sounds of sobbing. She wanted to retain the status of having undaunted strength and mysterious powers over evil. Gayle was quite familiar with the scent of her mother. Before looking up or turning around to face the bars of the cell, she greeted Sara.

"Hello, Mother," she said, wiping away the tears with her apron. "Where is me Papa?"

"He'll be along soon. He—he is just outside the door," Sara stammered. Instinctively, Gayle knew he was trying to pull himself together. He would never allow her to see him in tears or emotionally hampered.

"Oh Lord, I am so sorry child. I wish that I could be strong for you. I wish I could change everything. We know thou art no witch. This be Salem, but I wish it were not. I cannot fathom how the Reverend has named you as his tormentor. I now see that thou were right in the many years past. I bet it is he who is the evil one."

Gayle jumped to her feet and stepped up to the bars of her cell, both her hands cradling those of her mother's. "Hush mother, don't let any ears hear those words from thou," Gayle interrupted with a hasty whisper. "The Reverend is evil, that's true, but just the same, he will see you burn by the fires of hell for the words thou speak of now and long before thou sees retribution. I can guarantee that. Thou must be brave mother. I am not afraid to die. I weep for thou and father. Thou and father are my only sorrows of death, but don't fret my dearest mother. One day in the heavens of our God, we will be together once again as family. I guarantee that and if there be a way to visit thou and papa in dreams, I guarantee that too."

Gayle wiped the tears from her mother's face. At that moment, her father emerged from the darkness of the halls. He approached them both, reaching his large muscular arm through the bars, he harbored his daughter and wife with a loving stronghold hug.

"I love thee. I love you both." Gayle declared. The tears of her tranquil ebony eyes were beginning to show. From her father came no reply. He could only respond by pulling her closer into his huddle. This man of strength and courage was filled with so much grief, so much anguish and pain, that to speak would break his concentration, causing him to lose control over the dam that inhibits his tears. Though he did not reply, Gayle understood.

Soon Samuel and Sara were made to leave. The course of practice according to the laws of imprisonment for the town of Salem allowed for only one brief visit by the immediate family and it was already over extended. Samuel guided Sara out of the jailhouse as she found her legs weakened and sluggish. She cried in his arms throughout the walk home and throughout the entire night. Gayle returned to the familiar landing of the dirt floor of her cell. While sifting the sandy grounds in reverie of happier times with her family, she came across a hard stone. Still without conscious recognition of her find, she toyed with the stone between her nimble fingers. As she carried on in her stream of consciousness, the discomforting thoughts of losses continued to come to the surface. The loss of her mother and father were insurmountable. But second to that was something she had never thought before, that fact that she had nothing of her doing to leave behind, except that of the possible legacy of her performance in court that day. More importantly, love. Outside of her family, she had not experienced love and she would never come to meet the man she would have married nor bare his child. These thoughts saddened her. The stone soon became the outlet of her aggression as she squeezed it tightly in her hand. If she were truly a witch, she by this time would either have escaped from the cell of doom or cast the spell of plague as she threatened in court. Her aggressions accrued as she festered over the injustice brought upon her. Without a thought, Gayle throttled the stone across the cell with all her forces of fury. The impact against the wall left a large white impression. As she inspected it closely, she could see that the mark that was left by the stone was indelible. She then groped along the ground to find the stone once again. When she found it, she used it to mark the wall. Again, the stone left a permanent impression. With little recourses to vent her anxieties, she decided to leave a felicitous message on the wall of the cell for the people of her town to read long after she had gone.

THE DAY OF MY CHILD

Thou protection leaves no detection for those who chose not to pose.
To thee, foretelling the future is rebelling the suture.
With the end of my shaft, I point at the craft and foretell its crash by way of a hidden crack in the mast.
My vision was a mission from those of no commission.
And those thou cherish, are soon to perish.
Stop your travel, I say, or drown in liquid gravel.
But the town still frowns, for they can see no crown

of the one foretelling the yelling of those rebelling,
and soon fit for doom, by way of slow decay.

But first a spoken work, they say:
Your riddles and rhymes aren't worth the time, for
this fire is not mine.
And now it is time to pay for your crime.
And when you cry, you'll hope to die, for now you
will learn how it is to burn.
This meeting will now adjourn.
So...goodbye evil eye.
Her gift was set adrift.
Maybe to arrive somewhere not deprived.
It is just the wrong time for this prime of mine.
When your baby is born, try not to scorn.
Or that evil eye will learn to lie.

Abbigayle Harris

Chapter Two

Introducing

"Mike, what's the matter with you? I've been sitting here talking to you for the past twenty minutes and you haven't heard a word I've said."

"I don't really know mom," Mike replied with solemnity, "I just feel that high school's just so stupid, as though it were just a bigger elementary school. I hate it."

"You have to give it time, Mike."

"Time, time for what? I'm in my second semester of high school and it is no better than school nine years ago. Besides, it's like bad soup, you don't go on eating it hoping it'll get better."

"Perhaps not, but in this case, you don't have a choice. The day you quit school is the day you find yourself another place to live."

"Oh, give me a break, mom. Now you're starting to sound like dad. Don't worry, I won't quit.

There are others ways; somehow I'll work it out."

"Speaking of working things out, Mike. Don't go anywhere until after you've spoken to your father. He wants to discuss with you that little matter that happened in school yesterday. You do remember the episode with the stolen food in the cafeteria?" Mrs. Shane inquired.

"Yes, I do remember and it wasn't me who stole the food. I was just in the wrong place at the wrong time. Then they grabbed me because I look like a criminal."

"That's what you always say, Mike. You're always innocent and yet always in the middle of trouble."

"But it's true." Mike interrupted.

"Just make sure that you are in the right place at the time your father gets home. I am tired of your sorrow filled stories about your constant discriminatory misfortunes."

"I don't know why you choose to doubt me," Mike drawled. "I feel as though you want to believe that I am some kind of compulsive liar or something. Why is it you never believe me? What have I ever done to make you feel this way?"

"Save your song and dance for your father. Your little act of pleading innocence won't work on me anymore. I don't want to discuss it any longer." Mrs. Shane's jealousy of the relationship he had with his father was, no doubt the apparent catalyst. From weekend fishing trips to coaching the little league baseball, Mike and his father were indeed inseparably close. But by the time Mike was sixteen years old, his relationship with his father was totally destroyed at the hands of his nefarious mother. Mike's intractable anger and attitude were no doubt just. And the abandonment he experienced over the years only hardened his adamant opinion of his mother.

"Ya know? It's you I can't believe mom. It seems like you just love to make trouble for me. Especially between me and dad." Mike began to show his finely cultivated and impetuous anger.

"Keep it up Mike and you'll find yourself grounded for the next two weeks." Mrs. Shane keenly responded to Mike's ungoverned anger. If there was one thing she could do well; it was her ability to make the worst in him come to surface.

"Grounded for what? I'm just trying to talk to you and maybe understand what's wrong with you and maybe learn why you treat me this way."

"What's wrong with—Well, you spend the next two weekends at home and perhaps you might learn something. And that includes no guests, no car, no television and no phone." Mrs. Shane said, quite smugly.

"I can't be grounded. You know I have a date with Diane next weekend."

"Not anymore," Mrs. Shane quipped. "Maybe next time you'll learn what is wrong with me before you get yourself into trouble. Maybe you should learn to control that temper of yours."

"I can't believe this. I spent one hundred fifty bucks on those concert tickets. How could you do this to me?" Mike barked. "The Rockets are on tour for the last time. We have waited years for this concert."

"I don't care and I don't want to hear anymore out of you."

"Wait a minute! Is that it? You just cross your arms and that's that? A week's pay down the drain and no Diane?"

"Keep it up Mike," She played his rage like a trick card game. Mrs. Shane knew the foremost of Mike's weakness was his love for Diane. She had a good idea as to how he felt; his only refuge from the insanity of his mother was redeemed through Diane and the outside world. And she ought to know; she had taken liberties of listening through his door while he was on the phone with Diane, and on more than one occasion. "One more word out of you and you'll stay home for a month." She warned.

"This is so unfair, mom. Can't we just talk this over?"

"Okay, you just bought yourself a whole month." Mrs. Shane smiled.

"What? A month? At that point, Mike's unbridled rage became potentially dangerous to his social endeavors. "How about two months, mom? Wait—do I hear three? Four?"

"Well, Mike, when your father gets home you can also explain to him why you are grounded for two months now."

"Fine," Mike snapped. "That just suits me fine." Once again, Mike had allowed his mother to encroach upon his untamed anger. Mrs. Shane knew exactly what she was doing. After all, she has had years of practice. And Mike's patience was showing signs of constant weakening. Yet, somehow he managed the strength to pull himself away from his mother, the woman he and Diane would normally refer to as "the Witch." He retreated to his bedroom, anticipating the mitigating council of his father.

On most occasions, Mr. Shane was able to remedy the inflammatory situations by mediating a compromise between Mike and his mother. His expertise in the situation did not always culminate in Mike's favor, but at least Mr. Shane showed earnest concern toward Mike's side of things of which his attempts to do so were somewhat pacifying over his evil mother's doings.

After pacing the floor of his bedroom for nearly an hour, Mike couldn't wait any longer to hear from his father. Get a hold of yourself, Mike said to himself quite shakily. I'll just call dad and explain the situation to him before he gets home and before the witch tells him one of her notorious bullshit stories. At least dad's always tried to be there for me in the past. Dad would never take this concert away from me. Hell, he knows how important this is to me. Yeah, that's what I'll do. Mike crept out into the hallway, trying to avoid any confrontation from his mother. He located the phone in the living room, quickly dialed and carried on as quietly as possible.

"Hi dad. Are you busy? Well—I just called to tell you what's going on. Wait, dad, wait, wait a minute. What are you talking about? What do you mean, you're tired of my upsetting mom? It was she who was doing all that she could to upset me. No, I didn't cuss at her. I don't know why she would say that, except to try to get me into more trouble with you. Yes, I know the Dean from the school called you. I guess I was in the wrong place at the wrong time again. Dad, I have no reason to steal food. Yeah, I know it seems like a lot of coincidences lately, but I swear, I didn't do it." Mike could sense a new wall at work here, a wall of doubt or more to the fact, a wall of indifference. Also for the very first time, this horrifying wall of indifference was emitting from his once loving and caring father. Lately Mike had detected a bit of wear in his father's support, but never before had his father ever delivered such a blow of words favoring the witch.

"Mike, it's time you grow up and pay the price for your actions. Your mother and I don't need this kind of hassle with the Dean calling the house and all. And if you didn't steal the food, then why did the Dean feel the situation warranted detention for the remainder of the week on top of the phone call to us?" Mr. Shane questioned.

"I don't really know dad. But I didn't do it. And I don't know why you don't believe me. You know the Dean is a jerk. Remember the time he suspended Jimmy for flooding the boy's bathroom? And as it turned out Jimmy wasn't in school that day, he was out of town on a field trip with his class? The stupid Dean can't tell who is who without his glasses, and the kids are always stealing them as a joke. I don't feel that should be held against me." Mike protested.

"Mike, I'm tired of the constant stories. Next

27

time perhaps, you will figure a way of staying away from potential trouble. That is, if in fact you are not the cause."

Mike just shook his head while listening to the deterioration of a good relationship. The strange words coming from his father were no different than those of his mother's. It was now obvious that Mr. Shane is sporting a change of attitude toward the family setting. In past conversations, the witch had warned that she would win-over Mr. Shane's state of mind. After all, they are husband and wife.

"Okay dad, I guess I'll talk to you about it when you get home tonight." Mike abruptly dropped the phone to the receiver lest of allowing his father any further chastising and what Mike felt was the stealthy influence of his mother. Still in shock at his father's change of heart, Mike returned to his bedroom. His nerves were unsteady. As Mike paced the floors of his small cage-like bedroom, he began uttering. "I can't believe my father would betray me and give into that damn witch. How could he do this to me? How could she? Damn, I'd love to slap her arrogant face! Where does she get off telling him that I cussed at her? I hate her! I wish she were dead! Hell, if I hadn't spent all my money on those concert tickets, I'd have invested in a hit man. I should have figured it—she told me that she'd win him over one day and have him all to herself. What a sick pathetic witch! How could she take my father from me? Since when is a kid not allowed to have a dad? And not only that, she has now taken Diane away from me for two stinking months. The only thing worth waking for each and every rotten day is Diane. Remembering he hadn't yet called Diane as he habitually did each time he got home from school, Mike attempted to quietly make his way to the phone. In mid-stride down the hall, Mike was intercepted by the witch. She had appeared seemingly out of nowhere.

"Where do you think you're going, young man?" She asked.

"To the phone." Mike answered, still somewhat surprised by her sudden appearance.

"The phone is off limits to you—or did you forget?"

"Well at least allow me to call Diane to let her know what is going on. She doesn't know I'm now grounded." Mike reasoned.

"You can tell her tomorrow when you see her in school."

As the words came from her mouth, Mike could read the self-gratification spewing from her wicked face.

"What if she calls me?" He asked.

"I will tell her you're grounded and that you will see her in school. So you best just march your ass back into your room until dinner. And I don't want to hear another word about it. Understood?"

Mike couldn't bring himself to answering her. It would be self-inflicting to even show response, let alone to answer to her belittling admonishment. And Mike knew how his mother would be only too happy to be the one to deliver the message of bad tidings to Diane. Without a word or hesitation in stride, Mike took out his comb from his back pocket and began to stroke back his hair while turning his back to her. He then sashayed toward his room. Mike had learned that the only way to cope was merely by ignoring her. That is to say, when he's not arguing with her.

After quietly closing his bedroom door, Mike lunged his body across his bad, slamming his fist to the mattress. His body was rigid with bitter anger. Damn, I hate her, Mike thought. I have got to get out of here. I just can't live with this witch any longer. She's ruining my life. As far back as I can remember, she had tried her best to screw-up my life and take away my pleasures, my happiness and fun. Why me? Hell—I don't need this shit! I've done nothing wrong to her. I can't believe how she gets off on this crap.

While thinking in terms of getting off, Mike steered his train of thought toward Diane. The mere thought of her quickened his heart. I wonder what she's doing right now. God, I love her! She's so beautiful and caring, always there for me. I wish I were with her now. Dad was right; he warned me that there were two kinds of girls in this world. Thank the Lord I chose well. Who could possibly wait until a blind marriage, to find out what your lover is truly like? In everything people do, they first test or inquire about, or examine their merchandise before they make the purchase. Marriage is supposedly to be considered sacred, so why wait until it's too late to make a change. After all, making love is beautiful, especially with Diane. I knew from the first day we met, we were to be married. What guy couldn't love a girl who had all the same interests as he, as well as honest, dedicated, always uplifting in high spirits with fun and laughter?

Once, when the witch was out shopping, Mike and Diane were able to enjoy the day in total privacy, and not have to leave the house for refuge; they stayed in his room and talked while playing with his pet hamster, Lucy. As Diane was lying on her back across the bed, Lucy jumped from Mike's lap and onto Diane's shoulder. Her little paws tickled as she made her way down Diane's sweater. She then decided to rest in the warmth of Diane's bra. Mike couldn't blame her interest; he too had designs on that very location. After a couple of giggles from Diane, Lucy settled peacefully and soon fell asleep. Diane's character has always been so kind and fond of Mother Nature and her creatures. She thought it was sweet how Lucy would often play and runabout as though she were showing off her unlimited energies and finely trained skills. It was especially sweet when so many times; Lucy would find shelter in the strangest places. As Lucy fell asleep in the chasm of Diane's large and comfortable boobs, they continued in conversation. Tired by the strenuous workout of the running wheel and tunnel runs in her cage, the adorable little fur ball slept for nearly an hour as Mike and Diane carried on, forgetting all about her. After a few hands of cards, they decided to run to the take-out hamburger joint that was just a few miles from the house. The two of them were getting quite hungry, and felt it was a good idea to get out of the house for some fresh air. The streets were lined with mature sixty-foot tall eucalyptus trees. The aroma of the neighborhood was like that of a sweet nectar forest. The two stepped outside, took a deep breath of the fresh scented air and approached Mike's car at the end of the walkway.

As Diane attempted to get into the car, she felt movement between her breasts. "Oh my goodness! What about Lucy? I almost completely forgot about her."

Mike was on the other side of the car unlocking his door. "What did you say?"

"Lucy, I still have Lucy in my bra. Should we take her back in the house?"

"I'm sure she'll be fine. I know I would be." Mike glanced down her low-neck sweater. "Although, if she's going to be a bother to you—"

"No, she's fine. I don't mind her at all. I think she's gone back to sleep." Diane pulled at her sweater allowing Mike to get a better view.

"Mmmm, perhaps I should take her back into the house. I think I'm getting hungry for more than just hamburgers." His eyes were trained steady on her.

"Let's just go and hurry home. The witch should be gone all day with shopping. Your dad's at work and the house is ours," She placed her hand on his thigh and squeezed a hint of her desires. "So, what are you waiting for big guy? Let's go."

He started the engine and throttled the pedal to the floor. With Diane's sweet little fingers kneading close to his privates, he had no time to waste; having the house to themselves was indeed a rare occasion and should be taken advantage of.

The restaurant drive-thru was too long of a wait, so they parked the care and proceeded inside. As it was their turn to step up to the counter and order, the guys behind the counter would fall prey to Diane's beauty and voluptuous breasts. It would almost be comical to watch these guys try to keep from staring at her tits, as she would place her order. Then of course, Mike would step up to the counter alongside his girl to confirm the menu and intimidate the horny little devils behind the counter. At seventeen years of age, Mike stood five feet eleven inches tall and his weight tipped the scales at two hundred twelve pounds. But that was only half the intimidating factors. Since Mike was twelve, he studied with the best in the sport of weight lifting and bodybuilding. He had learned to harness the hatred for his mother and use it for the betterment of himself. The energies of negativity were redirected and guided to form a physique of rippling muscles and the strength of a high performance machine. When Mike stepped up to the counter from behind his girl, the guy suddenly had an attack of stutters; acting less proud of himself, he took the order from Diane. After he gave her the change from bill that

Mike handed him, he and Diane stood off to the side and waited for the order.

The restaurant was quite noisy with a lot of customers. Apparently the noise and the smell of food had reached Lucy, she started to stir beneath Diane's sweater, and as she did, a lot of attention was drawn to her, especially the guy behind the counter.

The guy's eyes grew wide and his mouth fell open as he handed them the order.

Mike leaned over the counter while urging the guy to come closer. Mike whispered, "Have you ever seen the movie Alien?" Mike looked at the guy quite seriously. "I bet you didn't know that it was a true story," Mike nodded. "That's what I thought, most people don't."

Mike laid across his bed thinking about the laughs and chuckles they got from that silly episode. They couldn't believe that the guy actually thought that they were serious. The two of them made quite an inseparable pair. Two months grounding without Diane after school was like a sentence of imprisonment with the devil. Mike stayed in his room with the door shut through the remainder of the day. That evening, like almost every evening, his dad came home and headed straight for the bar in the family room.

"Aren't you going to talk with your son? I thought we agreed that you would have a talk with him. This can't go on like this," Mrs. Shane said.

"I'd like to wind down first, Grace. Is that all right with you? I've had a long, hard day. What ever happened to: Hi, honey. How was your day? Can I get you anything?"

"Jack, those days ended when you decided to have kids. Particularly, one who doesn't mind or do as he's told. It's because Mike can't seem to keep out of trouble; our marriage has suffered terribly. Why don't you talk to him now before you—wind down." her tone wisped the familiar snide hostility towards Jack's drinking, "Before you can't talk at all."

"Damn it, Grace. Why do you have to make everything so difficult? Can I just come home to a peaceful house without any problems, just once— just once Grace?" with retorting hostility, he pointed his finger in her face. "I'm sure that you said enough to him already. What more needs to be said? He's grounded for two months, and his plans for the concert have been ruined. What more do you want? I think you just about covered everything, dear."

"Oh sure, make me out to be the villain when it's your son who's repeatedly caused trouble in school, and has brought trouble to his home."

"Why are you so hard on him? He's a normal kid with troubles and pressures just like any high school kid. He's no different from the way we were in school. In fact, if you recall, you were a lot worse."

"Yes, but we didn't talk back to our parents or treat them as equals. We respected them and their word without question. I treated my parents with more respect than Mike could understand."

"Perhaps then you should treat him with respect just as you would expect from him. Ya know Grace; I haven't heard you say a good thing about or to him since I can't remember when. Why is it so hard for you to see the good in him; like the good you find so easy to see in Jimmy?" Jack had already belted down two glasses of scotch and poured his third.

Jimmy was Mike's older brother, her chosen favorite. "We're not discussing Jimmy right now, but since you brought him up. Jimmy always shows respect for us. He's well mannered and has always brought home good grades. It's easy to see the good in him. He's a good boy and he's going to make something of his life."

"And so will Mike," he defended his son.

"Doing what? He doesn't do anything but listen to loud music; play with his animals in his room and workout with weights in the garage. How does that fortify a lucrative future?"

"He'll find himself, just give him time. What's the big hurry? Some people don't find their interests until late in their years. Besides, perhaps he'll decide to go back into sports. Maybe his knee will heal up. Anything can happen."

"Anything can happen? I'm talking about a future, not sports." Grace looked at him like he was crazy. Her idea of a future had nothing more to do with sports than owning a professional football team as a tax write-off. In her eyes, her son Jimmy could do no wrong. She thought he was quite the ladies man with his good looks and manners. Too many times, Mike had to hear her ask why he wasn't more like his brother. And now with Jimmy gone; already a graduate from college and living in his own apartment, and working in a law office as a paralegal, it would seem she had nothing better to do than pick on Mike for his failure to seen any interest in following in his brother's path. The truth is, as both Mike and Mr. Shane knew it to be, Jimmy could never make it in sports. He tried so many times to be the stud jock on campus, but he could never make it happen.

In Jimmy's senior year he stood at six feet tall and was of fair build. He tried out for the school basketball team but failed miserably. He was the first basketball player to be cut from the team in the history of the school's athletic department. He was so uncoordinated, the coach was afraid that Jimmy might accidentally kill himself on the court. For a guy who stood six feet tall, it was amazing how often he found himself looking at the kneecaps through the majority of the game as a result of tripping over the ball, or falling for no apparent reason. He barely had the stamina to last a game due to his self-inflicted injuries. Needless to say, the coach cut him from the team for Jimmy's own safety and to avoid a lawsuit from the parents of the other teammate's that inadvertently became injured by Jimmy's clumsiness.

Mr. Shane had worked with him for many years prior, trying to help him learn the fundamentals of basic athletics. He tried almost every game known,

37

but to no avail, Jimmy was a lost cause when it came to sports. He lacked the stamina and the drive needed to survive in the world of athletics. What seemed to make matters worse for him was the fact that Mike had a natural ability for sports. Although five years younger than his brother, Mike could out play, out run, out wit, out lift his brother at any sport by the time he was twelve, and proved it by joining every league available, from baseball, track and football, to wrestling; Mike did it all and more. It was never his intent to show-up his brother, for the most part it would have been to his advantage if he could have worked out and trained his brother. But as it came to be, sports merely turned out to be Mike's favorite past time, which also grew a strong, loving bond between him and his father.

"Are you even listening to me? Did you hear what I said? Are you going to talk to him or not? He just can't continue like this. Something must be done, Jack. What kind of future is there in weight lifting? You know what they say about those weight lifters, that they become over-infatuated with their bodies."

Jack looked at his wife with anger and utter disgust. "No Grace, but I'm sure you're going to tell me."

"One of the girls at the salon had read a report from a doctor that the hormones in men who lift weights too much become confused and start to produce the wrong kinds of sex hormones."

Jack was thinking that this was starting to sound more like a joke. "So, what's the punch line? You think Mike is going to turn into a girl?"

"No! Do I have to spell it out for you?" She looked at him like he was the one sounding a bit confused. "You see, what happens is that they become so infatuated with themselves and their workout buddies, they eventually lose interest in the female anatomy and choose to be with other men. Don't you understand? It makes perfect sense. They become gay."

"Oh for crying out loud, Grace! Are you for real? I really think you're losing it! And you're going to believe what some pencil-necked, hair styling, three dollar bill is going to tell you about manhood? He was probably telling you of his fantasies, his most desired wish, not a doctor's report. Listen, I've had enough of this discussion. I don't want to hear anymore about this cock-n-bull story. Mike is all male, always was, always will be. No amount of weightlifting is going to change that. It isn't the ones that weight lift that you should be concerned with. Now leave me alone and let me enjoy my drink."

"Is that so important, your drink? And I'll have you know, Francis is not gay." she said quite defensively, "Just because he's a hairdresser doesn't mean he's gay."

"Fine, Grace, go talk to your hairdresser, and leave me alone." The liquor was finally starting to take effect; he didn't seem to be as bothered by her nagging disposition.

"Why are you doing this to us? You're letting your drinking get between us. Ever since Jimmy moved out, you have been hiding from me in that damn bottle."

Grace couldn't have been more correct. The drinking had truly started the very week Jimmy moved to his own apartment. But little did she understand; Jimmy's departure was merely the prelude to the catalyst of his drinking. Jack was facing stress at work; stress that she would fail to understand, nor try to remedy with kindness or just a consoling word. It seemed that when Jimmy moved away, so did her best friend. Since that day, it seemed she couldn't speak a kind word. She blamed Jack for his moving out, but the fact was that she truly had no grasp of the truth. And Jack, of course, had his suspicions but failed to say anything. He kept to himself as Grace slowly wedged herself between him and Mike making their relationship more difficult and distant.

A loud crash fell upon the bar as Mr. Shane slammed his glass down. "Well, since you've decided that I'm hiding, why don't you let me do so in peace. I will talk with Mike when I'm good and ready. I think that you've said enough for the two of us." He turned his back to her as he stood from the bar stool, grabbed his jacket and briefcase, and then retired to the bedroom for the night.

Chapter Three
Jason's Dream

The world of Gayle's message showed its defiance and pride in that cell for a great many years. And over the years the words were read, deciphered and considered of its meaning by every person in that village.

The rise of the sun, on the day of Gayle's conviction and demise, arrive with little warning. The duties of the guards were carried out flawlessly. They approached her cell for the collection. The message on the wall meant nothing to them. She was pulled to her feet and guided out of the jailhouse. In the morning light her appearance was more tattered and worn. He wrists were bloody and bruised from the tight grip of the shackles. Dark circles had formed around her eyes. A nightmare of what was to be had kept her from sleep. The heavy chains had caused her to stumble. Her small and somewhat frail body endured the incumbency as best she could. As Gayle neared the pit of her hellish destiny, she was scathingly attacked by the hatred of her townspeople. She was pelted by stones, and those who possessed no stones, spat. The people continued with a battery of assaults as she entered the grounds.

"Burn the witch, burn the witch, burn the witch!" Shouts rang out, some chanted. "Evil must be gone with! Burn the witch! Our tormentor must die! Evil must die! Burn the witch, burn the witch, burn the witch! Thou art a witch, thou must die! Burn the witch!" The crowd continued to cry out with rage.

The guards pushed her along at full arm's length, as if they would contract some sort of contamination of evil by walking too close. Her sluggish body rippled with every blow delivered by the guards. The stones continued. One had grazed her shoulder, tearing her dress. Moments later, the blood from her torn skin began to show through; first, just her shoulder, her hands, and then her legs below her dress line. The people continued to shout. Wood had been collected from the forest and brought to an open dell where all the other burnings had taken place. There awaited more of the townspeople. The stones had finally ended when Gayle reached the sight of her demise. The guards removed her shackles.

She was bound to a large log that was half embedded beneath the ground. In methodical cadence, the people gathered handfuls of wood from the pile and distributed them at Gayle's feet. At a raise lectern, a safe distance from the soon-to-be fire's heat, the Reverend Parris delivered his last speech of condemnation. But the words that emitted from his mouth never reached Gayle's ears. She had called upon the Almighty to hear her prayers. While in a deep state of meditation, she slipped into a trance. The beautiful, young woman of radiant life and caring devotion to all nature possessed only prayer for salvation. But her prayers heard no answers. But the Reverend's command, the fire was ignited. The fire grew swiftly. The heat of the blaze became unbearable. Along with her screams the smell of burning flesh filled the air. In the dregs of her despair, Gayle succumbed.

A moment later a calming voice spoke softly, whispering its way through the dark quiet.

"Jason, I'm here honey. It's okay. Don't be afraid, sweetheart, mommy's here now. It was just another bad dream. Calm down sweetheart. Mommy's here now. I've got you my baby." Anne comforted her little man in her subduing embrace.

Jason's long johns were soaked with perspiration. His hands and face were flushed. Anne pulled Jason from his bed and carried him to the basin. She dampened a towel with cool water and swabbed his face, neck and cuts. Somehow during the nightmare he had acquired some cuts and bruises on his hands, legs and shoulder.

Jason was six years old when the nightmares first began. After a year, they still continued, sometimes as many as three times a week. All resulting in the same patterns of nightly screams and then waking in frightened delirium. With his tiny legs wrapped tightly around his mother's waist, and his face buried against her breast, he recited to his mother the events that took place.

"Don't let them hurt me, mommy. Please make them stop. Why do they hurt me, mommy?"

"It's only a dream, baby. Nobody's going to hurt you. It was only a dream. None of this is real. None of those people are real. Nobody is going to take you away. Mommy and Daddy wouldn't let any harm come to you. Don't worry, you're safe." Anne continued to console him night after night. For nine more years, Anne consoled her son as the nightmares continued. Throughout the years they grew more intense and incredibly more vivid. At the age of sixteen, Jason's nightmares had finally come to an end, but not before a summit of horror.

One evening, in the spring, Jason had experienced another one of his nightmares. Only this time, the loving warmth of his mother's embrace could not remedy the results. In the past, Jason's mother usually arrived seconds to his waking. On this particular time, he continued to scream long after his mother had entered the room. Her attempts at waking him were futile. As she tried to shake him from his sleep, Jason writhed and flailed all over the bed until finally, he fell from the bedding onto the floor. Jason hadn't awakened. His piercing screams were of pain and not fear.

The commotion was so loud that even Mr. Mathison; Jason's dad had awakened. He entered the room with a lighted lantern. At which time, he and Anne witnessed Jason on the floor convulsing in a seizure. Mr. Mathison hastily dropped his lantern onto the wash table in an attempt to help his wife gain control over Jason's rampant movements. They had never before seen Jason carry on this way or for this long. They expected him to wake up at any moment. As Mr. Mathison began to hold Jason's legs, the convulsions suddenly stopped. Mr. Mathison seemed confident that all was well. But Anne knew that something was terribly wrong. She could see in Jason's face that it was not over yet. He lay with his eyes open.

Anne shook him. A rank odor permeated the air. It was an unfamiliar smell and extremely rancid. The pungency seemed to be coming from Jason. Anne commanded Jason Sr. to bring the lamp to her side. Jason's body was so hot that it had been smoldering. The entire room had filled with smoke. Anne identified the smell as what could only be burning flesh. Before her very eyes, Jason was burning. His face and hands were blistered and swollen. Mr. Mathison reached for the washbasin.

He ordered Anne to take hold of the lamp and back away from Jason. The water from the basin was doused over Jason's body. As the water struck, his body steamed off the heat. From Jason's body the radiating steam and smoke slowly tapered to a halt.

Anne knelt beside him, checking for a pulse. His

breathing was shallow. She called to him several times as she and Jason Sr. sat his limp body up against the bed. Anne instructed her husband to ready the horses for travel. From the looks of the multiple burns and blisters, Jason was in need of emergency medical attention. The only doctor lived in town, about ten miles from the Mathison's farm.

Mr. Mathison was a blacksmith, a hardworking man. The money he made certainly wasn't much, but at least enough to suffice. Many of the people of their town were already driving the fancy new convertible cabriolet, while others were fortunate enough to have the first of the production steam-powered motorcars. Mr. Mathison was still sporting his trusty old buckboard. His pride kept him from telling the truth about his inability to afford a motorcar. He simply told his friends that it was a matter of preference. Most people knew better, but who was about to argue with a man who stood at six foot four and weighed over two hundred fifty pounds, and most times was seen with his sledgehammer in hand. He was a fond believer of old traditions and that's what everyone else accepted. Anne, on the other hand, was quite handy with the garden, and grew most of the family's food. Jason, who seemed to have a knack for caring for them, tended the farm animals. He would joke with his parents by telling them that he and the animals had a mutual understanding.

After hitching up the horses to the buckboard, Mr. Mathison hustled back into the house. When entering Jason's room he could see that Jason had improved considerably. He was coherent and responding to the pain. At age sixteen, Jason was almost as tall as his father, but not yet as full framed. His parents tried lumbering him to his feet. Jason was weak and crippled with immense pain. Struggling their way through the house, they somehow managed to make it to the buckboard. The journey to Doc Peterson's was dangerous. Without a moon's light and with the hasty lashings inflicted upon the horses for a quicker journey, it was a wonder that Mr. Mathison didn't topple the three of them. As the wind of the night air would wisp across Jason's face, the open wounds would cause that much more pain. Before the arrival to Doc Peterson's place Jason had quietly slipped into unconsciousness. He did not wake until the doctor had already treated the burns.

Just prior to his waking moments, Jason cried out several times. The tongue he spoke in was Middle English. Quite unfamiliar for the doctor to be hearing from Jason, the very boy that was born only sixteen years earlier in the very house he laid recuperating in. When Jason was born in eighteen thirteen the president of the United States of America was James Madison. The era which Jason's unconscious babble had derived from was nearly forty years prior to the first presidency. Nonetheless, he carried on in his tongue for several minutes, crying out the measure of his brutal torture. When finally awakened by his mother's voice, Jason sat upright. With his bandaged arms and hands, he pulled at his mother to come closer. He had declared to her that the nightmares were now over for good.

"Mother, I don't know exactly how to explain myself, but I believe that I understand now. Gayle is now dead and at rest. She's at rest within me. I know this must sound very strange to you and father, but I have somehow been allowed to see a spectrum of time normally forbidden from the conscious." Jason said, while still trying to cull the facts together in his head.

Mr. Mathison and Dr. Peterson stood looking dumbfounded, scratching their heads.

Jason looked around and realized he was not in the company of just his parents, nor was he at his home. The doctor then reached to Mr. Mathison's shoulder.

"Is the farm badly damaged?" the doctor asked.

Jason Sr. tilted his head. "The farm sustained no damages, doctor."

"Well, where did you say Jason was burned at?" The doctor looked perplexed.

"He was sleeping in his room. But neither the room nor the farm was on fire. It was Jason that was burning..."

"I don't understand," the doctor looked as though someone might while waiting for the punch line of a pathetic joke. "How could this be?"

"I have no idea." Jason continued, "Anne and I were hoping you could explain what has happened here. Jason's had these horrible nightmares for years, but never burned by them."

"Are you saying that Jason got his injuries from a dream? That can't be. I can't believe that!" the doctor said.

"But it's true," Anne spoke out in assistance to her husband, who seemed to have trouble with the facts as well. "Jason was asleep in his bed," Anne continued, "when we got to him his body was burning. We tried to wake him—" As her husband tried to describe what they saw, Anne bowed her head to look at the palms of her hands. With tears streaming from her eyes, she lifted her hands to be viewed by the doctor. Her hands and fingers were badly blistered.

"Anne, what happened?" Jason Sr. asked, lunging forward to grab her hands for a closer look. "Your hands have been—burned. Doctor what on earth has happened here? You can come to the farm and see for yourself, nothing is damaged except for my boy and my wife for trying to save him. What kind of a dream can do this?"

The doctor said nothing. He simply shook his head, and readied some ointment and bandages for Anne's hands. Twice he opened his mouth, but his words of explanation eluded him.

"It's okay, mother." Jason consoled. "The dreams are over with now. They won't happen anymore. Gayle is dead." As the name Gayle left his mouth, Jason realized what this must sound like to the doctor and felt that the subject was best to be discussed in private with his parents, namely his mother. Mr. Mathison didn't have much of an ear for his son's dreams. Jason resumed his composure. "The bad dream of Gayle is over. I'll be okay now, mother. Don't worry."

"Jason, who is Gayle?" the doctor inquired.

"Nobody," Mr. Mathison interrupted, getting extremely tired of hearing about a strange girl named Gayle. "She's just a bad dream, she's nobody."

The doctor finished dressing Anne's wounds. Soon after, the Mathison's left his in-house office with a thanks and leaving a promissory note of payment. As Jason had predicted, the dreams came to an abrupt and thankful end. And soon to follow were Jason's newfound interests in the super natural.

Since May twelfth, eighteen twenty-six, the night of his final bout with the horrid dreams of Gayle's execution, Jason's eyes were opened up to a very new and most misunderstood science. Although he was burned badly, leaving a great deal of scarring over twenty percent of his body, Jason was not sorry or regretful of his experience. To the contrary, the termination of the nightmares was merely the waking spectrum of his hidden talents. Much of Jason's new found interest had to be conducted in secrecy, except from his mother. For obvious reasons of skepticism and being outcast by his peers and relatives, including his father, he kept his interest and the truth behind his scars well concealed.

Chapter Four

The Phenomenon of Jason

By age seventeen, almost all of Jason's burns had healed. The only scars that remained slightly visible were those on his face, neck and chest; he looked upon them as an omen, perhaps even a message. When Gayle had died, something spiritual was born in him. His family was quick and grateful to put the nightmares into the past but Jason spent the rest of his life working to seek them out. Finding the answers to the many questions and mysteries of life became the all-important preoccupation. He spent his free time from his studies and chores learning of subjects that would ordinarily be difficult for the average person of his day to grasp or even believe. He was very clever and he truly enjoyed learning of new discoveries. To his good fortune, the family farm supplied a vast variety of schooling and unlimited curiosities.

He remembered a time when he was younger, he would be able to feel the heartbeat of a small newborn puppy with his fingers, as he would cuddle them and clean them. By the time Jason was seventeen, he had the ability to feel and hear the heartbeat of every unborn fetus of any given animal on the farm just by holding the pregnant mother. He also remembered his younger childhood of strange and unusual happenings. When he was three years old, his mother had a miscarriage. The child was to be a girl and her name was to be Sadie, but Anne developed complications and the child was lost. Jason's parents chose not to try having any more children. And, according to Doc Peterson, it was a wise decision because the miscarriage caused a number of problems with her uterus making it much more complicated for having anymore babies, and most importantly, another baby would no doubt endanger her own life.

Prior to the miscarriage, one early spring morning, a small young female voice had awakened Jason hours before the sun had come. The voice spoke to Jason, but he was too frightened to answer. The voice was calming and tender. After several minutes, Jason felt less frightened and was then able to communicate with the voice. Although he had no idea as to where the little voice was coming from, he accepted the friendship that she had to offer him. The communication was free of speech; somehow, communication was conducted via thought. It would seem that small children, such as Jason, actually possess less fear in the eyes of the unexplained; they learn faster, and have a better grasp at culling through the mortal boundaries of accepted beliefs. Many nights of friendly conversation took place between Jason and the young voice after the fear of mystery was long diminished. It wasn't until many years later and long after the miscarriage that Jason learned that the voice was to become his mentor and his savior through the horror of his nightmares. It was the voice that penetrated his subconscious and pulled him free from the grasp of the horrid dreams. Of course, when he would wake, it was his loving mother that consoled him. Jason also learned that not only was this mentor a mystery friend and perhaps a guardian angel, but she was also a vital source of his future; she was the voice of Sadie, his unborn sister.

A day on the farm consisted of rising early in the morning to feed the animals and milk the cows, dress and get ready for school and upon returning from school, Jason would do his homework if he hadn't already completed it in class. Once his afternoon chores were done, and if his father didn't need his help, Jason used his free time to work with a young girl named Millie Johnson. She was born blind and wasn't able to study and learn as the other children did; Jason took it upon himself to teach her of his own studies.

Millie was only one year younger than he, and very eager to learn. It was quite a challenge for him to work with her on the lessons. There is so much that most people take for granted, Jason thought to himself. He tried to fathom what it would be like to be blind, but found there was no way for him to imagine it. He worked with Millie almost everyday and he grew to understand her weakness and strength. Just as Millie was learning from him, he was learning some lessons from her. Millie taught Jason many of her secrets such as how she was able to feel the time of day and how she would learn everyone's voice. If she didn't hear the voice, she could identify a person by the way he or she would smell, or breathe or walk. Everyone has an individual identity and was easy to identify.

Millie could smell if Jason had done his afternoon chores; on the occasions when Jason forgot to do them, she would remind him to do them after her lesson. After a while it became easier for him to understand how she was able to adapt with blindness. One afternoon, Millie's mother had been baking in the kitchen when suddenly the hand towel that she was using as a hot pad caught fire from the heat of the stove and burned her hand.

Jason was quick to jump to his feet and grab the burning material from her hand. The flames were put out, Millie's mother ran from the house toward the water pump. Jason and Millie followed after her.

"No Mrs. Johnson, don't!" Jason shouted. "Don't put cold water on the burn. That will only make it worse. Here, let me help you." Jason took the bucket from the pump and instructed Millie to help him fill it with dirt. She dropped to her knees with her groping hands out in front of her. Jason put the bucket in her reach and told her he would be back with some medicine. Without question, Millie did as he instructed, with some herbs from the kitchen, he then ground the dried herb in his fist and mixed it with the dirt. Mrs. Johnson had begun to sob; her skin had already started to blister and swell.

"Just hold on Mrs. Johnson," Jason instructed with a consoling tone, "this will only take a moment." Once the bucket was filled, he then lifted it to the pump and filled it with water. Millie helped him mix the ingredients into a mud ointment. "This will take the pain away and keep your skin from scarring."

"Jason, are you sure of this?" Mrs. Johnson said, trying so hard to keep from crying aloud. The pain was becoming unbearable.

"Oh, yes Ma'am, it works well! I've seen it work many times before. Here now, give me your arm." Jason applied the mud to the burn area.

"It feels cool. You're right; it's much better already. How did you do that? I ain't ever felt anything like this." The last of her tears were wiped away with her apron. "How long should I keep the mud on?"

"Just until it dries. Most of it will fall off by itself."

"Is this something you learned from Doc Peterson?"

"No, but I wish I had. It could have saved me from a lot of scarring and pain when I was burned."

"Yes, I remember hearing about your barn fire last year." Mr. Mathison and the doctor told all the people in town a cover story about a barn fire. "Well, how did you learn of this medicine?" Mrs. Johnson continued to inquire.

"I learned of it on my own, at home."

She raised an eyebrow and looked directly at Jason. "Now, how could you have learned of something like this on your own? What were you doing to discover this?"

"To be quite honest with you, I wasn't doing anything, it just came to me as an idea for burns, and it worked; you said so yourself." Jason felt quite sure of himself as he gave his explanation to her, but what he didn't realize was the fact that the ointment was merely an adjuvant to the process of her relief. As Millie listened to the conversation of her mother and Jason, she thought that it was odd that she felt no coolness from the ointment, yet heard her mother concede its effectiveness. Millie reached for her mother's hand and attempted to feel for any coolness around the burn.

"How does it feel now?" Millie asked, "Is the pain gone?"

"Not completely, but it is much better. Your friend should be a doctor; he's got quite a feel for it."

The words she spoke made more sense than she probably realized. Millie held her mother's hand and she asked Jason to help apply more of the ointment on the burn area. Jason reached into the bucket and scooped another glob of mud. He slowly massaged the fresh ointment to mix with the old that was almost dry. As he did this, Millie held onto her mother's hand, hoping to understand the effectiveness of Jason's medicine. As she explained to Jason before, her lack of vision was responsible for the development of her other senses. What her mother and Jason didn't understand was what she could feel radiating from Jason's touch. Millie still couldn't feel any coolness, but what she did feel was a very different sensation from any she had ever experienced. From Jason's hand, she felt a strange vibration. She had felt his touch many times before, but never had she felt this vibration coming from him. She reached down into the bucket to retrieve more of the mud.

"How does it feel now?" Millie asked.

"The pain is almost completely gone," her mother replied. Millie held the mud out in Jason's direction and asked him to apply more of it to her mother's arm and hand. As he reached for the mud from her hand, Millie held onto him.

"What's the matter?" Jason realized that Millie wasn't going to let go.

"I just wanted to feel the coolness from your hand," she replied. But the coolness did not exist, nor did the vibration. Millie guided his hand to her mother, allowing him to resume his massage. The very moment his fingers touched her mother's skin, the vibration continued, slow at first, then stronger as he worked the remainder of the ointment over her skin. Within an hour, the mud had completely dried and just as Jason said, the pain was gone and there was no scarring. He had left to return home soon after the incident. It was getting late and he didn't want to worry his parents. That evening, Millie had given the situation a considerable amount of thought. She knew of no other person that had such a touch as his. Even Mrs. Johnson admitted that such a burn would normally have left some scarring, but was grateful just the same. The following day, Jason had many afternoon chores to do and wasn't able to work with Millie that day. Upon his return the next day, Millie didn't want to work with her schooling. She had much on her mind and was too excited over her discovery.

"What is it, Millie? I've never seen you with so much energy." Before he had the chance to set his school books down, Millie guided him into the kitchen."

"Look at my mother's hand," Millie instructed. Jason felt a bit uncomfortable; she had nearly pushed him into her mother acting jubilant and excited.

"Hello Mrs. Johnson how's your hand today?" He was standing so close to her, he couldn't see for himself without taking a step back. The burn was no longer visible. There were no blisters, not even the slightest red. The only remaining sign of the mishap was the missing hair from her arm that had been singed off.

"My arm is fine, thanks to you." Mrs. Johnson smiled as if to be holding back on a secret.

Jason turned to Millie, who was also smiling. "I'm glad to see you're feeling better," his voice sounded uncertain. He knew something was odd, but was almost hesitant to ask. "Is there something I should know? You both seem like you've got something to tell me. I hope it's good news, something like apple pie or peach."

"Nothing like that." Millie tittered.

"Well, come on now. I can't wait here forever. It must be real good news; you ladies wouldn't be smiling like two happy pigs bathing in table scraps."

"It's good news Jason. I think you'll be happy. I'm happy for you," Millie stepped closer to him to hold his arm. "Mother went to see Doc Peterson the other day to check on her burn."

"What did he say?" Jason asked, hastily.

"He said that mother's arm looked real healthy and that your ointment could help a lot of people in this town." Millie said.

"Oh well, that's wonderful." He thought it was a bit unusual for Millie to be so excited over something so simple. "I could make him a bucket of mud every week."

"That's not what he had in mind." Millie's smile was as gleeful and pretty as a small child on Christmas morning."

"The doctor wants to see you right away. He wants to offer you a job working with him in his office."

Times were hard, and most of the folks outside of town weren't doing very well financially. But the doctor gets many customers, rich or poor. And working as his assistant could bring him a fair amount of extra money to help his parents. Jason was pleased with the news. He hugged Millie, thanked her, and told her he should go to see the doctor before dark. Millie and her mother agreed, and bade him good luck. Jason dashed out the door and left the front door wide open as he sprinted to his horse. He climbed into the saddle and rode off.

Within less than a week, Doc Peterson had trained Jason on the basics of first aid and minor treatments. Going to school, working, doing his chores and helping Millie with her schoolwork gave Jason quite a full schedule. He promised his father that he would be able to keep up, and wanted very much to work with the doctor. He felt it would be good experience for him, and perhaps sometime in the future when he saved enough money, he would be able to go to school to become a real doctor.

Jason did as he promised. For several months, he continued on with his busy schedule. When Jason completed his last year of school, he went to work with Doc Peterson on a full time basis. Jason worked very hard with the doctor. He was offered all the books and materials needed to further his studies in hopes of becoming a doctor. Doc Peterson seemed pleased with his achievements and skills. He worked with the doctor for three years until he could learn no more from him. To further his skills, he would have to raise enough money to go to school. The financial burdens of trying to survive, run a farm and try to save money for school was a heavy toll on him. By the time he was twenty years old, he conceded that it would be too difficult to ever save enough money to go to school, and the time for him to find a place of his own was overdue.

A place in town would be better for him since it was more central for the townspeople to locate him. He grew to be a very respectable doctor with an auspicious future in his own right. He had delivered over three-dozen babies, mended every known bone, and treated hundreds of burns, cuts and bruises. The town accepted Jason as being a very capable doctor. In fact, many of the people preferred being seen by him. Since the day Mrs. Johnson was treated by him, word of his magic touch circulated around town faster than a hungry locust. The fact that Mrs. Johnson was the magpie of town spread his reputation.

After looking for a place of his own for a couple of weeks, Jason found a piece of property. The house was no bigger than a mountain cabin, and the roof needed tending to, but it soon became his home. The money that was intended to go toward school, helped pay for his land, home and restorations. The day he moved into his little house became the day of his house warming. Nearly everybody in town and outside of town surprised him by coming to visit and offer him good luck and gifts. His parents came to wish him luck, and even Millie came into town to visit him. But it wasn't the house warming that urged her visit into town, as she soon told Jason. After most of the guests had left, Millie told Jason that she needed to talk with him. The house warming party turned out to be quite a pleasant surprise, but not as surprising as the news that Millie brought with her. That evening, Jason made dinner in his very own kitchen for the first time. He was happy to share the special moment with such a good and close friend.

Millie turned out to be quite a little beauty and a homemaker of her own. She had met a man named Jonathan through a school that she had founded. She was quite skilled with her hands, and enjoyed working with children and crafts. Jonathan helped her to get the school started, and in time, she convinced him to stay on and help her with the school. Within a year they fell in love and were married. Since Jason already knew of her marriage to Jonathan, the urgency of her visit was still in question. Once the small talk was out of the way, Jason looked into Millie's face and could see that something was puzzling her.

"So if it wasn't a doctor visit that brings you out here, perhaps you would like to share your secret with me now?"

"I was visited by a friend last night, a mutual friend of ours." It seemed that her tone was unusually timid. It was as if she were trying to prepare him for some bad news. Jason had always respected her for her straightforward honesty and in accordance he prepared himself for the worst.

"Who is this mutual friend?" His expectations seemed of mixed emotions.

"Let me start by telling you what happened first. Last night, I was awakened from my sleep by a tapping at the front door. At first, I figured it was just a small animal trying to dig its way in the house. I became frightened, and it was just then, the strangest thing happened. At first, I thought I was dreaming. I've only felt this sensation once before in my life, but never with such power, such—overwhelming tranquility and—"

"What was it? Please tell me!" Jason interrupted.

"To be honest with you, I still don't know what it was. That's why I had to come to you."

"Why? How is it you feel I could help?" Jason inquired.

"I'm not here seeking your help." She held her hand out for him to hold. "I've been sent here to help you."

"To help me? Who sent you? Millie, you're not making any sense. What happened last night?" Jason was growing more impatient.

"She said you would understand, so let me tell you of something that I have never told anyone. Her face was pensive and serious with mystery. "Do you remember the time you healed my mother's hand?"

"Yes, of course I do. If it wasn't for you and your mother, I may never have been able to work with Doc Peterson."

"This may sound a bit strange, but that day when your ointment was on my mother's skin, I could feel no cooling sensation, and yet my mother was relieved of her pain and scars."

"Many of my patients claim that my medicine doesn't work, but each time I make a house call and apply the cure myself; it always works."

"I know Jason. That's the point I'm trying to make clear to you. Your ointment doesn't work. That same day my mother was burned, Doc Peterson applied the mud to another patient, and it did nothing at all. Do you remember your first day working with the doctor?"

"Yes, Doc Peterson asked me to put the mud on the old lady from the Johanson Ranch."

"And the mud cured her, didn't it?"

"Yes, it seemed to work."

"It seemed to work? Jason, you needn't act so modest with me. Your mud cured her from a disease that she had been suffering from for more than thirty years. You cured her crippled hands. Her fingers were bent, gnarled, swollen at the joints, riddled with pain and completely useless to her, but after two visits with you, she was cured. If she knew how, she would probably be playing the organ in church right now as we speak. But Jason, that's not the whole of it. The day my mother and I went to see Doc Peterson we brought the mud with us, and old lady Johanson was there in his office. So the doctor applied the mud on her hands several times and nothing happened. At first, the doctor felt that my mother and I were crazy to think that such a concoction of mud and herbs could possibly work, and that's when my mother challenged him. She swore that the mud took away her burns and blisters. But the doctor wouldn't listen, not until I told him what really happened."

"What really happened? I thought that was what really happened. I applied the mud to your mother's hand and the pain was soon to vanish. Just as it has worked on many patients."

"That's right," Millie said. "That's what I've been trying to explain to you. It works only when you apply the mud. Haven't you ever noticed that the doctor's never tried to use your medication without you?"

"Well—I figured that he was too busy."

"Doctor Peterson is never too busy to help his patients. You know that as well as I do." Her grip on Jason's hand suddenly tightened as she drew him closer. "There's something more I haven't told you."

"And what's that? Will I be able to make any sense of this either?"

"That depends on you, if you can keep an open mind." She said very seriously.

"I think I can—"

"I know you can. I told you that I felt a strange sensation last night; so strange, like some kind of vibration, and yet so pure and calming. There was only one other time that I felt that same feeling. And it came from you, Jason, three years ago when you touched my mother's hand. You have been blessed with a very, very special gift; which is why I'm here with you now. It's not the ointment that cures your patients. Your mud is merely what makes your gift work."

"Millie, I'm not quire sure of what you're trying to tell me."

"I wasn't sure either, until last night. Three years ago, I tried to explain it to the doctor, which was the reason why he had you come in, so he could see it for himself. Your touch is pervaded by a magic that I can't begin to explain. Your abilities are endless. You can heal the sick and injured like no one can possibly imagine. I should have told you this a long time ago, but I was afraid, and I guess that I was afraid of you as well."

"Afraid of me? Why me? I would never bring harm to you. I love you as I would my own sister."

"And that's why I'm here now. I should have told you the truth years ago, but it wasn't until last night that I learned why you were lying to me about your past."

Jason was beginning to get flustered. He had a past, that's for sure, but nobody but his parents and the doctor knew about it, and they swore to secrecy. "What past are you talking about?"

"I know about the barn fire, that there was no barn fire."

"How do you know about that? Who told you?" Jason asked emphatically.

"I learned it from our mutual friend last night, but I already had my suspicions long ago. I could always tell when you're fibbing. Without my eyes, I can probably see through everyone in this town. You're the most honest person I know. I don't blame you for not being honest with me about the fire. I had trouble believing it myself. The angels have brought us together for a reason, and it is time you take heed."

"Take heed to what? And who's our mutual friend?" Jason sounded confused.

"You have to open up your mind, Jason. It is very important. Many lives depend on you. Live of a future that neither of us will probably ever see. I know about the fire because I also know about Gayle, and I know that she still lives in you."

"How could you possibly know this?"

"I know because I saw everything last night. I saw how you suffered in the fire of doom. I saw visions in my head last night that only the angels could have sent. And one of them visited me last night. She told me that she loves you very much, and that she will always be looking after you. She is named Sadie. She tells me that there is also something else that you should know."

Jason said nothing. With his mouth open, he stared at her. It wasn't until that very moment that he actually believed without doubt that Sadie actually existed outside his own head.

"She wanted you to know that before you named her Sadie, her name was once, Sara." Millie could feel the goose bumps traveling over his body. "I also know how much she meant to you. I was there with you in your past last night. God, how she loves you! I never knew such a bond could exist."

Chapter Five

Introducing Rosemary

"Here driver, let me out here please."

"Are you sure madam? This area doesn't seem to be very safe. Would you like me to walk with you this time?"

"No, I'll be fine, thank you." The lady stepped out of the limousine, closing the door behind her. She seemed distant, and stared hard and steady. It was almost as though she were looking through everything as opposed to looking at the area around her.

After the driver returned to his side of the car, the lady walked a half-circle around the car and stopped ahead of the driver's side door, stating without looking at him, "You can turn the engine off, this looks to be the place."

"As you wish, Madam," the driver responded respectively and without question reaching in through the open window and turned the key.

The lady took a few short steps away from the car and began her meditative stare while walking once again. Less than sixty feet from the car, she came to an open field that was used as an old playground by the children of the nearby apartments. She studied an area of the field where a tree stump protruded from the ground just barely enough to be seen when close. She immediately turned back toward the car.

The driver responded accordingly by having her door open for her return. She climbed back into the car and quickly grabbed the telephone and proceeded to push the numbers. "Hi, its me, Rosemary," she said into the phone. "Yes, I'm fine. California is just what I had expected, smog, smog and more smog," she said while shaking her head. "No, I won't be returning just yet. I believe I'll be staying here for about two weeks. I'll probably rent a flat near the sight, and live like the commoners do. Don't worry about me, two weeks in California isn't going to kill me. I didn't live to be eighty-six years old only to be mugged. Besides, this is an opportunity of a lifetime I have to see for myself. I couldn't live with myself if I didn't at least try. I have to go now. Say hello to the kids for me. I'll see you in a couple of weeks. Bye, bye."

She hung up the phone and instructed the driver to turn the car back toward the apartment building that had posted a vacancy sign. Within two hours from her phone conversation, she was already settled in an upstairs apartment overlooking the field. Now, she must watch and wait.

69

Chapter Six
Introducing Mrs. Hunt

The two-month long punishment didn't quite stick as Mrs. Shane had planned, or hoped. Mike had a marvelous penchant and talent for discovering new ways to defeat his mother at her own deceiving tricks. Though he didn't go to the concert as she planned, it didn't faze him. Since the witch had grounded him, he decided to make the best of it. He certainly wasn't going to hang around the house long enough for his evil mother to get her talons into him again. It was his mother's idea for him to do something productive with his life, outside of raising pets and weightlifting. All too many times Mike would listen to her demand that pets are merely "prolific", not lucrative. When he was fifteen, he was able to raise enough money to buy himself a car by working for a friend of his, who owned and operated Scotty's Auto-body.

Before his father got home and drank himself into a stupor, he was able to sneak out of his room one more time to make a phone call to Scotty. After a short conversation, Mike was employed once again and out of the clutches of the witch. It was by her own word that he do something with his life and staying home grounded from Diane wasn't anywhere to be found on his list of priorities. Instead of returning home every afternoon from school, Mike would put in a few hours of work at the auto-body shop. Afterwards he would meet with Diane and stay out with her through most of the night. By early morning, Mike would return home to take his shower, gather some clothes and food and hurry back to school. A chaotic schedule, as he figured, was favored over further confrontations with his mother.

Diane's mother was very understanding of the situation and did her best to make things as nice as she could for her darling kids, Mike and Diane. She had met with Mrs. Shane a couple of times at different socials and all that Mrs. Hunt could reflect was her thankfulness that all mother's were not as Mrs. Shane. As one could possibly imagine, Mrs. Hunt was the nice 'milk and cookies' type of mother. Her house was where all the neighborhood kids would be playing. She seemed to have a magnetic appeal about her, especially attracted by the younger children. The comfort zone of Mrs. Hunt's home was soon to become the retreat of most of Mike and Diane's free time.

The passing of the two-month term came to pass

71

without a word from his mother. It was as though she wouldn't dignify him with the acknowledgement of his paying his penance.

Announcements for a dance were posted on all the bulletin boards around school. The invitation was a good opportunity to take some time off from work and be with their friends. Since his mother's last outburst and grounding, Mike made a special effort to keep from speaking with her as much as possible, and he knew that he would have to be particularly careful to keep her from finding out about the dance. Mike and Diane looked forward to going and having some fun. The previous year, they had attended the dance simply because of curiosity. But as it turned out, they had a very good time and by unanimous vote of all who attended, they were voted 'Class Couple'. Diane was crowned queen with a beautiful tiara made of dried flowers with baby's breath, carnations and gardenias. Mike was crowned king with a cardboard cutout resembling a dead fish. It was later explained that the purpose of the dead fish was to detour the queen from her king just long enough for the other guys to be able to cut in on her dance-card. It was lucky for Mike that the original plan was spoiled by the fact that a real fish could not be located that evening.

The passing of days just prior to the dance was surprisingly quiet. Each day Diane would ask him if his mother had mentioned anything relating to the dance and each time, he would supply a negative reply. The peace and absence of malice between Mike and his mother was unsettling. He could feel something brewing. Diane picked up on the perplexing vibes as well. Mike thought, "What was she going to pull next? How did she become this way?" It would seem hard to imagine how one person could become so unhappy with herself...with life itself.

From the old family photo albums, it was easy to see that peers from her childhood probably had a good time teasing her because of her obesity; she really was a sight from which to get a laugh. From the waist up she was somewhat normal looking for a kid, but for whatever reason, or for whatever joke the gods wanted to play, she developed the most bulbous butt known to the book of world records. To make matters worse and unbearably hard to restrain laughter, even for him and Diane when they first found the photo album stashed in a cache hidden under a stalk of old schoolbooks and antique relics up in the attic, was her most unbelievably large set of "Mickey Mouse" ears they had ever seen. She resembled a Saturday morning cartoon mouse; one that was perhaps stuck mid-passage through the exit of a mouse hole and had to live that way with only her buttocks sustaining the ability to grow. All she would have needed was a long tail and a set of whiskers and she could have made her parents a "lucrative" fortune as a sideshow act in the circus.

It was no wonder there were no other photos or

memorabilia of her childhood to be found anywhere, which also nullifies the idea that Mike had
about her being created in a lab by some mad scientist. But with further reasoning and the process of
elimination, it was postulated by Mike and Diane
that her goofy body couldn't have been what turned
her to the "dark side", her father spoiled her rotten
when she was a child, and her two-ton twin spheri-
cal buttocks had finally merged with her normal upper body growth by the time she was married to
Jack. Perhaps it was because she was spoiled as a
child that made things harder on her in the real
world of parenting. Countless times she would bray-
out in rage that her life was so much happier until
she had children; namely Mike. She had always
been the type of person who had to be the center of
attention, that is to say, outside of the attained
laughter from the audience of her fat butt and goofy
ears. Well...so much for monster-butt paranoid
schizophrenia psychoanalysis; whatever made her
this way, it was here to stay and there was nothing
that Mike could do or say to make things different
between him and his bewitched mother.

The day of the school dance, Mike made all the
preparations; he picked up Diane's corsage, his tuxedo and a few personal items from the drug store.
After the dance they were to go to the beach. A two-
dollar bottle of wine was chilling in a cooler and a
pile of wood for the bonfire was in his car trunk. It
was time for Mike to go home and get himself
dressed and ready while Diane would do the same

at her home. He instructed her to be ready by eight as he strutted down the pathway from her front door to the car at curbside. As he turned to wave good-bye, he found that she had followed him down the path. She grabbed him as a bear would a tree in the attempt to climb. She then pressed her body against his. Mike could feel her breasts pressing against his chest. With her legs wrapped around to the back of his, she proceeded to drown him with her kisses. He could feel the full weight of her body pressing him against the side of the car. It didn't take long before his affection had begun to swell.

"Hey lover, you get any bigger and we'll have to re-stitch those pants." Her long herbal scented hair fell to his face and she slow humped him.

He thought for sure if she had kept it up, his zipper would give-way, or the neighbors would complain, or her mom would pull in the driveway, or "E" all of the above, and probably all at once.

"What would you answer if I asked you to marry me?" The question was abrupt, but half so as her answer.

"I'd say yes," she answered, without a split second's reservation.

"Good, then it won't be long."

"Oh, there's going to be a priest at the beach to-night?" she asked, with a smug smile. "Boy, you have thought of everything."

Mike kept his composure, trying to be serious. "No, not tonight, but I want to marry you soon. Maybe even before we graduate. I wouldn't want to give anybody a chance of stealing you away from me. Besides, we love each other and I'm making money. We could get an apartment together and live as we wish, without having to worry about the witch or anything for that matter. Call me selfish, but girl; I want you all to myself. At times like now we shouldn't have to part just to get ready to be with each other.

"Okay, Shellfish, you got me. I'll be your mermaid for life, but first, I think you might want to put me down so I can get ready for tonight. I love the idea, but we should talk about this later. I have to make myself beautiful."

"Yeah—I might want to—put you down, and I may—" With her legs wrapped around his ever so tightly, there was one last slow hump and a concert of wet luscious kisses.

Just before getting home from Diane's house, Mike remembered the feeling of uncertainty. The feeling was getting incredibly stronger as he got closer to his house. Diane told him to be careful; she too could feel when the witch was festering with wile plans. He pulled his car to the front of the house. He took a deep breath as he looked over his shoulder in the direction of the front door. It's now or never, he thought. He made his way into the house with his rented tuxedo tucked under his arm and black polished shoes in hand, through the front door, past the entry, down the hallway and into his bedroom. He shut his bedroom door as quietly as possible and proceeded to dress. Once dressed, he marveled at his image. "Oh, that Diane is one lucky girl," he said aloud. The bowtie was in place, the cologne was applied—everywhere, the electric razor was slipped into his pocket for the drive back to Diane's house, every hair on his head was carefully guided into its proper place, with his curl lolling about his forehead, the shoes were spit shined...literally, and the disgustingly generic ebony glass and sterling-looking steel cuff links were clasped into position. The pelvic thrust in the wide stance was given a brief audition in front of the mirror, and of course, meeting his immodest approval, and his "hunka, hunka, burnin' love" was ready for the trek to reclaim his woman. He went out of his bedroom, down the hall, to the entry.

"Where do you think you are going?" An omnipresent voice rang out.

"I'm going to the school dance, mother." Mike replied, trying to sound matter-of-fact.

"And how is it you've come to the conclusion that you're going to this, so called 'school dance' without even asking me?" His mother's tone was sharpened and cutting.

"I already asked dad days ago. I didn't see the need in asking both of you. What's the difference?"

"The difference is, young man, you didn't ask me. Do you think I like playing these cat and mouse games?"

Mike thought to himself, and thought better than to say, "well, hell, you ought to know, mother. You spent half your life looking like some ungodly demented mouse." Instead he replied, "I don't know what you're talking about. I just want to go to the school with my girlfriend and be with my friends and have a good time dancing. What could be so wrong about that?"

"The rule of this house is, as you know it, you have to ask me if you want to leave this house, and you haven't asked me anything, and I haven't heard a thing about this dance. Are you sure that's where you're going? Or is this going to be another of your little episodes of trouble-making?"

"Would I be wearing a tux if I were going any-where but to a dance? Excuse me, mother, I'm go-ing to be late." He attempted to sidle his way past her, but just then, she put herself between him and the door.

"I'm sorry, but you're not going out this door, pal. It's time your father and I have a talk with you about your attitude."

"My attitude? I have a fine attitude and in case you haven't noticed, dad is...." Mike pointed into the direction of the living room where his father was passed out on the couch. "I don't think he's go-ing to be doing any talking tonight." Mike tittered, trying to keep from laughing at her aloud.

"You think you're pretty cute, don't you?"

"I guess I take after you, mother. "His curt tone blew his cover.

"No, if you were anything like me, you wouldn't be such a loser. You wouldn't have a slut as your companion, and only if you were very lucky, would you be half of what your brother is." The acrid words from her bitter mouth were coming from an evil he had never heard to be so cruel. She was no novice when it came to judging her prey in a duel of war with words, but this bout that she proposed was just outright truculent cruelty with little or no concern for Mike's feelings or pride. Her only intention, obviously, was to spark his anger as fast and as efficiently as possible.

"How dare you speak to me that way," Mike intoned, "I do not deserve to be treated this way. I really don't know what your problem is, but I've heard enough of it. Please move away from the door so I can leave."

At that moment his dad rolled over, falling onto the floor from the couch. "Maybe you should check on dad, he might have hurt himself." Whatever her plan for Mike may have been, she had no idea what was about to become of it. Perhaps her intention was to provoke him into striking her so that she could call the police and have him arrested, it would seem more her style. Her misjudgment of the situation was soon to surface. Mike could have simply grabbed her by the belt loops of her over-inflated Levis and lifted her to the side, tenfold. He didn't need to strike her. He didn't need to show any physical force.

For the first time, with a sudden development of some supernatural power, Mike looked deeply into his mother's eyes.

"Your father's fine. At least he can't hurt himself any worse. And I don't need you telling me what to do with my husband," She hadn't yet noticed Mike's meditative stare. "I have already told you that you are not going anywhere. You are going to stay ho---." She made eye contact. The words to complete her sentence were nowhere to be found. Mike's eyes were ablaze with an angry glare that was piercing at bay. An evil hatred exuded from his presence, as formidable panic of dread fell over his mother. With newly acquired power of seemingly omnipotence, Mike brewed his anger like a nefarious witch over his caldron coming to the rise of his nemesis. He had no idea what was happening outside of the fact he felt like he was becoming just short of some kind of demagogue, but it was working well against his mother. To see his mother's face pervaded with such fear made him even stronger. He fed on her fear.

Her face turned sallow. The front door was suddenly made available as she moved to the side, looking as though she were in fear for her life.

Mike took his eyes from hers just long enough to locate the doorknob and open the front door. Somehow, in that brief moment, she was able to gain back some of her composure. "I'll call the police, I'll tell them your car is stolen. You'll go to jail where you belong," Her words were so empty and futile with no effect at all. It surprised him to see her stoop to such puerile measures. She seemed so desperate to ruin his life. Why attack me? He would always want to know. If she had even taken the time to get to know me, we might have had a good time together. I'm not a bad person; if I were, I probably would have killed her by now, and probably without remorse. For all the pain she has put me through, she deserved worse.

"I knew you were no good. I look forward to seeing you in jail."

"Frankly, mother—"

"Don't you dare" she interrupted, practically begging him to commit the number one sin of the household, to use foul language.

"Mother, go screw yourself!" The words came from his mouth shocking him more than his mother. Mystified by his own actions, he turned his back to her and out of habit, he groped his back pocket for his comb and as he slowly and calmly walked to his car, he stroked back his hair showing no concern for his mother, whatsoever.

"You said what? To your mother? Are you fool-crazy? What got into you?" Diane asked excitedly.

"I don't really know what happened, it just popped out of my mouth before I knew to say it. I didn't plan it to be that way." Mike replied honestly.

"How was it, she just moved out of your way as she did? Now, I know your mother better than that. What could you have said to her that could possibly frighten her enough to keep you from walking through the door? She would rather die than give you any satisfaction." Diane said.

"Yeah, you're right about that..." Mike started to drift in thought.

"Well, aren't you going to tell me what you said to her, to make her move from the door?" she had to look to see if he was listening. 'Hey, what's the matter with you?" Suddenly a fearful thought came to her. Oh, no you didn't hit her did you? Mikey, tell me you didn't hit her, please tell me you didn't!'"

"You know me better than that." He said, waking from his trance.

"Thank God for that. Then tell me what caused her to move from the front door?" Diane inquired.

"I don't know what it was exactly, and if I tried to explain it to you—I think you might think I was losin' it."

"Try me." She moved closer to him after unbuckling the seatbelt.

Mike went into an explanation of how he perceived what happened. As he described all that he was feeling and all that he could remember, she just sat and listened quietly, she said nothing. And when he described the event in full to the best of his ability, he looked over to Diane who was acting strangely herself. She appeared to be mad, mad at him. It was as though she knew something about the event, perhaps more than him.

"You shouldn't have done that Michael."

Oh no, he thought, she called me Michael. She's mad and I don't even know why—women! "What is it, that I shouldn't have done?"

"You know what you did," she scolded.

"But I don't even know what happened, except that I gave her a look that frightened her and I was so angry, she probably thought I was going to kill her."

"You know better than that. Stop acting so smug with me. I know you better than that. This is serious. What you did was serious."

"Diane, I really don't know what I did." The sudden silence in the car became deafening. "Okay so I know what I did, but how was I to know that it was going to happen. It has never happened before."

"But you could have stopped it and you chose not to." She cast him a narrow sidelong glance, looking somewhat evil herself. "Haven't you figured it out yet?"

"Apparently not. Tell what's going on so we'll both know."

"You allowed your mother to get the best of you," she explained, "Your mother is mean and unhappy, and what you did was wrong. You called upon evil to vent your anger, and your hurt. You had a right to be angry, and you had a right to be hurt, she said some awful things, but that still doesn't give you the right to call upon the devil himself to strike her down."

Mike could pretty much see where all of this was leading. Diane had a strong religious background stemming back as far as her grandfather who was a minister just as her father was until he died. She had listened to enough of her father's sermons since the time she was a little girl, to know right from wrong and evil from God-sent.

"How do you know this was the work of the devil?"

"You, yourself said how you felt the evil, you tasted it and enjoyed it."

"That still doesn't make it the work of the devil. God works in mysterious ways. I felt I was doing what my mother would understand in her terms, on her turf, and it worked." Mike remained adamant about how he believed, something supernatural intervened and saved him from physically harming his mother.

"Damn your mother, and what she has done to you. Promise me that you'll never do this again."

This marked the first time he had ever heard her swear. "If it makes you happy, I promise." But he knew down deep that something was born in him, and it wasn't the work of the devil.

The two sat in silence as the drove to the school. The weather decided to show its authority with heavy drizzle and fog. Mike hit a switch at the dash. The windshield wipers came on, swishing against the glass. With Diane sitting close, Mike put her hand in his and tightened his grip as a sign of truce. She kissed the side of his face.

"You forgot to shave, Mikey," she whispered. Oh good, I'm Mikey again, he uttered in soliloquy. "I wasn't mad at you. I just wish your mother could know you as I do."

"She doesn't care to. Here babe, do me would ya?" He pulled his electric razor from his pocket.

"Anything else in those pockets I should know

about?" she cooed in his ear.

"All in good time my dear, all in good time." And speaking of time, I would have to say that mine has run out. I don't think that I'll be welcome at my house anymore. Perhaps now its time to find that apartment."

"Yes, perhaps it is," she replied.

"Damn, you're beautiful! You're going to have all the guys drooling."

Diane had made herself a lovely, long shoulder-less white lace gown with matching gloves. Her cor-sage was clipped to her bodice. Her silky, long blond hair was curled from mid-length at her shoulders.

"Are you nervous?" Mike asked.

"A bit." she shrugged her shoulders.

"You needn't be." He squeezed her hand, "you have me with you, to take care of you, to protect you, and to be there for you should you get so nerv-ous that you must puke."

"Hmmm, you're so romantic," she shook her head.

As they were turning onto the street just one block from the school, they could hear the band playing from the auditorium. The closer they ap-proached, the louder it became. As Mike completed the turn onto the street something caught his eye. In the darkness and fog, it was hard to discern. There was a flashing of multi-colored lights.

"Oh no," Mike uttered aloud.

"What is it?"

"You don't suppose my mother really did call the cops, do you?" Without waiting for her reply,

Mike barked, "That bitch, how could she?"

Diane said nothing; she just continued to look on, trying to recognize the image before them. As the beam of his headlamps reached the image, it was still too difficult to fathom. The colors were different from those of the police cars, and there was no definition. The entire street in front of them looked like some kind of aberration.

"What the hell is that?" Mike exclaimed.

"Mike—" Diane spoke with dread in her voice.

At that instant, the fog gave way. From beyond the glare of the headlight's beam came an enormous figure that was slow to define, but moving fast in their direction. The wheels locked-up with barely a squeal, but the car continued to hydroplane. They couldn't have been traveling at more than twenty miles per hour, but to their horror, the immense object was traveling at a far faster rate of speed. The multi-colors were coming to sharper view. At the street level, was a display of amber sparks caused by metal grinding against the pavement as it was sliding into their direction. The strobe of bright red incandescence was what came to view as a burning fuel tank that was about ten feet off the ground, also moving at an alarmingly fast rate of speed in their direction.

"Oh shit!" was all Mike could say as the terrifying picture of reality came closer; nothing could have been done at that point, it was already too late. A shocking blast of a scream emitted from Diane without warning. To hear her scream as she did was almost equally as chilling as the terror that was to fall upon them.

Concerned citizens of the city had made many proposals to move the interstate off-ramp away from its present location for the sake of safety on behalf of the students of the school and the residents that live close to the potential hazard, but unfortunately, the proposals of the past meant nothing to Mike and Diane as the driver of a dairy truck carrying the cargo of twenty tons of milk had misjudged his speed and the condition of the slippery road. His truck had toppled at the top of the embankment. As the rig jack-knifed, it flipped onto its side, instantly igniting the severed gas line from the tank when the exposed arcing electric brake wires came into contact with the spilled fuel. The already fast-moving truck gained more speed as it plowed its way down the sixty-foot embankment from the highway above, directly in the path of Mike and Diane. The last seconds before impact was a chilling rush of adrenalin for both of them. The driver of the truck was killed before his truck ever reached the street below, burned alive in the inferno of his cab. Its momentum had nearly doubled in speed as the thirty-foot long milk tank careened into the parked cars along the street.

The highly reflective, chrome surface of the tanker truck gave amplified display of each collision as it crushed and gathered every car in its path. The ever-present large body of the tanker consumed them just as it had everything else in its path. The tumultuous collision was thunderous with rage and undaunted fury of overwhelming force. Prior to impact, it all seemed to have proceeded in vivid, time-lapsed, slow motion and yet, happening too fast to react. Mike's car was dragged like debris entangled in the wreckage for three hundred thirty feet, nearly back to the intersection of where they first turned onto the street. Several minutes had passed before Mike came to. He found himself pinned to the steering column with the seat pushing hard against his back. He had no sensation of his lower body. As he made his first attempt to free himself from the car, he saw a portion of the broken steering wheel was impaled into his shoulder. There was no possible way for him to free himself from this horrid predicament. The crumpled sheet of glass that was once the windshield was resting against his face. He tried to turn his head in an attempt to locate Diane. The pain in his shoulder was severe. The thoughts fleeting through his head were scrambled and flustered with disbelief of what had happened. Had he had any sensation of his lower body, he would have felt the warmth of pooling blood in his lap flowing from his chest injuries. The awestruck crowd had gathered around the twisted wreckage once the flames had been extinguished. The band was no longer playing. The radio of the car was silent. The engine was dead. The rain had stopped. The only sounds to his fright were those of the curious onlookers gathering in the street.

"Whose car is that?"

"Do you think there's anyone in there?"

"What if they're still alive? Shouldn't we try to see? Maybe someone in there needs help."

"No way, no one could have survived this."

"Whose car is that?"

The voices continued in salvoes. They were talking about him, and there was nothing he could do to call out for help. He was barely able to breathe, let alone make any audible sound. A sudden sharp pain traveled throughout his entire body as he tried to turn his head toward the passenger side. As the glass crinkled and loosened, he was able to focus upon his worst nightmare, all that he lived for, and all that he loved in the world laid lifeless.

Mike reached for Diane. His hand was blanketed with the blood from his own injuries. Diane's body had been projected through the windshield. She was slumped over the hood of the car, emitting no signs of breath or movement of any kind. No, this can't be! Mike felt the sharp blade of reality making its cutting way deep into his heart. This can't be happening! This is a dream, and when I open my eyes, all will be well. While trying to call out her name, a stream of blood was all that drooled from the corner of his mouth. Why won't she move? What has happened? Diane, you've got to get up. Move damn it! Don't do this Diane! You can't do this. Get up, girl! Panic and shock was rushing him fast. Oh my God... how could this be happening? How can this be? Diane, don't you dare leave me. Don't die...

Shock overtook him, and he slipped into unconsciousness. His hand still outstretched for her to receive, his critically injured body waited for rescue. The crumpled car was embedded halfway into the tank of the truck with only the rear of it exposed to the people on the street.

Chapter Seven

Introducing the 'Lady in White'

A lady in white, with a warm, humbling smile seemed to be floating through the air. She's reaching out to me, but is too distant. Her face is familiar, but I can't recollect whom. She's fading away. Wait! Come back! Who are you?

The place was loud with kids running through the halls. Mike felt chilled. He had awakened from a dream wondering who was the lady in white. His eyes felt glassy, heavy and tired. The room took several seconds to come to view, in front of him was a wall with nothing to offer but a clock. To the right of that was a television protruding from a stand that was bolted to the same wall. As his eyes finally began to work properly with less blur, some fragments of memory staggered into proper order.

"Nurse, nurse, sleeping beauty has awakened."

That voice is very familiar, Mike thought.

"Billy—" Mike gasped; his voice betrayed him, almost choking him.

"Hey bro, don't try to talk just yet." Billy grabbed the jug of ice water. "Here, take a swig of this. This should help a bit." He reached behind Mike's head to help prop the pillow.

Mike took a shallow swallow from the straw. He didn't realize how thirsty he was until he consumed the entire pitcher of water.

"Well, that's a good sign." Billy looked into the container.

"Where am I? What's going on?" Mike asked, sounding raucous, but better.

"Let me ask you. What do you remember?" Billy replied.

"Not much, I sure as hell don't remember being here." He panned the room, hoping to remember something. On a table were a few get well cards and some fallen balloons of expired helium, nothing of recollection was available.

"Mikey," only his closest friends dared to call him Mikey. "There was a bad accident, the night of the dance. Do you remember anything?" The nurse walked into the room, but paused. As Mike looked into Billy's eyes, he could see the seriousness of the matter. He tried hard to remember any bit of information. It's common for the mind to void-out tragedy to protect itself from pain, but it was no doubt, so important for him to recover from what had happened, and the only way that this was going to happen would be soon after he remembers everything, as painful as it may be. This was part of the reason why Billy was there with him at that crucial moment to help Mike work things out. He had known Billy nearly all his life. They met playing Little League baseball at the age of seven and went on to play football and assorted other sports together. Billy finally lost interest in sports and decided to join a band. He was a good drummer and had no trouble making himself a success at it. In fact, it was his band that was playing for the school dance. That is to say, before the accident occurred.

When it was discovered that it was Mike and Diane that were involved in the truck wreck, Billy was the first to arrive at the hospital to keep vigil over things. He was like family and the doctor could see that Mike would have a better chance of recovery with Billy by his side than his parents, who never bothered to come to the hospital. It was lucky for Mike that Jimmy found out through Billy about the accident. Had it not been for his medical insurance with Mike's name on the policy as well, the hospital would have had the right to refuse service, thus sending him to a county hospital. And with the injuries that he sustained, the time it would have taken to transfer him to county may have made the difference of whether he would soon be able to walk, or ever walk at all. Bits and pieces of memory were slow to surface.

"Billy, help me out here. Tell me what happened." Mike said.

Billy pulled a chair next to the bed, "It's like

this, bro," he began. "You were driving to the dance, you and Diane, you got as far as Main Street, just below the highway off-ramp."

As Billy gave his report of the events, strobe-like pictures of events started to come back to him.

"And there was this truck, a dairy truck that—" Mike became pale. His memory was recovering rapidly.

"How much more do you need me to tell you?" Billy was hoping he wouldn't have to continue.

"You've got to tell me everything," Mike rasped.

"There isn't much more, buddy. You and Diane hit the truck and this is where you've been since. You've been in a coma all this time, until yesterday. This hospital has been taking care of you for thirty-eight days. You have Jimmy to thank for that. Thank God he had the foresight to put you on his medical policy."

As Billy was talking Mike felt the room seem to become dark with shadows. No sooner he had said the words "hit the truck", and it all started to come together; the staggered pictures of events and flashing lights, fire, sparks, the crash—Diane!

"Where's Diane?" Mike demanded to know.

Billy couldn't find the words. All he could manage was a brief shake of his head. There was a long period of silence. He stared into Billy's eyes as he watched the first of his tears begin to roll down his cheeks. A stifling lump in his throat kept him from saying another word.

Mike's body began to tremble as the vivid picture of his girl and their last moments together flashed before him. The nurse quickly left the room. Mike's face went into a trance with horror.

The doctor entered the room with the nurse close behind. The doctor reached for Mike's arm and administered a strong sedative into the I.V. "This will help you to sleep. You need your rest," The doctor announced, sounding somewhat perfunctory.

Mike never took his eyes from Billy's; the bond of friendship between them went deep. Until the sedative took affect, Mike needed Billy's strength to keep from crying out. In just a few minutes, he was asleep once again. The doctor checked his vitals.

"I'm glad you were here Billy," The doctor said. "He's going to need a lot of support from you." He placed the blood pressure cuff around Mike's upper arm and proceeded to squeeze the ball at the end of the tube. "One twenty over ninety." He reported to the nurse. She quickly responded by writing it down on the chart. "It's not going to be easy for him or you," the doctor continued. "The trauma of losing Diane will be the hindrance of his recovery. Once he accepts her death and if he regains the use of his legs, it could take months of therapy before he learns to use them. Between the bruised nerves and the atrophy and his losses, he's going to need a lot of your help.

"I understand doctor," Billy replied.

"It would be more detrimental for him to have you quit on him later on rather than if you were to walk out of here now. You must understand that his recovery is going to take a lot of time and patience to see your friend through this. We wouldn't blame you if you should feel that this might be too much for you. This is going to take a lot of dedication on your part."

"No doctor, he's my best friend. He'll be back on his feet in no time, with me be his side. You'll see. I know him real well. He's strong willed. The only hard part that I foresee is Diane. Hell, I'm not even sure that I've accepted it yet. You have no idea how close they were, how close we all were. I know this isn't going to be easy, but we'll get through this.

The doctor smiled with a show of pride for Billy. "I know you will, son. You're a good friend."

Mike dreamed of the lady in white again. What's going on here? Hey, who are you? How do I know you? Tell me, what is your name? Say something, please. But the image floated away as Mike began to wake.

"Good morning, Mr. Shane. My name is Lucy and I'll be your nurse this morning until twelve and then the afternoon shift will take care of you. Are you hungry?" She seemed almost too chipper for Mike to handle.

"I have a hamster named Lucy, or at least, I had one." Mike reiterated.

"That's flattering, and what happened to Lucy the hamster?"

"If I know my mother, as well as I think I do, Lucy is probably drowned in the sewer by now." Mike's voice dwindled.

"I'm sorry to hear that. I take it your mother's not too fond of hamsters?" The nurse trundled the bed table up to his lap. On top of the table was a breakfast tray. For hospital food, it looked pretty good to him.

"My mother isn't fond of life in general. We call her 'the witch'."

"So, you and your mother don't get along."

"To say the least. What's this suppose to be?" he asked, pointing to a side dish on the tray.

"That's supposed to be fruit cocktail. Haven't you ever seen fruit cocktail before?"

"Not like this." Mike managed to raise his lethargic arm to the tray, grab a fork and stab at the fruit.

"It's made fresh here. Those big pieces are apples, peaches, pineapple and orange wafers," she started to sound like a TV commercial. "Would you like me to raise your bed so you can reach your breakfast?"

He was preoccupied with his failure to work the fork with his fingers. "What's wrong with my hands?" Mike asked. "They feel weak. I feel weak and uncoordinated. What exactly is wrong with me, anyhow?" A thousand more questions began to erupt.

"I'll tell you what—" She said, flagging her hands for him to halt. "I'll get the doctor so he can explain all the tiny details to you. But as far as your weakness, that's quite normal for someone who's been asleep for over a month. It's called atrophy but its nothing to worry about. Your daily routines will get you back into ship-shape. Can you manage this until I get back?" She helped him get a better grip on his fork.

"Yeah, I suppose." Mike fumbled around with it until he figured it out.

"I'll be right back. If you need anything, just push the button." She pointed to a little remote box hanging from the sidebars of the bed.

As she left the room, Mike took a moment to think. Asleep for a month! Just the idea of being in bed for that long was frightening enough, but to have been asleep, that was too difficult for him to fathom. By the time the nurse returned with the doctor, Mike had nearly consumed all the food on the tray.

"Hello Michael, I'm Dr. Fargo." He reached to shake Mike's hand. "It's good to see you have an appetite. How are you feeling?"

"I was just telling Lucy that I feel weak and tired. How could I be tired if I've been sleeping so long?"

"It does sound odd," the doctor went on to explain. "But it's perfectly normal. Your body has gone through quite an ordeal; it requires rest in order to recuperate."

"So what exactly happened to me? Will I be okay? How long will I have to stay here?" He probably would have asked thirty more questions had the doctor waited that long to answer.

"Hold on now, one at a time. Let's start with the first and work our way through. You broke some bones and you sustained many cuts and bruises. Lucky for you, you should be able to recover from all your injuries, most of which have already healed." Something in his voice sounded vague.

"I should be able to? What does that mean?" Mike didn't like the sound of this.

"It means that your shoulder is doing fine, and the ribs will heal fine as they've almost completely done so. But you also broke your back."

"My back?"

"Three vertebrae of the thoracic section were broken. You were very lucky because the break didn't penetrate your spinal column. You should be able to recover from whatever bruises your spinal cord may have received. We know that you have sensation and movement, so there isn't any permanent nerve damage, but what we don't know is how long it will take for you to recover from the bruises. That is up to you. It will take time for your back to heal. We should have you in therapy just as soon as you are ready, we're hoping soon. As I said, you're very lucky."

The questions and answers went on for another twenty minutes. It was fortunate that Mike was strong willed and fit to endure such injuries, but the loss of Diane greatly affected him. The loss of his girl was too great to imbibe, and through the days to follow, at the very mention of her name, he would, each time hedge from disguising her by shunting the conversation with a change of subject matter. A very adamant subconscious block was at work. The concentration needed for his recuperation could not be divided. Although, it was to be just a matter of time when facing reality would come to surface.

Billy and the nurses watched him carefully; they kept a steady vigilance over him. He was being handled like a time bomb set to fall prey to the horrors of an agonizing and pain-filled waking at any given moment. He was offered psychological help through the hospital, but his bulwark of defenses denied the need.

The hospital procedures were methodical, pragmatic and most times annoying. Through therapy and a lot of determination, Mike was on his feet and walking by himself within two weeks with Billy by his side through every obstacle. To Mike, the process of recuperation seemed lethargically slow, but with such motivation and stamina, no one dared to tell him that never before had anyone healed as he had, and so fast.

To his surprise and fortune, he came to understand and get to know his brother in a completely new perspective. Jimmy came to visit on a daily basis. They reminisced of some childhood days and became friends, where before that friendship was impossible to nurture because of the constant interference from their mother. As kids, the two brothers were forced to accept a vague friendship of neutrality for fear that the witch would react with jealousy and vengeful rage. The witch would always find ways to wedge her way between each member of the family and cause interference, between Jimmy and Mike, there was always a stigma of condescending views. Now, with new understanding, the two felt different. Mike also learned that Jimmy suffered greatly at the hands of the witch as well. He was having trouble breaking away from her domineering influence, and unfortunately, moving away to his own apartment just wasn't enough of a detachment. He didn't even have the guts to tell his mother that his bragged about, lavishly designed and decorated penthouse apartment on the Ritzy side of town was no more than a rundown, ground floor studio apartment far from the Ritz, without a bedroom and a portable, single-burner, electric stove as the entirety of his kitchen.

Life was full of surprises, but none of which could undo the damage that Jimmy had sustained from his domineering mother. The journey of life's travels for Jimmy and his mother's damaging influence had been nothing but misery and self-degradation. Although new friendship had been found within the company of his recovering brother, the damage still remained permanent and deeper than Mike could have suspected. There was also an interesting side to Jimmy that Mike had never seen before. He had explained to Mike that life was merely a challenge, and whether one decides to accept that challenge in this lifetime or in others, the challenge will always remain. The challenge must be answered eventually, or forever return to face our fears and opposition, and forever be confronted with cowardice. He conceded that Mike was an old soul who had faced many of his challenges with intrepid staunch. He also conceded he was envious of Mike. The things that Jimmy spoke of were heard, but not quite understood by his little brother, just the same, it was good to hear those kind of bonding words from his newly united sibling and friend.

Once Mike was able to walk confidently and with less pain, the rest of his recovery went quickly. He got a lot of support from everyone, particularly the night-shift nurse, who went by the name of Miranda. She seemed to understand his every need, and even so before he himself did. Miranda was personable, unlike the other nurses who refer to the patients as "we". "How are we doing today? Have we finished breakfast yet? We want to get better, don't we?" With her long flowing, dark hair and deep, dark, compassionate eyes, she possessed a warmth and kindness that Mike found to be comforting. He found, through this companionable girl, that in times of need, friends are the necessary part of healing. Perhaps she was right, because in just four short weeks of therapy, hard work, perseverance and pain, he had gained back his strength, the twenty pounds he lost while comatose and the ability to walk; thanks to his friends and his brother's foresight to have placed him on his medical policy knowing that their parents would one day abandon him. Mike remembered laying in his bed on many nights, imagining just what it would be like to have been raised with a "real" family, the kind that shows love and compassion without reservation, the kind that can accept their fate, the kind that could laugh and have fun, the kind that he knew existed, but for the life of him couldn't figure how. He had never seen his parents laugh or have fun or kiss for that matter. The thought of them kissing made him want to vomit.

An hour before Mike was finally to be discharged from the hospital, Miranda came to visit and help him pack.

"So, its about that time, huh?" she asked, hiding something behind her back.

"Yeah, I suppose it is. I um—" The words seemed to stammer. "I...should thank you for all you've done for me."

"Yes, you should but why don't you tell me what you were first going to say."

"Well, I was just going to say—"

Miranda interrupted, not allowing him the time to think up a lie. "You were going to tell me that you would miss me."

Her words seemed to momentarily astonish him.

"I figured that we probably felt the same way about each other, that's why I made you this card." From behind her back, she presented him with a handmade greeting card. She had drawn a sketch of Mike on horseback, cantering across wooded terrain, dressed in Indian attire. The sketch was drawn well; he was quite impressed.

"Is this you, here?" Mike pointed to the girl in the picture, similarly dressed.

"Yes, that's me. And this is you." She pointed to the guy on the horse.

"Is she gesturing here that she will miss him?"

"Sort of, and sort of offering him luck on his journey."

"This is very pretty, Miranda. I didn't know that you were an artist and—"

"Among other things," she interrupted.

"Yeah, I was going to say—do you have Indian in you?" Mike was taken by her beauty, as she stood in the afternoon sunlight streaming in the window. He had never noticed the hint of red in her hair or the expression of mystery she was sending him. She also looked quite cute with her full, pursed lips and sporting her little Disney decaled bandage on her finger.

"My blood is one-eighth Indian, but of course it's the soul that possesses one's traits and knowledge."

"Now you're starting to sound like my brother."

"There's a reason for everything and everything has a purpose, Mikey." She looked deeply into his eyes as if to be trancing him with a spell.

He was caught off guard by her calling him Mikey. He put down his bag and stopped fumbling with his toiletries long enough to get a good look at her.

"Miranda, you're quite a special person and I truly appreciate all that you have done for me, but I feel foolish because I don't fully understand what you're telling me." Mike sat on the side of the bed, offering his undivided attention.

"It's nothing too complicated, really." She began to explain, looking and acting more and more personable with every moment. "Life in general conducts its cycles everyday and when certain things happen, good or bad, it's for a reason or more to the point, a purpose. Everybody we meet and all the faces we see in our life have purpose, its not just chance. Chance is merely the situations that we are not in control of."

"Such as?" Mike asked, drawn in by a side of her he hadn't yet been introduced to.

"Such as the unforeseen, the uncontrolled, and forces we are made to deal with. Your parents are a perfect example; they have nothing to do with your destiny unless you choose for them to be a part of it. If you choose, or need to, you could allow them to hurt you or you could continue on with your life by dividing the trail of life from them and going on with your own. It's up to you, and it is you that is in control of your life, and no one else can interfere with that fact unless you see a purpose for it."

"You're a fascinating girl. Why did you wait until now to expose this side of you?"

"Maybe—I just didn't want you to forget me." She was hedging from something as she looked away for a moment.

Mike reached his hand beneath her chin and guided her back. He sensed something special about her, but she was holding back. "Or maybe you were going to tell me that our meeting each other wasn't just chance?"

"There's a lesson that can be learned from eve-ryone." She was sounding too matter-of-fact now. Whatever she was trying to say, if he hadn't figured it out by now, he could only reason that it was best left unknown.

"I suppose you're right. From my parents, I guess I was to learn of humility, or perhaps how to overcome hatred. I can't believe they never bothered to come and see me, at least my dad anyhow."

"You're only fooling yourself if that's truly what you believe. I was the one that called your parents the night of your accident. You have been here over sixty days now, Mike. They haven't so much as made the attempt to call you. I think it's time to start believing, you have a whole life ahead of you, go out and learn something now." turning to better topics, "What do you plan to do? Do you know where to go? I mean—do you have a place to go?"

Mike shrugged one shoulder and raised his eyebrows. "I was invited to stay with Billy," he answered with question in his voice. "I'm just not too sure about the imposition that I would be on him and his other roommates."

"He wouldn't have invited you, had he not meant for you to come and be comfortable in his home. Do I dare say that it might in fact, be you who would feel imposed upon, that in fact, you have doubts about living with so many people or would I be too bold in taking liberties of saying such a thing?"

Mike's half-cocked smile was a sign of confession. "Oh, you truly are one gifted young lady, so perceptive of you or am I that easy to see through?"

"I think you should call Billy, get your life back

together, see what he has to offer and maybe when you've got your act together, you can come see me about the answer."

"Do you treat all your patients with such personal care?" Mike cast his narrow glance with a tight-lipped smirk.

"Only the special ones." She answered, rising to her feet, "only the very special deserve my 'personal care'. And speaking of care, I must get you checked out with your papers and such, and get on with my duties. If I don't see you when Billy arrives, I'll say 'good luck' to you now." She held out her hand for him.

"I thank you again, Miranda. You most definitely have made me feel special and I appreciate that." After shaking her hand, Mike watched her leave the room. He then finished packing his things and made the call to Billy.

"Why have we stopped here?" Mike asked, somewhat impatiently hoping to hurry to the apartment so that he could start in on getting himself settled, and then run over to Scotty's to confirm whether he still had a job.

"This is home, bro." Billy announced.

"This is home? I thought you said you lived in an apartment and with the band."

"I never said anything about an apartment. I told you that we have a place in town that we rent cheap, but I never said anything about an apartment. And yes, the band does live here too. We're quite fortunate to have a spoiled brat for our vocalist." He was

KS. Michaels

referring to Crystal, the lead vocalist and the pro-
prietor of the house.

"Spoiled brat?" Mike inquired.

"Yeah, I bet you didn't know Crystal is
loaded?"

"All I know about Crystal is that she's good
looking and she's got the best voice I've ever heard.
But I didn't know she had money. All this is from
her singing?" Mike leaned forward in the seat making every attempt to decipher just where the house
ended and where it began.

Billy laughed, "she's good, but we're not there
yet. Her ol' man, he's big time in the world of exotic perfumes." He pointed to the house and continued to boast, "He makes this in a week."

"So, how is it that you guys came to live here
too? I mean doesn't it get be uncomfortable living
with her parents?

"That's what I was getting at," Billy shook his
head, gleaming at the house, "her folks don't live
here anymore. They signed this place over to her
when she turned eighteen. They moved to some
mansion overlooking the beach, somewhere in
Malibu." Billy shut off the engine and looked over
to Mike. "Personally, I think he gave her the place
to be rid of her and save his own sanity."

"She's that bad?" Mike squinted one eye and
gave a lopsided smile.

Billy put his hand on Mike's knee, "well she
certainly has her days, but at least the rent is affordable and there's no more searching all around for a

place to jam. Until we can call ourselves rich, this is what we call home."

"I wouldn't complain, Billy." Mike couldn't get over the size of the place. He closed the truck door and marveled over every detail of landscape, the masonry, the stained glass windows, the twelve-foot high solid oak double entry doors with beveled leaded inlaid glass and the massive four-car garage.

"You haven't met Crystal. Oh and by the way, first rule of the house, no smoking inside, she'll scalp us all if she so much as smells a cigarette."

Mike shrugged his shoulders, "I wasn't ready to start any nasty vices anyhow."

"Lucky you." Billy stepped aside after opening the door, allowing Mike to enter first. "After you, big guy."

"Holy shit!" Mike stood stunned after having only stepped into the entryway.

"There's more...you'll get used to it." Billy quipped.

"Used to it? I don't see how!" Taking short, slow steps, Mike panned the sights.

"Take it all in, my friend," Billy announced, sounding like a carnival announcer, "'cuz this is what it's all about."

The house was nothing Mike had ever seen before. The house of grandeur stood with vaulted, high ceilings of over twenty feet with a royalty of dark hardwood beams. Skylights demanded majesty of open spaciousness. The carpet was so thick and full under his feet, it felt like a springboard. Even the large, custom-made potted houseplants that reached high to the skylights demanded attention, as they stood tall, strong and lush with the magnificent architecture. Each room of the house was as bold with opulence and the regal personage as Mike had only seen on television or in magazines of the affluent. From the outside of the house, there was no hint to the fact that there was also an upper floor. The spiral staircase of oak led to the one-thousand square foot master bedroom with private bath, kitchen and entertainment room, all of which belonged to Crystal. Thus, the second rule, no trespassing. Room by room, Billy proceeded with the tour.

"Who would have known anything like this even existed growing up where we did Billy?" his mind flourishing with dreams, fantasizing that this could really be what it's all about. And could he, perhaps one day, own such royal quintessence? All Mike had ever seen from the norm of domestic common living, was that of the stolid track-housing where every third house is the same as yours, with only the color of the trim and maybe the roof tiles to provide a change from the mundane. A home—two, maybe three bedrooms a couple of bathrooms and if somebody special on the block had money, they got a built-in pool in the cubical backyard, that's all Mike knew.

"This is what dreams are made of, Mikey." This is what gives us drive and the will to succeed."

"Yeah, but not in my field of work. I bet that the utility bills on this place alone come to more than what our folks are paying on their mortgages put together."

"So, we'll never see the bills. Daddy pays for that too."

Mike turned, wondering if his question would sound stupid. "Then why does she bother to charge rent if everything for her is free?"

"Daddy's rule; probably makes for a good tax write-off."

"Hell, he'd stand to make more if he just claimed it as vacant and unable to qualify a renter. Wouldn't be too hard with such a place as this. Ya know, Billy? He could easily claim a loss over three grand a month on this castle."

"You've got a fine head for business, bro. I think something like this is definitely in your future." Billy shook his head and smiled only as he knew how. "I can tell by the way you think, money is your destiny."

"I don't know whose tea leaves you've been reading, but bangin' bumpers and fenders ain't gonna get me this, buddy, I can tell you that. Which reminds me, I got to get over to Scotty's. I'm hoping that I still have a job."

"Before you go," Billy pushed open the door, "this is our room, a bit messy, but it's also home. You might have been able to score your own room a few months ago, but Crystal had the sixth room converted into an office. So, if you can handle bunking with me, I'd say we could make pretty good roommates."

111

"I'll make this up to you, pal, someday, you'll see." Mike said as he grabbed for Billy's hand for a firm shake of gratefulness.

"Do you need a ride to Scotty's?"

"No," Mike protested, kindly, "you've done quite enough for me, more than anyone. Thank you, but I think I'm going to walk this one. I need the exercise and...to smell the air once again. I've been caged up too damn long. Thanks again, you're true friend."

Billy slipped a house key into his hand and bade him good luck.

As Mike covered some distance from the house, he turned to imbibe another look at opulence. He smiled, shook his head and thanked Billy again, but only for him to hear. He walked for several blocks, taking in the sights, the passing cars and the sway of the trees. Life can be so strange, he thought.

"Mrs. Johnson needs her car back by this after-noon, guys. Let's get movin'; time is money. I want that Dodge out of here as well. I don't want Mike seeing it here. He's supposed to be getting out of the hospital today. Nick, I want it out now, please, do me the honors and tow it to the yard. If Mike shows up today, I don't want him to have to see it." Scotty's voice was powerful enough to be heard over the machinery and beyond.

"Sure Scotty, no problem." Nick responded to the orders.

There was no doubt to anyone who knew Diane

that the horror of seeing the crumpled car would cause anyone pain and especially painful to Mike. Scotty was better known as a businessman, pragmatic, frugal and punctual to no end, but under the stern facade, humbled a kind and caring man. He knew how much Diane meant to Mike. Anyone who knew either of them saw the inseparable ties. Scotty was fond of Mike and his dedication to his job and girl. He deeply understood what kind of man Mike would someday be, and he envied him. He had every intention of keeping Mike on as an employee. He knew it would just be a matter of time when he would find his way back.

A few hours after Nick had towed his car from the shop, Mike walked into the garage and presented everyone with a kind welcome. Working in the shop was Nick, usually referred to as Nicky. Chase, Scotty's oldest son, and Terry, Scotty's youngest. Now, with Mike back, the crew was complete. Everyone at the shop had their own duties: Mike, being the laborer, would dismantle and/or bang out the body damage and prepare the vehicles for Chase, who would mix and apply the bondo. Once the new mold had formed and dried or the new car part was affixed, Terry, the self-proclaimed artist would grind and sand out the rough spots and paint the finished products. During Mike's absence, Chase was given the laborious duties of frame and fender work. Needless to say, he was grateful to see Mike was well and back, ready for work. Nicky was the manager of the shop. His responsibilities were to the upkeep of the supplies, customer service, keeping the guys in line so Scotty wouldn't have to and primarily, he was the guy who wouldn't get dirty. He worked well as a manager and he did especially well with the customers. He was Scotty's right-hand man.

Mike made his rounds shaking everyone's hand. "I hope all of you missed me, missed me enough to convince Scotty to take me back," Mike scanned the garage, urging the workers to make comments. "I can see Chase is happy to see me."

"You got that right, my friend," Chase crawled out from beneath a badly rippled fender and proceeded to wipe his hands with a shop towel. "It sure is good to see you Mike." Chase seemed somewhat nervous as he walked up to accept Mike's handshake. With his young eyes of deep unfledged concern, he attempted to ask a flurry of painfully un-appropriate questions. "How are you feeling? Weren't you pissed that your parents didn't bother to—"

"Shut-up, Chase!" Nicky pulled at the back of Chase's shirt collar and gave a good yank, sending him back to his work. Scotty would have done the same, had he been closer.

Almost retching from having been briefly choked, Chase acted upon his habitual immaturity, "Hey man, you didn't have to break my neck! I can take a hint! Geeze-louise!"

"We missed you alright and we're glad to see you're well." Nicky consoled warmly as he turned to face Chase. "Some of us are just too shallow to figure out how to show respect."

"Thanks, Nicky." Mike wasn't really bothered by Chase. "Did Billy show you our place yet?"

Mike nodded with widened eyes, 'Yeah, he did!"

"Impressive place, isn't it?" Nicky nudged him with an elbow.

"Impressive is an understatement. How come you never told me about it before?" Mike asked.

"Why would I? I only bring women there?" Nicky, as everyone knew, had an insatiable appetite for the female gender, and since he wasn't bad looking, his appetite was frequently nourished. It was also fortunate for him that he was a decent bass player, as well. As Billy had commented to Mike more than once before, the only true reason that Nicky was in the band was for the expressway exploration of backstage passes and parties, thus, his ticket to paradise. He certainly had a way with the women, and he wasn't too modest to express that fact. Curiously, the very women that found him to be repulsively chauvinistic and too forward with the compliments, many times found his boast to be too irresistible to resist challenge, and ostensibly, found themselves prey to his well-mastered artifice of love and soon to join the ranks of his harem.

"Time is money," Scotty stood authoritatively in the threshold of his office while clapping his hands together, "Mike, come on in here. Let's talk, son."

"I'll catch you tonight, Mike." Nicky smiled warmly, knowing that the boss was just throwing his weight around, trying to feel important. He also

115

knew that Scotty missed him just as much as he.

Mike made his way into the office where Scotty invited him with a gesturing wave of his stout, muscular arm. He was no taller than Mike, but through the years of hard labor in the building of his shop, he sculpted quite a musculature of his own. He was known to be able to, with one hand, shear through sheet metal with ease using cutting scissors that most people would have had trouble using two hands to cut through. Mike had always admired the rippling girth of his forearms and had hoped one day through vigorous workouts, his too would be so strong and well formed.

"Come on in, have a seat here at my desk. How are you feeling?" Scotty looked genuinely concerned.

"I'm doing really well." He felt a little uncomfortable sitting at his desk.

"Are you ready to come back to work so soon? I certainly could use your help, but if you need time, Chase can handle things for a while longer."

"No, I prefer to come back to work as soon as possible. I need to for many reasons." Mike stared blindly through Scotty's chest.

"Work can be good therapy." Scotty placed his huge, calloused hand on Mike's shoulder. "If you're certain that you're ready, I'd be happy to start you next week."

Mike was hoping sooner, "How about tomorrow? I really need to work." Mike intoned as he stood up from the desk chair, now looking directly into Scotty's eyes.

"Tomorrow it is then, after school as usual?"

"Yes, that would be just fine. Thanks Scotty, I appreciate it." Mike felt comforted in the company of his employer and long-standing friend. When he left the shop, a large weight had been lifted from his shoulders. He wouldn't have blamed Scotty if he had hired someone else to take over his shift; after all, he had been away for nearly two months. Before he had left the shop, Scotty had slipped him his first week's pay in advance to help him along. The gesture of kindness and compassion was eagerly accepted. He was already starving and wondering how he was to manage through the week.

Mike returned to his new home after shopping for a few items. This would mark the first time he had ever done his own shopping. Even with the advancement of his first check, he quickly learned the value of the dollar. In the driveway of the house was Crystal's BMW and Billy's pickup truck. Hardly a compatible pair for bookends, he thought. He stepped up to the porch, still in disbelief over the size and grandeur of the house, the house that was simply given away as a birthday gift. The best Mike had ever done on his birthday was perhaps a ten-speed bike, second to that was a baseball bat and glove. As he opened the front door, he heard Crystal's operatic voice, rehearsing the scales. Her voice was powerful enough to reverberate throughout the entire neighborhood, had he left the front door open. He shut the door hoping not to disturb her. From all he had heard about her, he felt that it was best to prolong the introductions for as long as possible. Not a tenth of a second after the click of the door latch, Crystal, from high above, standing at the lectern of her banister, peered down and then placed both her hands on the rail. "Hello, I'm Crystal."

"Hello." Mike responded; surprised by how pleasant she was. The guys made her sound like a monster, yet I'm still alive; she can't be all that bad. He continued to stare at her, as the house grew silent.

"Do you have a name, stranger?" She asked, hinting a smug underside.

"Oh yeah, sorry. I'm Mike, Billy's friend." Mike just stood still almost as if to be waiting to receive orders from a drill sergeant. To make matters worse than what his friend had described, she epitomized the kind of woman that intimidates him: self-assured, confident in every way, self-managing, and independently complacent from a woman's needs for a man and all this, he gathered from her 'Hello'.

"I'll tell you what, I'll descend these stairs very slowly. If I go too fast, you just tell me. Then, I will make my way to the entry. If you wish, you may adjust the light with a switch to your left," she gestured with a tilt of her head, "should you require better illumination. Upon your signal, you may approach me or I will come to you. Shortly thereafter, I am certain that through thorough inspection, you will find no fangs, no green menacing scales upon the surface of my body, no wings for flight, not even a tail. I don't breathe fire. I possess no eviscerating appendages, or anything unpropitious for that matter, nor do I smell bad, thanks to daddy. So, whatever the guys may have told you, you won't find any dragons or brimstone here; I'm quite confident to inform you Mr. Mike. Although, if it would make you more comfortable, you could defend yourself with that pencil as your wooden stake that's on the table there below the light switch." Crystal's tone was begging for a response from him. Her monologue was still being deciphered as Mike took a second to gather himself. Her rhetoric qualities were to be commended; usually, through the practice of arguing with his mother, he would respond much quicker.

"Again, I'm sorry Crystal. I guess I just didn't know what to expect," from the distance he could barely discern the humor in her eyes. "But I really want to know what this unpropitious thing is. Do you commonly—I mean, are you, a writer or something? I thought I had heard it all, but you have a fascinating way with words. Unpropitious?" He concentrated aloud as he watched her descend each step of the staircase. "Considering the text and phrasing, my educated guess would be, perhaps weapons, claws, talons...things of that nature? Am I close?"

Less than ten feet away and with a very mischievous, half-raised, one-sided smile, Crystal answered with a question, "Are you close?" her low calm voice was a penetrating tone.

"Close enough to agree with you and your daddy." Her beauty inundated him, as well as the expertise of her father.

"So, you approve?"

The question seemed too vain and shallow for her intellect. He needed a clever reply, fast. "That depends." Mike said, trying to stall.

"On?"

"On the intent." he responded, nearly patting himself on the back.

"There's a motive?" she raised one finely penciled eyebrow.

"Motives are the essentials behind the given action, but you already knew that." Mike could see that she was one very classy lady, maybe ten years older than him at best, finely primped and preened to every detail. Even the outer ridge of her full lips was penciled in with a sharp detail of lipstick.

"So tell me Mr. Mike, how about if the motive or 'intent' were purely innocent?"

"I don't believe in innocence, or chance or even accidental voyeurism." his eyes just ever so momentarily dropped to peek at her cleavage, just enough for her to take notice. "As a philosopher once wrote: Chance is merely the situation that we are not in control of, and for every situation, there's a purpose. Therefore, purpose will, each time, preclude chance."

"Enough philosophy, Mr. Mike. Tell me, what is the purpose?"

"That depends on the creator." He was starting to evade the issue as he changed his grip on the bags.

"Doesn't the bearer have anything to do with the 'Intent'?" Crystal was allowing for no escape, she

just had to know more about this stranger, she enjoyed calling him Mr. Mike. She could see that the
shopping bags that he was holding against his chest
were getting a bit heavy after all this time.

"That depends." Again he was stalling.

She stepped closer and without taking her eyes
from his, she took hold of one of the bags and had
him follow her into the kitchen. "You're avoiding the
question Mr. Mike." She persisted, placing the bag
on the counter. With a facial gesture, she insisted he
pull the barstool from the counter from her.

Mike placed the bag on the counter alongside
the other. He was enjoying her game, it was a pleasant and refreshing change from the insipid and re-
pugnant 'high school life' that he so bitterly
loathed. He liked playing these kind of games, it
wasn't often he could find a worthy opponent. In
spite of his wicked mother, his skills were kept
sharpened, but never challenged by any other. There
were a number of similar games that he liked to
play as well; the comfort zone, for one.

The comfort zone game was something he
would often employ against his mother, particularly
when words were at a loss. Against his mother, it
worked every time. It was a very simple maneuver;
he would merely create an introspection of his present desire, implant it deep into thought, build it up
with generated energy and project it at will from an
energy emitting center-point, located at the center of
the forehead. In his case, generally toward his
mother, he would project an image of himself as

strong, overpowering, and somewhat formidable. The next step would be to encroach into her comfort zone, that is to say, approach her while projecting this energized manifestation of power, as if he were some kind of bulldozer. The intent of course, is to try to push her from her comfort zone without having touched her, to actually move her or someone with just a thought. With his mother it was, each time, very successful. In Crystal's case, his intent and introspection would not be of hate or of a power monger. Mike chose to try to decry her self-confidence, perhaps make her uncomfortable. She had a penetrating stare. To make her drop her eyes from his would show his victory over her and her concentration. She had a well-crafted skill of using her eyes as her tools, and she knew it too. It seemed that her backbone of confidence derived from her ability to stare-down her prey.

"Then let me reiterate," he concentrated on his thoughts and gazed deeply into her light brown eyes. Prior to him projecting his thought, he stepped closer to her.

Crystal didn't flinch, she stood adamant, waiting for him to pull the stool back for her. "You proposed innocence. So, if in fact innocence was your 'motive'—"

Mike stepped up to her, close enough to feel her warm breath on him. Her eyes flinched momentarily. He reached for the stool behind her as he projected forth with his power to weaken her confident stare. "You failed miserably." He stared her down with shearing intensity. Her eyes momentarily dropped from his, she began to fidget with the hem of her blouse. She tried to regain the concentration, but her efforts to redeem herself were futile. He broke her self-righteous will, as if he were breaking a feral horse of its spirit to its saddle and rider. Mike slid the barstool up to meet with the back of her legs, prompting her to sit back. He offered her a benevolent smile. She gladly accepted, returning the gesture with her habitual mischievous smirk, wondering to herself how it was that she had taken such a shine to this guy, and so fast.

"True Mr. Mike, I'm far from innocent as the same for my motives, but you didn't need daddy's perfume to tell you that." Her smirk was now more submissive than confident. "So tell me, what's a good looking guy like you doing in my house, when there's a million available women out there just dying to get their hands on you; ready, willing and able to support such a provocative stud as yourself? Surely, you don't intend to stay here long." Her manner was straightforward.

"As long as the invitation is open, and as long as it takes."

"As long as it takes?" Crystal inquired.

Mike felt a sudden, sharp pang deep in his stomach. His eyes swelled with glassiness. With all his efforts, he fought back the tears. "God, I don't know. I honestly don't know. My life is adrift right now. It would seem that only today I've come to the surface, but I'll be damned to say which direction to take. A shutter of a face flashed before him. It was Miranda's. He could here her voice and her words. "Perhaps that's why I'm here, Crystal." He looked at her face to read what she was thinking. For a moment she was quiet.

She leaned forward to gently land her hand on his. "Whatever it is you need, no matter what it is, you come to see me, Mr. Mike. I'm certain that you were guided here for a good reason. You are very welcome in my house for as long as it takes to find what you are looking for."

In her eyes, Mike could see warmth and compassion. The smirk she wore so well was just a tiny line at the corner of her mouth. For another hour, Mike and Crystal talked. She was picky about those she called friends and cared less for those who tried to befriend her, but didn't know the requirements to be so. As he got to know her better, it became clear that she was a perfectionist in every detail, including her companions. She had little patience for ignorance and fools. What Billy and Nicky misinterpreted as petulant mood swings was understood by Mike as simply her lack of patience. It was obvious that she required a certain provocative stimuli to sustain her interest. As far as Mike was concerned, he had found a new and interesting friend who had displayed patience in abundance for him. As the conversation escalated, Mike had to stop. He was getting tired and his back was showing signs of wear. He politely excused himself after informing Crystal of how much he enjoyed her company. She offered to put his groceries in the refrigerator. The pain was growing sharper as he stood from the stool. Accepting her offer and grabbing a container of orange juice from the bag, he carefully walked to the hallway, toward his room while groping his pocket for his pain pills. He half expected to see Billy in the bedroom, but was just as content to find the room vacant. He laid himself on the sleeping bag that Billy had loaned him, it was hard against the surface of the floor. Though with little concern for the rustic conditions, he pulled the bottle of pills from his pocket and guzzled a couple down with the juice. Seconds later he was asleep.

The band had been practicing for three hours when Mike was lured from his drug-induced sleep. To the sound of live music, he was lulled awake and impressed with Crystal's radiant singing voice. He had heard her sing before, but had forgotten just how beautiful it was to hear her sing. The band was well versed, as there were few mistakes that Mike could hear.

Slowly, he picked himself up off the hard floor. Looking in the mirror, he could tell that six hours sleep wasn't going to cut it for him. He would have to wait until the band stopped practicing. As he sat on the edge of Billy's bed, he took an interest in the music they were playing. Figuring that they probably wouldn't mind him watching, Mike stepped out of the room following the lead of the music. He hadn't even noticed at the time of Billy's tour that a small studio existed just to the side of the living room. It seemed as though the house was getting larger every time he closed his eyes. When he finally reached the studio, he was combing back his hair trying to look presentable.

In an instant, Crystal made eye contact with him. As she sang, the little smirk appeared on her lips. He couldn't help but smile back in response. Talking with her that day was a good healing for him. When he saw her up on the stage, he realized how much he really liked her. It made him feel good to know she was a true friend. The band completed the song and held a brief discussion afterwards.

They were called The Passion Seekers; Nicky played the bass guitar, Billy was the percussionist, Crystal was lead vocalist and the lead guitarist was Paul, and lastly, Tawny played keyboard and backup vocals. Mike had never before met Tawny or Paul, together they sounded like professional musicians. As Mike sat leaning against the edge of the couch, in front of the stage, he listened closely to the song that Crystal had picked. It was called When Love is Lost, You will Always Find Me. It was a slow love ballad, something he had never heard the band play before. Throughout the song Crystal kept her eyes trained steadily on his. Tiny little chills shot through his spine as she sang. Her singing was flawless, as to be expected.

As Mike was able to play games with energy forces, Crystal had perfected similar traits with an enchanting energy perceived through her voice. As she sang to him, she had him melting in the seat.

Deeper, he found himself sinking into the couch. He watched her every motion and expression. Her energy and spirit was being offered for him to relish infinitely. He had never heard her, or anyone, sing so effectively, so soulfully, and with so much passion. As the enchantress of song, she captured his undivided fascination. The lyrics seemed to be a message for him to understand. Throughout the song, Crystal never stepped off the stage, but to the dismay and shock to the rest of the band members, it was obvious that Mike and Crystal had a connection. She was accepted, praised and never challenged as the backbone of the band, the one to never lose her head or cool under any given circumstances. In accordance Crystal's added verses and extra-lengthened notes, the band stayed loyal with her lead. And with a look of confusion and wonderment, Tawny did her best with the band to accompany Crystal's advance. The song was performed, as it had never been before, with feeling, energy and compassion, something the band rarely saw from the habitually coldhearted Crystal.

In awe, Mike was captured by her beauty and unleashed talent. Her mousy, brown hair stylized to the recent Cosmopolitan fashion, her tranquil brown eyes, and her unmentionably costly streamlined attire all the way clear to her pedicure, all paid tribute to her fastidiously maintained beauty. The ballad was the last song of the rehearsal that evening. Afterwards, Crystal joined Mike on the couch. The remainder of the band members cautiously and quietly left the stage after dismantling and covering their instruments. Crystal and Mike were left in privacy. Crystal was never one to hold back on her feelings or opinion, so it came as quite a blow to the remaining band members as they were leaving the room to have overheard her coddling mannerism towards Mike. She was truly fond of him and he was made to feel special for that fact. As though the conversation from earlier that day had never ended, they talked. The topics of discussion covered a vast, but centered arena of common interest. They learned of the other's life interests. She could see beneath the facade, the inevitable crash or his reality would be a hard impact on him. As Dr. Fargo had told Billy, "it could happen at any time, and perhaps without any foreseen provocation. Until that moment comes, we walk on eggshells, hoping to be there for him for when that moment should finally arrive." Crystal's maternal instincts took heed to preparation. She wanted to be the one to catch him when he would finally come to fall. Hours after the band had stopped playing and had gone to their rooms, Crystal and Mike were still making new discoveries, and were bonding with friendship. By midnight, the pain in Mike's back had returned. Amid discussion, he excused himself to get another orange juice from the refrigerator to help swallow down more pain pills. As the bottle of pills was extracted from his pocket, he discovered that Crystal had followed him into the kitchen.

"Hey," she said, "didn't I hear you playing with

that bottle of pills earlier today?" In her own prying way, she was showing her concern. With merely a tilt of her head and inquisitive look, she was given the bottle for her inspection.

"You've got good ears too," he said.

She accepted the 'too' as a sign, but didn't make any comment. "Darvocet," she announced, reading the label aloud, "your back?"

"Yeah, that and a hell of a headache." Mike ran his fingers through his hair and pulled at the mane at the back of his head and neck to relieve the pressure.

"Perhaps you need something to eat. I'd be happy to make you something." She glanced at his bicep as it flexed with his movements. There was very little about him, if at all, that she could find unsavory. He could see that she felt a sudden urge to touch his arm, but saved it.

"Um, I don't know. I'm not really hungry. When I get like this, food doesn't help." Mike widened his eyes to locate the bottle in her hand. He reached and waited for her to drop it into his grasp.

"I know what will help, and it's not these pills." With her one hand supporting the underside of his hand, and the other placing the bottle in his palm, she held onto him firmly, waiting for his reply.

"Please, I'm open for suggestions." He was sensing a change in her.

"A massage, it will help." She could hardly keep from grabbing him, as she almost felt ashamed for the way she felt.

"Crystal, that's a fine offer. I wish it wasn't so

late, but—" He stepped back signifying his desire for the pills. "I have school tomorrow, and I think I should get some rest," he felt as though he should say something more, so not to hurt her feelings. "How about a rain check on that massage?" Though, he knew it would never happen. There was still the habit and contract of monogamy sewn in with the barrier of Diane's death.

"I'm here for you, should you need me," she relinquished the bottle and reached for a glass out of the cabinet. After she poured the juice, she handed it to him and gazed deep into his soul. "I mean that."

"Thank you, somehow, I know that you do." He gulped down two pain pills and watched Crystal walk from the kitchen. Unconsciously, he had stepped from behind the kitchen wall to watch her walk up the stairs. Without turning around, she stopped momentarily.

"Goodnight Mr. Mike." Came a subdued voice from midway up the staircase. And only after his predicted response did he realize, had he stayed in the kitchen to finish his drink, there would have been no way for him to have heard her low whisper all that distance away.

Mike walked back into the kitchen. Under their breath for no one else to hear, through her smirk, and through his gaped mouth of surprise, "Gotcha!" they both said simultaneously.

Chapter Eight

Rosemary

For a woman in her eighties, Rosemary had a firm grip on life and her wits. She was sharp and stubborn to no end. She had conducted her entire life in accordance to a format of her own liking, and there was no person or thing that had a prayer towards changing that fact. Her provisions of clothes, jewelry and such items were calculated for a two-week journey and an additional two-week stay in California. Once she found what she was looking for and was able to find herself a place to stay, with her chauffeur billeted across the hall from her, she kept her vigilance over the field from her second story window. After the first week had passed, the premonition became stronger, proving that the moment of truth was coming near. And the mystery of nearly two centuries was soon to unfold. She bought herself a pair of binoculars before leaving on her trek across six states. She had a dreadful fear of flying and being without the comfort and reliance of her own personal chauffeur would be too much to ask. With her binoculars, she focused on every face that came to the park. Most of those who came were too young to consider. And the ones that came with sports equipment were obviously the wrong party as well.

She was expecting a male in his mid-twenties and most like accompanied by his female partner of approximately the same age. She relied heavily on her intuition. What she thought was a couple of close calls were confirmed to be false alarms as she peered through her spyglass and could discern without flaw that the prospects didn't have the fire in their eyes to be the ones. Some of the visitors of the small park were regulars and often frequented the green grassy knolls, some everyday. One young and energetic couple would come to the same semi-secluded spot each day at three in the afternoon with their picnic blanket and beverages. Before long the two would be heavily engaged in an exchange of heated passion. Just as punctual as the young couple, hidden by the tall weeds of the hillside, were three young boys, one with thick glasses and an overbite, wrestling over their toy telescope, trying feverishly to get an education from the couple below.

From the superior view of her upper floor window, there was no doubt that those little rascals got an eyeful of what they came to see. Watching the world continue on from her perch and vantage point, she would reminisce about her own childhood and rigors of growing up as an especially gifted child; working hard as a young adult; becoming a wife to her childhood sweetheart; and the last decade of her life as a widow. It was a rich, full life of many pleasures and joys, as well as losses and pain, but she was proud to say she had done it all and regretted nothing. And now with one last quest to venture, she could die in peace after learning the truth of her progeny.

It was early, just after sun-up. Normally, Rosemary would still be sleeping, but this morning was like no other. She could feel her heart pound like never before. They were close, very close. There was no doubt about it; they were on their way. She nearly broke her glasses as she scampered about the room groping to find where she had left them; with a sweep of her hands she knocked them off the nightstand and onto the floor.

'Come on Rosemary get a hold of yourself,' she thought. You don't want to screw this up by staggering onto the street like some blind, drunken old biddy. Okay now, slow down and catch your breath. Take three deep breaths and you will be calm as a stone. She took three deep breaths and with the exhale of the last, she ranted to herself with flailing arms, what the hell am I wasting so much time for? They're about to arrive and I'm here cocking around playing blind Yogi. She lowered herself to her knees and with wide erratic sweeps across the carpeted floor she probed along the ground for her glasses. When finally she found them under the bed, she fastened them around her ears and onto her nose.

As fast as her gnarled arthritic fingers could dial, she phoned the chauffer. "Driver, it is time. Don't bother to pack, just get dressed and meet me downstairs with the car ready to go immediately." Without waiting for his reply, she dropped the phone to the cradle and scanned the room for her purse. She was acting as a child on the morning of Christmas, excited, in panic, full of bliss and joy and at the same time, she felt nervous like on the day of her wedding. So many questions would come to roost as she ferreted about the room for her clothes and shoes. Would they think I'm crazy? Would the believe me? Will they find it? Oh no, what if they don't find it? What if they don't show up? My goodness, I'm going to have to stop this craziness right now, or those nice men in white jackets are going to put me away in the funny farm for the loony and decrepit, that's for sure. The kids will show up, and they will find it, and we will get along famously. I'm a Mathison for God's sake... they have no choice but to believe me.

Chapter Nine
Returning to School

M ike's first day back at school he actually felt nervous. Returning to campus that day was an odd endeavor for him. He felt as though he were suffering from amnesia; the location of his locker, the combination to open it, the schedule of the classes and the times that they were to start, were all part of a faded memory of another life and time.

The first failure of the day was his inability to remember his locker combination. He spent so much time working with it, he found himself ten minutes late getting to his first class, and since he didn't get the locker opened he was forced to attend the first class unprepared without his books or note-book. He felt a like a fool walking into class both late and without his necessary paraphernalia. He also felt as though something were terribly wrong, as if everyone was staring at him. Whatever he was suffering from was happening only in his head. At the close of his first period he was only too grateful to leave.

Almost in a panic, seconds before the bell rang Mike dashed out of the classroom without a word. The pressure from an unknown source was too much for him to handle. As distant and unforgotten as all seemed to be, equally so were the faces of his friends and companions. As he would pass old buddies in the halls, he wouldn't know what to say, he just felt foolish and lost, and unfortunately no one seemed to know what to say to him.

His peers had not forgot his tragedy, and as hard as it may have been for them to articulate their feelings, it was worse for him. He felt like running away. The feeling of uncontrolled panic mounted with every passing second. Finally, he gathered enough strength to make his way through the halls to his locker. Once again, he attempted to work the dial, trying to remember the forgotten numbers. The movements of his fingers and hands appeared to be moving in slow motion, as if her were watching himself through a porthole.

Suddenly, a sharp pain shot through his back. Pictures filled his mind. He tried with all his will to block them out. The panic was moving swiftly through his body. He was losing a battle he had no idea even existed. Loud sounds of shattering glass filled his ears keeping him from hearing the passing footsteps behind him. Nothing seemed in place, like a harrowing nightmare. The locker wouldn't open.

He pounded his fist against the metal door, but all he could hear was shattering glass. His heart began to race and pound in his throat. He felt as though he couldn't breathe. He fell against the locker door with his face pressing hard at the cold metal. The pictures in his mind attacked in salvoes, coming faster and faster. The noises were growing louder. The screaming would not stop. The screaming was so loud he couldn't control the panic. His body was trembling. Sweat was pouring from his brow. The cold metal was pressing hard against his face, and it felt like glass. The pain in his back grew with crippling severity. He had to get away. He felt pinned against the locker. He could barely breathe. The noises were so loud, too loud. With all the strength he could muster, he raised his hands to the door and pushed himself away from the locker. He opened his eyes, and the noises stopped, the pictures vanished. All was quiet save the loud pounding of his heart in his chest. As the fog of sweat left his eyes, he witnessed the locker door finally swing open, and as each and every time that door would come open, Diane's hairbrush fell out onto the ground. It all remained silent and in slow motion. Until the hairbrush hit the concrete, there wasn't a sound on earth that Mike would have heard. Without warning, he found himself sitting on the ground beside the brush, his knees had buckled, leaving him lithe and without will. The tears streamed from his eyes as he stared blindly at the hairbrush. Strands of entwined long, blond hair were weaved through the teeth.

Diane was gone and there wasn't a damn thing he could do about it. Caring less about anything but her memory, he reached for the brush and clutched it tightly in his fist and drew it in, pressing it hard against his chest. The voices of his peers standing around him sounded as they did the night of the accident when he was trapped in the car. There was nothing he could do; there was nothing he cared to say. He managed to lumber himself to his feet. Leaving the locker door wide open, Mike left the campus never to return. He couldn't have been able to hide the tears had he even made the attempt. He walked straight home without stopping, to a home of what felt to him like total strangers.

His sluggish stride carried him to the front steps of Crystal's house. The front of his shirt was soaked from the constant flow of tears. Looking as though he were drunk, he inserted the key in the slot, turned it and opened the door. In a trance, he entered the house.

As usual, Crystal keeping vigil over the front door, peered down. "Oh no," she said with dread. As fast as her feet would carry her, Crystal came down the stairs.

The tears were still flowing but his emotions seemed distant and almost cold. He was headed for his room when she reached the bottom of the staircase. Standing in the entry, she called out to him.

With his back turned to her, he stopped. Silently he stood motionless. She walked up beside him and placed her hand on his shoulder to turn him to face her. His body turned, but he was only looking through her as if she wasn't there.

"Tell me what happened," Crystal said, feeling the pain he was suffering. "Talk to me Michael, let me help you."

There was no response from him. Looking like a shock victim, he felt the cold steel blade of truth jab deep into his chest through his heart. The lump in his throat had grown so large there couldn't have been any way for him to answer, even if he had made the attempt. Instinct took heed, as Crystal stepped forward, Mike's knees buckled. His struggle to communicate was slow to prevail as he found himself on all fours amid the entryway.

In her white, silken, taffeta outfit, Crystal stooped to her knees, gently pushing back on his shoulders. As he came to sit back on his heels, she moved in closer and took hold of the back of his head with the maternal embrace of both her outstretched arms and drew him to bury his face at her bosom. No sooner than he perceived her consoling touch, his body trembled and a surmounting deep breath was drawn. There was no holding him back now, with the deterioration of the barrier, there was nothing to protect him from the fact of reality, and nothing he could do, but concede his loss. The bray of his anguish unfurled with a blasting world of hurt. His Diane, his loss, was too much to accept. Crystal could barely understand his brash and muffled words of agony. But it didn't matter. The words would have been too painful for her as well. Her own tears were proposing a challenge to her strength. With the deepest compassion of her soul, she held him tightly in the harbor of her arms enfolding him ever so mournfully as she rocked him, pivoting back and forth on her knees. As his sounds of pain turned to words, she pulled him against herself with all her strength. The heat of his breath could be felt between her breasts as it penetrated the thinly woven material. Her heart went out to him as he cried out like a scared, lost waif. Huddled into her mothering shroud, Mike cried out the dregs of his pain.

"Why did this have to happen? Why Diane?" Mike demanded to know.

As the painful words came clear to be heard, Crystal cried unashamedly. And as he continued his demands to know more about the unfairness of life she cried even more. She searched for the appropriate answers but found none to offer. She wondered what could possibly take away the pain he was suffering so deeply. What miracle could she manage or create to urge him to recover from it spontaneously and shove the hurt to the past? Crystal held him with an embrace that she hoped would fight back her own tears. Her fingers ran through his hair. The heat of the sun was still present from his long walk home. As he slowly came to realize that it was Crystal's embrace that held him so tenderly, he responded by wrapping his arms around her waist, burying his head even deeper into her chest. She looked down, kissing the top of his head, feeling almost ashamed for the way she felt as a twinge of arousal shot through her while he held her so strongly. She could count every finger as they pressed against her back.

"What am I going to do? I'm lost without her! What am I supposed to do now?" The question seemed more direct and in need of solution and absoluteness.

She could offer neither of these things. There was no solution for the pains of loss, none of which that she could offer that time wouldn't heal on its own. Still, she felt that she had to say something. She had never lost anyone before, all the words that came to mind seemed impotent to his needs. She wanted desperately to take the pain and end his suffering. "I don't know what to say to you, Michael. I would offer you the world if I knew it would help. What would you have me say that would make it better?" The tears were in her voice as well as her eyes and face. The sudden pang of arousal traveled through her once again as he tightened his grip around her waist, as if to be making sure she wouldn't leave him. She gently planted two more kisses on his head. The heated saturation of his tears had literally soaked through her silk top and lace bra to her rising, goose-bumped skin. She almost felt ashamed of the way she was feeling. The man in her arms had lost all that he has known to live for. It seemed to her that her dutiful responsibility as a friend was to act accordingly with compassion and guidance, but instead Crystal wanted most to tear off her clothes and offer her body as the answer to salvation. It was becoming harder for her to rationalize her thinking. As Mike held her out of fright, Crystal thought how never before would she have given a thought to offer solace for anyone, it wasn't her style, it would make her too uncomfortable and perhaps most of all, it would take too much of her precious time. She was coming to realize how selfish and unfeeling she truly was towards others. She thought hard about who might be in her life that would cause her to hurt as badly as she was seeing in Mike. There was no one. As an only child, there were only her parents, and to the best of her knowledge the loss of her credit cards would be all that could hurt her enough to cause her to cry. Now, as she felt ashamed for two reasons, she told Mike how sorry she was and again could only offer her friendship to help him get through the hardship. Oddly enough, he responded.

"God, Crystal I don't know what I would have done without you here today." His face pressed against her breast. "Thank you for understanding. You know, it's strange, I feel as though we've known each other for a long time. Does that sound crazy to you?" Mike loosened his hold to see her eyes. He looked as innocent as a teary-eyed, young child who had lost his puppy.

"Not in the least," she shifted her stance and firmly pulled him back to the harbor of her breasts. "From the first moment I saw you, I felt the same way."

As the cool air came into contact with her wet skin, he could feel the hardening of her nipple as it pressed against the side of his face. Mike had no idea of what thoughts were rushing through her head. It was a wonder that he didn't comment on her pounding heart. "I just don't know what to do now," his mind was still adjusting. "I mean...I never imagined my life without her. I don't know where to go or what to do. I can't go back to school. The only reason for me being in school was to see Diane each day." His grip pulled hard at her waist. Flattening her breasts to his chest.

Her breath of passion disguised well as sorrow led the way for unfledged counsel. "You— don't have to continue with school and you most certainly do not have to go anywhere from here. I want you to stay and recover with me. I can help you. We can help each other." She said, sounding as though she were begging. But he wasn't listening to her words so much as her tone that consoled him. Her comforting embrace was truly what he needed the most and she wasn't about to release him without furthering her attempts at helping him recover from the memory of Diane. She could almost hear him drifting off into thought as the silence stilled the air. With all that she had ever known from the definition of loving compassion, she continued to run her fingers through his hair, and rocked him out of, perhaps, shame but mostly selfish passion. For more than twenty minutes the two were comforted in locked embrace. Her thoughts were pervaded with the curiosity and intrigue of her own actions. No man before was worth so much of her time and pity. She wondered what made him so different from the rest. What was it about him that was driving her passion? Maybe they truly were alike, or at least, alone in the world. He was thinking only of Diane, an impenetrable concentration that Crystal had to wean him from. Her knees began to grow sore against the hardwood parquetry flooring of the entryway.

"Michael?" her soft voice broke the silence.

"Yes, what is it?" The taffeta was filtering his words and breath.

"My knees," she answered, but not yet willing to let him go. "I believe they've fallen asleep. But I don't want to let go of you."

Mike wasn't quite ready to see the humor in the situation as he would normally. "Would you like me to make the first move?"

"If you can without letting me fall, I would be appreciative." Her tone sounded different, almost sedate.

With little effort, he kept his one arm wrapped around her mid-section while the other scooped under her legs. In two effortless steps, he was standing stout with Crystal carried in his strong arms. She felt as though she could melt all over him.

"Now I know that you wouldn't let me fall, so this is the least I could do for you to reciprocate." He looked into her eyes offering his thanks for her kindness with just a wisp of a smile at the corners of his mouth. "Where to, my kind lady?" The words were too unbelievably apropos for her to have planned it herself.

"I don't think I can walk just yet. Would you bring me upstairs, please?" Her knees were red as

144

Mike could plainly see, but if the timing were opposite, she, with her red knees and all the stiffness of rigor mortis would have carried him up the stairs to the zenana where no man has ever ventured, no man has ever been found worthy, until now.

As he took the first step toward the staircase, she held onto him tightly, nestling her face alongside his. At that moment, caught in the direct beam of the skylights, they both saw her very dark set of well-rounded nipples that had no problem giving defined shade and shape through wet lace and taffeta. Responding with reflex, she descended her hand from his shoulder and placed it across her breasts to minify the impulse of embarrassment. She looked into his eyes to read that he too was trying to hide his embarrassment. Her wrist pressed firmly against the wetness of her clothing. She could feel her nipples coming to harden once again as he stepped up each tier of the staircase. Her passion was quick to rekindle with nasty thoughts of her own selfish desires. She never thought she would ever rise to such verve for such a young man, a man probably ten years younger than herself. The mere idea of her wanting a younger aged boy made her feel old and domineering. Little did she realize, she had always been domineering in all her relationships.

Mike came closer to the upper level as her curiosities came to surface.

She wondered what he would do if she were to remove her arm from the veil of her dampened breasts and once again take hold of his shoulder; no

145

sooner the thought came to mind, impulse endeavored without hesitation.

Mike was certainly the gentleman, never dropping his eyes to meet with her intent. She could feel the material of her bra rubbing against her flesh. The shame that she felt before was soon to be overcome by selfish desire. Her mind was working fast to implement a plan. Her hand moved from his shoulder to the back of his neck, it was firm with strong, swollen muscles.

"You're tense." She said as her fingers methodically began to work at the tension as best as she could from the difficult angle.

They reached the top of the staircase. Mike panned the room in amazement. As hard as it was for him to believe, the upper floor was even more lavishly designed and decorated than the lower level of the house. Looking through her bedroom there was a wraparound redwood deck, just a step outside her bedroom and the remainder of the upper floor. As Billy had bragged, Crystal had her own kitchen, no smaller than the one downstairs. One of the upper twenty-five by thirty foot bedrooms had been converted into a dance hall-sized, walk-in closet. It too was furnished with assorted dressing tables and dressers with numerous mirrors. Behind the double entry doors, one entire wall of the closet, from floor to ceiling was occupied by nothing more than custom-made shelves accommodating what looked to him to be a minimum of three thousand pairs of shoes, of every color, style and brand. The interior design of the bedroom resembled the majesty of opulence found in magazines. The open, airy style and meticulous furnishings was much more to him than just breathtaking. Off to the right of the bedroom, divided by the hint of privacy via an antique armoire was the kitchen in all its proud glory.

Different from the design of her bedroom, the kitchen was rustic, almost provincial. A thirty-foot tall, A-frame structure bathed with sunlight from the massive wall of windows came to view as a warm side of Crystal. Outside the windows, beyond the deck were one hundred foot tall, strongly girthed pine trees. In the kitchen was an old-style, four-burner wood burning stove and from the looks of it, it had never been used. Copper pans and nearly a dozen baskets filled with dried flowers were fastened to the knotty-pined, tongue-and-groove wall above the stove and sink to add to the flavor of the rural country look. Old cook books, brass and copper fixtures, folk art collectibles, handmade crochet pillows in the chairs around the pine picnic table, kerosene lamps and a simple country hutch, not yet inhabited by the decorations of dishes and such were all the garnish of the rustic style Crystal had intended for this room. Out of all he had seen of the house, Mike appreciated the kitchen most, it seemed that the simplicity was more to his liking and comfort. She watched his eyes travel from room to room as he stood holding her at the top of the stairs.

"You're the first." She said, working her fingers at the muscles of his neck. He seemed to respond by tilting his head to give her better leverage.

"The first what?" Mike asked, becoming more entranced by her finger-work.

"That is to say, aside from the men my daddy hired to build this room for me, you're the first to bear witness to its existence." She seemed quite proud of her work.

"I have one inclination to offer that I hope wouldn't offend you, Crystal."

"And that is?" She inquired.

"That I would be more inclined to relish in the wilderness of your kitchen than anywhere else in this house. From what I can see from here, it's my kind of design. There's a side of you in there that I wouldn't have believed, had I not seen it for myself." Mike continued to walk around the room to locate the bed. As he proceeded towards the bedroom, Crystal knew she would have to act fast if she was going to savor the moment and make it last. She knew that he was enjoying the massage, with little strategy needed, she reasoned to simply continue with the massage until he would fall slave to her.

"Set me on the bed, if you would, please," she said.

He did as she instructed. "I hope your knees are feeling better. I want to thank you again for your friendship and kindness. It would seem my whole life has changed before my eyes. I really don't know how I'm going to get through it."

"You don't have a choice." She was getting annoyed with the thought of Diane.

"Excuse me?" Mike ensued, sensing a strange tone.

Making every effort to sound philosophical, she tried to elaborate. "You don't have a choice but to continue on with your life to find what God has in store for you. Perhaps God is the true philosopher enacting us as his puppets; intent is what you make of yourself, where chance is the assured directive to his motive."

"I thought you got enough of this talk yesterday." Mike placed her on the bed.

"True, I don't appreciate philosophy, but it seemed appropriate." She sat up from the bed, patting her hand against the bedding. "Here, sit beside me, I wasn't finished." She was referring to the massage.

He responded willingly.

Her strong, slender fingers worked effectively at his tension. He took a deep breath in reflex to a knotted muscle that her fingers tapped upon. She slipped back onto the bed behind him and with both her hands working in dutiful unison, she continued.

"That feels so good." His voice seemed to dwindle.

"I'm glad. You just relax and enjoy. I like you, Michael, I hope that we can become close friends."

If he had eyes in the back of his head, he would have seen that famous smirk painted radiantly across her lips.

"I thought we already were friends." He was just keeping up conversation.

"Closer, friends." She intoned at the back of his head.

He was still painfully sobering over the memory of Diane, taking less notice of the changer in her voice.

"It's good to have friends." He said, thinking aloud and less of Crystal. His mind kept reaching back to the tragedy. As she worked at his neck, shoulders and back he was soon reluctant to accept that it was Crystal behind him, and imagined it to be Diane. His better judgment was keenly susceptible to Crystal's intentions and growing desires, but he was torn by the moral of monogamy; seemingly too soon for him to even be thinking of another. Assorted thoughts filled his mind making it hard for him to call upon his virtues. The voice of Diane called on him. The strange words and pleasant voice of Miranda would then come to his ears. It was as if she were telling him to let go, let go of his fears and inhibitions. Images of many faces, all giving advice and empty words of solution, came together in his mind, melting together like some sort of memory induced kaleidoscope. As Mike knew Diane best, she would have wanted him to be happy without regrets. Billy, would urge caution, for he knew Crystal best, her insecurities, her shrewdness, her selfishness and worst of all, her attitude of expendable hearts. Nicky, could only be visualized, as he would so often be recognized with his big womanizing smile and two thumbs up. If Crystal didn't have such a bitter opinion for Nicky's pompous hormones, the two of them would seem most compatible. As the image of Miranda's face came to mind through introspection, he visualized her as the most noble and omniscient; with caring, dark eyes and an understood vision of her own, Mike could feel her presence, telling him to gain the most of life, and learn. One may never know what life has to offer until after one has accepted the offer, and lived it. With mixed emotions he just sat at the edge of the bed allowing himself to relax, as Crystal guided her fingers, searching out the tension in his neck. Her touch was as penetrating as those of the therapists at the hospital. And when it became too difficult for her to reach his lower back, her groping fingers reached around to the front of his shirt and systematically began to unbutton it.

"There is only one way to do this right." She said, trying to sound pragmatic and unaffected by his masculinity. From Mike there was no response, save that of a deep groan as he felt her hot breath at the back of his neck. Aside from him running down the stairs and out of the house onto the street, there would have been very little that he could have done at this point to detour her from her onward stride of seduction. Once Crystal's mind was made clear, there would be very little anyone could do to stop her determination or selfishness. In her terms, she defined it as 'survival of the fittest'. She removed his shirt and immediately continued on with her massage. She studied every curve of every muscle in his back as her fingers toured his form. He knew what she was after, and he was going to make her work for it. As she attempted to stretch her reach from his shoulders down to his arms that were resting on his lap, she allowed her breasts to come into contact with his back.

As she kneaded her fingers at the muscles in his forearms, her hard nipples rubbed against his back. Her top was still saturated with a clear view of her flesh beneath. Looking down on herself, she breathed a heavy sigh, just hoping that soon it will be his eyes doing their examination on her. Her efforts were in no way in vain, she truly had an effective touch and a way about her no man would easily be willing to refuse. Crystal was an exceptionally good-looking young woman. Her features were well defined, with her body-fat count kept to a minimum; her tone was trim and neat. The feature that intrigued him the most was her jaw-line; it was sharp with fine definition. Her smooth, silky skin was maintained every other day at the tanning parlor, followed by the work of her own personal masseuse. She had him feeling quite good—better than his therapy ever felt, but Mr. Bauslow, the chief hospital therapist didn't have the passion that Crystal was providing. Soon, she would have to make another move of seduction; she didn't want to allow him the time to think about Diane. Her move was somewhat bold, almost obvious, but she dared not to give herself away, just yet. She slipped herself off the bed, pivoting around him with her hands still working at his shoulders. She stood before him, his eyes focused with the looming vision of her gleaming breasts from beneath the taffeta.

He looked away and then looked up into her eyes. He didn't look away until he got quite an eyeful first. There was no doubt that he was interested in her anatomy, but out of curiosity and a ploy of his own, he played along, acting naive and respectable.

"Have you ever experienced the pleasure of a scalp massage?" She inquired.

"I can't say that I have." After having been given such a generous peek at her breasts through the material that was slowly drying, it was difficult for him to speak.

"Well then, please allow me to introduce you to the wonderful technique of stress relief and scalp sculpting." No sooner had the words left her lips, her fingers were combing through his head of thick, dark hair.

"Scalp sculpting?" he asked with a chuckle.

"Just relax and let me take care of you," her hands guided his head to face forward. Now, there was no excuse for him to show shame or look away. "In the Orient, it is understood that the pressure points on your hands, feet and head can be manipulated to cure a patient's ailments."

Mike didn't want to have to think to answer. To be able to stare at her breasts in peace was about all he could handle. To his surprise, her fingers seemed to find some pleasure zones. As she pressed and kneaded at certain areas of his scalp, he could actually feel similar sensations to that which her fingers would when she worked at his neck or shoulders, it felt unusually good. With her fingers strained through the body of his hair, she would press hard against the muscles of his scalp and then in the same motion, pull back at the handful of hair that was gathered in her grasp. A tingling sensation would, each time, surge through his entire body. With each tug at his hair, she managed to raise his spirits as well as his passion. As though it were a tapped magical aphrodisiac, she persisted to give him pleasure.

Crystal's plan was coming together perfectly, to the finest detail. Her arms were blocking the view of her eyes from his, to give all the privacy she could afford. In return, she took inventory over his manly chest and rippling stomach muscles.

The kaleidoscope of faces and cogent voices would return each time he would feel doubt or resentment towards his actions, as if his promiscuity would have a hand at insulting or degrading the memory of his departed lover. But as every masked move of compassion was exhibited through Crystal's fingers, Mike was coming to face with the fact that the memory will always live strong in his heart and the act that Crystal was playing upon him was strongly believed to be the therapy he needed. With a growing beat of passion, Mike's eyes studied her breasts, their shape, size and motion.

Upon a couple of sneaky peeks she found his eyes and attention just where she had hoped and planned for them to be. The material had not had a chance to completely dry. "Are you wearing shorts under your pants?" Without giving him the chance to answer or think about the question, she continued, "The reason why I ask is because, the only way to give you the full body treatment would be to also massage your legs. The feet and legs possess a number of pressure points."

"Well, I don't know about all that Oriental philosophy, but..."

"Here, just stand up, I'll help you," she said, "there we go, just step out of them and lay facedown on my bed." She seemed just as amazed as he, to see him obey her every instruction as if her mannerism was similar to that of the hospital staff. Her fingers were quick to work the buttons loose on his Levis. Followed by a sudden squat at the knees, she pulled firmly at each side of his pants and watched the fall accord. Next, as she had instructed, he had been patiently laid across the bed, waiting for his legs to be massaged when the sultry heat between her legs came to rise faster than she had anticipated. Because of the way he slavishly responded to her commands or by the way his penis bulged in his jockey shorts, the surge of her fever was more than she had expected by tenfold. She dove into massaging his hamstrings. His cotton shorts were all that kept him from being completely naked in her bed.

She was barely thinking straight as she tried to plan her next move. After several longing minutes of rubbing and squeezing his every muscle from head to toe, she further instructed him to turn over so that she could do the same to his chest, stomach and quadriceps. Perhaps she got carried away or perhaps it was her full intent, but when she was working so diligently at the muscles of his upper legs, she managed, several times, to brush her long manicured fingernails along the inside corners of his groin. With little imagination needed, the sequential evidence of her management came to unfurl as he did as she instructed and turned over exposing more swell in his pants than she had expected. Honing its thick shape and swollen size through the thin material, his organ showed its presence as openly as if her were showing her his knees. Goggle-eyed and with staggered breath, she proceeded to grope her fingers at the largest section of his thigh muscles, all the while staring unashamedly at the swell in his pants.

Mike acted as though he didn't notice. His attempts at controlling his emotions were failing desperately. Although with earnest efforts, he tried to sustain himself from any further growth, but as Crystal worked her euphoric fingers, it was to become a futile effort. By this time, the game could hardly be less obvious, but Mike was steadfast to see how far she would take the charade.

During the time he was faced down, receiving his back rub, she had managed to remove her pantyhose without raising suspicion. As her slender caressing touch traced his body over, she climbed up onto the bed beside him and straddled his midsection as she proceeded to knead his massive pecs. She had no man to compare him to. The men of her experience were less the physical type and more likely to spend energy formulating ways to buyout companies or sell them the same. As they were engaged with eye-to-eye contact, her patented smirk was more prevalent than ever. Once she regained her aplomb, she suddenly realized he was no longer in her thrall. The look on his face was all she needed to realize the cat was out of the bag.

"You've been counter playing me." With a pensive projection, she stared him down. "You knew—" Her eyes filled with fury and unspent rage.

"Tell me what I know, Crystal, that your compassion and lament tears were of true sorrow for me or for Diane? Or that the fabric of your blouse just happened to become transparent? Did you really expect me to keep my eyes shut the whole time? Girl, tell me I wasn't raised a fool!" As her anger festered from the harshness of his words, he grabbed hold of her at her haunches and forced her weight against him. It would seem her pride might have had her slap him or perhaps demand he leave her room at once, but instead she was now responding to his dominance. With his grip so taut, she grabbed his wrists giving passive show of resistance, but he knew better. She kept a wicked, drilling glare, enough to intimidate most men. What she knew and depended on was the fact that he was not just any man; he was no doubt, from the very beginning, her challenge, her counter punch, her equal in games of the cerebral kind and she wouldn't have had it any other way.

"You think you know me well, don't you?" She drawled, still showing signs of a struggle as she pushed hard at his wrists, applying all her weight. But in essence, all she was really doing was fortifying his and her intent. By pushing down on his wrists, her skirt crept up to her hips, exposing her privates, and subsequently landing her on his erection. She writhed about and couldn't have been more effective in causing heated friction had she been asked. Her pelvic bone pressed and rocked affectionately against his swollen penis. The hairs of her pubes were piercing through his shorts attacking his genitals as she continued to act resistant.

"I know that you are very wet." He said, breathing faster, "and I also know that you are a beautiful woman. What more would you like me to know?" Deeply he believed she truly was a beautiful woman with mature, feminine features he could easily grow increasingly fond of. The beauty of her revealing brown eyes ran deep with wonder, they always seemed to be talking or sending message, he loved reading them. And what she would soon come to learn, and learn well, was his acute ability to read those deep, big brown beauties with little effort. As she continued with her inert show of struggle, he could hear her breathing heavier and faster.

"And I suppose that's supposed to make me feel better?" She remonstrated like a well-coached actress.

"I was merely reflecting on what you had asked." She writhed on top of him. "And yes, its already feeling good, I don't doubt it'll get better." With a gesture intended to ignite the fury she truly needed to release, he continued, "Funny," he said. "I thought you would be much stronger."

"Oh, you conceited bastard!" Her performance

was worthy of rewarding accolades. She nearly freed herself from his grip with the strength of her reserves and a sudden show of fire. Her sweetened panting and whimpers were the accent of his pleasure. The struggle with her on top of him wiggling and grinding privates against privates, was the formula Crystal made clear to be her penchant. "Who the hell do you think you are?"

"I'm the guy who's going to be making love to you shortly," he said, almost laughing aloud as her struggle became a worthy bout of her slapping his arms and striking his pecs with her fists and making herself excited, more enviable. "The guy you brought up here to take advantage of." He said, returning her smirk while blocking another punch to the chest.

"You're mad! You're out of your mind!" The struggle was soon to become an all out battle of rampant wrestling and painless blows, and the more she fought with him, the better it felt for the both of them.

In her childish way, she preferred the act of making love to be conducted as an attack, an aggressive invasion and violation of one's consent and probably with no specifics over which party was to be the attacker or the attacked. Seemingly, rape was her fond form of copulation, something Mike was inexperienced with but learning. Her ravage struggle with audible, luring whines and seductive whimpers made him hotter. With little effort needed from Mike, Crystal worked her sultry haunches and succulently pulpy bush against his phallus swell with a glissading motion. Her skill in disrobing maneuvers managed to free his incredibly virile manhood from the veil of his saturated cotton shorts. Never losing pace, she continued on with her writhing accompanied with louder resistance.

Mike didn't know whether to cuff, whip and start slapping her to help her along with her obvious fetishistic behavior or search the room for the video camera that would undoubtedly incriminate him with rape charges, even though, for the most part she was the one who was doing most of the work. Amid her now, louder than ever ranting and panting grunts of bestial ardent, she let loose with a shuddering climactic wail. The resonance of her omnipresent shrill bounced off every wall of the upper floor. Once she regained herself, Mike looked at her arching his arms with a questioning gesture, as if to be asking with a very strong hint of banter, "Well, are we having fun yet?"

"Oh, shut the hell up and get on top of me." Her reply was as he expected. He did as she instructed and much, much more. After relieving her of the remainder of her torridly soaked clothes, he unmercifully ravaged her. Having not yet achieved the climactic goal that she so obviously had and without patience to wait for him, it was a near-miss to the brink when Crystal removed her top and then crossed her arms at the hip, in her clutches she pulled her skirt off over her head. The only anatomic secrets between them were what hid under his shorts and her lace bra. Once they too were removed, the fervor of ardor and mounting passion rekindled.

As he had only imagined, her silky skin was treated with the best care money could buy. With a tone of golden bronze, her body exhibited a flawless complexion and absent from any tan lines. Her lovely boobs of medium, yet plentiful size, gave a new perspective to the principles and laws of gravity. As firm as she may have built them to be through the workouts she endured at the gym three times a week, her buxom mounds of fleshy meat gave new definition to the art of bounce and ripple and jiggle. Taken by the supple loll of her breasts, Crystal found ways to restore him each time they played, simply by shimmying her sweet, tasty titties with dance in the direction of his receptive lips.

"Oh shit, is that the correct time?" Mike pointed frantically toward her wall clock.

Crystal intercepted his thought. "I can call Nicky at the shop for you. Stay here with me." Her offer was more than inviting, but he felt an obligation to Scotty.

"I'd like that, I'd like that a lot but I really need this job. I can't afford to screw it up, not now, not if I want to stay here."

As Crystal laid herself onto the pillow in the middle of the bed, her imploring eyes asked him to treat her just once more.

"You can stay here for as long as you wish, no one is contesting your stay." Her naked body contrasting against the light-shaded sheets was an invitation he could barely resist.

"You know what I mean Crystal," standing at the side of the bed, he searched the floor for his clothes. "I want nothing more than to be able to stay here with you, but I have an obligation to myself, and the shop," he reflected an inviting smile, "I'll be back tonight. Will I see you then?"

She pretended that she understood his responsibilities. "After the rehearsal." With eyes that sang the lure of siren, she watched him dress.

"I'd like that very much." He responded, briefly glancing at her while he attempted to step into his shorts.

She seemed impressed with herself by the fact that he was still quite hard, which made it difficult for him to fit her thrall into his scant jockey shorts. With a husky voice characterized as Mae West, she said, "Would ya like a hand with that, big boy? Perhaps I could help you tame that wild thing." She said, making sure he could see her fingertips brushing along the outline of her hardening nipples.

Mike stood up, looking down at his erection that was protruding from the elasticity of his briefs and answered her frankly, "No, I believe you've done enough already. I'll probably take three hours for the effects of your 'taming' to wear off."

"Well then, we'd better hurry, that only gives us one-hundred and eighty minutes to train." Her hands were busy at play, doing everything she knew that would make his escape difficult. Crystal had all the moves and the equipment to have kept him there if she truly wanted, or so she made herself believe.

Her teasing hands found other deeds to hinder him as Mike struggled to pull his pants up his legs without stepping on the cuffs.

She quickly sidled to the side of the bed next to him and conducted a game of titillation on the back of his legs with her fingernails. She wasn't about to make it easy for him. In her playfully energized banter, she exhibited a child in her that she rarely would allow anyone to see. Her meeting Mike was seemingly therapeutic for her own needs. What she wouldn't admit to anyone, much less herself, was the fact that being alone in the world wasn't nearly as painful as the suffering she endured at the hands of her father.

The son he had always wanted, the son to carry on the Worthington name, the son that would one day work side by side with his father in the most prestigious and profitable business in the world of exotic perfumes, and one day perhaps take over the business and quadruple its success, the son that would someday fulfill his dream, unfortunately, would never come to happen because when Crystal was born, Hillary, her mother and Charles Worthington's beloved wife, died giving birth to Crystal. When Charles Worthington remarried several years later, his work and his lifestyle would never allow for the time and dedication needed in raising a child. His only hope was that his only child would see the value of his wishes and fill the shoes of the son he never had. Perhaps by his own doing or perhaps through the ordain work of fate, when Crystal attended church when she was a young child, her father would make certain that she was the prodigy of every parents' envy. She would always be dressed in prim and proper form with her hair neatly styled in a pageboy and her poise well within the curriculum of a pristine, genteel lady. And when made to sing in the church choir at the age of nine, she did so as a gesture of politeness in accordance with her father's wishes. With the respect for the father that never learned how to love his little girl in the way she yearned so desperately and with the hope that he would hear her little voice through all the other choir members, she developed the singing voice that most could only dream of possessing.

But her father never cared to hear that voice. He didn't know how to care. Her little heart sang out to him every Sunday as proud and ebulliently as her tiny voice could manage. And with every bit of pride and bliss a developing young child should have, she would ask her father if her heard her sing, and each time in his perfunctory preoccupied manner he would answer 'yes, he heard her just fine'. Never in those years did he ever stop to think or realize that his little girl was begging to hear him say how well she sang or how proud he was of her. Those words never graced her precious and deserving, unfledged ears. She so painfully needed to find the way to her father's love and appreciation, but nothing could penetrate the enigma that would elude her. Though she never would capitulate to frustration, her heart was broken many times by her father's lack of understanding.

Then finally, one spring Sunday morning when Crystal was sixteen years old, she was asked to sing solo. With her finely trained and disciplined singing voice, she was the only member qualified to deliver the hymn. As she and her father attended church that day, she kept it a surprise from him hoping that he would see how hard she had worked in preparation for the song, and over the years. That beautiful Sunday morning with the resplendent sun glinting through the stained glass dormers, Crystal accepted her cue to stand before her audience and sing her part as proudly and gleefully as ever. Indeed, she sang so well that day. And as usual, the congregation was with her from the start, singing praise to the Lord right along with this enchanting, young girl with a voice of pure gold. Her song reached every ear with a driven passion of love for her father and the faith in the Lord, her Savior. She was to sing all five verses of Amazing Grace with her powerfully vibrant voice in lead echelon, but before she had completed singing the first verse with her fellow worshippers, the cathedral of hundreds of other voices dwindled to a quiet stir. And before she had realized what was happening, it was only her voice and her voice alone, singing a cappella. Her song pervaded the ears of the entire congregation, including her father's. She was magnificent and enthralling to all those who watched and listened in awe. Her captive audience listened intently until the very last note with admiration, honor and praise.

165

With her spirits elated and the adrenalin rushing through her body, she knew for sure that her father would be pleased and that her auspicious future in the vocation of singing to the people was undoubtedly her calling.

It was as though she had told her father that she wanted to run naked through the streets for a living. He looked at her that evening before dinner as if to say that she had gone completely crazy and refused to accept her idea and dreams to pursue her desires of becoming a singer and perhaps an actress. He told her that singing was meant to stay in the church and anyone who thought different was obviously twisted or without sense. He added that those who pursue a singing career outside the church are losers and never amount to anything. "You have the best future ahead of you that anyone could ever ask," he boasted. "You'll be working with me of course. Singing like some kind of trollop on television isn't going to get you anywhere. The only thing that comes to those movie types is booze, sex and drugs; they all end up becoming losers in the long run. Nope, my little girl is not some simpleton floozy. I don't want to see you wind up on the streets begging for miniscule parts in those trashy programs where all they do is exploit the woman. You don't need that kind of nonsense; you're too smart for that. You'll work for me and that's final."

Crystal was crushed. For more than six years she did what her father had asked of her, to sing in the choir and do her best at everything. All she ever wanted was to hear her father say she had sung well and to make him proud. She worked day and night trying to please her father in the only way she could figure how. She thought for sure he would have been as excited as she when the entire church stopped to listen to her sing—only her. No one else made a sound. She could see it in their eyes; she captivated them. She was a good singer and she could feel it to be true, but daddy didn't care. That wasn't the life he had planned for his one and only daughter. As the months came to pass after that painfully hurtful speech from him, Crystal grew hard and distant. She had worked so hard to please him for all those years, it seemed that there was nothing left to give. There was nothing that she could do to make him proud, to make him realize that she was alive, that she had thoughts and feelings like anyone. What makes his damn job so important that he could just cut out her heart, drop it to the ground and step on it as if to be snuffing out one of his smelly cigarettes? How could he not see her dreams, or her need to please him? Why was he such a fool to hurt her so badly? By the time she was seventeen, she had finally given up on trying to gain his love. As far as she was concerned, he didn't deserve it. He failed her and she was determined to prove him wrong.

Two months before her eighteenth birthday, daddy remarried. All hope of any relationship between her and her father, had there been any, would certainly have diminished from that time on. Her stepmother, who Crystal refused to recognize as such, was only seven years older than herself. Her name was Goldie, but Crystal called her digger, denoting exactly what she was—a gold digger. The first two months of the marriage was disaster but as far as Charles could see, Goldie was everything he had ever dreamed of, it was as though he reached his second phallic stage. And Goldie, well, as long as he paid for every sex act with at least the reciprocation of a diamond bracelet, she was contented. The feuds between her and Goldie were fierce from the start, as Crystal is not one to hold back a punch, or in this case, afraid to call a prostitute a prostitute. There was no communication between the two females, save that of spiteful acrimony and only to cease immediately when Charles should happen to come within hearing range. There was no need to aggravate daddy since he was now living a whole new life, in his own new world. In fact, he became more oblivious to Crystal's needs, once he was wed to digger than ever before. Her stoicism was all she allowed her father to see. The cold, curt personality of this teenaged gamine was soon to become her now famed repertoire. It had been nearly fifteen years since the last time she was able to smile, play and laugh as she now felt comfortable and less inhibited to do so in the company of her new friend, Mike, who was making every effort to get to work.

"You're going to make me late if you don't stop this teasing," Mike said, almost hopping from the bedside to get clear from her reach. It was hard enough to try to squeeze into a pair of pants that were already too tight to manage. Nonetheless, too tight was just how Crystal liked it.

"You fascinate me," he said.

"How is that?" she said seemingly preoccupied by his buttocks and then by something she snatched from out of Mike's back pocket that caught her eye as it seemed to work its way out when he was hopping about.

"I'm not sure exactly, I just keep thinking that I know you from somewhere, something in your eyes calls out to me, but I can't seem to figure it out. What I do know is your eyes seem to tell me everything about you."

For the moment her eyes looked playful. "And what are they telling you now?" She tittered, fussing to unfold the leather looking envelope.

"Right now is obvious, but just a while ago today and all day yesterday, I saw what seemed to be pain and loneliness. As much, if not more than what I feel for Diane. I don't make any claims to know what your losses are, but whatever they are, I can feel the heavy toll in your eyes." He read her correctly and was just as correct discerning the signs of her unwillingness to talk about it. She kept her pain close to her heart locked up tight in a deep, hidden place of her mind, waiting to one day prove her father wrong.

She wasn't willing to confide in Mike; instead she shrugged it of as if to say his premonitions were a complete mystery to her. She was enjoying the

169

moment far too much to allow the flux to be spoiled by the past.

Reading into her adamant self-denial, Mike didn't persist, but he could see something desperate in her eyes, something so powerfully destined, and yet, he couldn't make the call. Something about her was dangerously wrong. Almost as a sixth sense, his ability to read Crystal was growing stronger with magnitude. How uncanny, he thought, to be able to actually read her mind. Until that moment, he hadn't bothered to give it such a thought. It just seemed to come to him like magic. Nevertheless, without pressing on with his strange intrigue, he hurriedly put on his shirt and shoes lest he would make a bad impression on his boss. Looking towards Crystal as he tied his shoelaces, she was still fumbling with a familiar looking swatch of leather.

"Hey, where did you find that?" Mike cast an inquisitive look.

"Found it," she supplied, working with her long, slender fingers to open it. Once it was open she knew just what she was looking at. And finding it very odd to be in his possession, she inquired with curious, knowing eyes, "How did you get this?"

"Do you like it? A fair likeness too, I'd say."

She didn't answer. She studied the picture as if she were reading the strange foreign lettering to herself. Her interest in the picture and seemingly all the little detailed graphics made it seem somewhat important, like there was actually something significant about it.

"It's just a get well card the nurse from the hospital gave me," he said

"A get well card?" She looked at him oddly.

"I suppose that's what you could call it. That's supposed to be me on the horse, there." he boastfully pointed to the portrait.

She passed him a look of annoyance. His naiveté was pressing hard against her patience. Or so what he thought that was what he was reading from her. She knew more about the picture than he, and somehow, she wasn't pleased by it. The playfulness on her face seemed to fade as she continued to study the leather.

"How well did you know this nurse?" she inquired.

"Not too well, really. We talked a lot while I was recovering in the hospital. She took care of my room and all those hospital formalities. Why? Is there something I should know about it?"

"Did she tell you what this was?" She seemed to draw even more annoyance from her already established tone.

He shrugged his shoulders. "Just what I told you. What's the big deal anyhow?"

"My father is an art collector—"

"Do you suppose there's some value in it?"

Her wry expression projected petulance, ignoring his interruption and continued, "Out of all his artifacts, the Western Indian collectibles are of the least valuable, yet the largest of his collection and the most interesting. You truly need to understand the nature of the Indian and their beliefs and way of life to understand their art, their tools weapons and drawings."

"Wouldn't their art and drawing be one in the same?"

"Not necessarily, they use drawings as we would perhaps use letters on paper to communicate words and stories and such. What you have here, Mike is something similar to what is called a Mandela." She continued to study the drawing as she spoke to him. "It signifies much more than what she told you."

"Do you know what it means?"

She wasn't sure if she wanted to tell him. Not because she wanted to save him from hardship, on the contrary, there was nothing hurtful or ominous about the drawing, it was just that her driven selfishness didn't want to expose the truth, or the whole truth, as it were. "In accordance with the beliefs of the Indian people, the Mandela represents a shield of luck for the one who possesses it and his family. From the power of the gods, it is to shield you from harm, illness and it will bring you joy." Mike didn't remember Miranda mentioning anything similar. "There must have been something she told you in reference to the meaning of her having given this to you."

"She said something about wishing me good luck for the journey, but that's about all I can remember. If I'm missing something in the translation, shouldn't you tell me what it is? Perhaps it could be important." Professedly, something was being withheld by Crystal, but as she reasoned to herself that the true translation of the message was obviously not too important to the nurse since she didn't bother to give Mike a justified explanation for why she gave him such a card, a card Crystal knew a great deal about was not willing to tell him, not yet anyhow. It was odd however, that a nurse of mere platonic relations would give him such a significant message. The card indeed was well drawn and the writings were quite similar to those seen in her father's private gallery, but a Mandela, as she told Mike, it obviously was not, similar but different in many distinct ways. The format and design of his card was not of just a good luck symbolism, it also offered more. The leather, with its fullest intent is a powerful and spiritual blessing between only the conjugal and given to the spouse with only one intent and that is to guide the other through the journey of the seen or unforeseen dangers.

Once the drawing is made, traditionally by the wife, she then goes into private quarters and prays to the gods of protection and asks them for their guidance and magic to see her husband through the battle or journey, and in so doing, she also must offer the gods her most valued possession in reciprocation. Once her prayer is complete, she is to sign the contract by letting a small amount of her blood join with the leather. Afterward, she presents it to her husband with her love and blessing. Should he lose the leather or not return it to her, it would be considered an act of blasphemy and risk retribution by the gods and permanent relegation by her people. In every case known through history, the offer that she makes to the gods is that of her own spirit, her life. Should the husband die in battle or on his journey when the two are apart, the gods respond by restoring his life. If they do not respond by redeeming him with the breath of life, it is understood that the wife was not worthy or she shamed the gods at one time or another in her life. The gesture of the leather is a very sacred belief. A woman to believe herself and her love for her husband worthy of the virtuous gesture must believe with all her heart to be true or the gods will take her spirit as retribution. Upon the rising of three suns after his death and should the gods not respond by allowing him to breathe once again, the wife is to be sacrificed. If the gods do respond by giving him back his life, the wife was obviously found worthy and they are allowed to rejoin, but the two will have forfeited their spirits to the gods, therefore never being able to return to the mortal world thereafter. It's considered an honor to live among the gods of the heavens once the spirit is forfeited. And for obvious reasons the gesture of the leather is very special and not used with vague intent. So why would this near stranger give it to Mike when he didn't even know of its vital significance, and take such a chance with her valued spirit? There was no way to make a mistake with its meaning, if she knew enough about how to make it, blood letting and all, she would have had to know of its meaning and consequences.

"For whatever reason she might have given you this leather, aside from wishing you good luck, I think you should at least consider keeping it in a safe place so not to lose it."

Mike nodded strangely in answer and wondered where a safe place would be. If he were still living at home he would most likely stash it in his closet without a pass or protective gear for obvious reasons, when one might see what dangers lurk in his closet. Similar to that of a battlefield's obstacle course where men are trained to expect the unexpected, no one including Mike himself, would know exactly what dangers were ready to pounce once the closet door was opened. From basketballs, footballs shoe boxes filled with baseball cards, paper bags categorizing dated Playboy magazines and a set of bongo drums to fishing poles with the dried, dead worm still stuck to the hook from the previous years' fishing trip, all would shift, crackle and creak like the stammer of the ground just prior to an avalanche in the mountains, ready to come crashing down on whoever would open the ominous closet door. Perhaps that would have been the best place for his leather, but he was reminded once again of the many changes in his life that have taken place and what felt like just had happened in the past few days. The closet filled with memories and trinkets and his desperately needed clothes were far from reach.

He folded the leather and stuck it in his back pocket. The thought of returning to his home to collect his things was a depressing thought to say the least. Having to face his mother could result in a number of unfriendly scenarios, although he knew that he would not be able to prolong the inevitable for much longer. He was in need of many things; things that he hoped his mother hadn't already thrown out or destroyed in spite. Until that final moment of confrontation, he chose not to think about it.

"What's that look for?" she said somewhat wistfully, wrapping herself with the bedding as she gathered her clothes up off the floor.

"I was just thinking about something Miranda said and she was right. I need to get my act together. There's so much I need to do. I know that I should feel lucky to have such good friends such as yourself and Billy. And I should feel fortunate for a lot of things, but I'm having so much trouble understanding why things happen as they do. I don't know if I can explain it fully, I'm not sure I understand it myself, aside form the fact that I don't feel so fortunate. I'm not sure how I feel." He wanted to say so much more, but he didn't bother. The burden of his losses was his to bear and his alone. He could see in Crystal's face that she was growing less interested in his problems. Her heart truly was cold with apathy. Whatever tainted her heart must have made deep impressionable cuts into her soul. He wondered if he would one day learn more about her and her detachment from compassion. And then he wondered if he would want to live long enough to find anymore answers to anything.

"Time is what you need. Time is all you need." She said resolutely and bluntly, although she said it out of experience, it was obvious now. Something or someone must have caused her great pain. "When all else fails you, you always have yourself to live with, to try to please, to keep company with when you are alone and afraid, to be friends with, and if you can ever find peace with yourself, you may also learn to love yourself."

Mike turned to face her as she spoke. She sat on the bed with a sheet wrapped around her looking like a Sarong and her dress clutched in her lap. Her eyes were glazed and serious.

"Have you found peace with yourself?" he asked, "Living alone without the love of another? Did someone hurt you so bad that you turned to the reclusive life for solitude? Is this what peace within yourself looks like after the annals of time and pain? Is this what I have to look forward to?"

She could have lied to pacify him She could have said anything to perhaps show a spark of compassion that might have been salvaged in her pitiful heart. But instead, her veracity cut straight through the cushions of warmth and tenderness. "I don't know if anyone does," mercilessly she continued, "we should have been born with less fragile hearts, that way it hurts less when the venomous truth strikes. Perhaps it's only the lucky ones who find peace and happiness, and perhaps they pay for it in the long run. Time, Mr. Mike; I'm still doing my time and you have just started to do yours. Who knows, maybe one of us will get lucky. Don't get me wrong, I'm hopeful, its just difficult to be anything outside of pessimistic when life continually treats you unjustly and without remorse," with her bleakness she looked over to the clock. "Look, it's getting late. Let me get dressed and I'll drive you to Scotty's."

Perhaps it was contrition that made her offer, or maybe she felt it her duty as a friend. It was evident that after her little speech she had done little to raise his spirits. He said nothing as she disappeared behind the closet doors. Moments later she emerged from the darkness of the closet looking only slightly sympathetic. She bore the burden of her misery like an armor shield of protection against anyone who might find an interest in her. For what it was worth, the time they shared in her bed was merely a transitory symbiosis between two people who shared a similar misfortune, but as Crystal said, only time succors.

After she had taken him to work, he spent much of the day thinking of his life and the changes he will have to make. And with a briny grain of salt he tried to keep from blasting into impromptu fits of tearful hysteria. It was an emotional battle within him stirring and festering with little relent. He felt as though he had done wrong by allowing himself to make love to Crystal so soon after losing Diane.

Much to Crystal's upset, he chastised himself by staying celibate for the next six months while still battling with his painful emotions and fitful cries in the lonely hours of nearly every night. The memory of Diane's love and tenderness was hard to just wash away. What they had was very special and it was obvious that there was very little anyone could do for him. There were days he would wake up hoping it was all just a bad dream, but each time he found himself mummified in a sleeping bag in Billy's room it would cast away doubt. To keep his mind from dwelling, he enrolled in night school and took on full-time hours at Scotty's. The money was useful and the long hours kept him busy and his mind occupied. The relationship between he and Crystal was amicable and growing closer every day, but the void in his heart was ever-present. He wondered if he too would soon become as cold and austere as she. In time, he learned that her escape from the loneliness and pain was pacified by her music. It wasn't until then that he realized how serious her music was to her.

Hours of every day of every week were spent training, perfecting her singing voice and abilities. Her stamina and perseverance were commendable and exemplified a secure role model for him to follow. He applied the same efforts toward his work at the shop, working hard and long hours with little rest. Within six months he was promoted with a substantial raise in pay and in eight months he graduated from high school. The work and efforts were grueling but at the very least he had something to be proud of and for the first time, he was truly on his own and making it, contrary to his mother's last words.

Chapter Ten

The Passion Seekers

The Passion Seekers were on the rise for an auspicious future in the professional world of music entertainment. Crystal's personal perseverance had her working night and day, perfecting her to flawless endeavors. The rest of the band was equally enthused and motivated to one day see their names up in neon lights. Although their original intent was to be rock and roll band, somehow the mood-swing and unforeseen preference came to light when the chemistry of their music took a turn in the direction of a more soulful sound, jazz-rock with fantastic instrumentals and the phenomenal sound recognized as Crystal's passion for perfection. She was unbelievably gifted with a beautiful voice.

When they would perform at the local clubs trying to land a contract or gain the interest of a reputable recording label, they would give each performance their all. Crystal seemed to have the knack for conveying the painfully sad songs. It was as if with little effort she could have the house crying along with her and moments later elate them to euphoria. The Passion Seekers were good, better than the clubs they were performing in but as Mike and Billy would say, "ya have to start somewhere."

In the summer of 1980, one year after Mike moved in with Billy, the magic of things began to happen. The Passion Seekers and their original sound were the talk of the up and coming.

One Saturday night, after performing in a small club in North Hollywood, Crystal was approached by a man named John Blackmore, who had followed The Passion Seeker's itinerary for three weeks. He claimed to be the owner of The Star House, a well-known club on Sunset in Hollywood. He liked their music and the fact that they had a vast song list. He needed a band that could perform weekdays at his club and keep his clientele entertained without having to hear the same songs played over and over again each day. Word was getting around that The Passion Seekers were climbing to the top of the 'unknowns'. The 'unknowns' were those who were not yet recording or contracted, but were regularly getting a lot of club gigs. John Blackmore offered The Passion Seekers a contract for three months, weekdays only and contingent upon their performance. The offer wasn't instant stardom, or for that matter anymore money than the other clubs, however, it was a steady job and has been known as one of the clubs that has been the springboard for many other bands that went all the way to recording with notorious labels. The contingency of the contract was based upon the three-month probationary period, just as he would contract most of his other performers. If in the three months time, attendance was good and liquor sales were up, the band was found to be good performers and dependable, the contract would be extended and with the higher pay incentive of working weekends. This was truly the break that the band needed to gain more publicity and to get motivated. After a brief discussion with Billy, Nicky, Paul and Tawney, Crystal agreed to sign with John Blackmore to perform at The Star House for three months. The band was ecstatic!

Nicky grabbed the first strumpet that was within reach and proceeded to get drunk with her in celebration. Tawney and Paul left the club together as usual. It was apparent that after living together for nearly two years, they were quite fond of each other. Although at first, they tried to deny the rendezvous between their bedrooms late at night and scampering back early in the morning, it became futile and without cause to continue in hiding, as their affection accrued.

Billy was enjoying himself that night and especially so after the great news. He decided to stay at the club until arrangements could be made with the manager of the club to continue working weekends. The band had agreed that they could use the extra money. Crystal wasted no time in packing away her equipment for the night and dashed out of the establishment without a word. It would seem that she was pleased with the contract and wanted to share the news with Mike, who was working late at Scotty's. Scotty entrusted him with the keys to the shop, allowing him to pick up some extra hours. Many times, Crystal would find Mike at Scotty's working late into the night.

On occasion, she would come by to coax him into coming home with her, thus terminating his six-month long term of celibacy. A six-month term was all that he could endure. After she shared the news with him, Mike locked up the shop and accompanied Crystal at a quiet all-night coffee shop. She didn't seem very excited about the news of the contract. As Mike soon found out, the news of the contract was just a ploy to get him away from the shop. With gaunt eyes, she tried to hide a hurt that she desperately wanted to tell someone. Crystal had been living in reclusive solitude for so long that she had almost forgot what it was like to have someone to talk to, to depend on, to confide in and share dreams. After befriending Mike, a heavy weight had been lifted form her fragile shoulders, Even though she had never told him of her life in great detail, it was just the mere fact that she could confide in him if she needed to, that gave her the boost of spirit.

She ordered a sandwich and a glass of orange juice and Mike ordered a dessert. No sooner had the waiter walked away, she poured out her water into a planter and pulled a liter of vodka out of her purse. She made herself a screwdriver to the tune of a fifty-fifty ratio mix. Mike could see a long night ahead.

"How about if you give me the keys now so I don't have to wrestle you for them later?" Mike asked, reaching over his hot fudge sundae.

"With pleasure," she acquiesced with a gruff tone. Her throat was still a bit raw from her performance. "I had planned on getting blitzed tonight, making you the designated driver. Providing you can handle that much sugar." Her eyes held question as he poured the dark stream of hot fudge over his ice cream.

"I can handle it." He watched as she gulped down three quick swallows of her drink. She took one bite of her sandwich and then proceeded to inhale the remainder of her drink.

"Are we ready to talk yet, or do we need more fortification?" he said.

She poured herself another drink in answer, this time omitting the orange juice. After two good gulps and a wry wrinkle of her face, she peeved, "Almost, and you need not be so condescending with me. I know for a fact that you still carry around those bottles of pain pills."

"Because I still have pain." He retorted.

"In your heart or your back?" She quipped back seeming more than condescending.

"I take them for my back." Mike dropped the spoon in the dish and pushed it aside. "Crystal, let's cut the bull now and get to the bottom of this.

What's wrong? Why are you being such a shit? Look, it's me you're talking to, so talk to me. Who pissed on your parade? Who would cause you to drink this stuff?" Finally, the right question, her attrition had worn through as a stream of tears ran down her cheeks. Mike seemed shocked to see her crying. It was the first he had ever seen from her.

She had caught him off guard, staring pensively at her tears for several seconds as if to be making sure she didn't just get lint in her eye, or perhaps a reflection of glinting light gave way to an aberration of shimmering tears on her face. Surely, the girl of no emotions or feelings could not be crying real tears. Surely the intrepid facade could never release such a dam of tender, teary emotions. But in fact, they were and for the first time she opened up to him, exposing herself vulnerable almost in an angelic way. In the passing of mere seconds, Crystal became unashamedly somber and seemingly human.

"My father, he called me this morning." She replied through her sobbing, "I don't know how to make him love me. All my life I have tried to make him love me and he refuses to acknowledge me." She lowered her head to wipe away the tears with her napkin.

Mike took a moment to gather his thoughts. He couldn't understand why a woman of her age, nearly in her thirties would be so concerned about her father's affection. It wasn't as though she would have to show him her report card each semester. All this time he had thought she was so strong-willed and independent. Why was it so important to her? And why wouldn't he be proud of her? She's intelligent, motivated, well bred, beautiful and a lovely, talented singer. What more could he want from her—to be a brain surgeon or a rocket scientist?

"What makes you think that he's not proud of you? Is he nuts or is this another one of your ploys?"

Crystal looked up at Mike. Her eyes were already red and her makeup was smudged just a little. For a moment she didn't know how to answer, and then suddenly in salvoes the story finally surfaced. She told him of a time that even Billy didn't know about. And he usually would know about all the happenings and seemingly, almost before they'd happen. If Billy weren't such a good drummer, he probably would have wound up as a world-renowned gossip columnist. As Crystal told him of her painful story the pieces fell into place, making it easier for him to understand what she had been going through. For five months, she was engaged to be married to a man named Thomas Justiano, whom she thought she understood and loved compassionately and unselfishly. Formal arrangements were made for the families to be joined at the wedding ceremony. Since his family lived in Rome, Italy, Charles Worthington went through a great deal of trouble making all the preparations to have Thomas' relatives flown in and billeted at the Beverly Hilton.

Five hundred guests were to attend the lavish wedding. The ballroom spared no expenses. The caterers were paid in advance to a tune of over one hundred thirty thousand dollars. The centerpieces at every table were heavenly. Digger had appointed herself the bridesmaid and ordered the most expensive gowns for the wedding party. The flower girls were well rehearsed and primly fitted in matching gingham dresses. Nothing was left to chance; all was prepared down to the finest detail by her father's love for his little girl. Until three days before the wedding, Thomas claimed to be cool as a cucumber, but she could see through the facade that he was nervous and more in love with his bride-to-be than anyone could have dreamed possible. It was to be the happiest event in Crystal's life and she could see the pride in her father's eyes. Finally, she was to gain the fairy tale of dreams come true, her father's proud love and a wonderfully loving and clever man to live with happily ever after. Two days before the wedding Thomas announced that he would be meeting his relatives at the airport and help set them up at the Hilton. He told her the truth that he was in fact, especially nervous about seeing his relatives after such a long time of living in the states for almost ten years. Without a hint of alteration in his being, accepting a kiss and a passionate embrace from his beautiful and resplendent bride, Thomas got into his rental car and drove to the airport.

As his car drove away, Crystal blew kisses and gleamed a smile that would glow around the world. She was indeed more beautiful than a spring bouquet of nature's best red roses accompanied by the delicate hint of white baby's breath. Her radiant charm was unmatched by any other. Her day had come and she didn't have the slightest suspicion of what was to come. After Thomas arrived at the airport, he stopped at a safety deposit box. He pulled the key from his pocket and unlocked the door. Inside were three airline tickets and a briefcase filled with nearly two hundred, thousand dollars cash; monies for the travel arrangements for his alleged family. A familiar sound had found its way to his ears.

"Daddy, daddy..." An excited and jubilant little girl with long, blond curls and crystal blue eyes shoved her way through the crowd with open arms toward Thomas. Following close behind was the little girl's mother, Thomas' wife of ten, doting years.

"Hey, how's my sweetheart?" Thomas held her tightly as she jumped into his arms.

"I'm fine, now that you're back. Mommy and me must have been watching for you on the wrong plane, we didn't see you get off the plane."

"Well that's okay, I'll forgive you," he said, furtively. "Did you miss me while I was away at work?"

"Oh yes I did whole bunches. Mommy did too."

"Hello Sam. How was your flight?" The tall and thinly framed woman asked as she planted a small kiss on his cheek, suspecting nothing odd about not having seen him get off the plane. "Did they change planes on you again?"

"As usual, it was too late to call you, you guys had already left to come get me."

"Did you have to wait long, honey?"

"Not long, thirty minutes, tops," he replied, tugging at his cuff to expose his watch, playing out his deception down to the minute details. "Well, are you girls all packed and ready to return home?"

"Oh, I suppose. Though it wasn't much of a vacation without you."

"You knew I had business to attend here in California, but you still chose to come along. And hey, at least we were together on a few weekends."

"I know...you don't need to remind me. Last vacation was a business trip to Paris...and the vacation before that was a business trip to London, I remember each vacation only too well. So, Mr. Real Estate Tycoon, how did you do on this business-trip-vacation?" She smiled at him wryly.

"Not as well as London, but at least this client paid in cash." He boasted, patting his hand against his briefcase. The three boarded another plane chartered to leave the states once again. And that was the last anyone had heard from Thomas Justiano.

"He just disappeared, vanished without a trace? Did you call the hospitals or the police? Did he at least make it to the airport to receive his relatives?" Mike's emphatically brash number of questions blasted like rain pelting the memory of her anger and anguish into her face.

"Yes, of course. Daddy made all the appropriate calls and when the telegram arrived, he called the police and hired a private investigator." The cold anger was returning to her eyes.

"What telegram?"

"Thomas had sent me a telegram before he had left for the airport; I received it the morning of the wedding, daddy had already suspected something was wrong when Thomas didn't call, but I begged him not to make a scene. I was foolish enough to believe that Thomas was just busy with his family and that he was so nervous about the wedding he simply forgot to call me. Then the telegram arrived." Crystal's eyes took on a coldhearted fury with festering, bitter rage. "The son of a bitch didn't even have the balls to tell me to my face, not even over the phone for Chris' sake. I had wished he were in the damn hospital. If I had known what he was...I would have killed him myself."

"What did the telegram say? Did he bail out on you from nerves or something? Was it cold feet?"

"Worse! His telegram thanked me for the best screw of his life and the best sex, better than his wife. That's all the little weasel said."

Mike cupped his hands over hers, "Oh God, Crystal I am so sorry."

"And can you believe that the tenacity of that damned telegram wasn't what hurt me the most?" She was shaking her head with a blind stare. "The dregs was what my father said to me when I needed him the most—when my heart was crushed by some heart-stealing, rip-off confidence man. When I needed a kind word to help me get through the shock, my father told me I was a fool, that I should have seen it coming and that he...was furious because he...had been taken for more than a quarter million fucking dollars. Since that day, I do not know who I hate more, Thomas, for using and humiliating me before my entire family, whom I, to this day cannot face, or my father for not knowing how to be a father and making me bear the brunt of the blame. I don't even know if I truly ever loved Thomas. I agreed to marry him because I thought it would make my father proud of me—to be a wife and one day be a proud mother with her own lineage."

"Did the private investigators ever catch up with Thomas?"

Crystal took a deep breath and shook her head. "Thomas has been at it a long time. I'm not the only one he's done this too and let me tell you, that only aggravated my father more. According to daddy, I should have been able to foresee the situation. No, they never found him. They know where he's been for the past fifteen years by the reports, descriptions and method of operation, but no one can predict where he will strike next. It's all part of a very clever and cunning operation with precision, skill and timing. Apparently, I was sought out because of my father's wealth, as the many victims are wealthy. My meeting him wasn't just by chance or fate. You see...Thomas and his people first scrutinize the affluent, then they investigate the personal history of their target and that is where Thomas comes into the picture. He is one of many for the various jobs he is appointed. For some it is real estate scams and insurance frauds and for others, the assignment is to con and swindle young, available, unsuspecting, naive women into marriage. The investigator believed that I was merely one of three operations conducted to culminate that same day I was to be married and all by the same clan of con artists. Neither of the other two parties had any suspicions either. It would be hard to catch these thieves without the help of a crystal ball or a fortune-teller. And to complicate matters to the worse, Thomas had stolen all my photographs of him prior to his disappearance. All I could offer the police was a description of him. The police artist was able to make a sketch from what he was able to discern from my description and from the description from some of the other victims. It's been nine years, Michael," somberly she pushed her plate away. The smell of her sandwich seemed to offend her. "He has eluded the police thus far, I doubt they will ever catch the son of a bitch. For nine years I have been living with the loss of my father's money and the humiliation from Digger. My father has reminded me of the nightmare every time we speak. If it's the last thing I do on this God forsaken earth, I'm going to pay him back and make him eat his money and words."

"It wasn't your fault, Crystal. The private investigator told you that himself."

"I am fully aware of the facts, but that does not change a thing with daddy. The burden will not be lifted from my conscious until he gets his money and every damn penny of it. I'm going to earn the money by means that only he would understand. My father has made it a point to tell me what a loser

I have been all my life, because I have chosen to be a singer instead of one of his minion perfume sales operators. He had badgered at me since the first day I decided to sing. His belief is that singing is for peasants and commoners, but not for the Worthington lineage."

"Maybe he should hear you sing. I think you're fantastic! No one could deny that you're the best. You're no loser, Crystal." He said...and maybe if you weren't always such a moody bitch, I'd marry you myself. He truly was moved, seeing her humble for the first time.

"Thanks sweetie, you really know how to calm the festering fires of hatred in a girl's broken heart, but the fact is, he has heard me sing. I was young then, but capable enough. Before I had completed the last verse of Amazing Grace he marched out of the church in total shame."

"Then he's a fool and doesn't deserve your love." He raised his voice, "It shouldn't be so important to you to gain something that is less important to him. Who the hell is he to dictate your life?"

"I'm his only daughter, the one living in his house and the one deeply indebted to him."

"You owe him nothing." Mike smacked the table with resoluteness. "He gave you the house. The wedding swindle was not your fault; there was no way that you could have known. He has no right to blame you for that. What the hell is so important about a mere couple hundred grand to a millionaire?" Mike quickly shielded his hands in front of him. "I know, I know, don't say it. It's the principle of the matter and not the money. Well, let me tell you something, sister, he could have been taken just as easily; it was just your misfortune that you got caught in the ploy of their snare. They went after him and they got him. If your father was so keen on suspecting him from the beginning, he should have conducted his investigation prior to the fact and should not have laid the burden of guilt on you. No one is to blame, least of all you, and you owe him nothing. If he can't be a father to you, then to hell with him, that's his loss and making him the only loser."

Crystal knew the words to be true and they sounded most resolute, but the many years of daddy's ridicule and show of disappointment had her inured by unjust fate. "Are you finished?" She asked.

"Yes, unless you want me to yell at you now for being a martyr."

"I'm not being a martyr and I was referring to your dish of melted ice cream." She pointed with a nod of her head.

The nuance of his hostile attitude lightened up. "Oh, ummm, yeah, I guess so. It wasn't that good anyhow."

Just then the waiter stepped up to their table, after detecting Crystal's eagerness to leave. "Shall I get a doggie bag for you, Miss?"

"Not unless you plan to eat this un-kosher trash."

The waiter's teeth nearly fell out of his face onto the floor with his mouth a lolling gape. "Excuse me, Miss?"

Crystal grabbed the check from the waiter who looked as though he were about to suffer from an embolism. She took a quick glance at the eight-and-a-half dollar bill and wedged it and a twenty-dollar bill in between the two sandwich halves on her plate. Looking to Mike, almost stepping on the waiter's toes as she pushed her way by him, she ranted loud enough for most of the patrons to hear her squabble. "I ordered a corned beef on rye and these insipid little mullets ladled out a disgustingly greasy ham and cheese sandwich, with American cheese, no less." Her bicker dwindled on as she was led out of the restaurant by Mike's lead.

After Mike and Crystal left the restaurant they continued the discussion in the car while heading back to her house. There was no way that he would have been able to convince her that the whole ordeal was not her fault, but it was obvious that her imperious father felt different or at least needed someone to pour the blame on. The more he heard of her father the more he hated him as well. He could now understand why it was so important for her to enrich her career as a singer, if not for her own pride and enjoyment, it was to defy her father and lastly, to pay him with the earned monies of her defiance. To Mike, the irony was dismal and most disturbing. He couldn't rationalize how a father could be so abusive to such a young and innocent mind. He could almost picture her face as a little girl, trying so hard to be daddy's little girl, to try to make him love her, make him proud and then to have him shit on her every time. Just the thought of it was so disheartening. It was to no wonder why she was the way she had turned to be. At least I had my father's love, Mike thought, when he wasn't too drunk to say it. That poor girl, what she must have gone through while growing up with a monster like that. It just doesn't seem fair. I have now seen through the facade of her bravery and the curt wall of protection; there truly is a little girl in her, crying and suffering, in desperate need for a father's love but the fact is, it's never going to happen. Even when the money is paid back and she should become a starlet, he will never know how to provide her with the affection and support she needs. With a rueful grin, he tried his best to bolster her spirits and drove her home. That evening she drank the remainder of the vodka and told Mike another horrible event that happened to her just two years later; after which, she cried herself to sleep. Although he tried, there was nothing that Mike could do to patch things between her hurt and the cruelty of her father. He wished that there were a way to take away the pain, a way to perhaps make her forget.

Unfortunately, the resolution was nowhere to be found. She was determined that the only way to appease herself and her father would be through working herself sick until the money was procured and back in her father's hands. For nine long and hard years Crystal had finally worked her way through to The Star House. Before she had met Billy and the others she was scraping tips as a singer in a seamy cocktail lounge, hoping that someone would discover her talent. After four years of suffering through the squalor of that rancid bar scene, one of the clientele who was a personal friend of the owner of the establishment had taken liberties with what was not the property of the lounge. The patron had paid a rather healthy sum of money to the owner in exchange for a night with Crystal. The problem was, no one told her about it. It wouldn't have mattered anyway. That evening as she was making her way to her car, the repulsive man with his squinting eye approached her, as the wafting smoke from his cigarette would cloud his vision. He was a brutal sort, with greasy unkempt hair and was in need of a shave. His clothes looked and smelled fusty as they hung on him like a clothesline.

"Hey there, purdy girly. Let's say you and me go for a drive in that fancy car of yours." Before Crystal had purchased the BMW she had been driving a Jaguar XKE. She poured her hard earned cash into savings until she could afford the sporty car of her dreams with the intent of motivation and mind conditioning; think rich, think rich. Unfortunately, this guy was not a casting director or a vocal mentor.

"I beg your pardon?" As he stepped closer she could see that she was suddenly in a desperate situation.

"You can grovel if you wish, that suits me just fine." He rasped. Before she realized he was even close enough, he had his hand on her breast and was squeezing it painfully hard.

197

"Get the hell away from me!" She pushed him back a step, "Who the hell do you—" A crashing blow of his right fist connected with the entire side of her face, throttling her to the ground, nearly putting her into shock. She never would have imagined that the straggly little, pathetic vermin of a man could muster enough strength to do so much damage with one punch. Her body fell numb to the ground as if she had been shot. The punch was felt clear to the back of her head and through her entire body with resonance. Suddenly, the fate of her existence was his to do with as he pleased. She could taste the blood from her split lip as it streamed into her mouth and across her tongue, as she lay helpless against her car door, palsied and trembling with fear. He knelt alongside her and smeared the blood over her cheek.

"You've been bought and paid for, girly. You're mine tonight. What do you gotta say about that?" Her thoughts were scrambled and barely coherent. The next thing she knew, she had been taken to a secluded parking lot several blocks away. Since her compact sports car was too small to accommodate his horrid deed, he dragged her from the car and almost effortlessly hurled her onto a small greenbelt. After smacking her senseless one more and final time, he raped her. The second blow had knocked her unconscious and totally unaware of what had happened until she awoke the next morning in the hospital. Her near-lifeless body, with tattered and bloody clothes wasn't discovered until the following morning. She had sustained a fracture to the sphenoid bone in her face, a near-fatal concussion and numerous cuts and bruises. After a two-night stay in the hospital she was allowed to return home. Her eye had swelled shut and stayed that way for three painful weeks. Her car had been recovered the same day she was admitted to the emergency room. It had been totaled and abandoned at the bottom of a deep ravine in Topanga Canyon. Crystal followed through with filing a report with the police, but the effort to find the attacker was futile. He was never found, but she swore to herself that the vendetta would someday be repaid.

Six weeks after the attack and rape, when Crystal regained enough of her strength, she decided it was then time to pay a visit to her boss. She reasoned that the only person that her assailant could have been referring to as to her 'being bought and paid for' and the only one who would be deceitfully low enough to sell her like some community meat, had to be Roman, her boss at the lounge. She had a lot of time to think about her woes and a lot of time to imbibe the possible ramifications. Six weeks to the day, it was time for her to act. She dressed herself appropriately and arranged to have a cab pick her up from across town. Her visit with Roman was to be unannounced and with precision and methodical itineration, she had schemed out her plan. As it were, she hadn't saved enough money to dole out for another car and her expenses and debts were accumulating fast. With good reason, she had too much pride than to ask her father for a loan; she couldn't possibly inform him about what had happened to her. In her whirring, mounting thoughts, she could already hear her father's ridicule and insensitivity. He probably would have told her that she was responsible for that too. His discovery of the rape would only have made her life more miserable. The only alternative was to follow through with her plan.

Before leaving her house, she made one final call to a car dealer located not far from the lounge. Crystal was dressed in baggy sweatpants and shirt, with running shoes, as if to resemble a common jogger. She directed the cabdriver to drop her off at a grocery store, which was also strategically located about three-quarters of a mile from the lounge. Once the cab was out of sight, she proceeded to walk the remaining distance. She had never done anything like this before and prayed that she would be able to follow through with it. Each time her jitters would cause her to weaken or fret over the possible circumstances and ramifications of the act she was about to commit, her anger toward the man who took her, mercilessly beat and violated her would rekindle a fiery, molten blaze within her soul, completely obliterating any nervousness, reservations or fear. At the backdoor of the lounge, in the privacy of a cul-de-sac alleyway, she removed a paper bag from under her shirt and then proceeded to remove her sporting attire. In the bag were her high heels, a small matching purse, some cheap costume jewelry and a padlock. Beneath the sweat clothes was another outfit of tight Levis and a revealing, sheer zephyr top with a see-through, push-up support bra beneath, something Roman would never be able to resist. From her back pocket she extracted several pieces of chewing gum. Purposefully, she shoved them all into her mouth and began to chew. After hiding the bag that was filled with her former disguise, she took a deep breath and knocked at the backdoor, knowing that Roman would be the only one inside at that time of the day, preparing the bar for another evening's work.

"Yeah, who's there?" The voice answered, it was definitely Roman.

Crystal responded, with a heavy New York accent, "Ah...yeah, hi there, I'm here to see a Mr. De-Palma about my audition."

"Go away, I'm not holding any auditions today."

"Are ya sure? A mutual friend told me that you would be interested in me."

Roman, being the paranoid, creepy wimp that he was, was always suspicious of unplanned occurrences. Crystal thought, knowing how he came to be such a successful, creepy, low-down, no good son of a bitch, back-stabbing, swindling, bastard parasite, but I'm not the least bit bitter...I just want to scratch his eyes out and shoot his kneecaps off and skin him alive and emasculate him and lastly, hear him scream in agony until he should succumb from mortal torture. "That is to say, if you wanna open to door and take a look for ya self." She thought to herself, of course you want to take a look, you womanizing piece of shit, that's what you live for, you intestinal scum of the earth. The dead bolt cracked out its release and there stood the puny milksop of her rancor, cowering behind the cover of the door. He peered over her shoulder to make sure no one was with her before he conducted his habitual and repulsive meat-gawking-once-over on her. Without even looking at her face, his eyes immediately focused on her billowy, wire-propped breasts. Her top was unbuttoned to the depth of her entirely exposed cleavage. Without giving it further thought the door suddenly opened, offering her passage to come inside for one of his notorious office couch auditions. No doubt, he was pleased.

"Can you sing?" He asked, as if it would matter.

"Oh, sure no problem." She entered the threshold, brushing her breast against his arm. The difficult part of her plan was now over. Getting inside was all she needed to be able to conduct her business. No sooner the door was shut and dead-bolted once again, she lured him into the office where she knew the hidden safe was located. As she had so cleverly planned, Roman had no idea what he had gotten himself into. He didn't have a clue as to who she was.

"So, what's your name gorgeous?" He so triumphantly asked, watching her shapely rear-end as she led him into the office.

Before answering him she removed the gum from her mouth and fasted it to his leather desk chair.

"Why Mr. DePalma, I do declare, I find it hard to believe that you don't recognize me." Just as quickly as snuffing a match, her New York accent was gone, replaced by a sassy southern accent. "Why, shame on you, you horny little devil of a man," she wagged a finger in his face. "Why it was just six weeks ago you fixed me up with a fine gentleman caller. Don't you remember me now?" Roman's face was a stolid blank, much like usual. He didn't know what to make of it. He truly had no idea as to who she was, but it was to no wonder, he had a hard enough time keeping his hungry eyes off of her honing breasts that gave such luscious, supple shape through the transparent material of her top.

"Please tell me your name? Who was it that I fixed you up with? I'm sure I would remember. You must understand that I see a lot of faces in this joint and it's hard to keep track of all that goes on here," he directed his constant stare at her breasts. It was as though he were talking to them, forgetting that she had a face. "I'm a busy man, you know. I've got so many girls working for me...it's so hard to keep track. You know how it is." A familiar glint for her wares appeared in his eyes, as he stepped closer for a better view of her.

"Perhaps I should give you my name to help jog your memory," she knew she didn't have much time before she would end up as another notch penciled in on his couch diary. His disgusting crotch was already showing swell. There was nothing she could do to remove the makeup that she had piled onto her face for disguise, but she was however able to remove the blond wig to expose her long, silken, brown hair. She reached to the top of her head and removed the bobby pin. In her own naturally deep voice she announced, "I am your old friend and employee, Crystal, you vile, impish sack of feculent squalor." Now, he took a closer look at her face and to his total disbelief, the girl whose progeny resembled everything that was classless, cheap and promiscuously available with the poise of a cow and the personality of a dead fish, just the way he preferred them, had suddenly transmogrified into the cock-softening nightmare. Once her identity was discovered, Roman made an attempt for the phone.

"Yes, Roman, call the police for me. Actually, I'm surprised that they haven't been here already. I guess we must have forgotten to give them your full name."

"What are you talking about?" He stopped from dialing, but hadn't yet released the receiver. "What would the cops want from me?"

"Come now, Roman. You can't be as stupid as you look. You must have heard what happened to me?" she replied, calmly dropping the wig to the desk from a deliberate and conspicuous two-foot drop, just inches away from the phone.

"I had nothing to do with it. I was here the whole night. You have nothing on me. I have witnesses," He declared adamantly.

"Well then, dear Roman, I'm pleased to be the bearer of such terrible tidings, it would seem that your statement is quite to the contrary of his statement."

204

"I don't know what you're talking about. Whose statement? If you don't leave here at once, I'll call the police."

She could see the panic in his seedy little eyes. "I urge you to do so." She then cast him a wicked, long glance of a truculent hellhound. With a deep drawl she imploringly said, "I dare you...make the damn call, Roman! I want to be there when they arrest you. I want to be there when they cut of your briny, little balls in prison and feed them to the inmates as a delicacy. Who are they going to believe, Roman? You, the owner of some sleazy, barfly trap like this, or some innocent victim as myself? Let me tell you a little secret Mr. Roman DePalma, when the cops found me raped, bleeding, beaten, broken, unconscious and left for dead, those officers personally promised me retribution." Her voice was now seething with unspent fury. "Those cops that found me, can't wait to get their hands on you, pal."

"But I had nothing to do with it."

"Do you know anything about the law, Roman?" She didn't allow him the time to answer as she stared him down with the venomous intent of a cockatrice. "Do you know what the term 'accessory before or after the fact' means? Got any ideas, Roman? Let me help you to understand the facts as they were explained to me this morning by Officer Randow after I identified your partner in the lineup. Your partner fingered you as the one who set me up with him, that makes you an accessory before the fact and because you did not have the intelligence to confess to the police after you heard of the incident, that makes you an accessory after the fact." Roman's commonly recognized chauvinistic grin scrolled across his creepy little face, as he slowly replaced the receiver, the dial tone suddenly silenced. "So, the way I see it, you are just as guilty as he and without even having been there."

"I don't believe you!" As the ugly man that he was, with his dark, beady eyes set too close to even look possibly normal; he continued to make himself sound even more inept than he already was, "How do I know you're not lying? What do you want from me? You are one crazy broad! Whatever it is that you want from me, you can just forget it. Kiss my ass!" His composure was still a bit leery, as he continued to look down on her as just another female bimbo and absent of any true cognizance.

"Why don't you call the cops and find out? I'm sure they would love to hear from you, the partner who's about to serve twenty years for rape charges and grand theft auto and—attempted murder. Which reminds me, let me tell you more about the law, Mr. Roman. Officer Randow was nice enough to take the time to teach me a few things about the law, it would only seem right that I do likewise and devolve the same information to you, you vulgar, pathetic scum." The acrid jabs at his species were just a reflexive response to his macho facial gestures. Now, the fury was to the boiling point. Just having to see him again made her want to knee him where he stood. To see him cringe in pain was, for the moment, all she desired. "There are three categories that suit one's qualifications for the charges of 'murder one' and 'attempted murder', one is premeditation and it is pretty obvious that you took the time to set this shindig up. So, I would have to say you qualify there, second, is deliberation and it seems obvious to me that this was not a rash decision or something that just happened to occur accidentally. Third is willfulness. Now, that is the most obvious of them all, Mr. Roman because you did accept the money from your partner. I truly doubt that you could convince any jury members that your partner had forced you to take the money, especially under the circumstances. It looks to me like you qualify for all three categories. My vote would have to be guilty as charged."

"This is bullshit! Get the hell out of here or I'll—"

"Or you'll what? She brayed out in his face. "You'll beat me? Rape me? Something along those lines Mr. Roman? Accessory?" She could see his insipid little mind churning. Her ploy was, suddenly without warning, not quite going according to plan. It looked as though he was going to become violent. His ugly little nostrils were flaring and his eyes sparked with greed. The little man with an inveterate, womanizing right hook stepped towards her and raised his hand in an attempt to smack her. A blasting surge of adrenalin raced through her body allowing her to step away, miraculously, saving her from another onslaught of facial trauma. "I wouldn't attempt that again if I were you," she warned as she unbuttoned the top button of her Levis. The timbre of the cocking small pistol that she extracted from within her pants echoed with intimidating and righteous clarity. She pointed the gun toward his crotch. "Since it is so hard for you to understand your predicament, let me reiterate for your remedial facilities. All I have to do is finger you as the guy your partner already turned evidence against and you are going to do just as much, if not more prison time than he. You see, it's quite simple, really; you scratch my back and I'll scratch yours. You fuck with me and I will have your ass thrown in jail so fast it would make your puny little pea-brain spin. Or would you prefer I just blow your balls off here?"

He threw his hands out in front of him in fearful response, as if he believed that fibrous muscle, soft tissue and phalanges bones could hinder the explosive penetration of a three thousand mile per hour projectile. "Okay Crystal, you win. What the hell do you want from me?"

"Certainly, you must have figured it out by now, Roman, I have not been paid yet. If you're going to treat me like some sleazy whore, you best follow through with the formality of custom. I have come here for my paycheck. We'll call it our own little secret agreement."

"How much will this 'agreement' cost me?

"Open the floor safe and I will decide then, fool." The fire in Crystal's eyes were less a passive bluff than Roman cared to challenge. It would seem that a mere seventy-eight hundred dollars wasn't worth losing his balls over. Once the safe was opened, Crystal took all the cash and then doled her simple instructions. She informed him to stay put in his office and forget about the money. Should he just happen to forget the agreement, she would finger the procurer to the rapist and use the money to have him killed in prison. For good measure, she tore the phone wires from the wall and slugged him in the gut with everything she had stored for six long, recovering weeks. As he lay on the floor of his office in the fetal position gasping, Crystal, with her bag of loot and Derringer in hand, ran out the backdoor refitting the wig on her head. Just outside the door, she recovered her bag of jogging clothes. Using the padlock, she locked the backdoor shut with the same cleat he would use to fend off would-be burglars. She took heed to all precautions and just in case he was stupid enough to try to catch up with her, the lock would fetter his attempts just long enough for her to make her escape. Once she was dressed again in her jogging attire, she trotted over to the car dealership a few blocks away. She had already arranged the purchase of a used BMW. As she pulled out of the dealership parking lot in her new, used car, she had only one regret...that was not having been able to do the same, if not worse, to her attacker; the man who stole from her something she would never be able to redeem.

Upon arriving home after the eventful day, she took a tranquilizer and smoked a joint to calm her nerves. Through the remainder of the day, the gun never left her hand for a second. That evening passed quietly and uneventful, denoting Roman's defeat. Had he meant to, and she knew him well enough to know, he would have already retaliated. The next day, she culled through the classifieds ferreting out the new job possibilities. At the time, choices were grim.

For a year she worked stringently as a waitress. The year after that she challenged a ten-month long position as a secretary to a lesbian mogul, who was more chauvinistic than all her worst dates molded into one. After a heated altercation with her, she became unemployed. Her next venture was sought through temporary placement agencies and a sorted variety of job search programs. For two years, her search for work was aimless and she meandered with discontentment and lack of interest. Her true passion was to be a singer and without the spirit of song in her life, she faced the world naked, vulnerable and without will. The emptiness of her soul suddenly evoked anew, that she believed came to her through prayer and the scant preservation of her deprived dreams. Scathed by time, but not completely forgotten or forsaken, the verve of ambition was rekindled by the negativity set forth by one of many of her father's oppressive phone calls. It, like magic, came to her as a blinding light from God himself. She took out an ad in her local newspaper summoning any band that was in need of a lead singer and chose to be auditioned at her residence, to call her at the posted number. The response was immediate and inundating. She had scheduled three or four bands each day of the following week and for two more weeks thereafter to audition in her living room. The overwhelming response from the vast talent was truly inspirational. These were people much like she once was—ambitious, motivated, full of energy and the drive to conquer the world with a song. For days she wondered why it had taken her so long to perceive the idea. By the third week of the auditions she had seen all that she needed. There were many to choose from and many that suited her. Although, one band in particular was well groomed, for the impression she wanted to convey as a band and they had an outstanding sound that showed a lot of promise. They were called The Passion Seekers. They had a singer but they knew she lacked the power and finesse needed to bring the enthralled to their knees. It was now up to her to convince this band that they needed her. She called them back to return with their equipment a second time. She offered to pay them four hundred dollars, one hundred each, just for doing her the task of returning. Once they arrived, she asked them to perform their favorite song. After hearing it, Crystal had a verbatim account of the words. Without a flinch of nerves or a hindrance of confidence of any kind, she requested that the band play it once more with her as lead and if they were the least bit dissatisfied with her as their replacement as lead singer, the audition would be over and she would bother them no more, paying them as promised. Upon their response, all the band members had moved into Crystal's house a week later for the nominal rent of one hundred dollars each, thus redeeming their audition pay and a permanent and private place to practice on a daily basis. The arrangement was ideal for each of them. The rent was more than affordable, making it easier for them to concentrate on their music and the band was also saving a small fortune on practice halls. For Crystal, the rental income was just enough to get by on while working part-time. Finally, she too could dedicate all the necessary time and energy required for her music practice. Within three months, Crystal learned and perfected all the songs the band had already written as part of their performance material. Fifteen months later, she aided in doubling their material and gave the band more hope and reason for the expectation of success. As a team, they worked well together and all had a hand in the writing of the material. As professionals with the compatibility of their talents, their relationship with Crystal was amicable, pragmatic, business-like and tolerated. It was as though they were living with Dr. Jekyll and Mr. Hyde. No sooner the band would end a performance, Crystal was back to her cold-cutting self with little tolerance or patience. They learned that as long as they abide by her house rules, refrained from any small talk with her and most importantly, never miss a band practice; the home-life in her beautiful castle nestled high in the Hollywood Hills of Nichols Canyon would be endurable. They had little idea as to why she was so curt and bitter toward any and everyone, but as long as the music was prolific and the living arrangements were sustained as agreed, Billy, Nicky, Paul and Tawney were content to bear with her personality. Over the months Tawney had made several attempts at communicating with her. She had wondered if maybe Crystal was simply in need of a female companion, but all attempts failed. It seemed that she needed even less from a companion of the female gender and her contending with Nicky was dealt with immediately. He was the first to arrive for the transition of moving in. The poor guy didn't even get the chance to attempt his best. Upon his arrival to her house the day he was to move all his belongings in and with a heavy, armful of neatly pressed suits and shirts, which was his first load into the house, Crystal intercepted his path, blocking him from proceeding down the hall to his room. Her adamant disposition was not to be contested. With fire in her eyes, she gave her warning to Nicky who never yet said more than 'thank you' or 'hello' and stood in befuddled shock, listening to her drawl.

"I know who you are and what you are...therefore, I give you this one warning and I will only say this once to you. If you see fit to come within ten feet of me or even so much as attempt to talk to me about anything other than what pertains to our music, I'll have my daddy incarcerate your hormones in prison on rape charges, faster than you could imagine the time it would take for you to be raped by your new boyfriend in jail. Savvy?"

His response was uniform with the first impression most men have of her. Unable to close his mouth or look her in the eyes, as she would stare him down, he just shook his head in agreement and proceeded to sidle past her. Had it been in his agenda to make any attempts at coming onto her, they certainly were abolished by her wicked speech. She had perfected a way of making men hate her and that suited her just fine. As it turned out, Nicky was more than inclined to obey her wishes; he preferred women with less brass and more breasts.

All things considered in general, Crystal was pleased with her plan and her goals for an auspicious future in music and entertainment. First on their calendar of events, Billy and Nicky had set-up a few performances at the local high schools and soon worked their way up to nightclubs and private parties. Seemingly trivial and a waste of such good talent, Crystal reluctantly agreed they would have to start somewhere and in time work-up their references and résumé. When Mike moved into her house, eighteen months after the band, it seemed to be of good omen for everyone. He had a wonderful personality and had a knack for taming fires that were quick to fester within Crystal. It was as though he were the mediator and bonding agent between her and the other band members. If there could've been anyway to take away all of Crystal's hurt and anguish of the past, they all may have been considered as close as a family.

Chapter Eleven
Jason and Ceenatanee

His life of secrecy and mystery was suddenly exposed like a billboard sign with little regard for the promises in the noble oaths of silence. In near shock, Jason stood from the table and began to pace around the tiny kitchen. Flurries of emotions and scattered thoughts came to his mind. Not until Millie had made the connection between Sadie and Sara, did Jason ever figure it to be so. But it made perfect sense; he could feel the truth in Millie's words and he knew then there was meaning behind all the nightmares and all the happenings since the night of the supposed fire. As Jason was gathering his thoughts while pacing around the kitchen table, Millie intercepted his path by reaching out for him.

"What are you feeling, Jason? What are you thinking?" Though she couldn't see, her eyes tracked him.

"I'm thinking how lucky I am to have a friend like you, Jason and I'm feeling strange about all this. I don't know how to react, as it was, and has been for some time. I was alone with these thoughts of lunacy and unnatural happenings, and today I'm visited by a friend who only now informs me that she too knows of such odd phenomenon."

"It's not odd," Millie said. "It's very human, very natural and very real. I now know why Sara chose to speak through me," her pretty eyes continued to stare as if she could actually see. Her hands clutched at Jason's arms so to feel the truth permeate with vibration through him as well. "Last night, for the very first time in my life I was given the ability to see. I could see pictures and faces and sadness and laughter. It was a transitory gift of magic that I will always remember. Sara showed me more than what the seeing people will witness in an entire lifetime."

Jason lowered himself to his knees and her eyes followed him. With his hands now placed in hers, he looked deeply into her face. "How could this be?"

"I don't really know, but I do know it happened and it's very real. How could I have known of the color red before last night? Or any other color for that matter? I saw everything, Jason! I even saw you, in the agony of your past." Her hands traced lightly over the scars on his face. "And I've seen you in the happiness of your future."

"Sara has shown you the future? My future? But why?"

"As I said before, the future of many lives depends on you. But that's not even the half of it.
There's more to the mystery of life than you and I
may ever learn in just one lifetime. I was given a
night of splendor and travel and vision, all from a
moment's visit from Sara. And I passed through
many lifetimes, Jason. Sisters and brothers of gen-
erations we will never meet with in the flesh. And I
know that you know exactly what I'm talking about,
because I felt you last night just as I can feel the vibration in you now. Our subconscious abilities are
limitless, and you are not the only one who shares
in these powers. All those who breathe are capable,
but only the chosen few know how to develop, nurture and shape the powers of our subconscious.
You're one of them, Jason. You have a blessed soul
of many angels. They watch after you, as you will
do the same in good time...in good time..." from the
nape of his neck to the top of his head, a vibrating
chill rippled beneath his skin. It felt as though his
hair was standing on end. "But for now, there's
something, rather, someone waiting to meet with
you." Through his fingers, and straight to his gut, he
could feel a vibration of her own coming from her
gentle touch.

"Who? Tonight?"

"I was blessed with the gift of sight last night,
maybe for only a short while but I do know this." A
smirk came to Millie's lips, her face seemed to glow
with a secret pride. "Tonight is as good a night as
any. She's a very special girl, Jason. You have no

idea how happy this makes me—to be the one bringing the two of you together at last..."

"At last? What does that mean?" Reading the expression on her face, Jason was bubbling with enthusiasm.

"She's traveled many miles to find you. By herself, she sought you out through the vision of her own. Sara guided her to me. From a far world, through storms, snows and even the treacherous Appalachian mountains this girl had come to be with you."

"Who is she, Mille?"

"Her name is Ceenatanee."

"She's Indian," Jason's voice gave a hint of distant recognition. "What does Cenatanee mean?"

"It means, with fire in hair. You see, Jason, the red I saw was the glow from the sun's light through her hair. She has told me, through the help of Sara and her own magic potion of smoke and herb-roots, that you are her spirit-destiny. She is beautiful and colorful, Jason. She is also the one that you have been looking for. She comes to you in the night, in your dreams. You've seen her, haven't you?"

He shook his head in disbelief. "This is not what I had expected to hear from you this evening. When you said that you needed to speak with me, the first thing I thought was perhaps you needed advice or medication or—I don't know what, but never this. This is so hard to believe."

"It shouldn't be. Nothing that I have said to you is untrue."

He nodded in response with a distant gaze. "But until tonight, these dreams were my own, shared with no one and thought to be nothing more than just dreams. And now, you tell me that the woman in my dreams, the woman who's face I've never been able to find in my waking quest is now here to meet with me? You're right; this beautiful and colorful girl has come to me amid many, many nights. And I have also seen the fire in her hair," his voice began to dwindle with his mind wandering and in reverie. "I just don't know what to say. I thought that perhaps she wasn't real, only a dream. This is quite a revelation, you know? There was a time when people were imprisoned and tortured for saying and believing in such things."

"And burned" Millie added. "You owe it to yourself to meet with her, tonight." There was eagerness to her voice, which made him slightly nervous.

"What if I'm not the one? What if she made a mistake or something?"

"She didn't sacrifice a complacent and comfortable life with her people to exile herself and travel through what most healthy and strong men could not have survived to have made such a 'mistake'. There is no mistake. How could two people share the same dream? How could I have known of your secrets, had this been a mistake? Has Sadie ever been wrong?"

Jason's heart was pounding with excitement. He couldn't sit still; his nerves were jittered with unfledged emotions. A blind date was not something he was readily prepared for. He paced around the tiny kitchen, circling the table a few more times.

"Well, Mr. Mathison? Do we get to meet with this Indian girl of destiny, or are you going to continue to besiege me until I relent with a confession of witchcraft?"

"I'm sorry. It's just that I'm so full of jitters."

"I'm sure she feels the same. Just take a drink of milk and let's be on our way. Jonathan isn't going to be happy about being made to wait for me all night long ya know."

"Ah, yes ma'am." After following her instructions, he cleaned himself up and prepared for the journey, harnessing the horses and wagon and bringing along a leather pouch filled with some of his secret potions and trinkets.

Ceenatanee was camped just a few miles outside of town. She had only arrived in town three weeks prior. As Jason and Millie rode through town, the amber sun was setting with half its resplendence hidden behind the neighboring mountain range. With Millie guiding the way through the memory of her vision, Jason followed her precise directions. He marveled over her abilities to have been able to see and remember every little detail that came to pass on the trail out of town. She named all the buildings of the town as they would pass each one and she had even made comment on the landscaping along the terrain. Sara had given her quite a gift for one night, more than she would ever be able to express to anyone, but none more than the gift that Jason would be giving to her in a couple years to come. As she had told Jason, she was given a chance to see not only the past, but also the future--the same future that involves her and many others, in a very big way. Riding on that future, with all the precarious factors, is the major role that's played when Jason was to meet with Ceenatanee. Just as she had predicted, there was a small camp just outside of town. Below a steep mountain ridge there was a campfire with a few cooking utensils, tools and blankets in the area. It was clear that someone was preparing to cook a meal. There was no sign of Ceenatanee, but Jason knew through instinct that she was near. He could feel her presence and smell her handmade skin lotions. Within a chasm of a small cliff just about thirty paces from the fire, was a cavernous shelter deep in the mountainside. As the horses drew nearer, their presence was obviously heard. From the grotto of the rocks emerged the most beautiful and enchanting image of a woman. Before the mouth of the cave, she stood silent, proud and strong, watching the two strangers approach. She was dressed in a bleached deerskin robe. It was bleached, no doubt, to camouflage her presence against the snows that had blanketed much of the path on her long journey.

Once Jason was close enough to see her eyes, he knew that Millie was quite right. The girl of his dream was standing less than fifty feet from him in all her splendid beauty. Her skin of bronze was satiny and smooth with a perfect complexion. As they made eye contact, the two smiled as if they were old friends. Her eyes were as tranquil as a stream running through a wooded forest. Jason slowed the horses to a halt.

"She's here, isn't she?" Millie asked.

"Yes, she is." Jason was unable to take his eyes from hers, "just don't pinch me. This is one dream I never want to wake from."

"You won't have to, she's real. Just as real as you and me." For a brief moment, just long enough to help Millie down from the buckboard, Jason took his eyes from hers. Together, they approached her. Meeting them halfway, Ceenatanee offered guidance to Millie. It was as though she knew them both and needed no explanation of her handicap. The night was beginning to get chilly. Around the fire, they all sat on blankets. Judging from the arrangement, she was no doubt, expecting them.

"Ceenatanee?" Jason asked, earnestly.

She smiled and responded, "Jason?" Her accent was similar to French. She had answered in a way that he could tell she was playing with him, almost bantering. These vision-quest occurrences are likely common amongst her people, but to him this was something of a miracle.

"I can't believe I found you." Jason just couldn't stop staring at her. Everything about her was so familiar, so true to his vision of her.

"Hah!" She retorted with a show of resentment. "You found me?" Her eyes drilled him for being so blind to the facts, "for three years I send you my spirit to bring you to me. And you do not come. For two years I traveled to find you in your world, and you—you claim credit." Truly, she wasn't mad or spiteful. It wasn't in her nature to be of either. Behind her eyes of contempt hid a strong-willed woman who was more than just wise and pretty. While she spoke to him, she kept hold of Millie's hand. It would seem the two were enjoying watching him try to explain what he meant.

"No, of course not, I mean, you traveled for two years just to find me? Wasn't that dangerous? How did you know where to search?"

She described some of the ways of her people and how it came to be her destined journey to find him and make important medicine together. She explained that through the spirit world, anyone could transform into any being they desire or find most comfortable to transform into. The eagle, for example, can travel great distances and report back with far away journeys of medicine, plague, famine or drought. The tiger and the wolf can do well in the search for food and in the protection of the clan. She claimed only to be of a small finch-like bird capable of flying short staggered distances. To claim more would be an act of projecting too much self-importance in the eyes of the male tribesmen. Even among the Indians there was much chauvinism to contend with. Jason watched her closely as she spoke of her people and her beliefs. He still couldn't fathom her having traveled so far just to find him. Millie seemed to accept everything as if it were as

223

natural as being able to walk. In fact, the two girls had developed an instantaneous rapport without having to say much at all. They even seemed to be able to communicate through simple touch. There was so much he wanted and needed to learn from her. What was thought to have been primitive practices of medicine in the Indian techniques were quite intriguing and very effective sources of healing. In the short while that they spent together, Jason had already learned much more. From the moment their eyes met, he knew there was a strong connection between them. He hated to have to leave her that night, but it was getting late and he promised he would take Millie home before Jonathan would have a chance to worry.

Upon her invitation, Jason returned to see Ceenatanee the following morning. They spent the entire day together, getting to know each other, and learning of her medicines, travels and lifestyle. He was taken by this intelligent, beautiful, young and undeniably independent girl, who seemed to have more experience in the trials of life than one could possibly imagine. He continually found himself hoping that it all wasn't just a dream. The morning he returned to see her, he was relieved to find her camp still nestled close against the mountainside. The smoldering embers of her fire were glowing with a small mirage of heat rising with the image of her face within. As he arrived at her camp that morning, he was approaching from the east. The full radiance of her splendor was stunning in the morning sun. She had dark green eyes and long, lanky brown hair. It wasn't until she stood between him and the sun did he finally see the red fire in her hair. They spent the next several days inseparably enthralled in each other's lives. It didn't take long before Jason grew protective of her. He didn't like the idea of her living in the hills unprotected and too far from him, even though she had traveled on her own for two years and over two thousand miles without his protection. When he suggested that she move into town, she unashamedly suggested that she move in with him. Jason couldn't have been happier. In his dreams, he already loved her. Now, with her living with him in the realm of reality, he loved her more. In less than a year, they were married and planning a family. When Doc Peterson passed away shortly after they were married, Jason became the town's fulltime doctor. Like a puzzle, Jason and Ceenatanee seemed to fit together perfectly. The people of the town accepted her immediately. In fact, the people were grateful to know her and be treated by her as well. Where Jason was at a loss with his practice in medicines, Ceenatanee filled the voids with her knowledge. As many of the townspeople had said, the two worked like magic together.

Within two years of practicing medicine together, Ceenatanee told Jason that it was time for them to start practicing spiritual medicine together. He had taught her everything he knew about the western medicines and now, it was time for her to go a whole lot further and teach him of her forefather's magic. Once she opened Jason's eyes to her world, it was like waking to an entirely new and very different life. The vibration that Millie could feel in his touch was only a small fraction of his spiritual prowess. With the development of his skills, Ceenatanee promised that the spirit gods of medicine are of the most powerful. When one has developed his meditation and is visited by the medicine gods, only the sacred cures are then revealed and offered to the mortal man. The rewards of their cures are infallible and never to be questioned. In response to his training and her teachings, he studied hard and worked endlessly to achieve the terminus of spiritual healing. Through meditation and silence, fasting and suffering through the strenuous weather conditions and changes in the sweat lodge, day after day for weeks on end, Jason continued to work toward the higher spirit world. He had to relinquish and dispel his former beliefs and myths involving the scoffed rumors of Indian magic. His faith in the spirit world had to be kept pure and untainted. Only then, by the will of the gods, would he be enlightened with the ultimate gift of the healing touch and the open door of passage to the gods. In the trails of Ceenatanee's efforts to reach the spirit world, she learned through the gods that she would never be whole without the integral of a distant counterpart—Jason. The gods showed her how to call him and she worked hard in doing so. Because he failed to respond accordingly, she was forced to leave her people and seek him out on her own. In doing so, she would never be allowed to return; it was a choice she didn't hesitate to make. Once the gods showed her the importance of her healing powers and the destiny found in the partnership of her counterpart, the choice was clear and noble, destined after having been privy to such persuasiveness through the eyes of the gods. There are matters of destiny that even the fatalists of time cannot fully explain; the path is just obvious and the one to quest must follow accord or die without learning any of the truly necessary values in life, and no doubt, be made to go through it all again in another challenge of life. And now, she found her counterpart through the help of the gods and the angels of Jason's protection. For two years she studied his medicine and then, he studied hers. Spirit relations were taken very seriously among the Indians. Jason had to learn and study without any former training, save that of his own visions. And when the day of revelation finally came, the two rejoiced like two young blissful hatchlings just given the ability to fly. It was a strange and different encounter from anything Jason had ever known. Speaking with the spirit gods was only the final phase of his being accepted. First, they tested his faith with a formidable labyrinth of deception and confusion. It was as though he had strayed and ventured through the gates of Hell. He relived the torturous burning of Salem. Then when he thought he had embarked on a reprieve from the spirit gods, they challenged him again and again. The brimstone and the hell-fires had pushed him through the gateway of Hell where the devil himself; a fawn looking creature with horns and steely talons, tried desperately to bedevil him. They tested his will through his own fears, but he never gave up. Undaunted, he continued through the spirit journey. Second, and lastly, he was tested for his compassion and love. And the spirit gods were obviously pleased with his answers. The gods can be equally formidable as they can be kind, loving and abundant with knowledge. Once they approved of him as they found and knew him worthy, he was accepted as a student. As his mentor, they took him to far away places of majestic lands and never before seen quintessence. His travels felt to have lasted merely fleeting seconds, but a week later, after waking from his trance, Jason learned different and was congratulated by his wife. During his travels he had been proudly given his transcendental form. It wasn't until that moment that he realized the meaning and the vital importance of his given form. He found himself taking the form of a tiger with powerful hindquarters and lasting endurance. From the midsection and beyond to what was supposed to be his head, Jason found his companion and counterpart. Ceenatanee was the proud and intrepid eagle with a wingspread of nearly twenty feet. Together, they formed a whole. United, they were omnipotent. As one, they were called, the Griffin.

Chapter Twelve
Opening Night

Tension was especially high on their opening night at The Star House. Making matters worse, Crystal was still sobering over the two-week past telephone conversation with her father. He had an uncanny and malignant way of resonating the anger in her. It was to everyone's misfortune that Charles Worthington would infallibly call each month making like miserable for everyone in the house.

That afternoon, Mike was visiting his brother, Jimmy when Billy had called. He asked him to come to the opening night to help calm Crystal down. At the time, Jimmy was going through a crisis of his own. So, in hope to solve two problems with one effort, Mike asked his brother if he wouldn't mind coming to the club with him. Mike just simply assumed that Jimmy was going through a mild case of depression and that getting out of his tiny, cramped apartment would help to allow him to think clearly. It was hard for Mike to understand all that his brother was going through. It seemed he was having trouble at work, and yet, it seemed like his problem was more personal. In the past year, there had been three other outbreaks of depression with his brother, and each time, Mike paid a visit to try to help bolster his spirits. He couldn't understand why Jimmy found it so important to please his boss. He was going to school fulltime at the University of California in Los Angeles to one day become a lawyer, while working part-time as a paralegal for a small law firm in East Los Angeles. It behooved Mike to see the reason why it was of such concern for Jimmy to even give it much worry about his boss' personal opinion of him; when in three years, he will have acquired all the credits and completed the dissertation needed for the privilege of passing the State Bar on his own, thereby being able to open his own practice, because there was much more to be said than simply his brother's worrying about some guy's sentiment over the minion office-help of an understudy-paralegal. Unfortunately, it was beyond Mike's grasp to read between the lines, and Jimmy didn't have the nerve to expose the whole truth to him, and each time, leaving Mike more confused about the complexities of his brother.

Reluctantly, Jimmy agreed to go, but insisted on taking his own car, his leased Lincoln Town Car, just in case he might want to leave early. From Scotty, Mike had purchased a small, ugly economy car that was badly in need of a paint job that nobody seemed to like, except Mike. He was complacent just knowing he had reliable transportation. When they got there the club was already packed. The Star House was notorious for hosting good performers. There were a variety of new faces in the crowd, apart from the regulars of the other clubs that would often come to see The Passion Seekers. It looked as though they were already acquiring a dedicated fan club.

It was early and the band was still setting up their equipment. Mike and his brother got themselves a table by the stage, thanks to Billy, and ordered drinks. When the band was finally ready for their opening performance, Mike excused himself, telling his brother that he wanted to wish Crystal luck.

At first, he was hesitant to approach the stage. In all the time that he knew her and her manic-depressive behavior, he would still have to stop and read her. Many times it was as though he was meeting her for the first time, not knowing exactly what to expect from her. As he leaped onto the stage and slowly closed the distance between them, he could see her glazed eyes clearly and read the signs. Her movements were perfunctory and slovenly. It wasn't like her at all to be acting in this manner.

Billy, who was standing off to the side of her peripheral vision, called Mike's attention by waving his arms. He mimed raising a bottle to his mouth and then pointed to Crystal. As Mike stepped closer to the rancor of her breath, it was obvious that Billy was right and she was blatantly drunk. It would seem that after two weeks since her father's phone call, she was still harboring the bitterness.

"Don't you start on me." She beat him to the quick, avoiding the liaison of eye contact.

"I haven't said a word."

"You don't have to. I've already got an earful from Billy and I just knew you would be next. My faculties are acutely intact. You needn't worry about me, I'm fine, as you can surely see," she said.

"You've been drinking a lot lately. It worries me, it worries all of us. You know, whether you like it or not, we care about you."

"Your sentiments have been noted and I appreciate the concern, but your worries are unwarranted. A medicinal drink now and again will not jeopardize the future of this band. They can stop fretting over their careers."

"You've got it wrong Crystal. It's you that they show concern for. Don't you understand? You've done so much for all of us, and we know how much this means to you. We don't want to see you—"

"They know nothing about me," she abruptly scolded. "...And you, I have told too much." She continued with a disturbing tone of lost friendship. She had a distasteful way of crawling inside herself when she became distressed.

"Damn it, Crystal, I only wanted to help you, girl, to be your friend and companion. Obviously, I care more about you than you could appreciate. The other night, for the first time you opened up to me. You made me feel like a true friend. There is nothing wrong with opening up, and there is nothing wrong with having friends who want to listen and learn of your troubles. But I'll be damned if I'm going to continue to stand her and be shit on by you."

She continued to fight off his eye contact.

"I don't know exactly why, Crystal, but I'll always love you, even if you choose to be a beautiful, wicked, little bitch." A very small, but apparent smile came to form at the furthest corners of her lips as she stepped closer and hugged him. The tears were beginning to stream as she buried her shameful face in his chest.

"Oh, Michael Shane, will you forgive me?" she asked through her tears, seemingly somber. "I know how difficult I've been lately, or probably always. It's not intentional, I don't want to hurt anyone, least of all, you. I just have so much trouble dealing with it. There is so much more to it. It hasn't been easy for me. Perhaps I have been weak. It's always been so hard for me to figure it out. And then I meet you..." the notorious smirk, appeared, looking enticing and vibrant as ever. "The guy who makes everything seem so simple and easy to understand. You have a magical and rhetorical way of making things all better. Even your tender touch possesses a healing quality for me. I wish I could be so optimistic." She pulled away and finally looked him in the eyes. "And, the reason why you love me, is because I am—such a bitch. I have yet to see you stand-down to a challenge." The tears were glistening over her cheeks as her face never looked more innocent with resplendence. "I love you too.

And please accept my apology." She tipped her head, offering a kiss of truce.

Mike accepted and wished her luck, then stepped off the stage, taking notice that most of the seats of the club were now filled and standing room was filled to capacity. The place was loud and thick with cigarette smoke.

"Well, well, well little brother...when did you and Crystal become so close?" Jimmy nudged a sporty closed fisted tap on Mike's shoulder. "Something serious, perhaps?"

Mike's attention was drawn to the stage; he couldn't take his eyes off of Crystal. She possessed a magnetism that would always intrigue him. "It's not that way, but we are close; as close as we were meant to be, I suppose. But it's not exactly the way you're thinking. It's strange," Mike shook his head and turned to face his brother. "There's something between us alright, but I'll be damned if I can figure it out."

Jimmy put his hand on Mike's wrist and with eyes of all knowing and a smile to match, he said purposefully, "I know exactly what you're talking about. Those are the relationships that compliment the virtues and quality of life. They're rare, and yes so vital."

Mike suddenly and proudly knew that his brother understood him precisely. In the past year, Mike had learned so much more about his brother. He was proud of him and his stringent efforts to become someone important and successful, even if it was mostly to please the witch. Jimmy would one day make a fine attorney. He possessed all the admirable qualities a lawyer should be—honest, kind, determined and understanding. If only they could have been friends when they were younger, if only it could have been allowed, if only the witch could have been liquidated years before, if only their dad were of brazen loins, who would stand up for them and help nurture their needs. But the hypothetical wonders of their youth had long passed; the present time was consolation enough. Mike felt fortunate to have at least been given the chance to meet and know his brother at all. Had it not been for the accident, Mike may never have had the chance to get to know his brother and probably would never have made the attempt once he was freed from the clutches of the witch. As the many disheartening stories of their adolescence unfurled over the months, both Mike and Jimmy became stupefied by the misery they both shared at the hands of their mother. When he was young, Mike hadn't any idea that his brother was going through such similar anguish as he. It was, however, of a different nature, but as painfully abusive just the same. It wasn't until Mike's eighteenth birthday that he saw Jimmy smile and laugh for the very first time. He was nearly caught by surprise when the revelation occurred. Ironically, it was when Mike was reciting to Jimmy about when he and Billy went to get his belonging from the witch's house. At the time, Mike was nervous about what confrontations might take place between he and his mother, and he had no idea if any of his things would still be there. It had been two months since he was released from the hospital, nearly five months since the last encounter with his mother. Billy stayed in his truck waiting for his return, making sure all was well once Mike was in the house. As he curiously stepped onto the porch, he was struck by the oddity of not knowing whether to knock on the door or just walk in. Without further ado, he turned the knob and opened the door.

"Hello, is anybody home?" The house looked the same but felt very different. It was dark, cold and absent of any hospitality.

"Well, I'll be...the long lost prodigal son has returned," her voice was weak and unfriendly.

"I have only come to pick up my things, mother." He replied, trying to trace where her hoarse voice was coming from. As he made his way through the hallway, he could see the silhouette of her ominous image looming in the darkness of her bedroom.

"I was wondering when you would be along...now that you have dropped out of school and undoubtedly found yourself living on the streets of squalor and poverty. I know you would eventually come back. You'll probably need to sell all your junk just to survive another day as a pauper. So, what's it like being a total loser? With no friends, no place to live, no money, no food, no l-o-v-e-r?" Her cutting words were nothing less than what he had expected from her. As the burry brashness of her voice exuded the air, Mike felt as though a major change had taken place. It was as though his mother was without any prowess or effect on him, as if he had somehow outgrown her childish game. He didn't fear her; he didn't feel threatened by her. He didn't feel anything at all, save a miniscule measurement of pity. He suddenly discovered that there was nothing she could possibly say that could penetrate his well-being. He had fostered a new attitude, a new life, a new world and milieu that was so far beyond her wicked reach. For the moment, he thought perhaps, she had missed him, if for no other reason, at least to harass, badger, ridicule and torment.

"I'm sorry you feel that way." Mike made his way to his bedroom with his mother following at a distance, emerging from the darkness.

"What do you care what I feel?" He flipped the switch turning on the bedroom light. Surprisingly, nothing had been removed or changed. "I killed the rat you know. Take a look for yourself, its dead carcass must be in there somewhere."

"Did you now, mother?"

"I wasn't going to feed it. So, it's dead."

Out of a habit of his past, Mike leaned over the cage and peered into and along the many trails. "When are you going to stop playing these games, mother. We both know that Lucy is not in the cage." By her shadowed expression, Mike realized that she truly didn't know that Jimmy had come the week of the accident and picked up Lucy, knowing that she would leave her to die or flush her down the toilet,

237

that is to say, if she wasn't so frightened to touch Lucy. Over the years, Mike had other hamsters and had accumulated many integral cages and a rather extravagantly large Habit-trail. Jimmy didn't want to be bothered with the complexities of the contraption, so he bought a small, manageable cage from the pet shop before he came to collect her. Since the cage was still there, the witch figured Lucy would still be inside, dead from starvation.

"What are you talking about? Of course it's in there. The little rodent is probably nothing more than a pile of bones." She literally felt proud of herself to have been able to say she was the cause of his grief.

"Don't you know anything about hamsters, mother? Lucy wouldn't still be in there, she's carnivorous." As he was bustling to gather all his belongings to the center of the room, his mother came into the ray of the light.

"So what if the little rodent was a meat eater? It's still just as dead." She hadn't even bothered to dress, save to throw on an old, musty robe. Her hair wasn't combed or washed. Her disposition was equally as unsavory as her appearance.

"On the contrary, mother," Mike brushed by her as he made his way to the front door with a bundle of clothes in his arms. By her standing in the light, Mike could see why she had the house in total darkness. She was obviously suffering from another of her allergy attacks. She had dark crimson rings around her eyes, and her nose was as bright as Rudolph's. Aside form the nose; she could have passed as a demented raccoon. She was a comical sight, to say the least. For a brief moment he almost felt sorry for her, but quickly regained himself. "The jaw and bite structure of a hamster is over seventeen-hundred pounds per square inch."

"So..." She followed him all the way to the front door, where Mike had flagged Billy to come in and receive the handful of clothes.

"So obviously, Lucy must have gnawed her way out of the cage, as all hamsters do when they get extremely hungry. You should have fed her, because now there's no telling where she will show up." He knew what she was thinking and beat her to the quick. "And I wouldn't bother with those mouse traps or poisons, they're too smart for either." The wretched look on her face was well worth the effort of his prank. As he continued to pack and transport his belongings to the truck with Billy's help, his mother had a few more hostile and bitter things to say, but Mike ignored her. When he was finally done packing and loading, he pulled a piece of paper from his pocket that had a number scrolled across it. He walked into the kitchen where his mother was trying to inconspicuously inspect the cabinets.

"I'm living in Beverly Hills now, mother. Should you need me or find Lucy—I can be reached at this number. The best time to reach me would be early morning; I work fulltime now during the day and I'm going to night school in the evenings. Oh, and one more thing, when I was deliriously sick over at Park View Hospital, I may have gotten a few digits wrong on dad's medical insurance policy number, but don't worry, they assured me that the collection department will be able to correct the matter without any further delays. You should be hearing from them any day soon. Perhaps, they will be working out that moratorium deal as they mentioned. I'm not really too clear on all the formalities of the paperwork, but they did say something about me being a minor and you and dad as sequentially liable, or something to that effect. Well anyhow, I have to press on. With my hectic schedule, it's hard to imagine that I still have time for therapy three times a week." With a bantering salute in her honor and a quick pivot, Mike turned toward the door and played the role one last time, taking his proverbial black plastic comb from his back pocket and slicked back his hair and exited from her life. The look of worry for her pocketbook was apparent, and the unspent anger towards Mike was, no doubt, festering deep in her peptic ulcer. She looked as though she were about to become an insolent statistic.

On the way back to Crystal's house, in the prestigious Nichol's Canyon of the Hollywood Hills, Billy and Mike got a good, triumphant laugh, but not as hearty a laugh as when Mike told Jimmy of the incident. Only he could truly know and appreciate the justice of malice played upon the witch and how she had a dreadful fear of small furry animals with steely teeth and beady, vigilant eyes of hunger. And only Jimmy could understand how Mike felt about his parents abandoning him to the whimsical chance of the bureaucratic red tape involved with hospitals and their insurance policies. She must have suffered such dread and worrying about the collection department's phone call and the outstanding insurmountable debt to the hospital. Had it not been for Jimmy, Mike's injuries could easily have culminated in paralysis or worse.

Crystal started the band off with a slow love ballad. The acoustics in the club were adequate as she first relied on the microphone to carry her voice to the people. The second song of her choice was faster with much more punch. The microphone was no longer needed as her singing voice accrued with sinews of authority and appeal of sirens, and the audience watched in awe. The stunningly beautiful woman with the powerful song delivered a night of music and song that no one present would easily forget. And the response was proof of that. It was clear to see The Passion Seekers were well on their way to fame. After performing for an hour and a half, the band announced their fifteen-minute break and exited the stage. Nicky headed for the bar where he saw an available-looking, voluptuous blond. Paul and Tawney went backstage to release a privy urge, Billy and Crystal joined Mike and Jimmy at the table reserved for band members and their friends only. Mike introduced his brother to Crystal, and the two seemed to connect. Very few

people had the ability or personality to render interest to her requirements.

He wondered if perhaps she was merely showing
respect for his being Mike's brother, but as the conversation between them progressed, it was quite to
the contrary of his former thoughts. Jimmy was an
interesting person, and she seemed to appreciate it.
An interesting thought in Mike's plotting mind was
held for further consideration; perhaps what Jimmy
needed in his life was a serious relationship. The plot
thickened as he gestated a theory. Maybe Crystal
would be good for him; perhaps they would be good
for each other. From all that Mike had gathered from
his brother through conversations at coffee shops, his
apartment and everywhere they would go, he was
without a doubt, a very lonely guy and without much
carnal companionship. In fact, he couldn't recollect
his brother ever having been with a woman on a date
or in his apartment. He passed it off as usual, postu-
lating that his brother is very dedicated to his work
and studies. Obviously, he just didn't have the time,
for a time-demanding and time-devoting relationship, and yet he possessed all the classic signs of being extremely lonely and in desperate need of that
very sustenance. When Crystal and the band returned
to the stage, resuming to their enchantment of musi-
cal prowess, Mike tested the waters by asking his
brother what he thought about Crystal. His response
was less promising than he had hoped. And almost
coming to him as a shock, he felt strangely about attempting to fix his brother up with her, the woman

who would only, hither to, share her secret intimates with one man, himself. The flurrying confusion of mixed feelings, jealousy, ego and compassion were soon remedied when Mike conceded to himself that Crystal would never have him as her husband. Nor did he feel that way about her. Deeply stored in the passages of their minds, Mike and Crystal knew that they had a bonding relationship of heated sex and intellectual intrigue, but would go no further.

What would please him most, as he gave it a great deal of consideration, would be to see his brother and Crystal make a go of it, together. Two of his best friends, who both suffer from the similar ailments of loneliness, finding companionship and love, through his efforts, would be the most rewarding bestowment of his kindness and affection Mike could possibly offer.

"What do you mean, she's okay?" Mike asked. "She's gorgeous and talented, intelligent and single, and in case you didn't notice, she took a shine to you." Mike took a couple swallows of his beer. "What more could a guy ask for?"

"Yes, you're quite right. She's got the finest qualities of a woman to be sure. But you know how it is. You've seen my apartment; you know how hectic my schedule is. When would I find time for a relationship? There's too much involvement with relationships. It's hard enough trying to survive these days, much less complicating things worse by adding fuel to the fire with a committal relationship."

"But that's the point." Mike pointed the mouth

of the beer bottle in Crystal's direction, "with a fantastic woman like that, a commitment should be welcomed. She's struggling to make her career, just as you. She battles with the hands of time just as you and everyone else. So you arrange your schedule to accommodate accordingly. One helps the other. Survival is easier with a companion."

Jimmy already knew this to be true, only too well. "Why are you so determined to fix us up?" The question seemed wistful.

"To me, the both of you are special, and I think you two have similar interests. You, yourself have said many times to me that your life is missing 'that something special'. And I think a woman like Crystal is 'that something special' worth looking into, she's not going to be single forever, you know."

"How do you know that we wouldn't be as you two are, relationship wise? What makes you think that we would get along any different than you two do?" For some reason Jimmy was hedging from his true feelings, much the same as when they would talk together at his apartment.

"I don't, but unless you try, no one will know. Besides, our friendship is worth whatever trouble it might cause with scheduling. Like I said, brother, she's a fine woman. And I admire her and cherish our friendship. If your relationship with her should go no further than ours has, then so be it. It would be worth the venture with nothing lost and a true friend gained. She is special, I'm telling you."

"Mike, I believe you. And I know you're right

but to put it frankly, she's not my type and I'm not hers...please don't ask me to explain." He looked sternly at Mike with forbearing eyes. Forasmuch as it were a mystery that Jimmy wasn't yet willing to confide, Mike would concede to his wishes by abstaining from furthering the discussion. Once again, Mike was confused by his brother's actions. Perhaps Jimmy wasn't capable of handling rejection, assuming she would do so. Or maybe he was right and she simply didn't meet his womanly criteria, and by saying nothing more, Jimmy spared his brother's feelings. Mike only admired him more for being so proud and for having the ability to stay in control and committed to such high standards. He liked and appreciated his big brother more everyday. And everyday, he hated his mother more for having kept them apart through the years of their childhood.

The performance on the opening night was outstanding with John Blackmore the first to give a standing ovation. The mystery of their all-important questions had been answered. And without fail, the questions were asked no less than ten times a day...Are we good enough? Will we make it far? How much longer will it take? How far can we take it? With the answer seen clearly on the faces of their audience and in the responses of the excitement that filled the club, there was no longer any doubt, they had the magic that it would take to succeed. After three encores, the concluded the opening night with

"When Love is Lost, You Will Always Find Me". With the same demeanor and effect as when she had sung to Mike the day they met, she did so again and with the same luring enchantment. Throughout the song, she never took her eyes from his. She made him feel special and all-important in that crowded place filled with so many nameless strangers. Mike felt a chill of her splendor shoot a tracing path throughout his entire body.

After the show, the club would remain open for an additional hour. In that time, Crystal joined Mike and Jimmy. Jimmy soon commented that it was late and that he would be getting up early for work in the morning. He wished Crystal luck with her singing and bade them both a goodnight. Once the band had stopped playing, most of the people left or were readying themselves to do so. The two remained seated, talking as if in reverie as the bustle around them dwindled to a quiet. Crystal could feel the lingering adrenalin pulsating within her with verve.

"You were fantastic, Crystal. It won't be long now."

She gleamed, "I should hope not! I don't believe that I could go much longer without some kind of reward for all our efforts. Nevertheless, it was exciting and—" she nodded her head with wonder and confirmation, "fun too. I actually had fun. I could most definitely get used to this."

"I bet you could. Then there's no doubt in your mind that it was meant to be?"

"None, never a moment's doubt. I never felt better. I'm glad you were able to make it. I was hoping you would. And again, I'm truly sorry that I was such a shit to you earlier. I guess I was worried about the opening night and that you might have been spending the night with your brother. I suppose I am being selfish."

"Not at all. It's nice to be needed, especially by you and my brother. You two keep me on my toes. And speaking of, what did you think of him?"

"He is very interesting. I can see why the two of you get along so well. What does he do?"

"He's studying to become a lawyer. Right now, he's working for a law firm in East Los Angeles as a paralegal, and he seems to be having a rough time. Actually, I was hoping the two of you would hit it off."

Crystal looked at him curiously, "Why?"

"Why not? According to your own admission, he's interesting and I could see that the two of you had a lot to talk about. I think you would make a good couple. We haven't had a whole lot of time together, but I think he's a wonderful person and a good brother."

"Before you go further, did you discuss this with your brother?" Mike was hoping that her inquiry was for personal interest.

"Sort of."

"And when he told you that he wasn't interested, did it surprise you?"

"What makes you think that he wasn't?"

"A woman's intuition."

"I don't understand. In less that fifteen minutes

time, you could tell that my brother wouldn't be interested in you."

"Michael, before I came to sit with you and before you introduced us, I knew that your brother wouldn't be interested in dating me, seeing me, befriending me or ever seeing me again, for that matter."

"Why? How did you know all this? Have you guys met before or something?"

"When you run off to rescue your brother from any of his fits of depression, has he ever told you why he's in such a state?"

"He works hard, doesn't get much rest. He hates his little apartment and I believe he's lonely. It's usually the same old story with him." Mike was totally off and Crystal didn't know just how to tell him.

"And that's all he told you? You didn't hear him say anything else, even between the lines?"

He looked at her vaguely, shrugging one shoulder. "He seems to complain about his boss a lot. He feels that the guy doesn't give enough recognition or praise. But once he starts his own practice, he won't need to worry about such trivialities."

"But why do you think he does worry about the trifling?" She was hoping he would figure it out on his own. Coming from her, he may not believe her or understand.

"I don't know, perhaps he's insecure." It was probable that he just didn't want to read into the truth, that perhaps it was too perplexing, too menacing, too vulgar or repulsive.

"If I tell you something that I know and understand

to be true from the standpoint of an outsider, will you promise not to be offended or angry with me?"

Mike had no idea as to what this was all leading up to. "Yeah, sure. What is it?"

Crystal didn't enjoy being in the predicament she had put herself in, but as a friend to Mike and his brother, the facts would have to one day come forth—no time like the present. "Does your brother have a girlfriend?"

"I don't think so." Mike responded.

"Have you ever seen him with a girl?"

"Not that I can remember. Why? Do you think he's a virgin or something? Is that what this is all about?"

"No, it's not, and no, he's not a virgin either nor has he ever been with a woman."

"What are you talking about? You're not making any sense."

"Michael, I wish you wouldn't make this so hard on me. I realize that you're fond of your brother and that is fine, but he has a serious problem and perhaps you'll need to be there to help him through it. That is to say, when he comes to realize the facts with himself.

Mike's face turned pale. Suddenly, he realized what she was trying to say, "You can't be serious."

"I'm very serious and for the very reason that he hasn't admitted it to you, leads me to believe that he's having trouble dealing with it within himself."

"For Chris' sake, tell me I'm reading you wrong, Crystal. Tell me you're not saying that my brother is—" The words were stuck in his throat, waiting for her answer with a last second hope for error.

"Gay, Michael. Your brother is gay. I'm sorry, I wish there was a less blunt way of telling you. Doesn't it make more sense to you now? Do you see why your brother is having such a hard time?"

Mike kept shaking his head, "I just can't believe it. I don't see how. I mean he's tall, good looking and smart." As the word passed his lips, he found himself listening to his own ramblings. Tall, good looking and smart men can by gay just the same.

"It happens to a lot of guys, Michael, it's like a congenital chemical imbalance. It has little to do with his mental or physical workup. It was inevitable if it was to have happened at all."

"My brother was born gay? Are you sure? He's never said anything to me about it." He dropped his hands to the table, palms up. "This is all so unbelievably and inconceivably bizarre. I can't reason with what you're telling me."

Her look of sympathy denoted her confirmation.

"How did you, or rather, your 'intuition' derive at such a conclusion? What did he say or—"

"Call it a feeling, an innate feeling of his chemistry. And perhaps now, it makes more sense to you—his loneliness, his continual depressions and concerns for his boss' appreciation, the absence of women in his life."

She offered her apology as she gently placed her hands into his. "I'm sorry to have upset you, but you had to learn of what was bothering him, he's going to need your help and understanding. He's alone without you and he's deeply bothered and burdened by his predicament."

"How would I be able to help him? I don't even understand it myself."

"It's not necessary for you to understand, just be there for him, allow him to tell you in his own time, and let him know that his preference doesn't matter to you. He is what he is, and the fact is, you can't change that fact. So, show him your acceptance. Right now, he's feeling like a pariah and it's an isolating and frightening feeling. Believe me, I know what I'm talking about." From beneath his chin, she lifted his head to meet with friendly eyes. "Are you okay?"

He was looking sickly with uncertainty and concern. "If it was anyone but you to have told me this, I wouldn't have believed it, wouldn't even have considered it as a possibility. I'm trusting in your intuition, I'm still having trouble believing it, but you've been right about a lot of things. I respect your judgment and intuition. I can only hope that you're wrong but unfortunately, I expect less from the outcome of hope. I just wish I knew why, why the man upstairs plays such games with our minds and bodies. What lessons, do you suppose, are to be learned from this episode in the trial of life?"

"The lessons aren't always clear." Crystal got up from her chair and slipped behind him. Wrapping her arms around him compassionately, she kissed the side of his face and whispered in his ear. "There could be countless books of biblical zealotry written by the gods themselves with thousands of

251

chapters pervaded with postulated theories on life's lessons to be learned. And we could spend a thousand lifetimes reading those books and never find anything more than conjecture and consternation, whence finding ourselves right where we are now. And who is to say that we even have the right to read those books? Let life take its course, Mr. Mike. Your brother will take the path that is best suited for him and he will be looked after by the vigil of his guardian angels. We can sate our lives with the incumbencies of life's worries and complications, or we can accept the life we have been dealt and simply try to make the best of it."

Mike came to realize that he didn't already know all there was to be learned about the woman who would embrace him amid a stygian, smoky nightclub with warming, consoling passion while giving rise to new horizons, sharing the same air they did breathe, sharing an intimate and transitory moment and giving life a perspective of philosophy different from any parameters previously discussed.

"I thought you didn't like such philosophy." He reflected, taking great pleasure in the realm of his being alive...and being alive with her.

"And yet, it haunts me," the huskiness of her beaten voice and the scent of her perfume mingling with the traces of vodka from her breath seemed to turn him on. She slipped her hand down over his chest inside his shirt, cooing in his ear. "Come-on baby, take me home now. I want you. I must have you tonight." Her persuasive rift in conversation roused him like an added catalyst.

In his thoughts, he was already making love to her, imagining her nakedness against his. As similar to the magic of her vibrant song, her cogent sexual lure was unmatched by any with sinews of sultry passion and seductive crave. After brief accolades from John Blackmore and the packing of instruments, Mike and Crystal left the club.

As for the first time that she was to take a ride from him in his jalopy, it seemed incongruous to see her looking so primly attire in her commonly favored designs of Chanel, Givenchy and Dior against the contrasting dismalness of the weather-beaten interior. With little concern for the decrepit nature of his vehicle, Crystal boarded.

When they got home, smoking tracks were laid to her room. Midway up the stairs, she had already removed her designer heels and earrings with Mike stalking close behind. As the evening progressed after a savage course of bestial copulating deluge, they laid silently for a while, staring up at the tongue and groove beamed ceiling, sated and breathing heavily in the flux of repose. For a while, they talked about their dreams and plans for the future. Mike's dreams and desires were somewhat vague and unpretentious. He thought that perhaps his hidden talents were shoved to the side because of the lack of tangible reality. His dreams were hardly feasible when he had neither hardly the time nor the resources to be able to commit himself to such a dream. Although, he thought of it often and hoped that perhaps one day things would dif-

253

fer allowing him to venture to his fond aspirations, one day far in the offing, but not yet tangible. After some persuasive coaxing and prodding from Crystal's banter and curiosity, Mike finally divulged his dream. To one day be able to divorce himself from the financial worry and concentrate on being a writer.

With so many chapters to speak of from the trials of his own life, he felt confident and eager to tell his tale of woes, anguish, conquests and adventures.

When the time is right, he thought, one day it will happen for him; when the trial of life has been furthered and enriched with experience and knowledge, when the storylines unfold after properly incubated gestation, and when he knows the time is right to pursue a dream. With Crystal, it was different; her financial burdens had been lifted, partly because of her father and mostly through her own hard-working endeavors. Now with the years of dedication to her music so ripe with close rewards, it took less than a moment to fathom that once her father was paid in-full for the house and the wedding, her indenturing self-written obligations would then be freed at last, thus commencing a yearning dream of freedom from guilt, independence from her father, pride in herself and contentment with life. But of all the mentioned dreams and desires, never before had Mike heard her say with such pain, condemnation and contention in her voice that her deepest wish, if life could possibly bestow the kindness, would be to have a child.

This was, no doubt, another blow to the journal

of Mike's mental diary. A child—he couldn't fit the picture in his mind. Seeing her with a baby, tending, caring and consuming time into such a responsibility, seemed almost as incongruous as seeing her in his car; like a Harley Davidson with training wheels or a formal Bellingham English tea party with all the quests clad in the nude, save cloth napkins. The wonders of Crystal were many with the latter, no doubt, the most difficult to have ever suspected.

Moments after, she drifted to sleep pervaded with the revelry of motherhood, he pondered the variety of scenarios, Crystal pregnant, Crystal giving birth, Crystal...raising a child? Imagining her pregnant, complicating her already petulant personality, seemed the hardest to conceive. The obstetrician would probably slap her with a parturifacient in her early months just to mollify her and shut her up. But after taking the time to seriously consider the matter less objectively, Mike then wondered if a child wouldn't be the very antidote to her habitual petulance. Perhaps a baby would, as he could hear her say, alter the pathological chemistry of her body enough to make her more patient and endearing to the needs of others. With that being the case, looking over at her sleeping peacefully and looking as lovely as ever next to his side, he bade her his best wishes and prayers in finding the perfect man to fulfill her deepest desires.

The months to come were a learning experience for Mike. When coming to the clubs as often as he did with Crystal and the band, he came to meet a variety of sorts. He and Billy were not even old enough to drink alcohol and yet, they and the other band members were catered to and extolled like kings and queen. Mike wasn't even a member of the band but it didn't seem to matter, he was associated with them just as though he were, and with the persona demanding respect and recognition. He possessed a personality that everyone liked and appreciated. He was the kind of guy that people would love to know and befriend and be next to. There was an aura of importance and majesty that followed his name and surrounded his person. In an innocent and pure way, he was the epitome of honestly, kindness and compassion. When he and Crystal were together, they would bring out the best in each other's personality. It was often mentioned that they were quite a compliment to each other; he was the halcyon stabilizer of her being and she was the hope that someday he too will find himself and his success. He certainly had the makeup of a successful businessman.

Once Chase, at the body shop, had quit to further his studies in school, Mike took over his position, stepping up the ladder of seniority and later was rewarded with Nicky's position in management, once he had quit to pursue his music career, as it was becoming too difficult for him to work for Scotty and keep up with all the bookings that The Passion Seekers were acquiring. The day before he was to start at his new position of shop manager,

Crystal, as his acting big sister, treated him to a tour and an expensive splurge on her personal bank account to her preferred shops of Beverly Hills. If he was to act as a man of responsibility and high-ranking position, according to her philosophy, he must dress accordingly and learn the proper etiquette of class and style, and understand just how to wield it properly and effectively. Any fool could own and wear a five hundred dollar, Armani suit but it takes a true beau to work with it, walk with it, to exhibit it with distinction and elite breeding. And what better mentor to show him the ropes than the woman who was raised with the golden spoon in her mouth?

Before the three-month contract between The Star House and The Passion Seekers was ever reached, they were getting offers from all over town. Out of the chosen favorites for the betterment of success, they would soon take on an itinerary of performances at The Whiskey of Hollywood and the Roxy of Hollywood alike. The name and reputation of The Passion Seekers were well on their way to a promising future.

John Blackmore agreed to the new unbinding time-contract, allowing them to perform at his club with an open calendar at triple the former pay. With an open calendar the band would be able to pick up other club offers at a higher pay scale without having to pay a penalty to John Blackmore for last minute cancellations or sacrifice future gigs with Mr. Blackmore.

With the increase in money coming in, Crystal was also able to quit her part-time job with the referral service. With the new successes of new clubs and better money, came undivided dedication to the band and the writing of more songs. Should the offer or opportunity arise, they would have enough material to cut several records.

As family and friends, including Mike, The Passion Seekers shared in the pleasures of success. Within a year following a busy itinerary of as many as three different clubs a week and as many as seven nights work a week, Tawney and Paul planned to be married and had saved enough money to apply a down payment on a small two-bedroom house in North Hollywood. Nicky was still saving and collecting all the funds that he could eek from all sources to partake in a co-ownership of a nightclub that was to be built in Westwood, close to the college. Billy had only one dream and one plan, that was to go all the way to the top with The Passion Seekers and hopefully, once success was satiated with dozens of records and hours of radio airtime, be able to retire on the income of his royalties. Almost a year from the first signing with The Star House, it would seem they all knew just where they were coming from and had every intention of going all the way to the top.

On a warm, rainy day in June, just a couple hours after their kick-off performance at the Roxy on Sunset Boulevard, the epitome of Hollywood and the famed milieu that is generally ambient, a

man introduced himself to the band as Peter Walbrook, an independent financier and manager of
many talented artists. In latter discussion with him,
it was learned that he already had been and still was
the manager of several prominently celebrated and
brilliantly talented artists, of which were signed
with recording labels, such as Electra/Asylum Records, Atlantic Records, Arista Records, Columbia
Records, Geffen and many more. His business
proposition was to the point, as he seemed a pragmatic man. During their first break, they held a pre-
liminary discussion backstage, planting the seed of
thought. Mr. Walbrook then left the club to attend
other business in town only to return in a long,
black, Fleetwood Limousine after their performance. It was quite obvious by the witnessing of his
mannerism and volubility that the man knew his
business thoroughly and wasted little time hashing
out trivial matters. He announced with clarity and
assured absoluteness that upon their agreement of
terms, a seemingly high percentage of the proceeds,
he would produce their first record deal followed up
with a number of concert performances at some
rather large clubs in New York, Chicago and numerous places in California. He already knew that
they had the talent to be successful with the recording of their music and that they would have
plenty of material to be able to follow up with future recordings, should they agree to do so. His contract consisted of signing them for one year,
obligating them to his assigned itinerary at his travel

and board expenses and of course, he would collect his percentage of all live performances as well. Nevertheless, he had guaranteed a base rate of pay from their performances of his itinerary to exceed their present rate of income by fivefold in writing, and that didn't include the royalty income from their recording contract sales or radio airplay. He then explained to them that the reason for his short-term contract consisting of only one year was to allow them to understand and experience the primrose path of success in the music business world. What might seem glamorous, stately and manageable to them now, will no doubt, as he has seen it happen before with other clients, become exhausting, over-burdening and draining as the days of performing accrue and the hours of each day grow old and longer with the relentless work schedule. Mr. Walbrook further explained by elaborating with unsavory anecdotal case histories experienced by some of his previous contract performers, going into detail over the taxing hours of work and restless travel, which are synonymous with the stellar life.

"The money is more than just lucrative," Walbrook stated, "and the fame comes hand in hand with all the touring you'll be doing to expose and circulate your music and names." He winced with intransigent demeanor, looking over each of their faces carefully and chidingly. "But it doesn't come easy by any means. It doesn't come easy for anyone in this business. There is no personal life for a performer, especially for those just starting out. And the only time that you will have to yourselves will be the time it takes to ready yourself for a performance, as many as seven days and nights a week for the full year of our first contract together. Of course, I won't be there with you, but my associates will and they will be in close touch with me, should any problems arise. If there is any extra personal time allotted, you will find yourself wanting only to rest or sleep in preparation for the next performance. It is not my intent to daunt or discourage you from signing with one of the best management programs in the East, I certainly wouldn't be here wasting my time if that were the case. I stand to make a sizable share of the profits from your talents, that's my job and I know how to do it well, but if for one minute, any of you feel that a hectic twenty-four hour a day schedule is too much to handle for whatever your reasons, let that be your basis for declining my offer, because once you have signed with me, you're mine. You can see, my cards are on the table and I foist no ambiguities. Like I said, I know my business and a breach of contract with me due to failure to perform or any such complication could lead to a detrimental future of being black-listed and unemployed in this field of work. I can guarantee that. So, we work together for a chaotic year to be filled with experiences the likes of you young, talented folks have only dreamed of, or you tell me that you are not interested and I will leave your lives as they are now, because there is no in-between status. You're either with me on this side of the road or you stand alone on the other side, because standing in the middle will only get you hit. I can tell you from experience that litigations of a contract breach can be very painful, taxing and costly."

His professionalism was stern with little leeway to falter. Beneath the core of his business approach, he seemed to be a reasonably fair and honest man, and no doubt dedicated to his work. He appeared to be in his mid-forties, healthy with a considerable amount of energy and well dressed in what looked to be the threads of the London designer's finest. His jet-black hair slicked back and his pocket watch, attached to a swag chain of gold tucked neatly in his vest fob, would ordinarily have him spotted and characterized as a wealthy gangster. But he carried himself with a poise of good education and breeding. Before departing to the airport to seek out more new talent, he congratulated The Passion Seekers as being the best of novice he had seen in years, and then proceeded to inform them that they would only have two weeks to decide their fate. Handing Crystal his card, he departed with his first and last show of personality as with a parting smile. Non-plussed and still trying to ingest all that was said by Mr. Walbrook, the five of them just stood silently watching him leave the club. No sooner the door had closed behind him, Crystal looked to the members of the band, with wide open eyes, "Well, he seemed to know his business and you heard him, only two weeks to decide. This is the culminating moment of many hard hours. I for one will not require two weeks to decide on what I have worked so hard for. If any one of you feels differently, you had better find a replacement for the rest of us."

With almost the same look of bliss and apprehension, Paul and Tawney looked at each other, shrugging their shoulders as if to say, this is what we have been hoping and wishing for. There was no doubt that Nicky was in favor of going all the way with signing with Mr. Walbrook, even though, he looked a panic as if he were feverishly trying to figure out how he would be able to stow members of his minion harem along the trips abroad. Billy's distant stargleam of reverie was answer enough on his behalf.

"So, do we need time to think about this further or would a call to Mr. Walbrook in the morning seem appropriate?" With the look of a virago Gestapo, Crystal threatened her inquiry with intimidation. Happy with their responses of affirmation, her greedy little grin shone through with exaltation and a jubilated perk.

It was time once again to share the news of good fortune with her pal Mike. As usual, he was working late at the shop, figuring accounts, filing forms for accounts payable or overdue, and generally doing all that needs to be done in the ranks of management. There was more responsibility dropped into Mike's lap since Scotty's wife took ill. She had contracted a cancer and was having to go through radiation therapy to try to stay ahead of the malignancies. As a result, Scotty was spending less and less time at the shop and relying on Mike more. Fortunately, he didn't mind the long hours, but his concern was for the shop and Scotty's well being. Since the day his wife was first told of her condition, Scotty took the news hard. In his face you could see the worry and trouble he was going through. Since he was self-employed and never took the time to consider the consequences of his choice in medical policies, he soon learned that his medical insurance for him and his wife wasn't quite adequate for his wife's needs. Within the first three months of her treatments, Scotty was already liquidating assets to keep from having to spend their savings that was intended for their retirement. Soon, there were no more assets to liquidate. All the old, rebuilt cars that were stored on the lot had been sold. One of the spray booths had to be leased out on consignment in order to bring in more income. And he had also sold all of his own personal items from his home in order to keep up with the mounting medical bills. As his funds would dwindle over the months, Scotty seemed to be coming apart at the seams. When he would come into the shop to check on things, sign checks and sign for materials, he would bustle about the shop in search of less vital materials to either hock, pawn or sell. He was becoming a desperate man and certainly no one could blame him. He loved his wife very much and would stop at nothing to ensure her the best medical treatment, even if it meant having to spend their retirement funds.

Crystal pulled into the shop with her BMW. She was beaming with radiance when she told Mike the news. She sat patiently, taking periodic sips from a vodka bottle that was meant to be hidden by the cover of her rather large purse, the same purse that seemed to be with her quite frequently, waiting for Mike to finish up with his work. The two then climbed into her car in trek for the nearest, all-night fast food place. Feeling rather high-spirited, and after insisting that she was fully capable of driving, Crystal proceeded to regale Mike with a side of her humor that he had rarely been given the privilege to see. She didn't want to hear any chastising from Mike about her drinking, so she pertly went about parrying by way of her humorous jokes and mannerism. As she was somewhat tipsy, she had a way of delivering her jokes of inebriation with considerable authenticity, and cleverly avoided his chiding confrontation. Aside from the fact that sometimes she was a bit more tolerable and amicable when she had been drinking, she was also quite a jokester. She had a penchant for imitating people, and quite a talent for doing so as well. While Mike was locking up the shop, she started in on him with her first act as Scotty.

"Let's get movin'. Time is money, sister." She gruffly barked. While clapping her hands to rush Mike along, sounding and acting very much like him as she has seen many times when visiting Mike at the shop. "I'm not paying you to be a loaf. If I wanted a loaf, I'd go to the bakery for a baker's dozen. Let's get movin'." As she climbed into the car, with slurred articulation, she acted as if she were drunk and playing the part of Dudley Moore from the movie Arthur, only at this moment, getting on a ride at Disneyland and inquired to Mike about her inability to find the safety bar to engage and begin the ride.

At first Mike was a bit hesitant and worried about her disposition, but soon figured out that her jokes and actions were too funny for her to be truly drunk. In fact, she had him laughing harder than he could remember. Next, she was playing the part of Sylvester Stallone from the movie, Rocky, portraying him as the somewhat shy and unfledged guy with Adrian. "So...ahhh...ya like turtles?" She asked with a deep remedial voice, portraying him excellently, even with the raised upper lip action. "Ya wanna come to my house, I show ya my turtle? Hey, yo Adrian...I got a good idea. We could go get a pizza...and, eat it." As Mike couldn't stop laughing, listening to her wonderfully entertaining homage to the stars of Hollywood, she continued to add-lib and acting as Rocky. "Hey ya...you didn't happen to have beans or Pepsi for lunch, or anything flammable or explosive like that didya? 'Cuz ya know, this car ain't insured for such road hazards if you should just happen to explode from all that laughter. Ya know, you're startin' to turn blue over there..." Mike truly was enjoying her comedy and perhaps he really was turning blue or at least, red anyhow. "Are ya gonna be okay? Can I get ya anything, a barf bag? A marshmallow? Maybe a bullion cube or a shovel?"

In hysterics, Mike asked, "What would I need a bullion cube or a shovel for?"

"Well, I don't know for sure. It was something I saw in a movie, except that was the part when I left the room to feed my turtle some beans and Pepsi."

Through the laughter he could barely ask, "And the marshmallow?"

Still portraying Rocky, she answered, "well ahhh, my mother, God bless her soul, knock on wood, throw salt over the shoulder, always told me to keep a marshmallow handy in case you get sick, ya know? That way you can sit on it if you should feel uncomfortable. Well, I think that's what she said." Mike was laughing hardy with tears pooling in his eyes, marveling over her acute sense of humor, almost in disbelief that she could be the same girl that he lives with, that behaves so differently in the presence of other people, and that was almost never heard laughing. She was a clever and amazing girl with many hidden traits and talents. It seemed a shame when he realized that the only times she would either open up to him or act human with a fair personality would be through the bolster of alcohol. She could be such a wonderful person, Mike thought, a wonderful wife, perhaps even a wonderful mother too. He wondered if she would ever be able to let go of the past and live her life for herself. Crystal pulled behind a fast food chicken restaurant. Normally, she would have parked in front of the place, but she wanted to have a little more fun with her companion in the privacy of her car. She was

feeling frisky and proposed to tempt the 'unfor-
given' in her car with him. With Mike still laughing
from her entertaining dialogue, he was nearly driven
to shock when she so abruptly leaned over and
kissed him on the side of his face while her hands
were busy unbuttoning his pants. In an act proceeded by none other, she then laid her head in his
lap and relieved him of any inhibitions. Why she
did what she did and in the way she did it was a
mystery to say the least. She had never before displayed such pleasure in such a giving carnal act. If
anything, she would be the one insisting on oral
copulation to be done to her, if not simultaneous reciprocation. Nonetheless, her delightful rift from the
norm was welcomed without protest. And soon after
ingesting the last of his briny tap, she was back with
the jokes. No doubt, alcohol has its different effects
on each individual and the effects can vary in relation to the amount consumed, yet with Crystal,
Mike would never know what to expect from her after her drinking, no matter what the amount. Most
times, her father's phone calls would be the reason
for her escape to the bottle, but as of late, Crystal
was drinking for all occasions. She was becoming
as predictable as winning lottery numbers when
Mike would try to foretell her mood-swings and the
coming results of her inebriation. And unfortunately, there was very little he could do to detour
her from the primrose escape. As Crystal climbed
out of the car while unintentionally resuming her
Dudley Moore routine she promptly fell out the

door onto the hard pavement, subsequently scraping her knee. From the passenger side, Mike quickly ran around the car to help her to her feet and tend her small wound.

"Damn...somebody did it again, Bitterman." With clever response and without allowing for the lapse of one second, she enacted her add-lib and luring Mike to play along.

"Did what again, Crystal?" He was almost hesitant to ask, to result in falling prey to her humorous punch line.

"What are you, blind? Somebody forgot to trundle the stairs to the plane. I fell out of the plane Bitterman. Don't you hate when that happens?"

While wiping away the dirt and small pebbles from her knee, he couldn't help from laughing. "Yes, Arthur, it's a tragedy when they do that."

"Oh, and Bitterman... the next time I have you make me a margarita, hold...hold the salt please...too much salt," She connoted with ribaldry, and playing the part down to the finest nuance of facial expressions, she mocked Arthur's perplexed and pensive look. "Perhaps that's why they call you...Bitterman. By the way...would you happen to have a marthmallow? I think I'm going to be uncomfortable."

As they approached the restaurant from the back parking lot, the big flashing, neon chicken sign caught their attention. The two continued laughing quite skittishly. Crystal was laughing more so from the reaction she was getting from his laughing so hard. Tears were streaming down his face as she continued to play the jester for a night. "Hey, speaking of chicken, Bitterman…why do people want to know which came first?

"I don't know Arthur, why?" He chimed in.

"I don't know either," She drolled on with her drunken act. "But quite frankly, I just want to know which one got laid first."

Laughing hard and loud, Mike grabbed his side to pamper his aching stomach muscles. Just then, the pain in his side intensified, as a sharp and extremely painful jab. The humor in the situation dwindled as the pain increased by the second. He stopped to catch his breath alongside the building and to get a hold of himself. "Damn, this hurts."

"What happened?" Still chuckling, she ambled toward him.

"I'm not really sure," Mike was gasping in pain. His hands were clutching at his side just below his ribs. "I must have been laughing too hard. Lord knows we don't do that often."

"And not often enough. This has been fun. We should really do this more often. You make a good audience," She began to ramble on, as if to be talking to herself. "I wonder if I should change my vocation to stand-up. I could hire my own claque to get me through the tight and rough spots."

"With you, as I see it, there wouldn't be any rough or tight spots. Once you get going on a roll, you never take a breath." He spoke to her gruffly, trying to control the pain.

"Yes, you could be right. Can the claque. Who the hell needs them?" She looked into Mike's face. "Hey, are you okay? You're looking quite pale. What did you do, break a rib from my impressions? That's just great! My new career is barely off the ground and my audience is already dying on me. I could just see it now, the Surgeon General will be forcing me to put warning labels on my albums," She scrolled her hand across the air. "It will probably read, something like: 'Warning, the contents of this album can be dangerous or harmful. Can cause exploding ribs and excessive gasping...maybe worse. Are you passing gas, too? Oh, wouldn't that be a kicker? The exploding rib might ignite the gas. It would go on to read: Can also be the cause of spontaneous combustion, and gosh maybe brain damage or suicidal tendencies. Oh Michael, I can't record this album; it's already costing me a fortune in litigations and negative publicity. Golly, I'm so glad that you exploded first and showed me the light. I think that I will just have to stick to singing. Well, for now anyhow, or at least until we figure out how to package a bodice with every disc, tape and album."

"For Chris' sakes, Crystal, where's your off button?" Unable to laugh anymore through the pain, Mike gave an almost wry smile as he straightened up, trying to make light of the sharp, jabbing sensation that was penetrating with a paralyzing effect. "If you keep trying to make you laugh you're going to end up a beneficiary, and you just may have to put a death warning on that album." Crystal looped her arm through his to help guide him to the front walkway. After two steps, Mike grabbed his gut once again, falling to his knees in severe pain almost taking her down with him.

"Hey Michael...what's going on here? Are you alright?" Suddenly, the seriousness seemed to outrank the humor.

"I don't know what's going on. This sharp pain in my side feels like a broken rib or something," Writhing, gasping and clutching at his side, Mike winced as if to have been repulsed by something horrible. "Oh my God!"

"What is it?" Crystal demanded to know.

"I'm not sure," he sounded in panic. "I don't understand it. It's a feeling...a bad feeling..."

"In your side?"

"Yeah, there too."

"What do you mean, 'there too'? Where else does it hurt?"

"It's the rib that hurts, but the bad feeling is from within, like some form of ugliness or danger. Oh Hell, I don't know how to explain it; something is terribly wrong. I think we should leave here." Seeming more assured of himself, he realized that the source of danger was close at hand. "Yeah, that's it, we have to leave here now." A bitter taste of dread and despair seemed to permeate his body. A formidable feeling that he could not yet explain had left an indelible impression of disgust and an overwrought feeling of nausea. And yet, there was a very clear resoluteness to the problem, he knew they would have to leave immediately, before the feeling of pain and dread would leave.

"I thought I heard some laughter coming from back here. Hey fellas, come take a gander at this little cutie."

A very deep and omnipresent voice exuded the air with a very formidable resonance. The moment his voice met with Mike's ears, the pain and feeling of dread had vanished as though it were all just a sick dream. Under her breath, directed for him to hear and take heed, Mike heard Crystal say, 'oh shit, we're in for it now'. He was now able to stand without hindrance, but it didn't matter, for the reason became clear as he looked in the direction from which the stranger's voice came. One after another, they came in legion; each one was bigger than the last as they all came to enquire. From the front of the building, they came around the corner in echelon. Their ominous presence was clearly the source of Mike's dream-like premonition of forthcoming danger. There was no doubt in his mind that there was going to be serious trouble, as thirteen bikers, clad in sleeveless Levi jackets, leathers, chaps and boots approached with feral eyes of lusting hunger directed at Crystal, who was clad appropriately for a performance at the Roxy, in fashion labels of Gianni Versace, a sort of risqué, trendy, leather and lace look.

"Now look guys, we don't want any trouble. We just came here to eat at the restaurant." Mike spoke out with a crack in his voice. He stepped in front of Crystal to shield her with his body. More than half of the bikers began to chuckle with a nuance of disgust toward his futile attempt at protecting her from their encroachment. The smallest of the litter stood at no less than six-foot and two hundred fifty pounds. With his tattooed skull and cross-boned biceps, he stepped forward gleaming his gold-capped incisors and a cheek-full of chewing tobacco that could be seen through a 'shit-eating grin' with his head held askew.

With a sensation of smallness, Mike felt like a little boy mittened and scarved to contest against the full-charging onslaught of any angry avalanche pervaded with a world of hurt. No sooner than the biker was close enough to act against Mike, the familiar jabbing pain in his side had returned. He fell back against Crystal, clutching with both hands at his side. The only memory he would recall thereafter would be that of seeing that biker with the same grin, fall supine against the ground, with a bullet hole in his forehead. From behind the cover of Mike's back, Crystal was able to retrieve her gun and take careful aim. Mike never even heard the blast of the gun.

"I have one more in this gun. Who'll be next?" Crystal shouted with her raucous voice while pointing the gun indiscriminately at each of the bikers that still remained within her range.

One of the cooks from the restaurant cautiously peered around the corner from the front of the building to see what the commotion was about.

"I don't care which one of you thugs gets it next. I'll get satisfaction enough just knowing that I got two of you before you got me," she drawled with a penetrating glare of bitter hatred. "So decide now, which one of you fuckers gets to die next; I didn't come here to be fucked with." The cook then disappeared from sight, no doubt, to call the police after seeing a man laying dead on the ground and a ranting, crazy woman wielding a smoke-wafting gun.

"Now get the hell away from or so help me, I won't care what happens next."

The bikers were of mixed responses. In their eyes, she could see that some of them were merely waiting for the right moment to pounce. A few of them had already decided her fate and destruction. Only one of them was indifferent to the matter, and he laid dead on the ground with a small sanguine stream slow in flowing from his forehead.

She reached for Mike, who was sitting limp and dazed against her legs, while training the gun on any movement with her peripheral vision. She locked her hands under his armpits to lumber him to his feet. She had no idea as to the reason why Mike had collapsed, but she had a suspicion that she would soon find out, that is to say, when or if she would be able to take her eyes from theirs. As luck from the gods would have it, the succoring squall of police sirens gave way to the essence of hope. The familiar sound of the boys in blue gave positive flux to the situation. The cavalry was on their way and she could clearly see that only a few of the bikers had the same interests in her. Retreating back to the front of the building, where their bikes were parked, some would sashay showing remorse only for leaving a job undone, others scampered in fear of prison life, no doubt, acquired through unsavory experience.

"Can you walk?" Crystal whispered in Mike's ear while keeping her eyes vigilant and the gun ready.

"I think so, but I'll need your help." The deep resonating rumble of their hogs had begun to start up with a procession of roaring thunder. In scattered directions, they took to the streets with throttles fully opened. Within seconds, the reverberating thunder of the hogs was a mere fold into silence as the sound from the sirens prevailed.

She dipped her head to fit beneath his arm, securing his stance to balance upon her as they too made a desperate attempt to escape. With almost all his weak and lithe weight incumbent upon hers, she struggled. It wasn't until she got him to the passenger side of her car that she saw the extent of the damage that Mike had sustained. Surrounded by a basketball-sized stain of fresh, Ferrari-red blood, impaled deeply into his side was a black-handled stiletto with only the exposure of the hilt protruding rigid and ominously as proof of the inflicting weapon. She fumbled with the keys in panic to get the door open for him. She knew not to remove the blade lest the extraction would cause more damage or perhaps cause him to bleed more profusely than he already was. From the looks of his shirt, he had lost a lot of blood, and there was very little time to waste. To be confronted by the police that were soon to arrive might have only caused complication to his survival. Crystal knew that it was up to her to get him to the hospital or Mike would, undoubtedly, bleed to death within minutes. To avoid the cops, she fled from the scene by driving the surface streets just one block parallel of the approaching sirens. Once she had passed them by, she was then able to speed the rest of the way to Cedar-Sinai Hospital.

Her heart was pounding as she entered each intersection that impeded her plight. Once traffic was clear, she sounded her horn and hastily swerved, darted and raced around traffic. Within minutes she located the hospital and was pulling into the emergency pad with screeching tires. She screamed at the security guard to help her pull Mike from the car. In response, without a word, the guard grabbed a wheelchair and helped pull Mike into it. Thereafter, it was out of her hands and a desperate feeling of hope. As Mike was being wheeled into the emergency room, he was no longer showing any signs of consciousness. Crystal was made to wait in the waiting room. She let go of his hand to fall back into his lap with a wet slapping sound. The river of blood had already traveled its path, blanketing his front all the way to his knees. She watched as he was trundled away. Crystal cried out, "I know you can hear me Michael. Don't you dare leave me! I...I love you! I need you!" Her braving face would no longer have any reason to resist the inundation of emotion. She dropped herself into a chair in the waiting room amid a dozen other people, lowered her head into her cradling hands and with tears already streaming down her cheeks, began to sob unashamedly and aloud while a small trickle of blood dripped down her leg, from her having scraped her knee in the attempt at making her best friend laugh.

Chapter Thirteen

Miranda

There she is again. "Hey there, don't go anywhere this time. Come talk to me. I know you
can hear me. You hoo..." She had a beautiful and
familiar smile, dressed in all white with long, dark,
flowing hair, she was graceful, slender and mysterious. Her dark eyes could, no doubt, tell tacit tales of
mystery, as she would waft through the air on a carpet of clouds.

"In good time, Mikey...in good time..." Her lips
never moved, but her voice and message was as
clear as she was beautiful.

"I knew that you could hear me. Why are you
making this so difficult? I want to know who you
are; please, tell me."

Her warming smile pervaded with a powerfully
humbling sensation that permeated deep in Mike.
She then rose into the clouds.

"Hey, hey, hey don't do this again. Wait! In good time—what? What will happen in good time?"

In through the rift of silence came her whispering voice, "In good time you will learn of all the mysteries that are yet to be understood. For now, be patient and remember." Her voice was omnipresent, but she was nowhere to be seen.

"Remember what? Wait, come back! Where are you going? Come back. Please, come back...come back..."

"Good morning. Mr. Shane. Was she pretty?" The voice was familiar. Mike opened his eyes to find himself in the unsavory recollected setting of a hospital with all the sterilized smells that accord with hospitals. Wearing a gown and covered to the waist with stiff, starchy sheets, he remembered just how much he hated being in a hospital. The IV needle was pierced into his left arm with tape holding it into place, and from it was a long, skinny tube reaching to a plastic bag of nourishment. And there stood a pretty girl with a smile that clearly possessed an embarrassing grin of premise.

"Who was pretty?" Mike growled, obviously upset having been awakened.

"The girl you were calling out to." Once Mike took a closer look at her face, he recognized the mysterious beauty that was related to the voice.

"How do you know it was a girl?" Mike smugly quipped. And in response, her grin grew obvious with a secret too soon unfold. Her calling eyes gestured towards his lap. Mike glanced down and to his embarrassment, saw his erection rustling beneath his sheets. In reflexive response, he raised his knees while supporting a crimson face.

"A girl has a way of figuring these things out, Mikey." Her manner was guile, as well as cute.

"Okay, so you know she was a she, and yes, she was pretty...very pretty, and if I'm not mistaken, she looked a lot like you."

"Yeah, right. I've heard that before."

"So, tell me Miranda; where the hell am I and how have you been?" He had lost a lot of blood but not his ability to remember a pretty face.

"This time, you're at Cedar-Sinai, and I've been just fine." She held up her hands, staying any further questions from him. "My turn. Are you following me?" She painted a stern look to play-act her facade.

"If I had any sense, I would. And how do I know it's not you who is following me?"

"Then I would have to say that your observations need therapy."

"Why is that?"

"Well, I've been working here for nine months, between fifty and seventy hours a week, and correct me if I'm wrong, but I believe its you who is at my place of work. It was you who found me, pal. I wouldn't have a clue as to where to find you, and how long has it been anyhow; a little over a year now?

Mike raised his had to scratch his head. The pain in his side reminded him of his injury. "Has it been that long already?"

"It has," Miranda's eyes looked just as wholesome and warm as they were a year ago. "and I can see that you have met some new friends."

"Oh yeah, those guys. What an experience that was."

"I heard, the whole hospital heard."

Mike looked at her strangely. "Why would the whole hospital have heard of my being stabbed. Doesn't this sort of thing happen everyday? I mean—this is a hospital."

"Oh yes, we get stabbings, beating, shootings, all kinds of injuries, but never before has there been an assault on an officer in our lobby before."

"Wait a minute. I don't remember anything about attacking a cop."

"Not you," she protested. "Your lady friend, the one that brought you here."

"Crystal? She attacked a cop? Why?" Mike tried to sit up in the bed, but Miranda stayed his efforts.

"Just lay back. You're not ready to be moving around yet." She fluffed his pillow. "She was really worried about you and when the police arrived, well, she became upset. Actually, rather violent."

Miranda read the worry in his face. "She's okay, don't worry. She just made it known, known to everyone, that she wasn't ready to leave here, police business or not, until the doctors could assure her that you were going to be okay."

"What happened?"

"Apparently, they wanted her to go down to the Beverly Hills police station to fill out a report. The guy she shot died last night before the ambulance got him here."

"Yeah, the guy who did this to me. Christ, I didn't even see it coming, it happened so fast. Are you sure she's okay? I mean, they know that it was a clear case of self-defense, don't they?"

"Yes, everything is fine now. His prints were on the knife, there were plenty of witnesses."

"Witnesses? Where the hell were they when I was being made into hamburger? If it hadn't been for that gun, do you know what they would have done to Crystal? God, I can't believe what has happened. I can still see his pathetic face. He was willing to kill me just to get at her."

"It happens, Mikey, more than you know. I see it everyday."

"Well, I don't, and I still can't believe that this has happened to us. I knew we should have gotten out of there."

"What are you talking about?" Her eyes seemed to grow wider, strangely intrigued.

"It's hard to explain, but I had this weird feeling just prior to the attack and—"

"Then why didn't you leave?" she interrupted, "If you knew this was going to happen, why did you hang around?"

He found it very strange that not only did she believe that he had the premonition, but she thought nothing strange about his ability to have acted. As if to say he could have cheated fate. "I don't know. I guess because I never felt that way before. I didn't understand it."

283

"But you will recognize it, should it happen again?" Her eyes were filled with wonder that Mike found to be very different from anyone.

"Without a doubt." Mike nodded, flashing back to the feeling of dread.

"What did it feel like? How did it make you feel?"

He looked at her and knew that with whatever difficulty he would have describing it, she would still understand. 'It was a sharp pain in my side—"

"You know I'm not referring to the pain. Tell me about the feeling you had." She asked as though she already knew the answer, but merely wanted to hear him say it.

"Well, it was very odd...very different from anything I've ever experienced. This may sound gross or repulsive to you, but it was like a feeling of total and utter disgust and yet worse than anything I could think of. If you could imagine how you would feel if-- Are you sure you want to hear this?"

She looked at him wryly in answer.

"It's like this—there was this time when I was a young kid on my way to school with some of my buddies, including Billy, and suddenly a dog ran out in traffic and a car hit it, throwing it clear across the street where we were. And as the dog hit the curb, it sort of exploded on impact and splattered all over us with a pelting rain of blood, guts and fur. I felt that dog all over me. It was so gross, so nauseating, I ran home as fast as my legs would carry me and I must have puked three times before I ever made it to the front door."

"And that's the way you felt last night?"

"Yeah, but it was actually worse."

"Why was it worse? What else did you feel, or have sensation of?

Somehow, she knew what he was going to say before the words would leave his mouth. "I don't know how you know so much about this, but I find it strange that you not only understand all this but you seem to know how I felt."

She said nothing, just waited for his answer.

He took a deep breath and solemnly answered, "after the pain in my side and after the ugly feeling of that dog on me again, I could also hear its heart-beat, its last. When I was young, that didn't happen."

"There's more though, isn't there? I know just what you're going to say, just come out with it."

Without asking her any foolish questions, he an-swered, "I, ummm, I could also taste it." Mike shook his head in disgust as he could remember everything to the finest and most minute detail. "I don't know how or why this has happened, but I know for a fact and without any doubt, last night, I could taste the flavor of death and I heard it and I felt it all over me."

"But you didn't see it." She further inquired and seemed somewhat disturbed by his inability to have seen it beforehand.

"No, I didn't see it, not beforehand anyhow. "Why?" His voice was calm and somber, "What happened to me last night? You seem to know what's going on with me." He stared into her dark eyes. "And do you want to know something else? I know that you're not going to tell me that this happens a lot here at the hospital, because until now, no one's ever spoke of this sort of thing to you."

Her eyes were almost smiling with pride.

"Ya know, Miranda...I'm not quite sure how I know this to be true, but, I know it is, and it can't be disputed. So, tell me what you know. Tell me how suddenly I've become a sort of mystical psychic, and how you and I seem to connect. You know don't you?" It would seem, Mike was putting a puzzle together in his head, and coming with more questions than answers.

Standing alongside the bed, she placed her hand over his. Even her touch seemed familiar, and yet, from a distant memory too far to recollect. "You and I are like little Lucys in a labyrinth."

Mike was impressed that she remembered his hamster and then remembered that she was the one that told him that he was not to worry about her fate at the hands of his mother. Without knowing that Jimmy had gone to the house to pick her up, Miranda was certain with her placating assurance that no harm would come to Lucy while he was in the hospital. At the time, he figured she was just trying to mollify and comfort him, but now, there was a new understanding. "You're right, we do connect and as we travel through the labyrinth of life, we connect with others and the endless cycle continues. You should have taken heed to your first instincts last night, but I'm glad I got to see you again. Oh, and you're not a mystical psychic. You had a vivid and well-developed premonition. Most people choose to ignore them, fortunately for you, yours are too strong to ignore. Next time, it might save your life."

"I hope there won't be a next time."

"But you shouldn't think like that. Premonitions foretell good as well as evil or danger. You never know, a premonition may be what dictates your future, and perhaps brings you happiness. They come in all forms, Mikey. And you have a long way to go in learning how to direct and use them."

"How about you? Do you know how?"

"I followed you here, didn't I?" At first he thought she was joking to be cute and possibly hedging from a secret that was deep within her soul, but then, a strong vibration in his being told him otherwise.

"You did, didn't you?"

"Perhaps we followed each other," she was indeed hedging. And somehow he understood it to be so that she knew she would find him again. "So, do you still have it?" She was referring to the leather.

"The get well card? Yes, I still have it."

"Good, I'm glad. Keep it close, it means a lot to me."

"How's that?"

"I don't give cards to just anyone. You know that."

"Yeah, that's right, I'm special."

"That you are, Mikey and probably more than you know," her voice held a tone of curious mystery and challenge.

"So, when do I get out of here anyhow?"

"In a day or so. Why don't you want to be with me?"

Mike looked deeply into her enchanting, ebony eyes. "Probably more than you know."

"Oh yeah, that's right. You claim she looked a lot like me."

"Look, let's let that subject rest. I feel embarrassed enough. Truthfully, I do like you. I find you most interesting..."and familiar he thought to himself. "I hope to see more of you."

"I'll be around, I practically live here. So tell me, how do you feel?"

"I feel okay considering some shit tried to carve me like a turkey."

"I'd say he pretty much succeeded in doing just that. Lucky for you, those two little ribs down there deflected the blade away from your liver and lungs. Aside from losing a lot of blood, you're really quite lucky. And lucky for you, that feisty lady friend of yours got you here when she did. Is she your girlfriend?"

"Not really, but we are very close, and she means a lot to me."

"Well, I assure you, the feelings are mutual. She was willing to go to jail for you. That is to say, after smacking a cop downstairs in the lobby."

A proud smile came to Mike's lips. "Yeah, she's a tough cookie alright," he allowed himself to chuckle while holding his hand against the bandages that were wrapped around his middle. "She's been through a lot, and not one to take crap from anyone."

"I know."

Something in the way she said, 'I know' drew upon a curiosity. "And how is it that you know about Crystal? Aside from last night?"

"And this morning. She was here this morning and cussed out the nurses for not letting her in to see you before visiting hours."

"Oh, Crystal." Mike sighed.

"I could lose my job for telling you this, but I have a feeling that she may have already told you this. It happened a few years ago. She told you she was attacked once before."

"Attacked, raped and badly beaten." Mike said angrily. "It was then when I met Crystal. I was her nurse here when they brought her in. 'Tough cookie' would hardly be the definition. It was bad enough that she was having to deal with her pain and suffering, but when the complications developed, well, I'm sure you know her just as well as we do."

Mike wasn't quite sure just how to ask, but he had to know. "She didn't tell me about any complications. What else happened to her?"

She looked surprised. "I wonder why she didn't tell you. Apparently, the guy had hit her in the stomach, which caused her to hemorrhage internally. The only way to save her life was to perform an immediate hysterectomy. And when she found out about it the next day, we thought she might try to take her own life. She was so distraught, she took it so badly."

Mike looked ashen. "My God, she's been through so much hell, I can't begin to imagine. More than anything in this world...Crystal wants to have a baby. And she can't, never! I guess that would explain a few more mysteries about her. And speaking of mysteries, if you've only been here nine months, how is it, you were her nurse nearly six years ago?"

"My first three years in nursing, I worked here. And then I transferred to Park View for some additional training. Then, by no choice of my own, was made to work at Good Samaritan Hospital in the cardiology department and I don't mind telling you, those people were a bunch of jerks. After three months of working with those fools, I gained the training that was necessary to further my career in nursing."

"I take it you didn't like working for them at Good Sam?"

She snickered, "Just be grateful that you don't have a serious heart condition at Good Sam. I just couldn't deal with their egos and their lack of compassion. I was only too happy to be transferred back to Park View after that experience. And that was when I met you and now I'm here. It's the life of a nurse, you see."

"And a busy one at that, I'll say. And I might add, I'm happy to have been able to meet you through such busy training schedules."

"So am I. I couldn't have planned it better myself." After talking a while longer, she returned to her duties and Mike lay back in bed wondering why

Crystal never told him. He thought perhaps she hasn't yet faced the truth or perhaps it makes her feel less adequate as a woman. Whatever the reason, he decided it was best that he didn't mention it to her. Any bit of pain he could spare her in the next thousand years, couldn't be enough remedy to take away the misery of what she'd already been through. It was best to say nothing at all. Maybe the hope, dream or wish is all that she has to hang on to.

By eight AM sharp, Crystal appeared in the doorway of Mike's room. She looked bereft. He assured her that he was well and told her that he would be out of the hospital in a couple of days. He was happy to have her there with him. They talked over the episode a dozen times, and still, the two of them couldn't believe what had happened. Crystal had taken a man's life and probably would have killed another had it not been for the sirens.

Neither of them knew that those sirens were for another call, a jewelry store burglary. The man with a bullet in his head was lying dead for nearly forty-five minutes before the police responded to what took place at the restaurant, less than a block away. The whole event was a totally shocking experience for them and yet, may not have meant much, other than the passing of another mundane day, to the bikers.

Crystal went on to tell him of everything that followed when he was being operated on, including the situation with the officer. He didn't tell her that

Miranda had already told him. He wanted to allow her the full pleasure. She spent the entire day with him, ordered specifically prepared foods to be delivered to save him from hospital food and helped him with his trips to the bathroom. She remained by his side until she was forced to leave that night by the hospital staff.

Miranda had arrived to work her night shift and to regale him with more stories, anecdotes and facts about the many curiosities of the world of psychic phenomenon. She was infinite with knowledge and fascination. He had gained a rapport with her that he thought was a great deal, even after he had been released from the hospital.

He decided to visit with her at the hospital when he was to have his stitches removed, two weeks after his release. To his disappointment, the nursing staff told him that Miranda was transferred across town the day after he had been discharged. They claimed that they had no idea which hospital she would be working at and she left no forwarding number where she could be reached. He felt like kicking himself for not having the foresight of getting her number when he had the chance. He didn't even know what city she lived in, but he checked the phone listings in every city within a hundred mile radius from the hospital. There wasn't any number listed in her name. She vanished without a trace. When he returned to the hospital he learned that none of the other nurses knew much about her. They seemed aloof about his interest in her, simply reporting that many nurses come and go from the many different departments and hospitals and that it would be almost impossible to track every staff transfer that takes place everyday. Almost broken-heartedly, Mike left the hospital, wishing he had acted sooner, never thinking that this might happen. Over the next several months he called the different hospitals that she mentioned and a few others, hoping to track her down, but to no avail. She had become a bigger mystery than ever, with no clues to her whereabouts.

The following months became especially lonely for Mike when The Passion Seekers accepted the contract with Peter Walbrook. For a full year they took to the road with an itinerary no less than what they had been warned. Crystal and Nicky, the two who complained the most, claimed the worst of the tolls. Tawney, Paul and Billy seemed to be the true troopers, enjoying every minute of hard work and lavish rewards. They were making more money than there was time to spend it.

Three months after the tour began, Mr. Walbrook had allowed for a seven-day rest so that they could return home from Chicago and take care of whatever personal affairs might need attending. Most of their time seemed to be occupied with performances in Chicago. Most of Peter's big connections were there and they were connections, to say the least. It was there that The Passion Seekers met a few talented artists and famed names as Kitaro, Mickey Hart, Andreas Vollenweider, Jean-Luc Ponty, Hiroshima, Phil

Collins, Don Henley and Sade, who was preparing for her Diamond Life recording.

For the seven-day break, Crystal and Nicky were the only ones to fly back while the rest were contented to stay, rest and take in the sights of Chicago. Crystal had seen the city before and thought less fondly of it each time she'd visit. Nicky could have cared less where they were. His involuntary celibacy had him looking wretched, weak and in great need of female companionship from his chosen many back home. Upon returning to her Hollywood Hills home, Crystal didn't have to search hard for her buddy, Mike. He was working at Scotty's, racking his brain trying to make ends meet with a budget that was barely feasible to run a shop half its size. Scotty had cut he budget to the bare minimum in the attempt at saving his wife's life. The situation with her cancer was grim. She was spending more of her life trying to survive the therapy in the hospital than she was allowed time to rest at home. And Scotty was quite worn out as well; six months of her illness had seemed to age him ten years.

Mike could remember the first time he had met him, it was through an ad in the classifieds, which Scotty had placed for a part-time, fill-in position. Mike was a spunky, chock-full of optimistic energy. He wanted to be able to make enough money to buy a car. He was willing to take a bus across town just to have a job, and yet, he didn't have the slightest idea about auto repair. He did however, possess such a passion to work and learn that Scotty took him in under his wing and made him a deal. Mike was to work a thirty-day probationary period without missing a day's work and he had to be able to strip a car of its fenders and bumpers as fast, if not faster than Scotty himself. At the time, Mike didn't see the challenge as much competition...granted, he was a young-looking, mid-forty year old, but Mike's cockiness and over-confident youthful boast, had him believing that Scotty was over the hill and the job would easily be his. During the thirty days, he didn't miss a day in attendance. Then Scotty set up two closely, related type of heaps to be dismantled in a race. At the drop of a wrench, the two began, Scotty, working calmly and deftly, kept a fair pace. Mike was fumbling and ferreting for proper tools. He blasted through the ordeal in about twelve minutes, which was a fair amount of time according to Nicky. Scotty was standing in front of his car with his arms folded. It had looked as though Mike had won, but looking at the faces of all the guys in the shop, acting as though they could barely restrain laughter, he figured something was odd and perhaps, not to his favor. Mike lumbered to his feet, all the while looking at Scotty's car. The bumper and fenders were still attached, seemingly untouched. So what was the joke? With one swift and powerful kick, Scotty throttled the bumper of his car with his boot. Not only did the fenders tumble to the floor, but the front and back bumpers, the hood and the driver and passenger doors all came crashing down with an explosion of noise. It was like something out of a used car cartoon. Mike had plainly lost the race and thought to have lost his job as well. With a somber look of defeat, he offered a handshake to Scotty, figuring he would have to relinquish his job.

"No one has beat me yet, my friend, and everyone here has been challenged with the same probation," Scotty announced with a warming smile. "Congratulations, you got yourself a job." That was the day Mike became friends with Scotty, the strong man, full of youth and skills of his own.

As soon as Crystal arrived at the airport, she arranged to have a cab take her to a Chevy dealership. Before she had left for Chicago she made arrangements for a custom van to be completed by the three-month break. The exterior had an extraordinary twelve hundred dollar paint job, Mag wheels with chrome rims, tinted windows and miscellaneous extras. The interior was decked out as well, with an Alpine stereo, TV, mood-lights, lush carpeting, built-in bed with matching cabinetry and a wet bar. To the relief of the dealership, Crystal was happy with the work that was done and paid them the balance of the purchase price in cash. She brought the van home after picking up some things from the market. When she got home she took a quick shower and the prepared the van for the evening.

Mike would generally return home from work anytime after midnight, so she planned accordingly.

When he arrived at the house and attempted to pull in the driveway, he was curious to know who was visiting. Crystal hadn't told him of the three-month break or her arrival in town. He backed his car to the end of the driveway in the attempt at keeping access clear, all the while, wondering who would be at the house. Walking up the drive, he got a good look at the van. It was black with gold pin striping and trim. Painted in script lettering on both side-windows were the words 'Crystal's Angel'. Wrapped around the entire girth of the vehicle was a huge, wide-banded white ribbon with a rather large bow on the roof. He had no idea what this was all about, but whatever it was, the van was parked in his spot and he wasn't happy about having to park so close to the street after working such a long, hard day. As he entered the house he almost immediately recognized the familiar two hundred dollar an ounce fragrance.

"Crystal?" Mike called out, looking around the house to see the lights were all turned off as he had left them to go to work that morning, but there were a number of candles burning throughout the lower level.

"Upstairs, Mr. Shane and do not keep me waiting." Her voice sounded more raucous than ever. It was quite a turn-on for him. He raced up the stairs cantering over three steps at a time.

"Why didn't you tell me you were going to be in town?" As he reached the upper floor he realized there was absolutely no lighting whatsoever. "Where the hell are you?"

"Just keep walking straight forward." A deep

voice answered from straight ahead, "and follow my voice." He did as she instructed with his hands stretched out in front of him, fingers splayed, groping the darkness.

"Okay, Crystal, what's this all about?"

"Just a little closer, Mr. Mike..."

It had been three, long months since the last time they had been together and the five, very long distance phone calls they shared during that time, couldn't possibly have cooled the smoldering embers.

As his eyes adjusted, he could barely discern her outline against the faint moonlight that was illuminating the sheer, airy curtains behind her. The slight and gentle zephyr of a September night was billowing the curtains through the open sliding doors. As he came closer to her, her image loomed a feminine presence.

Her silken hair was down and caught by the breeze. The cast of light showered her widened stance. Her nakedness was apparent and most inviting.

His first touch upon her came to caress her satiny shoulders. He pulled her into his tight embrace and kissed her passionately. Her flesh against his fully clad body gave wonder to new sensation.

"If I knew you were coming, I would've come home sooner."

"We have seven days." She answered with resoluteness.

"That's all? Why did you bother?"

"Shut up and kiss me." Or so help me, I'll do to you what I dreamed of on the plane.

"How is it I feel there's more to that request?"

He did as she instructed, and more. Her feral ambitions had him unrobed and near panting in seconds. Three months of torrid passion and aggression was unfurled through to the following morning. Lucky for him, he had the weekend off. What he didn't yet know was that had also been arranged by Crystal. Nicky promised that he would spend the entirety of the weekend with worshipping bedmates; they were blessed with two days of privacy to do with each other, as stamina would permit. As sun-up had shone through the curtains, proving the dawn of a new day, Crystal jumped from the bed and quickly dressed herself.

Mike could tell that she was having difficulty with her hangover; the proverbial purse accompanied her into the dressing-room closet. When she emerged perked and dressed, Mike could smell the lingering of vodka. In habitual response to his admonishing glare and disappointment in her drinking, she avoided liaisons of eye contact with him and proceeded to leave the room to descend the lengthy staircase.

"There is something you might want to take a look at," she said.

"Am I required to get dressed?"

"Only if it bothers you...to be outside in your birthday suit, birthday boy."

"So that's what this is all about. But my birthday isn't for another two months."

"That is very true, but I won't be here then to give you your gift. So, do we cover Mikey Junior or do we take our chances in the wild and venture the neighborhood in the raw? It is all pretty much the same to me. In fact, I would definitely enjoy watching you dangle for my delight."

"I don't think so, Junior is shy. A skinny-dip in the hot tub would be more like the summit of risk."

"Well, whatever you decide, please hurry; the suspense is killing me. I hope you like it. You had said once that you wanted one."

"I can only remember requesting a dozen more like you." Mike shouted and gesturing with open arms in the direction of the stairs.

"Honey, the one you have is hardly containable."

"Do I get a hint?"

"Yes, of course, let me see. There's an eight and four. They are not sold in Hong Kong. It would not make a good centerpiece. They come in all colors. They rumble, growl, roar and can screech, yet they are not of the living. You might find one floating, but it would not be for long. They have..."

"Never mind, forget it. So far—all I can come up with is a beached whale. Thanks for the hint." Mike approached the staircase to find her standing impatiently in the entryway, leaning against the door latch, twirling her keys around her finger and staring up at Mike with her famous grin. "Where did you learn to give such descriptive hints, from Helen Keller?" There was no reply, just the suspicious grin of hers and a gimlet-eyed stare.

He saluted her tacit demands. "Yes ma'am. On the double," Reading her message clearly, he scampered down the steps as quickly as possible. "Let's go outside to see an eight and/or four ton beached whale. He looped his arm through hers and opened the front door.

No sooner had the door swung open, Mike remembered the van. He was so surprised to find that she was back in town that evening, he completely forgot about the van in the driveway, in his parking spot, with the big bow and ribbon. "And the four and the eight?"

"Cylinders and tires, of course. I hope you like it. You have always been such an angel, like a precious little gold nugget, to me. I wanted you to have something special from me for your nineteenth birthday."

"Like it? Crystal I love it! My God, this is something I would never have dreamed about. This must have cost you a fortune. Why would you do all this for me? This is too much. I've never seen such a beautiful machine," his face was glowing with radiance and blissful surprise. He turned to her and nearly hugged the breath out of her. "Crystal, I love it, it's beautiful." Grabbing her hand, they circled the van three or four times, trying to imbibe its all.

"Well, are we going to look inside, or are we going to circle it until it gives up?" She asked.

Mike took a deep breath. "Okay, sure, let's take a look inside now." She handed him the keys. He unlocked the side sliding door, pulled the handle and opened the door. He was struck with awe. The soft, velvety, burgundy interior with all the works was gorgeous. It was obvious that the van had been custom built to the specifications that he had mentioned to her in passing conversation many months before. To fulfill every aspect of his dream vehicle, she had remembered everything and had it built for him. As he stepped inside groping the plush interior, Crystal was close behind. After removing the ribbon so the door would close, she slid the door shut behind her, climbed into the bed beside him and reached to the bed console, flipping on one of the switches. A section of indirect, soft lighting illuminated the ceiling through recessed receptacles. She hit another switch that operated another set of lights. And after turning all the switches, she had the stereo on, the television on, over a dozen different lights and the electric pump for the sink. It even had a CB radio with an external PA system.

"The van is equipped with two batteries so you can run all the accessories without worrying about draining the main battery. And," she opened a door to a small cubby located just above the sink, "it has a microwave oven."

"The oven works off the battery, too?"

"Unfortunately, no. There's a small locking cabinet on the other side of the van. Inside is a thirty-foot extension cord. Once you plug that in, all the accessories automatically switch to AC current, and then you can operate the oven. It has almost everything you need for camping, for sleeping out," her voice suddenly became very suggestive, "for being romantic at places like the beach...or maybe even...in a driveway." The long t-shirt that she had slipped into was all that she was wearing. She then slipped it off over her head. "Time to christen the vessel, my love." She laid back and made herself comfortable and enviable. "I hope that Junior will be able to overcome his shyness. It was not until this morning that I learned about the hot tub. Perhaps one of those could be installed too...at a much later date..."

"That's right, we've only six days left. We'd better hurry." Mike replied emphatically, stripping away his clothes with a rush of frantic passion shooting through his veins. Seeing her suddenly in the nude and looking as sexy as he could handle, was far too much to allow for any shyness...if there was any to be found. Just as ever, she selfishly took him into her embrace, making him please her in the manner in which she taught him. And taught him well. Before long, it became hot and uncomfortable in the van. Mike suggested they go for a test ride. Crystal suggested, with an insatiable tone, he open the windows.

"Come on...just a quick cruise around the neighborhood. What's the sense in me having this big play-toy if I can't play with it?"

"You can play with it in six days. I'm still due payment, my dear Mr. Mike."

"Why Crystal, do you know what that makes you sound like?"

"Horny?"

"That wasn't quite the word I was thinking of." He cast a look of shallow doubt.

She cast him back a venomous look.

"Come on, please!"

"Very well, but you owe me Mister."

"More than you'll ever know, Crystal." Mike grabbed the keys off of the nightstand and proceeded toward the front of the van. "Aren't you coming up front?"

"No." She replied, reaching for the stereo knob to find a decent station. "You go and have fun. I am going to stay here and enjoy this bed."

"Suit yourself."

I usually do, she thought. As Mike had straddled between the bucket seats, he noticed a small battery-powered refrigerator incorporated in between the seats. It was all so fantastic. The van seemed to have everything, like a little home on wheels. He started it up and felt the roar, rumble and growl, but wouldn't allow for any screeching. To him, that machine certainly felt as though it were among the living with so much personality and stylized comfort.

"Oh, what they're missing in Hong Kong."

"Oh, what you're missing back here..." Crystal retorted.

"I can just imagine what you're doing back there." Since there were no rear windows, Mike was getting himself adjusted to backing up using the side mirrors.

"Instead of imagining, you should be here with me."

He pulled onto the street. "Oh God, Crystal, this thing is beautiful. It rides so smooth. I love it!"

Mike parried. After driving for a couple of miles, he wanted to share the wonderful experience with her sitting up front with him. "Come on, Crystal, come sit up here." Before he knew it, he was already out of the canyon and driving onto Sunset Boulevard. "Oh my, aren't you a bit out of attire for a drive on public roads, Miss Cadiver?"

She joined him up front. After looking to see where they were located, she simply replied, "For Sunset Boulevard? I would say that I'm dressed somewhat appropriately." It was an amazing feeling of both freedom and privacy for him to be driving around in that van with dark tinted windows offering absolutely no visibility to anyone who might want to gander within. In the passenger seat, sitting completely naked and within the total privacy of his new van, Crystal made it even more difficult for him to continue driving. About four miles was all he could stand of her, within reach and her sexual coercion. Behind a hospital and some apartments, Mike pulled into Barnsdall Park and almost in a feverish deluge of panic, parked the van. In an odd way, the placed looked strangely familiar to him, but with passion on the rise, he didn't allow it a second thought. After checking to make sure that all the doors were locked, he closed the drapes dividing the back from the driving compartment in the attempt to keep anyone from taking peeps through the windshield, the only non-tinted window, save that of the visor. They resumed their acts of carnal splendor in the back of the van until finally, Crystal agreed to a break. And that was due, probably only because of exhaustion from her hectic tour schedule, the long flight back and the night without any sleep upon arrival. The christening of the van was by far, the ultimate of any dream-state he could recollect. Throughout the entire day, the two of them drove all over the valley with a nomad itinerary. When they returned home, it was only to shower, get clean clothes, grab some snacks and take off once again to tour the town in the carriage of splendid royalty. Crystal seemed pleased that he liked her gift so much. It was probably the first time she had ever taken such pleasure in an act of spontaneity, free of inhibitions.

Saturday evening, after dressing appropriately in comfortable dance clothes, they decided to go to a new dance club that was celebrating their month-long grand opening. There was rumor that the club was a tad weird as far as the regular clientele, but it was said to be equally as fun just seeing those that usually attend. When they got there, Mike was a bit hesitant to leave his new toy unattended in the parking lot, but Crystal assured him that the alarm system was one of the best, another part of the gift that he didn't yet know about. The place was crowded and nonetheless fulfilling of it reputation.

Outside the club were a number of odd sorts standing around talking and gawking at one another. There were a vast variety of multi-colored, spiked Mohawk hairstyles with attire to match. There were bald women, bald guys, gay couples, guys with only one patch of a long, braided tress sticking out from one part of their head or another and some had a date groomed likewise to match.

As Mike and Crystal walked through the crowd of weirdness, they thought that perhaps they too should have dressed accordingly; it seemed to be the type of place where anything and everything goes, no holds barred and power to the freaks. As strange as it was to be there and dressed straight, looking like black beans in a bowl of granola, they came to have a good time and dressing straight would be their acting repertoire for the night. Since Crystal was already drinking and feeling less inhibited, the task of mingling with the granola-type crowd of nuts, fruits and flakes seemed natural for her. After nearly fighting the loitering crowd to get in the place, they could see there was no band or any source of real entertainment outside of two disc jockeys in separate booths suspended from the high ceiling, playing records. The sound system was loud, bassy and powerful. It was surprising that they didn't hear the music miles from the club. That is to say, if you could call it music. It seemed to be a cross between sadistic rock and roll, punk and to their surprise, fifty's oldies. Inside the place there was standing room only with no tables or chairs. There were no waitresses, which was probably why there were five strategically located liquor bars, two by the restrooms, one at the immediate entrance that everyone had to pass through in order to get their first free drink and be able to enter the place, and the other two bars were planted in the middle of what seemed to be a half-acre sized dance floor.

After seeing the layout of the club, Mike told Crystal that Nicky should check the place out as a good possible idea as a business prospect. There was very little overhead, not even furniture, and it was plain to see that liquor sales were lucrative, to say the least, and the place was packed. Multiply that times the five dollar cover charge and Nicky could be looking at better than twenty grand a night. Crystal agreed to mention it to him the first chance. After drinking their free beverage, they tossed the cup into one of the many trash containers. They proceeded to cut through the crowd to the dance floor. The music, as odd as it was, had good dancing rhythm and beat. They dance for about an hour.

Both Crystal and Mike saw her at the same time. She was tall and skinny, wearing a ridiculously hideous wig with clothes to match. Standing awkward on her feet, the striking resemblance was far too close to being just uncanny or coincidental. Even the makeup on her face couldn't cover the truth. Both Mike and Crystal stood palsied as they saw her at the same time. She would have been hard to miss as she was making a fool of herself trying to sustain her aplomb, as she would dance unsuccessfully due to her inability to maneuver in her pumps. When she slipped and fell between them, looking as though they had all seen a ghost, they just froze for several seconds. They acknowledged her identity the moment they saw her face, and she knew it as well.

She looked at Mike and Crystal as though they were bearing down on her with a gun. She scuffled to her feet only to fall with a tempestuous collapse to the floor once again. Mike reached down to help her up. It was difficult for him to even simply find the words while attempting to help her up. "Here, ummm, let me help you."

Pulling away from his grasp, she growled, "I don't need your help. I don't need anybody's damn help. Just get the hell away from me, damn it."

Mike didn't need to hear her sadly disguised voice to confirm his fears. Her clumsiness alone was confirmation enough. Having no prior experience in these matters, Mike forcefully grabbed her by the shoulders and brought her to her feet. In pumps, she stood nearly six inches taller than him. "Jimmy, let me take you home so we can talk." The secret was out and there was no use in furthering attempts to hide his identity.

"What is there to talk about Mike?" Speaking with his true voice, he was near tears and fighting them back with every conceivable effort. "It's pretty clear, isn't it? I have nothing to say to you or anyone else. Just please, get the hell away from me." Jimmy pushed his brother back, only to clumsily fall to the ground once again. Spurning off the hindering shoes, he crawled away from Mike and Crystal, wedging through the crowded dance floor.

"Crystal, help me. What do I do? Should I go after him?" He asked in panic.

"Let him go for now." She put her arm out,

309

keeping him from going. The music was loud and she had to shout with her already hoarse voice. "Later tonight, we can stop by his place. By then he will have settled down."

"If you don't mind, I'd like to leave here." He promptly announced, supplicating with weary eyes.

She smiled in response and the two made their way through the crowd to the exit. As Mike surveyed the many faces that crowded the establishment, he soon realized that his brother wasn't the only guy dressed in drag that evening. There were probably a great many more that were a lot less obvious. Nothing could have prepared him for this, even though Crystal had already told him of the months before, it was still much too hard to gather his thoughts, to accept what had happened and what he saw; to rationalize the situation when seeing him this way, effeminate, bemused and lost.

Breaking through the crowd and out the exit doors, Mike wedged a clearing-way out of the building, holding tightly onto Crystal's hand, who was close in following tow. As they reached the fresh air and the satiate of capacious offerings, they exchanged expressions denoting a wonder of why they ever thought to attend such a stale and crowded environment in the first place. Perhaps it was just curiosity or perhaps it was fate. As soon as they were able to extricate themselves from the club, they located the van and drove directly to Jimmy's apartment. When they arrived he wasn't there. Mike was worried and inclined to wait until he would finally arrive. Crystal didn't seem to mind too terribly much, after all, she had Mike, her booze privacy, and a van full of entertainment, it was what she came back to California for anyhow, whether it was outside Jimmy's place or at the park or in her driveway or at any of the three other dozen places they shared time together. After a three-hour wait parked outside Jimmy's place, they decided to head back home and perhaps make another attempt at finding him in the morning.

The remainder of Crystal's six-day vacation break was slightly less than euphoric. After abandoning their surveillance, Mike wasn't as pert and attentive to her needs as Crystal would have normally expected. Fortunately, it wasn't too difficult for her to hide her animosity toward Jimmy's ruining her vacation. However, after her drinking excessively the next morning, she had little restraint over her tongue and the dialogue in which she chose to speak to Mike in reference to his "troubled" brother.

"I just want to check on my brother, he's not answering his phone and I'm worried. Why don't you come with me? If he's not there we'll come right back. How's that?"

"I have already told you, Michael. I don't want to go anywhere today. I wanted to stay here with you, that was the reason for my having flown two thousand miles, that and celebrating your birthday with you. What happens if your troubled brother is home? Would you have me sit in the van for hours on end?"

"I think you're being unreasonable. Actually, I was hoping you could help me to help him. Through your own admission, I was said to be an important factor toward helping him through this. He is, after all, my brother."

"Fine, but why does it have to be today? Why can't you wait until I'm gone?"

"Because I'm worried. I have a bad feeling about this. He didn't have the nerve to tell me about this in the first place, I can just imagine how he feels about me finding out about it in the way that it happened. Crystal, listen to me, we have nearly an entire week together; let's not ruin it by arguing and—" his voice dwindled off.

"Well, why don't you say it? Does my drinking bother you?" With dulled and fogged eyes, she intoned with a meanness that Mike found to be unlike her and most unbecoming from a woman of her stature, pride and beauty.

"Yes, more than you know. I watched the evils of alcohol destroy my father. I also know that the driver of the truck that killed Diane was intoxicated. All I have left in this world is you and my brother. My brother needs my help and you need to stop this drinking before it kills you too. I don't want to lose you, Crystal. I wouldn't be able to handle it."

"You need not worry your little self over Crystal. She's a big girl and has been on her own far longer than you have been around here."

"Is that how it is?"

"How what is?" In the duration of time that she

stood in the entry arguing with Mike, the alcohol in her system began to take stronger effects on her.

"How it is with you. Distant, third party—like it were somebody else's problem. Can't you see how important you are to me? How your drinking is screwing with your head?"

"I've been getting screwed all my life. It most certainly had nothing to do with drinking." Her tone was growing bitter with petulance towards him.

"No, but it certainly complicates things. You are so close to accomplishing your dreams and desires, girl. Why let something like this get between that?" He placed his hands on both her shoulders to steady her rocking stance and to make every attempt at getting through to her. "Hey, I know about a lot of the pain that you have suffered." He didn't dare mention the hysterectomy. "We've spent a lot of time talking about such injustices. You once told me that you would try to take a way the pain I was suffering from the loss of Diane, if you only knew how. Well, the truth is now obvious to me. No one can erase the past, but we can learn to deal with it." Glassy tears swelled in his eyes as he brought her to attention. "I know how you've suffered. I've listened to you and I have felt your pain. I've cried over your pain because I knew you couldn't. I knew that you would never allow for it. I'm telling you this whether you choose to believe me or not," he could see that she was getting through quite effectively.

Her normally stiff and stout-worthy chin was not quivering. Her sobering eyes were drawn to his.

"I can't—I won't stand by watching passively and do nothing when someone, who I love, is in danger of destroying her life. I would hope that that same someone would have the love enough to call out and wake me if I were resting on the railroad tracks of doom with a train thundering down on me."

Little, narrow streams of tears began to flow down her crimson cheeks. She unfolded her arms and reached out in surrender.

"I would never let anything happen to you, my sweet angel."

With her tears flowing, she cried aloud the words, "I am sorry that I'm such a bitch all the time. I just—I don't know—I can't seem to find myself. I have so many problems. How could you love me? What man would possibly want me?"

"I've never complained."

"That's not what I meant, not completely." Her defensive barriers had fallen away, leaving her vulnerable, hurting openly, and crying uncontrollably in his embrace. "I don't know if I could ever please a man. I'm already thirty-one years old and I have nothing to offer."

Mike was a bit confused, but then wondered if this was a prelude to more anguish she hadn't yet told him about. "Excuse me? I don't know of any man who wouldn't find you attractive with plenty to offer, intellectually, sexually, whatever. You have more to offer than any woman I have never known."

"And what about maternally? Could a man love me, if I were incapable of giving him a child?"

"Listen Crystal, I have a strong feeling I know what this is leading to and I don't know exactly what kind of crap your father has filled your head with, but let me tell you from the heart. It isn't going to be your lineage he, whoever he may be, falls in love with. If you can't bear a child, then to hell with those who employ that as a requisite; what you've been through requires no explanation to anyone, especially your father or anyone like him and his kind. This maniacal madness with breeding, posturing and pragmatic progeny is just a whole lot of bullshit. You have spent so many years building this shell around you, filled with rules, regulations and the haughty, pompous and aristocratic beliefs of your father. It's time you grow up, girl. Live by your own damn rules and to hell with the rest. If they can't conform to you, then they're not worth your time."

"I know what you're saying is right, but I have lived and conformed to those rules and beliefs for so many years. It is not something that just washes out with the laundry. I do not know of any other rules to live by. I think it would be impossible for me to turn my back on my father, he seems to have this stranglehold over me."

"Then just break away."

"It only sounds that simple. I owe him so much—"

"You owe him nothing. We talked about this before. He gave you the house and you have been supporting yourself ever since—"

315

"It is not just the house—or the wedding. He's my father and he raised me. I at least owe him the respect of love from a daughter."

"I think he has you brainwashed. The sooner you break away from him and his ridicule, the sooner you will breathe with freedom from his stranglehold. You can still love him, but just tell him that you have a life too, with your own beliefs, your own values and with your own dreams. You must make him understand this or he will continue to hound you. Stick up for yourself; you have a mouth, one hell of a mouth, I might add so use it. Make him understand that you're a person too. You certainly don't need anymore of his guilt trips laid on you."

His answers to everything seemed so resolute, but unfortunately it was very difficult for her to talk to her father without falling back into the same fearful, slavish responses to his overbearing persuasion. In her heart, she knew she would never be able to boost her nerve enough to talk to him in the manner in which Mike had dictated, and yet she knew that he was right.

"Yes, you are right. He has always treated me like a little girl, too young to know what is good for me," she released her hold from around his waist and wiped away her tears. "Perhaps it is time I spoke with him as an adult. Hey, did I ever tell you how I came to get this house?"

"Aside from your father giving it to you for your birthday?"

"Sort of. I found Digger's real birth certificate when we were packing to move from the house. As it turns out, she had lied to all of us. When my father married her she was still a minor."

"She was only seventeen?" He cringed with disbelief. "Couldn't you see that she was that young?"

"Aside from her being three inches taller than me, she looked every bit of thirty. She'd had a rough life, moving from foster home to foster home and then back to Juvenile Hall when there was a dearth of foster parents. Her biological parents were drug addicts and lost custody over her after a bad car accident when she was three years old. Apparently, the tumultuous childhood had aged her. Anyhow, after I found the certificate, I showed it to her, you know...teased her and gave her a hard time about it. Well, she got pretty upset; in fact, at first I thought she was going to have a heart attack. I had never seen anybody get so fired up over a piece of paper. Judging from the type of life she had led, I guess she figured that I would use it as blackmail against her. After she was able to catch her breath and lose the hysterics, she finally confided in me. When she was seventeen, she was put in the custody of a family in Canoga Park. They had a couple kids of their own, a house, a yard and all that, but the man of the house, some brutal, beer-bellied pig tried to have his way with her many times. After six months she had all she could take and ran away. A few months later she met my dad and you know the rest."

"How did that get you the house?"

317

"Hey, I had the goods on her. One word from me, and the Digger would have been h-i-s-t-o-r-y, looking for a new home and she knew it. So, knowing what kind of a man my father is and what kind of a girl she is; not about to go back to a life of cat and mouse, living in squalor, she did what she knew how to do best. To get me out of her life and to assure her privacy of avarice, she talked daddy into taking the house off the market, subsequently presenting it to me as a gift. Kind of ironic, isn't it?"

"In which way?"

"My father treating me like the little girl and then he marries an adolescent who has been posing as almost fifteen years older."

"Yeah, I suppose so." He was still trying to get over the idea of the twenty-five years age gap. He could see she was really starting to feel the alcohol run its course. "Are you going to be okay?"

"I'm fine. You go and see about your brother now. I'm going to go upstairs, watch some nasty videos. When you get back, perhaps you could join me?"

He could see that grin infiltrating through the booze. "Yeah, that would be fun. I'll be back as soon as possible, I promise." He kissed her on the forehead and she grabbed him, kissing him on the lips.

"It was just a little snippet of gin. I won't poison you, 'I promise'."

"I'd rather you promised me that you won't drink anymore," he said, trying not to sound too admonishing.

"I'll try." Her grin was still ever-present. "Now

get out of here so you can hurry back to me." Mike
did just that. He hurried over to Jimmy's to find that
he hadn't yet returned. He knew this because his letter was still wedged in the door jam. He saw no use
in hanging around, so he returned to Crystal, who
had decided to drink a great deal more. He made the
effort of preparing her breakfast, but she wouldn't
eat much of it. It was growing more apparent everyday that her drinking was no doubt, alcoholism. She
would deny having been drinking and in that same
breath would go into the bathroom only to drink in
privacy. The remainder of the six-day vacation with
her was like none other. She had become so inebriated that sex was sluggish and unappealing, and yet
she thought she was fantastic, even when she had
fallen asleep in mid-stroke like someone suffering
from narcolepsy. By the middle of the week, it
wasn't even the sex that she wanted. She just wanted
him there with her. She would give him a hard time
when he would leave for work and then would bom-
bard him with sloppy kisses when he would return.
There was almost no talking to her. By the time her
vacation was over, he was exasperated and just as
happy to see her go. It was a horrible feeling of hope-
lessness for him to want her so badly and yet, under
the circumstances, to want to be clear of her and her
near sloven inebriety. He didn't know whether to
write her a letter, asking her to please stop drinking,
or lock her up in a cage to prevent her from doing so.
After dropping her off at the airport, he breathed a
sigh of relief. He may even have enjoyed the van

more had things worked out better that week. Help-lessness and sadness was all that seemed to lie ahead, with a positive glimmer of hope that she would just snap out of her tolling binge.

In the months that followed, her drinking per-sisted in salvoes. According to Billy, who had called Mike several times, in hopes of being able to pacify her outbreaks and binges, Crystal was drink-ing more now than ever. Billy and the other band members feared that it would soon start affecting her performance on stage. They couldn't understand what was happening to her, what she was going through, or why it was coming to this. She was be-side herself, depressed and showing no relent in hostilities; even Mike had no effect on her. She would either refuse to talk to him by simply hang-ing up the phone without even so much as a 'hello', or she would arbitrarily deny all that they said to him. It was also apparent that she was tired of them continually running to the phone, to call him every time there was a problem or mishap. Billy and Nicky were desperate enough to have paid for the flight to get Mike to Chicago, if they knew it would help. Although it never came to that, because they knew that it wouldn't have mattered; especially af-ter hearing that most times she wouldn't speak to him. And with all that was happening, Mike was having troubles of his own.

There was something very strange going on with Jimmy; he could feel it deep in his soul, but there was nothing he could do to help. Again, he was feeling that twinge of helplessness. He checked by Jimmy's place dozens of times, trying to find him and find out where he had been. Since that Saturday night at the dance club, Jimmy was nowhere to be found. After the first week of his disappearance, Mike thumbed through the yellow pages to find Jimmy's place of employment. After finding the law office and speaking with his supervisor, he became extremely concerned. He hadn't returned to work after that weekend. Out of desperation, Mike checked with the hospitals and police stations to locate his whereabouts, but to no avail.

Jimmy was nowhere to be found and Mike was getting upset with panic. In his gut he could now feel that something was horribly wrong. After the second week of his disappearance, he filed a missing persons report and by the third week, he checked with his landlord who had already evicted him for not paying the rent and thought he had abandoned the apartment. By the fourth week, Jimmy was still missing and Mike had learned that the police were a useless source of information; they had done nothing to investigate his disappearance. After a great deal of research on his own, he did learn that Jimmy had returned his car to the leasing agency, but from thereafter, there were no more clues. When Jimmy's landlord had so hastily evicted him, he also had all of his things hauled away. There was no way of finding more clues as to where he might go or with whom he might have associated.

Scotty was demanding more of his time, which

was making matters worse. It was hard, if not impossible, for him to allocate the time needed to find his brother. The shop was starting to go downhill. Scotty had pinched too many funds and cut too many corners. There were no more tools or options to sell. There were absolutely no more funds to eek from any more sources. Half of his retirement was already gone and his wife was getting worse with no signs of a possible recovery. After two and a half months, Mike spent his birthday alone, Crystal didn't call, Jimmy was still missing and the shop was in dire hardship. All the guys including Mike had taken a cut in pay and still, Scotty didn't have the funds to meet payroll. That's when the jaws of Hell seemed to open up and swallow Mike up whole. Five months to the day after Jimmy's fateful night at the club, Mike received a call from a Sergeant Dougherty. Apparently, Mike was needed to render his services at the police station. They needed him to identify a body, possibly Jimmy's.

Chapter Fourteen
The Suicide

Five long months and not a word from Jimmy, nobody but Crystal could have understood the worry that Mike was experiencing. She was becoming too difficult to talk to, especially since the phone was the only means of communication. With every passing day, it was becoming harder for him to ignore the signs, the most obvious being when the lady in white appeared in his dreams once again. She had confirmed his feelings and dreadful premonitions then vanished as mysteriously as she appeared. After speaking with Sergeant Dougherty over the phone, Mike placed the receiver onto the cradle in a trance-like state. He hadn't even taken a step and yet, in a phantasmagoric vision, his mind took him through the entire trek, through the streets and to the police station, to the downstairs morgue and to the unveiling of Jimmy's body. It was as clear as his most recent memory.

When he got to the station, after waking from the trance, every waking event came to pass like deja vu. Every word that was spoken, every step that was taken and every face he came to see were all as exact as the vision he perceived. When the Sergeant led him to the basement, Mike was answering his questions before they had been fully asked. It was as though he were some kind of witch.

"Pending the investigation, we'll need—"

"I'll leave my parent's telephone number with you before I leave here. I have no desire to speak with them. I will leave that part up to you, Sergeant."

The Sergeant opened the door to the morgue. Against the far wall were twelve retractable body drawers. Without a clue or hesitation, Mike walked directly to the one marked John Doe, Hollywood reservoir and stood waiting for the Sergeant to open the drawer.

"If you don't mind, Mr. Shane, how—"

"On the phone you told me my brother was believed to have drowned, I guess I could smell the chlorine," that year the Hollywood Reservoir was in the process of being heavily treated with chlorine to fight back the bacteria. Through his vision, he could smell and taste the chlorine, just as Jimmy did. "And yes, we were very close. What I don't understand is why there would be a need for an investigation."

The Sergeant stepped up to the sliding cabinet, put his hand on the handle and asked him if he was ready. Mike nodded. No sooner than the drawer was opened, a chilling wave of cold refrigerated air exuded the room with an odor of chlorine. The cop then clutched at the sheet, taking one last look toward him. Gritting his teeth, Mike nodded once more. The sheet was drawn back; there were no surprises, no possibility of mistaken identity. Looking blue, cold and motionless, as he had envisioned, Jimmy's suffering was covered.

"I'm sorry, but I need to ask you a few more questions."

Mike said nothing. He couldn't take his eyes off of Jimmy and the Sergeant closed the drawer.

"Did your brother have any enemies?"

"None that would do this, if that's what you're implying."

"Do you think your brother could have been suicidal?"

"I know that my brother has been very upset. Sergeant, my brother has been going through an emotional trauma all his life. He had no enemies and he seemed to get along with everyone. What would make you think that this was anything other than suicide?"

"What was the trauma that he suffered?" He asked, sounding routine and perfunctory.

Mike felt odd talking about his brother just inches away from him. "Can we talk about this upstairs?"

"Certainly." In a calm habitual manner the Sergeant lead Mike upstairs to his desk. After a brief discussion, Mike had learned that Jimmy had attempted to have a sex change operation. Forensics was able to determine that Jimmy had the operation just four weeks prior to his death.

There would have been a few more follow-up operations had he lived to continue. The investigators were not yet convinced that his death was suicidal since he had already gone so far to change his life. It was explained that in most cases, a homosexual male in this situation would most times choose not to live because of the shortage of money and inability to pay for such an operation. Jimmy was more than three-quarters of the way through the expenses. There wasn't much for the police investigators to go on, he admitted. As far as the Sergeant was concerned, through experience of many similar scenarios, it was a clear case of suicide. But to make sure as best they could through formalities and protocol of an official investigation, all sources had to be checked out in order to close the file.

As the evidence and information was divulged, Mike could feel his brother's emotions. Sudden flurries of brief pictures came to him. It wasn't until then that Mike realized his premonitions were not just smell, sound and visceral feelings; they were coming through in visionary form, very detailed and very real.

Miranda foretold that these abilities would soon develop within him and that it was just a matter of time. In fact, it wasn't just Miranda who had told him that mysteries would unfold in a matter of time.

As the Sergeant was speaking, Mike could see and feel his brother, looking gaunt, pale and feeling desperate and alone. Jimmy had run away in hopes

to make his world change. He had saved enough
money to follow through with what he desired most.
He had intended on changing everything, including
his name and his past. He wanted absolutely no re-
minders of his horribly confused life, prior to the
new changes to come. That's why he abandoned his
apartment and returned his car. Unfortunately, he
made one tragic mistake that he didn't count on.
Through the vision, Mike could feel the elated final-
ity in Jimmy's emotions soon after his first operations were complete. For the first time in his life, he
actually felt normal, as though a correction had finally been made. A new life was at hand and no one
could take it away. Or so he thought. His mistake
was encountered through a phone call. For whatever
reason, he had misjudged a vital factor. In all his
ebullient glory, Jimmy called his mother with the
good news of his sex change, but much to his crushing demise, his mother couldn't have been more
cruel and impetuous with her brash and insensitive
opinions. As Mike truly knew the witch best, Jimmy
should never have told her of his operation. Of all
the people in the world he chose to confide in, she
was by far the most wrong, the most guileless, hurtful person to have gone to. Subsequently, it cost
him his life.

When he realized how disappointed she was, he
could think of no other alternatives. There was no
way to turn back and he most certainly couldn't go
back to living as a man, even if he wanted to.
Jimmy took a cab to the Hollywood Reservoir. Af-

ter ingesting a handful of sleeping pills, he walked along the shoreline path that encircles the water. Through Jimmy's eyes, Mike could clearly see the faces of the joggers, as they would pass. He could hear them breathing heavily and feel their pounding feet vibrate the ground beneath his. His heart was racing with fear. Once he reached Mulholland Dam there was no more chain-link fencing with barbed wire at the top. Although Mike had never actually been to the dam, he was now able to see everything, as though he were there. Facing the south was Hollywood, through the smog and haze he could barely see Capitol Records and the many homes nestled in the hills. To the north, high on the side of the mountain was the famous Hollywood sign. Below that were more homes, with a view of more than two billion gallons of blue waters.

Jimmy walked up to the railing that was only waist-high. As the soporific pills had taken the edge off his fears, caused him to become drowsy and distant from himself, he looked down on the glassy, turquoise waters. While waiting for the stronger effect of the pills, Mike could feel Jimmy resisting the pills to the very last, to assure the inability to feel the impact of drowning. Finally in a limbo state, he rolled himself over the steel railing, plummeting nearly thirty feet and almost lifeless already, Jimmy hit the waters below. Mike felt the chill of the surrounding waters as Jimmy stopped breathing. With wide-open eyes, frightened, alone and lost, looking through the fog of abyss, he felt his heart beating slowly to its last. Finally, Mike felt his brother die. There was nothing more that he could do to help his brother.

We knew that further examinations would soon detect the sleeping pills, thus termination of the investigation. After jotting down his parent's telephone number, Mike left the police station, knowing that the funeral would take place in three days. As he was leaving the station in a state of hurt and remorse, he glanced at the side of the building where squad cars enter the jail with arrested prisoners. A sudden vision of a familiar face flashed before his eyes; it was his own. He saw himself in the back of one of the police cars, handcuffed, frightened and desperate after being arrested. Then suddenly, the vision disappeared. He couldn't perceive why such a vision had come to him, or why he was arrested. It had to be a mistake, he thought. With a shake of his head and a dutiful rub of his eyes, he passed it off as a fluke.

When he got home, he checked the answering machine in his and Billy's room. Billy had left a message of good news. The Passion Seekers were finally signed to record their first album. Six months on the road and already they were contracted with a recording label. The news was indeed fantastic in every way. They had worked very hard to reach such success. Mike was less than elated. It all seemed distant and incongruent after just returning from the police station and dealing with Jimmy's death. Instead of returning the call, he left the house to take a drive, trying to better his state of mind.

Little did he know, the jaws of Hell had opened just a little wider, ready to cause him more hardship. While driving his van, he decided to stop by the shop to check on things. He figured the only way to get over his sorrow would be to bury himself in work. As he pulled onto the street, expecting to see Scotty's big sign in the front of the building, the tow truck parked out front and the few cars being worked on by the guys, he was first, confused that he might have pulled onto the wrong block and then he was horrified, as he pulled into the driveway of what was indeed the shop, or what was left of it. The building was roped off with yellow police tape. The bitter smell was still heavy and thick in the air. Unable to pull the van any closer, Mike parked just outside the barricade where Chase and Terry were talking with a police officer. There were two official-looking types, looking through what was left of the shop. Apparently, they were looking for clues as to why the building had burned down. The cop was then called over to speak with the detective and that was when Terry turned and saw Mike standing there. In that brief moment, they both could feel each other's losses and shared in solemn exchange of glances.

"What on earth happened?" Mike asked, in total disbelief of what he was seeing. The place was leveled to a two-foot high pile of black, charred rubble. The only thing standing was the midsections of the building that were constructed out of block and concrete, which even some of those crumpled under the stress of the extreme heat generated by the blaze. Even the tow truck was blackened and completely destroyed; the tires had burned, the windows of the truck had blown out and the interior was gutted.

"They're still trying to figure it out. It could take days before anyone knows what happened here." Terry's voice dwindled as he looked over the destruction of the building.

"When did it happen? Was anybody hurt?"

"Last night. Nobody was hurt, thank God!"

"Does your dad know?"

"Yeah, he's with mom at the hospital. He called me this morning. Listen Mike, my dad told me about your brother, I'm really very sorry—"

"So am I. I feel as though we never really got to know each other." Mike breathed a heavy sigh and continued looking over the ruins. Trying to keep his mind on the present, "Tell me something, Terry, do you think your dad will re-open the shop?"

"Re-open? No, I doubt it." Terry tugged at Mike's arm, guiding him back toward the van. "Between you and me, since mom took ill, my dad has been acting real strange. I'm sure I'm not telling you anything new." Mike nodded. "But as far as the fire is concerned—this place was my dad's life and only you'd know if there's any hope, if he was still current on the fire insurance and I'm sure the inspector over there is going to ask you the same. Tell me, Mike, was he? Was dad still insured for this?" Terry looked as though the entire world was riding on this million dollar, suspense-chilling question.

331

Suddenly, Mike remembered his vision back at the police station. The chilling suspense was now relative in a whole new light. He was falling prey to his own fears for himself, wondering if the investigators might arrest him for suspicion of torching the building to perhaps collect on the insurance.

"He cancelled a lot of policies and sold nearly everything, most of which was not on the records. But one thing I do know for a fact, and that is your dad was most certainly insured for fire—heavily insured."

Relief showed in Terry's eyes, "well, we can thank God for that." Terry said, wiping away the sweat from his brow.

Mike wasn't sure if the sweat was from the heat of the smoldering ashes or perhaps over the worry of whether his father was sane enough to have kept up with the insurance policy. Mike was already two steps ahead of him, the vision of himself in the squad car kept infiltrating into his every thought. Just watching the investigator tooling around through the ashes with his pocketknife was making him very nervous. He wondered if Scotty did it. With the amount of coverage he had on the place, there was no doubt that Scotty would get a very large sum of money and would be able to afford enough treatments for his wife to last another twenty years or more. Mike could feel his heart beating faster. He too, was now sweating and he hadn't done anything wrong.

"Hey Terry...?" Mike called out, looking pale and skittish. "I'm going to go home. Give me a call tonight at my place. I need to go get some rest now."

"Excuse me, are you Mr. Shane, Mike Shane?" Both the inspector and the cop approached him, walking gingerly through the smoldering evidence. Mike froze in consternation.

"Yes, I am." He was surprised he could find the words.

"Could I have a word with you? I'm Lieutenant Fisk." Without waiting for an answer, he went on to ask his routine line of questions. The man looked somewhat sloppy in his manner. With a stubby cigar askew to the corner of his mouth and smoke wafting into his face, he reminded Mike of a television cop. "Would you happen to know if Scotty kept a safe on the premises?"

"A safe? No, not that I know of, he kept his paperwork in his briefcase and the cash in his register box."

"Would you happen to know where that box is now?"

"I would imagine it's with Scotty. He picks it up or takes it home with him every night."

"Are you certain that there wasn't a safe on the premises?"

"If there was, he never told me about it."

"Thank you, Mr. Shane, that's all I need to know for now."

Mike was wondering if his pounding heart was noticeable or the streams of sweat dribbling down the sides of his face.

"If I need to get a hold of you, can I call you at home?" The Lieutenant pulled his little pad from his breast pocket and quoted Mike's telephone number.

"Yeah, that's it." Mike was trying to sound matter of fact as he climbed into his van making every attempt to leave. To his surprise, the inspector didn't ask anything further and Mike was able to escape unscathed. After reminding Terry to call him, Mike started the van and was happy to get the hell out of there. He nearly had himself convinced that he was going to be arrested on incendiary charges. He drove straight home. In a way, he was happy for Scotty. Whether Scotty intentionally burned the building or not, he stood to make a great deal of money. Since the shop was going under and business was poor, it would seem that he had finally found a way to come out ahead. From the look on Terry's face, it was fairly evident that he didn't suspect his father in the least. And as it turned out, the report on Scotty's place was completed and closed within thirty days. Within sixty days from the fire, he and his family were compensated nearly a quarter million dollars for the loss of his business and possessions. Again, Mike figured that his vision of himself in the police car must have been just a strange fluke. It was discovered that one of the welding torch tanks had possibly fallen over subsequently releasing the gas into the building and ignited when a portable electric floor heater went on. Since the fire, Scotty had retired and was able to spend more time with his wife who was recovering nicely due to a new treatment procedure.

Mike was pounding the pavement, looking for a

new job. Scotty had written him a good letter of recommendation, but it didn't seem to help much. Nobody was hiring in his field of expertise. He accepted a job at a fast food restaurant just to stay afloat for a while. The job, it's responsibilities and low pay was degrading and humiliating, but few with alternatives he was forced to stick with it.

After The Passion Seekers were signed to record their first album, they were permitted to return home. Mr. Walbrook had arranged for the recording to take place in Hollywood. Soon after they returned to California, Crystal found out about Jimmy and made every effort to appease Mike. Seemingly, there was nothing that could keep her from drinking, or from having her impromptu mood swings with fits of petulance, rage and hysterics and then sloven attempts at compassion directed toward Mike. All that was humorous, desirable and appealing about Crystal was fading away with the merging blend of alcohol.

In two months time the recording was completed. Mike and Billy were surprise that she was able to do it. By luck of some sort, she would enter the studio each day as drunk and belligerent as ever and then suddenly sober up just enough to conduct an adequate day's work. When the album was completed everyone was relieved to see it over. It was assumed that it would take much longer, thus allowing them a three-week break before having to return to the road. Paul and Tawney had moved out into their new home and seemed to be very happy together. Billy and Nicky and decided that they had enough of Crystal's faults and took advantage of the three-week break to move out into their own apartment. They invited Mike to come too, but he declined. He felt as though he would be deserting a friend in need to leave her now. Although the decision was tough to make as she would so often remind him of her insecurities. Realistically, Mike couldn't afford to move out. Crystal could have cared less whether he paid her the rent or not. What she seemed to want was to have him at her beck and call, day or night. She would have been willing to pay him just to stay with her. It hurt him terribly to see her like this.

There were still some days that she was like an angel, a bit tipsy, but more like her playful self. It was those few choice days that made it worthwhile to be with her. He never lost the glimmer of hope that maybe she would somehow see what she was doing to herself and everyone around her, that perhaps she would be able to stop before it was too late. Seeing her fall to waste made him realize how much he truly loved her and couldn't stand to see her throw it all away.

One evening, Mike asked her out on a date, making her promise not to drink more than what she had provided herself with in her purse. For what it was worth, she agreed. As it turned out, their evening out was one of their best. He then knew their relationship was worth trying to save at any cost. With only alcohol as her downfall, it would seem something should be able to stop her from going on with this act of degradation. They had dinner and a quiet evening together then went for a drive to the beach. It had been a long time since either of them had seen the ocean or run in the sand barefoot. The cool breeze with a light spray from the ocean was a bit chilly, but nonetheless, was a great adventure while walking in the huddle of each other's embrace. After taking a romantic stroll along the coast in the wake of frothy, shallow waves, they returned to the van to dry off.

While the romantic setting offered its splendor, Mike took her in his arms demanding that she promise not to drink. Knowing that his futile attempts would be scoffed or ignored, he tried to impress upon her that he would have to leave her; he would not be able to continue being her friend if she continued to drink. In the manner in which he could not convey over the phone, as he had tried before, he caused her to cry. It would seem that without his constant guidance over her, he would never be able to stop her from drinking and even then, it would have been questionable. She cried because she didn't realize what hell she was putting him and everyone through and the pressure she was putting on their relationship. She cried because Mike threatened to leave her and she cried because she knew he would. With the stereo on and the sliding door left open facing the beach and the crashing waves, Mike and Crystal made love as if it would be their last time together. After momentarily falling asleep to the melodic sounds of the beach and the music of the radio, they were both awakened from their restful calm. It came over the radio like some sort of distant dream. At first, neither of them so much as flinched; they had heard the recordings so many times before, but this was the first time they heard her beautiful voice over the airways.

"Congratulations, Crystal!" Mike announced with pride.

"This is the radio? They're playing The Passion Seekers? That's me on the radio?" With the slight fog of sleep in her eyes, she sat up, smiling with bliss. "We did it Mike! We finally did it! Oh, this is so fantastic!"

"You made it, girl, you're famous! How does it feel to be on top of the world?"

"It feels wonderful! I couldn't be happier." She nudged herself closer and planted a passionate kiss on Mike's lips.

The song that was played on the radio that night was Mike's favorite; the very first song Crystal had ever sung for him, When Love is Lost, You'll Always Have Me. For as long as Mike shall live, he knew that he would never forget the night he first heard her sing it to him, or the night they first heard it played over the radio in his van. It was her special song to him, meant for him. On their way home from the beach they heard it played two more times, as Crystal flipped the knob from station to station.

For the next several weeks, they heard the songs of The Passion Seekers played continually. The band's spirits were elated before leaving to go back on tour. Within two months from the album's first release the title song went to the number five spot on the record charts, nearly three hundred thousand copies of the single had been sold. To follow up with promotionals and sales, arranged by Peter Walbrook, Crystal and the band had taped a music video of their title song that was released the same week that the recording was completed. It was aired on MTV, VH1, More Music Videos, Canada's Much Music and many others all over the world. Truly, stringent dedicated work had paid off, providing The Passion Seekers with the ultimate in success they had only dreamed of, and more.

Inasmuch as Crystal's drinking hadn't interfered with scheduling or her performances as yet, Peter Walbrook agreed to sign them for another year of touring the country and promised to set some time aside for the recording of their second album. Mr. Walbrook was very leery about the contract in so much as Crystal was no longer making the effort to hide her condition. He wasn't the type of man to be taken advantage of either. He had warned her prior to the signing that he would not allow her to renege from the contract. But for whatever reason, he had taken a great deal of leniency with her. Where many times, Billy and Nicky thought he would be furious with her actions, Mr. Walbrook would surprise everyone by allowing Crystal to step all over him. She would constantly disagree with him, counterman his decisions and argue with him in public like he was her little brother. And that's when things started to make more sense. Instead of traveling from one city to the next looking for new talent as he normally was inclined, Peter Walbrook was spending a lot of personal time with Crystal. It appeared that her drinking didn't seem to bother him inasmuch as her performances were never once hampered by her constant condition. Three months after their second year contract, Peter and Crystal announced their engagement to be married. It happened after a fall-out between Crystal and her father. The final goal that she had planned for so many years was finally at hand when her royalty checks exceeded the amount needed to pay her father back for the wedding and the house in Nichol's Canyon. From her personal account she sent him a check and a tape of her first recorded album.

Deep inside, she felt that all burdens of guilt would soon be lifted and a self-satisfied jest of "I told you so" would then prevail, finally proving to her father that singing was indeed her calling, and that she didn't need his money to be a success. Here she had proved to him that she was successful on her own and by her own doing. But her check was returned and the tape was never opened to be heard. Her father didn't even bother to listen to the tape or even acknowledge her accomplishments. Without a reward of compliment or even a letter of congratulations, Charles Worthington III, the proud, pompous son of a bitch that he was, scrolled a brief note across Crystal's check stating that the tainted money from which it came and what it represents was not worthy of his acceptance; the little girl he raised was not intended to be a "Rock and Roll" star. His note crushed her like nothing he had ever done to her before. It took no time at all for her to fall apart once she received such spiteful words from her father. Yet, somehow, Peter was there and able to help put her fallen, crumpled pieces back together. Seeing them as a couple seemed almost a clash. If anyone was to be more correct for her Billy, Nicky, Paul and Tawney had hoped it would be Mike to become her choice of husband. They even seemed to resent the two of them for having done such an injustice to Mike.

When Mike found out about the engagement, he was actually very happy for her. What the band never knew or couldn't understand was that the relationship they shared could never have been more than what it was. His love and admiration for her ran very deep, equally as deep as the new curiosities that seemed to be unfolding with more mystery and more development of his hidden talents. Unfortunately, his talents were not helping him financially. Since Scotty's shop had burned down, he was barely able to hang onto his jobs. In a year's time, he had quit two jobs and was fired from one. He couldn't seem to keep his mind on his work. His mind just seemed to be continually preoccupied. He started to keep a journal to keep track of all the strange occurrences that would take place almost everyday. Visions and feelings of distant places kept coming to focus in his mind. Many times, he could hardly keep from trying to investigate, to keep from trying to find these places that would suddenly flash before his eyes in fragmented images. At first, it was as though he were losing his mind. After a while, it was like fitting a large-scale jigsaw puzzle together in his head and everyday would bring him a new piece to help solve the mystery. His only regret was that he didn't take advantage of the time he had with Miranda. Somehow, she seemed to be an important part of the missing puzzle.

Three months after the announcement of their engagement, Mike finally met Mr. Walbrook. Between them there was an instant aversion. Mike knew from the start that he wasn't right for her; he was weak and unable to see her true needs. Peter could only see Mike as competition. The tension between the two was irreversible. Mike knew what had happened between Crystal and her dad. He didn't need to be told, he saw it in her eyes. What Peter could never provide would soon prove to be Crystal's biggest downfall and Mike's biggest loss yet. There was no way Mike could continue to live in the same house with Peter and since Peter didn't have property in California, he naturally found himself residing at Crystal's place, which soon became full-time. Mike could see what was happening, but Peter could just as well have been blind. He had no idea how devastating it was for Crystal to finally become completely alienated by her father. Once she had persuaded Peter into canceling the tour for that year it was all so very clear; she had given up the war was over and she had given up the fight to go on. There was no reason to go on. It was not to be a transitory rest as she had told him at first. This was it for her. If Peter didn't force her back in the circuit immediately, he would lose her ambition forever. Now, with Peter by her side, willing to accept her as a winner, loser or quitter, it didn't matter anymore. She knew that she could control him, and as far as The Passion Seekers were concerned, she knew he could afford to write them off as a loss.

The second album never came to be. The tour was cancelled and just eighteen months after Mike and Crystal first heard The Passion Seekers over the radio in his van at the beach, Crystal announced she was quitting the band. The news was devastating to everyone. Mike hated Peter for allowing it to happen, knowing a real man would have seen it coming, would have known what to do to help Crystal through it and yet, Mike remembered the desperate words of his own admission once said in confidence to Billy, "I don't know if I or any man could stop her from drinking. She's trying to bury a lot of pain that I couldn't begin to describe. She needs help but I'll be damned if I can figure out how to get it to her. First, she has to be willing to accept it and she's not even willing to admit it, much less, accept help for it. I lost my father the same way. It's going to be the worst day of my life to lose her."

Chapter Fifteen
Jason and Ceenatanee and the
Portal of Time

To the knowledge of the Indians, the mighty and most powerful Griffin was known only as fable. Such transcendental forms as: the bear, fox, deer, eagle and such, even the worm, all have been known to take place through the endeavors of traditional ritual. But the Griffin was unheard of and yet to have been seen in form. Especially when the efforts of conduct require two spirits to equal a whole as in Jason and Ceenatanee's case. The fact that one in the spirit of a female made matters less believable and hard to accept by the fellow tribesmen. One of the reasons that Ceenatanee was not permitted to return to her people was because she had made such horrendous and pretentious claims. But this didn't matter to her. Those who know the truth need not to explain, the truth will undoubtedly prevail, especially in the spirit world. Ceenatanee, no doubt, knew this to be fact. In the spirit world one can visit the past as well as the future. In transcendental form, one can make himself seen and known at will. With the sight of an eagle ten times stronger than that of a man, medicines from the furthest distances across the lands could not elude the Griffin. And with the sinewy wings to carry it effortlessly to these destinations, the healing prowess of the Griffin was unmatched by any. The bloodline of the tiger gave the Griffin qualities of endurance, cunning, patience and the will to succeed undaunted and impervious to all elements and all other predators. Once joined as a united force, the two were inseparable. They soon learned that in the realm of time and its continuum, they had never really been apart. And they never will be, because the spirit world is eternal with no beginnings and no ends, only a journey. The destiny of their journey took them through endless doors of mystery, heavenly quintessence, and to the catalyst of healing, which was the root of their destiny. They made medicines together with the guidance of the gods and over the eternal years, those gods had cured endless numbers. Together, Jason and Ceenatanee would enter their sweat lodge and in a matter of time, they would emerge with the miracles of healing. Answers to plague and famine and never before seen illness would eventually come through the guided visions of the gods. From the rare precious herbs of the earth to odd and untraditional applications, the healing powers were delivered to the Griffin, and people were cured.

It was two years, seven and a half months since Millie had brought the two together. That was when the calling came. For the first time, the gods spoke to Jason and Ceenatanee without the need for meditation and prayer guided inquiry. They came and delivered a cure. From herbs of a neighboring town and the combination of medicines for common ailments, they prepared a two-part medicine. Then they sent for Millie Johnson. When she arrived, exulted and excited, it was obvious that she was well cued to what was about to take place. They learned that the reason why Millie was never able to see was due to an impaired blood supply to the retina of both her eyes. With the inflammation and narrowing caused by the abnormalities of the blood vessels, a blockage of sight was inevitable, even at birth. Millie had absolutely no reservations when consulted by Jason and Ceenatanee. She had every intention of following through with the procedure that Sara had told her would one day take place, changing her life drastically. She was made to relax in the examining room. Ceenatanee had mixed a small portion of her herbs with a diluted serum of scorpion venom. With her body relaxed by way of Ceenatanee's own teas, Jason applied the gelatinous potion to the inside of Millie's eyelids. In time, the formula had successfully penetrated both the sclera and the ciliary's body. Once it reached the retina of her eyes, the formula was intended to temporarily paralyze any inflammation. With a second application of Ceenatanee's premixed remedies, the penetration of medicine was stimulated by the first, thus causing an instant liquidation of all inflammation and break down of the blockage and the inertia. Through the enwreathe of the optic nerve, the infectious fluids then infiltrated with exudation back into the blood stream with no danger or harm to her blood, save that of a small loss of protein. The discharge from the blood vessels from within her retina lasted a duration of several minutes. The procedure, as it was, could not have been conducted less painfully, but Millie was brave and courageous. Anyone who didn't know Jason would not have believed the results. Millie's mother could hardly contain herself when she heard the news. More than two decades of Millie's life was spent in total darkness with no hint of what life looked like, what a rising or setting sun looked like, what colors were, what an insidious smile looked like when cast with penetrating direction from across a crowded room to its intended target. She had no idea that a simple field of view could take days to travel through. Just two hours after leaving Jason's examining room, all these things and more were now hers to witness. All she witnessed from that day on was exactly as she had envisioned through the help of Sara on that fateful night. It was no less than a miracle to see this young girl who was once totally blind and dependent upon others for sight, suddenly walking, skipping and running down the street without any aid whatsoever, talking to everyone with jubilant radiance like a small child boasting her new toy. Once word was out, via Millie's mother, that Jason and Ceenatanee were miracle workers of sorts, telegraphs and letters from all over were flooding in for cure and salvation. The course of destiny was then made pellucidly evident. This wasn't to say that all people were miraculously cured of any and all diseases; there were a few that could not be treated. In fact, there were those who the spirit gods would not answer for; it was hard for the Griffin to accept this fact, but the reasons were cogently obvious, as destiny would always prevail over all powers. Those who were not cured or could not be cured were made to accept their destiny as a trusting fatalist. Unfortunately, very few of the patients that could not be cured of their affliction or terminal illness would be able to readily accept Jason's failure to heal, especially when so many were seen and cured without having had any problems in the process. These may have been hard facts to reason with, but as it had been said, the gods are not to be questioned. With so many miracles in abundance, Jason wasn't going to challenge Ceenatanee's sacred traditions.

Within just a few months, the workload at Jason's medical office was overwhelming. Strangers were arriving everyday from far and near places to be cured of their afflictions. After a full year of the hectic scheduling and hard work and non-stop treatments, Jason and Ceenatanee knew that they would have to make a serious change in their lives. Although the town and the medical facility had soon become very prosperous with all the travelers coming through, the strain was becoming too much to continue.

Out of desperation, Jason spoke with the gods in hopes to remedy the situation. He wanted to be able to heal all the sick with his gift, but there were too many. With concern for the future and the health of he and his wife, Jason had turned to the gods for answers, but they offered no solution. For another year Jason and Ceenatanee worked together, helping all those who needed their guidance. They were loved and honored by many and rewarded handsomely by those who could afford to. In that time, a larger medical facility was built and then, a hospital. Once the hospital was built, the sequential episodes gave Jason his answers. Qualified doctors were coming in to answer to the needs of the people. Soon, a medial training school had been built in Jason's honor. With the facility fully staffed within its first year of operation, Jason was able to organize his time accordingly. He continued to study and eventually was able to take the time to document many of his procedures. Eventually, with his methodical documentation, he was then able to perform and duplicate all his procedures for the staff to learn as well.

In 1843, the first School of Chemistry in the state of Massachusetts had opened in the name of research, test, synthesis and analysis. It was never questioned as to where Jason gathered his information. His processes were studied and chronicled in

the first known journals of drug therapy. The town
continued to grow larger and prosperous. Job opportunities were many. And the sick were treated by
the hundreds. Jason and Ceenatanee had made quite
a name for themselves.

In 1850, at the age of 37, Jason became a Pro-
fessor of Medicine and eventually he wrote several
books on his research. The spirit gods were pleased
with the progress that Jason and his wife had made
and rewarded them in many special ways. Somehow, during the time of all the hard work, research
and study, Jason and Ceenatanee raised three girls
of their own, Melissa, Mary and Sadie, on a large
ranch just on the outside of town. The ranch was a
richly sylvan splendor, nestled against a small
mountainside that revealed a small cave at its base.
The very cave that Ceenatanee had emerged on the
day when they first met.

At the age of seventeen, Mary died of heart failure. She was one of the many sad and unfortunate
ones who could not be cured by the miracles of her
parent's healing abilities. The gods told Jason that it
was her destiny to move on.

In 1859, the year Sadie was born, Jason and
Ceenatanee's destiny had taken a change of course.

Nearly all their work in relation to medical research was completed according to the spirit gods. It was now time to move on to other duties and other destinies. Jason and his loving wife had a lot to be proud of. As Millie had predicted, a great many lives were, in fact, touched by the work of the gods via the Griffin. Millie and her husband continued on to work with the children and had opened several different schools for the handicapped and learning impaired.

Jason's parents shared in the wealth and continued to reside on their small ranch, but did build a much larger house and barn. They too were very proud of their son and Ceenatanee. Anne and Millie seemed to be the only ones that Jason could confide in, as far as the methods of their healing procedures. He wouldn't dare discuss these subjects with anyone else for obvious reasons. Miracles or not, history has been known to repeat itself. An example of proof is revealed by the fact that the Witchcraft Act was not repealed in England until the late 1950's, more than one hundred years after Jason retired from the hospital. And as recently as 1944, when the allied armies were invading Europe, the Spiritualist medium Mrs. Hellen Duncan was charged with witchcraft and subsequently sent to prison; a prosecution which brought forth caustic comments from the then Prime Minister, Winston Churchill. At age forty, Jason and his spiritual guides extrapolated all facts from given information, leading to the yet-to-be seen future and conceded that his retirement from the hospital and his medical research were necessary. In compliance with his visions, Jason was able to devote more time to his growing family. The doting love that he and his wife shared was an inseparable pact of heart and soul. Ceenatanee idolized her man. He was her hero, her dulcinea, and she was his. The retirement from the hospital wasn't an end to his studies or his relationship with the spirit gods. He went on to learn more about himself and the world with its many complicated mysteries. The three girls were raised with the philosophies of both their parents. All the facts of the spirit worlds were shared with their children. Jason spent just as many hours with his children as he did studying alone. And that which he learned upstairs in his private study, was almost immediately taught to his children. Nothing was spared from the knowledge gained from the trials of life. If the children would choose to pursue the spirit world, it rightfully should be their decision to make.

In Jason's later years, his interests in the future of things seemed to intrigue him most. He spent most of his spiritual time consorting with the ideas of evolution and its capricious properties. As the sage that he was, he developed an insatiable hunger to learn everything that the gods had to offer, and more. He would spend the day on end studying the claims of his visions and their etiology. It wasn't enough that the gods were providing him with travel, knowledge, insight, foresight and endless varieties of unfledged powers to be developed. He always had to know and learn more. It almost seemed that the answers he received only urged more questions. But the gods never halted communications with him and until his dying day, he was remembered most by his love and devotion to his family, friends and the spirit gods.

At the age of 59, Jason traveled across the states, guided by the spirit gods. He was destined to find his roots. Fourteen months later, he returned home elated by his discoveries.

At the age of 80, the very day Sadie gave birth to his grand-daughter, Rose, Jason died in a state of prayer and meditation. Painlessly, without any regrets and with a look of contentment on his face, he simply drifted away. His family believed that he merged with the spirit world and continues to communicate through all of us. Many claim to have felt his presence, years after his death; none more than Ceenatanee herself. She promised that she would find him again, in the spirit world or here again on earth; when she died three years after him, her family believed she truly would. Ceenatanee believed and made claim that through the portal of time, love will return.

Chapter Sixteen

The Confrontation

"I don't know why you're still hanging around here, and quite frankly, don't give a damn why. I just want you out of here. There's nothing for you here. You're obviously one of those leech types, who sucks upon the good fortune of others, rather than work and try to earn a respectable living on their own. So why don't you just collect your tin cup, get in your van and go harass some other family. Or better yet, why don't you do what your kind does best and go file a claim at the welfare department and collect your riches. Certainly, it would be a more resolute and lucrative move for you since Crystal, obviously, won't be doing you anymore of her philanthropy." Peter's tone was curt and seething with jealousy.

His true colors toward Mike would, each time, surface only when Crystal was too distant or too drunk to hear his searing tongue. The only way Peter could get up enough nerve to talk to Mike in such a manner was after he had his fortification of brandy.

"Peter, you know as well as I do, the only reason I've stayed here for as long as I have was only because of the 'welfare' of Crystal." At first Mike appeared calm and in control, "now, as far as I interpret the situation, you are either too blind or too inept to see the malignancy of Crystal's condition."

"You don't know what the he—"

"And when I am talking, I expect respect from those I am talking to," Mike was already preparing to pack and leave. He was on his knees, rolling the sleeping bag into its wrap. Since Crystal was in a vodka-lulled sleep in her room, Peter decided to take advantage of the moment by badgering Mike once again. Because Crystal was asleep, Mike saw no reason to hold back his true feelings from Peter and his belligerent state of mind. It was time he saw just what ominous forces he was dealing with. As he was rolling the bag along the floor, he had his back turned to Peter. Slowly, Mike rose to his feet. And as Peter thought himself so bold to interrupt, Mike stood before him, inches from his face, and with a drilling stare, he said his piece.

"Perhaps its time somebody teaches you about the etymology of respect," Mike continued. "It's a Latin derivative, in case you didn't know. The word doesn't only mean to regard the status of honor or esteem. And it doesn't only mean to show courteous considerations and politeness for one' feelings. It is also defined as knowing when to avoid intruding upon or interfering with others in respect to their privacy. Perhaps no one has taught you this. Or perhaps you forgot. " With a stout, projected index finger pressing hard against Peter's bony chest, Mike pushed forward with the force necessary to push Peter back out of his room. "Or maybe you feel that your cynical and elite upbringing doesn't warrant such amicable trivialities. Whatever the excuse may be, for your lack of etiquette, frankly, Peter, I don't give a damn why. The fact is, you now know exactly what the definition of respect means and I expect you to exercise this knowledge whenever you speak with me or about me. And should you happen to forget this little lesson, well, I think you have the idea. I would hate to think that someone like you, 'of your kind' could be too stupid to remember such a simple task." Mike's eyes were heated and he had pushed Peter five steps back, into the hallway with the force of one finger drilling into his chest.

Peter was no match for Mike, mentally or physically. There wasn't enough brandy in the world to equip him with enough gall to resist Mike. His bitter hatred for Peter's cowardice was accruing with force as Peter continued to relent and cover. The look of fear was painted all over his milksop face.

"Long before you ever came into the picture, Crystal was cared for and loved by me," Mike said. "As a brother and a best friend, I will continue to look after her at any cost. Obviously, you're incapable of handling such a woman, or pleasing her for that matter. Because of your inadequacies, someone has to look after her. I'll be leaving here today and it's not by your request, not by any means. It's because of the fact that I can't stand looking at your stupid, insipid face, nor can I tolerate seeing Crystal suffering so. When I return to check on her and I will, I promise you that and I will kill you if Crystal has been harmed by you in any way. That also includes her drinking. Make her stop or I promise you, you won't live long enough to regret it. Yes, Peter, that was a threat but try to prove it, I dare you." It was a powerful blow of words that he delivered to Peter, but they were the only kind that Mike knew he would take heed to. Soon afterward, Mike packed all that he could in his van. Most of what he owned was merely a large pile of clothes. Many of which were those that Crystal bought for him. Without being able to say goodbye to her because of her three-day long condition, Mike walked out of Crystal's life. As he drove out of the canyon, streams of tears flowed down his cheeks. The sounds of Crystal's voice and laughter kept rising from his subconscious. The smell of her perfume was still present in the van.

In a state of depression, and with Lucy in her cage in the sink running on her spinning wheel, Mike drove for days without a destination. He found himself going to the places where he and Crystal had been. The pressure of pain and loss seemed to mount with no end in sight. He had no job to vent or detour his anguish. He had no older brother to turn to, and no prospects, save that of the strange visions of a girl in white. And she wasn't offering any advice.

"What do you mean, he's gone? Where did he go?"

"He just packed all of his junk without saying a word and left. What's the big deal? You know he was just a leech and a loser. I wouldn't be surprised to find that he was probably stealing from you too." Peter could hardly hide the joy in his face and voice.

"What did you say to him, Peter?" The look in her eyes was mostly of hurt. She hadn't yet begun to get angry.

"I didn't say a thing. I didn't have to. His kind knows when to leave. There was nothing more for him here, so he left. Honestly, my darling, what's the big fuss? He was nothing but trouble. Can't you see that? You know, I heard about the fire at his last place of employment. Don't think for one minute that I don't know about his kind. I wouldn't be surprised if he had something to do with that as well."...He's nothing but a gigolo. His thinking about Crystal having been with him just made him fester with more unspent anger.

At first, it was as though she couldn't hear anything he was saying. Sitting up in her bed with her nightshades propped up on her forehead, her eyes still trying to adjust to the morning light bleeding through the curtains, she stared beyond Peter into space. A reverie of images passed before her. She remembered his tone and the look in his face when he gave warning that he would have to leave her if she didn't stop her drinking. She wouldn't allow herself to believe that she had drunk him away. For a moment, she felt as though she were totally alone in a world of faceless numbers. This was the closest she would ever come to truly knowing what a loss felt like.

She thought of Diane and the sorrow-filled tears Mike shed for her. She remembered the look on his face in the entryway the day they met. She thought about the first time they made love together in her bed. The same bed she was sitting in, and at that moment, wishing he was with her then, loving her, caressing her and filling her ears with philosophy. She remembered his infallibly candid sense of humor. A smile came to her face when she flashed back on the time she had stormed out of a restaurant because they prepared the wrong sandwich for her, but not before he had dulcified the situation and his embarrassment by explaining to the horrified waiter and patrons of her grief. Even though he was far from base, she had a great deal of trouble trying to keep from laughing or allowing him to know that she had heard his remarks. As Crystal was still bickering aloud with her back to him while he helped her with her sweater just moments from the time she had delivered her bitter spout to the waiter, Mike turned to the waiter and patrons and said, "Please understand, Miss Hamilton isn't always like this. Just moments ago, I had to inform Margaret that we can't make it back to Kansas because unfortunately, somebody dropped a rather large house on her sister. She was from the east, you know." As they made their way to the exit of the establishment with Crystal still mumbling more of her garbled obscenities, Mike had made eye contact with one of the patrons, an elderly lady accompanied by her husband, who had witnessed the entire event and found it be very entertaining. For the most part, she too was having trouble keeping a straight face as Crystal stormed by in a huff. She was obviously a person who enjoys a good laugh. Pushing Crystal ahead of himself, Mike leaned over toward the woman, looking her dead in the eye and whispered with almost too cogent a sincerity, "You have to understand her position, she was rather fond of those slippers."

Crystal blasted through the exit as Mike was delivering his final departing lines. At that same moment, the woman and a few other people opened up with unleashed laughter. Even Crystal almost lost her balance of equanimity to laughter. Had it not been for the dulling of her sense via the vodka, she might have lost the battle of sustaining her anger long before.

"Hey, I'm talking to you. What's the matter with you?" Peter waved his hand in front of her face. "Anybody in there?"

Falling back to reality, the angelic look on her face faded quickly to emptiness and then, turned to a simmering anger, "Peter?"

"Yes, dear." He answered, sounding self-assured.

"Do not think for one moment that you can fuck with me...I am no fool. And I can have your balls in a vise by simply snapping my fingers. Now, tell me where he went."

"I honestly don't know."...Hopefully, to hell he mumbled.

Slowly, Crystal pulled the pair of nightshades from her head and allowed it to drop to the floor. She didn't care that he could see the tears flowing from her dark, weary eyes. She grabbed her purse off the headboard and blindly groped for her bottle of whiskey. She allowed the purse to roll onto the floor as she twisted at the cap. With the bottle inches from her lips, Peter intercepted her attempt at a medicinal sip. "I don't think you should be drinking anymore, Crystal. It really doesn't become y—"

At that moment, she cast him the ultimate look of death. A man like Mike would have seen and been able to read the signs. He probably would have wrestled her for the bottle, or mocked his shield from her deadly stare and ultimately end the act by turning to stone in her arms swaging her anger to a calm.

Peter just froze in consternation.

"Get your hand off me or draw back a damned, bloody stump."

"Honestly, Crystal," Peter said, trying to make light of his sudden fear of her. "Why are you acting this way? Get a hold of yourself. Why don't you do something different today for a change, like get out of bed, get dressed, perhaps put some makeup on or something."...Do some fucking thing for a change.

After taking in the majority of what was left in the bottle, she looked at him in disgust. What did I ever see in you, she thought. "Just get the hell out of here," No matter how fast he may have responded, it wasn't fast enough for her. "Did you hear me? I said, get the hell out of here." She threw the bottle inches from his head. It landed with a dull thud in the carpet. "Go away. Leave me the hell alone." She didn't possess the kind of voice that could scream at high decibels. But if she had, she would have probably squalled him deaf. Instead, Peter could only hear her raucous bray of her demands exuded with the rancor of stale alcohol coming from the bowels of her fermented liver. Even the pores of her silken, pale skin smelled like bitter, rancid alcohol. Her entire body was tainted by the poisons of her past, and yet, she continued to search the room for more bottles. Peter obeyed her wishes and descended the stairs to watch television in the den after making a few business calls over his briefcase cellular phone.

"Hey bro," Billy said. "Where've ya been? Hey Nicky, come take a look at what the cat dragged in." In response, Nicky emerged from the back room.

"Well, well just a matter of time, eh Mikey?" As painful as the truth may have been Nicky couldn't have been more correct or guileless. As far as he was concerned, no woman was worth the trouble or worry, he simply figured that every guy should think his way. "There's a couch with your name on it, big guy. It folds out into a bed. Pretty nifty, huh?" As Nicky stepped close enough to shake his head, he gave Mike a wry smirk. "Ahhh, I suggest that you take a shower first, my friend. You smell a bit ripe, guy. What happened? Did she throw ya out without the soap, or did ya have trouble finding your way to your old pals?"

Billy could see that Mike wasn't taking the humor too well. "Hey bro," Billy said. "It's good to see ya. Let me show you around the place before you introduce Nicky to the dark side. This complex has everything a bachelor needs. Even those who don't know what they need." Billy placed a friendly hand on Mike's shoulder.

Mike knew that he could always count on Billy for being a good friend. After showing him their apartment, he took him downstairs for the guided tour of the complex. There were two swimming pools and two hot tubs. One of each was either inside for the winter months and the others were, of course, outside for summer. Saunas, a workout and weight room, a billiard room, a mailroom, even a membership to the golf course was part of the rental package offered at the complex. No known amenities were spared for the opulent living of the wealthy.

"Ya know Billy, I don't think it's such a wise idea just to throw away all that hard earned money from your royalties on a place like this. You need to invest. You need to—" With his dirty hair and unshaven face, Mike laughed in distress and shook his head. "I don't mean to be telling you how to live. Hell, look at me, who am I to be talking?" Billy just smiled with a look of confidence and pride in his good buddy.

"Damn, it's good to have you back, bro. I really missed you and your head for business. I was almost worried that you would never find your way here. You are going to stay with us, aren't you?"

"Well, I haven't even given it much thought. I mean, where would I be able to get the money for the rent or food or—" Mike was obviously letting the pressures of the situation get to him. He looked as though he were about to pass-out from lack of nutrition and faith.

The blast of of Mike's revival came in a fashion of shock through what Billy had propositioned him with. "Look, Mikey, there's nothing to it and it's good money. It'll only be for a short while. You see, once we get up enough money, we'll invest it, just as you said; we just don't have enough cash yet. But if you help us out, it won't take us as long to get there and just think of it, you would be partners with us of equal shares. We would never have to work another hard day in our lives. Nicky already has the plans for the place; it's just a matter of finding the right property, buy it and build on it. Word will get out fast enough, and the money will be rolling in. You'll see."

"Yes, I know that Nicky's idea for a nightclub will work. I have yet to see one fail, but Billy." Mike looked deeply into his eyes, searching for the truth. "Are you joking with me? How did you ever get such an idea as this? How do you propose to pull it off? It's not even legal, is it?"

Billy laughed aloud at his innocent naivety. "Your candor is priceless, little brother. Of course, it's not legal, at least not in this state. Don't worry; no one is going to get caught. Nobody cares about this sort of thing. Hell, it's hardly a crime; think of it as an offering therapy to the ladies in need.

"Billy, I don't know about all of this. The club sounds great, but the other...I don't know. I would have to think about it. I've never heard of such a thing. How did you find out about it? Are there others?"

"That's what I've been trying to tell you. Yes, there are many others. It's a regular business and it happens a lot around places like this. A friend I met in the weight room recruited me a month ago. After some training, he started me right away."

"You're already doing it?" Mike looked as though Billy had shot him. "And they trained you too? What is this world coming to?"

"Once you've met Dorianne, you'll understand the purpose of the training." Billy said with absoluteness.

"Billy, my God, are you sure about this?" Mike wanted to give it some considerable thought.

"More than sure. Tonight I'll be making two hundred dollars an hour. I'll probably make a grand tonight. With this kind of money, between the three of us, we could have enough funds to start building the club and open in less than a year from now. It's a sure thing, Mikey. No one's ever been busted yet. You have a smart head on your shoulders, bro, we need your business savvy with us." A big smile painted it's way across his face as he looked into Mike's innocence and waif-like qualities. He reached around his pal and gave him a meaningful hug. "Damn, it's good to see you, Mikey. You have no idea how happy I was to see that you found your way here today. I just know that things are going to work out for us. You'll see, little brother, you'll see." After the discussion of business proposals and the tour around the complex, Mike went upstairs to take his needed shower. The loss of Crystal had him driving endlessly and lost for three days.

The proposal that Billy had spoken of was the most different sort Mike had ever heard. He thought that such transactions only happened in the movies. Billy had indeed met a man in the weight room— his name was Clyde.

After his shower and a bit of rest, Billy introduced the two of them. Clyde was tall and stout, like a strong, satiated tree. His mannerisms and etiquette were well educated and finely trained in every primping detail. Mike almost felt insecure being in the same room with such a prototype of perfection and refined distinction. Clyde obviously had a penchant for fine clothes; Mike recognized the cut and style of his suit. Crystal had educated him well in the finer threads of style and this guy's jacket alone must have cost over five hundred dollars. Mike soon learned a great deal more about the soon-to-be, new partner in crime. For nine profit-able years Clyde has been in the business of prosti-tution for the wealthy women of Beverly Hills. He's recruited more than a dozen men to take on the workload of his growing list of clientele. Business was obviously doing quite well, the man owned his own home in the hills and drove an all white on white V-12 Ferrari Daytona. He claimed that he would retire as a millionaire by the time he reaches his fortieth birthday.

Poor thing, Mike thought, what's he going to do with all that money since he already has everything. Perhaps since business was so good, he'll probably need it to buy himself a new pecker.

After meeting with Clyde and listening to the pros and cons, and according to Billy, there were no cons; Mike decided that he still needed a little more time to think things through. Somehow it all seemed too primrose to him. Surely, there would have to be some kind of drawbacks. Clyde claimed that in the nine years of operation he had never been arrested and that he never had any problems with the IRS. Furthermore, Clyde claimed it's all legal as a rec-ognized escort business. Even his clientele often use his business visits as a tax deduction. The operation is clean, well run and lucrative beyond any doubt. The names of his clientele were kept confidential, except to the escorts only. Clyde, a very clever and good looking French black man, knew exactly how to run a provocative operation. Mike was tempted, but not yet willing to commit.

Chapter Seventeen

Dorianne

*M*ike wasn't all that keen on the idea of selling himself out for pay. Although Clyde made sure that he understood that not just any guy is as readily qualified as he. The men he would hire were potentially the best, once trained accordingly. The first week after the proposal of carnal slavery for profit, Mike tried his best to tour the entire city for a legitimate job. He put applications in everywhere. Unfortunately, no calls had come through with any openings. All his funds had nearly dwindled away. It was bed enough that he had stepped all over his own pride by applying for jobs of less requirements than his abilities, but when he found himself offering his services for less than the going rate just to be employed for food, he realized he had hit bottom.

He couldn't stand taking handouts from his buddies. Nicky and Billy would always offer and didn't mind helping him through the rough times, but he still found it very hard to accept. He would rather steal than take philanthropy from his friends. Mike found himself so desperate and hungry, he would continually ponder the ideas of stealing food. He tried figuring ways of doing it with the least risk of getting caught. Knowing that his situation was merely a transitory fallback, he figured a few stolen meals wouldn't get him thrown in jail or executed. On occasion, he would drive his van behind some of the affluent restaurants in town and rummage through their trashcans for food that had been scraped from the plates of the patrons. Bread rolls, crackers a half-eaten pork chop or steak would sometimes be found mingled in with old register tape, vacuum bag contents, broken glass, soiled napkins and whatever gunk winds up in the trash bin. But when suffering from nutritional deprivation, one doesn't think so hard about the little trivialities that come with eating out of the squalor of trash receptacles; one thinks mostly about the pain in his gut and the remedy that is found sometimes in places less savory than others. With many unfortunate people doing the same as him, many times, there would be a fight or struggle to be the first to foray through the findings, or there would be merely nothing edible left to find. There were however, many restaurants to choose from, but unfortunately, the same situation of other's destitution prevailed there as well. It was then, and out of starvation, Mike parked his van outside the Ralph's grocery store. He searched through his clothes for an appropriate choice of attire. Once dressed in an, obviously expensive suit, Mike stepped out of the van and approached the establishment. With his heart beating hard and loudly in his chest, he walked through the entry doors, grabbed a basket and proceeded to shop through the store. Item after item was dropped into his basket. He even had a shopping list in his hand to add to the effect. While shopping, reading labels and comparing prices, Mike would calmly open some of his items from his basket that were to be purchased once his basket was half-full. He ate to his satiated capacity when nobody was looking in his direction. The empty containers would then be buried in his basket deeply beneath his other items. And as normal and habitually as anyone would, Mike stood in line to purchase his basket of goods. Just as he got to the register, he realized that he didn't have his wallet, or so he wanted the cashier to think. He groped all his pockets and then in a blush, would apologize to the cashier for having forgotten his wallet at home. He asked her to put the basket aside and reported he would be back momentarily, stating that he lived close. The plan worked well. He left the store, got into his van and drove away never to return. Mike believed that it was only a matter of time when the phone would ring and a job would be made available to him and the stealing of food would only last for as long as he were in the desperate situation. On occasion, the trash bins would provide just enough to keep him from furthering his criminal activities. There was many nights that he couldn't muster the nerve to go back to the apartment and face his friends. They could see it in his face—he was losing his self-confidence and endurance, but not yet willing to sell his flesh for cash. Although he had resorted to stealing food, Mike felt that whoring himself would have been a more offensive attack upon his virtues. In his mind, he just knew that something good was about to happen; something had to happen.

On a Friday, after his second week spent in the van traveling in search for job opportunities and food, Mike thought heavily about Crystal. He wondered if she had yet noticed him gone, if it mattered to her. He could no longer smell her scent in the van. The cedar woodchips in Lucy's cage had taken over the scents of the past. The memory of Crystal was strong in his mind. For a brief moment, he suddenly felt her presence, her pain, her emptiness, and then her capitulation. As a foolish notion of desperation, salvation and heroics, he thought that maybe this one last time he would be able to save her from the evils of alcohol. He hoped that maybe his absence was indeed noticed and warning enough to help her fight for a better life, to want to live and be healthy with friends who love her and care about her. He ignored intuition and ventured one last attempt at saving Crystal. It was as though his nutritional deprivation was playing tricks with his mind. Or perhaps his hopes and aspirations were the blinders that kept him from feeling the truth. With only enough money to ration purposeful travel in the van, Mike dutifully drove to the nearest restaurant to clean himself. Using the bathroom to wash his hair, face and body, he proceeded to tend to his needs as though the bathroom was his own. In the unsavory month of destitution and homelessness, he had grown used to the idea of using public bathrooms to conduct his personal business. As he made the finishing primps to his appearance, he flashed back on the memory of doing the same in front of the mirror when preparing for the school dance. In a strange way, it seemed like a thousand years in the past, and yet, he remembered it as yesterday. He thought of Diane and he thought about the fact that he never had the courage to see Diane's mother after the tragic accident. He found himself wondering why he was thinking of Mrs. Hunt.

Confused by the signs, he again, ignored intuition and pushed the memories of the past out of his mind. With his comb, he slicked back his wet hair, including the Elvis curl and then packed his toiletries back into his overnight bag and exited the bathroom. As he left the restaurant and proceeded to walk to his van in the parking lot, he continually received visions of Crystal. It was as though he knew that there was an importance to his seeing her, but not for the reasons he had figured. The drive to her house made him nervous. He didn't know how he would handle Peter or what he would say to Crystal if she were drunk. As he pulled into her driveway, he rehearsed the phrases and replies of probability in his head. He parked the van in what was once his parking spot. He also noticed that Peter's limo was in the driveway along with Crystal's BMW. With a deep breath, he pulled at the door handle and exited from the van. His heart was pounding in his chest with dizzying effects as he knocked at the front door. It was as though he were going on a blind date, not knowing exactly what to expect. The door latch clicked and the knob slowly turned. As the door came open, Mike was relieved to see Crystal standing on the other side. In the time the band had first gone on tour and hither to, Crystal has stopped going to the tanning salons and the gym. As she stood wavering in the threshold, he could see her pale skin looking pure, natural and fresh. But as he looked into her dull and lifeless eyes, he knew that nothing had changed.

"Hello, Crystal," he said, forgetting all that he rehearsed to say.

"Why are you here?" She stood hanging onto the door for stabilizing support.

"Won't you let me in?"

"No, it wouldn't be a good idea." Her voice was curt and without feeling. "Peter has thrown out all that was left behind in your room. There's nothing here for you, Michael."

"Not even friendship?"

"You never even said goodbye."

"How could I have?"

"You could have called." She scolded.

373

"Both times that I called, Peter told me that you wouldn't talk to me."

"Peter never mentioned to me that you called." Her voice held a challenge of doubt and resentment toward Mike.

"Well, I don't know what to tell you, girl. I never would have believed that after all the time we had spent together, you would choose to doubt my word." He was trying to hide his hurt. Being doubted by Crystal was like being accused of murder. There was a time that he could have told her that he and she were the incarnate of a thousand lifetimes together and she would have believed him wholeheartedly. As she stood against the door with a glass of what looked to be scotch, Mike couldn't even convince her that he had called.

"So, why did you come here?" she asked.

"My God, Crystal. What the hell do you think I came here for?" There was a hint of panic in his voice. He couldn't understand what it was that made her so spiteful toward him. Surely, the alcohol can change one's state of mind, but this attitude that she was brandishing was different from that.

"I don't know. I already told you that there's nothing here of yours."

"Damn it, Crystal," Mike grabbed her shoulders and slightly shook her. The ice in her glass sounded against the sides. "I came to see you, to see how you were doing, to perhaps find out if you have given up drinking, to see if you even cared about me enough to give up drinking."

She was looking weary and disheveled, dressed in her nightgown and robe. Her hair was uncombed, parted at the side and hanging at the sides of her face. Aside from the dullness in her stare and the dark rings around her eyes, Mike would always find her pleasing to look at. As he held her shoulders in his firm grip, the tie of her robe came loose and the view of her front came freely. Through the thin material of her nightgown, he could see all her unveiled beauty. Seeing her again in such form had sparked a thousand memories.

In the slumber of her daily habits, she hadn't even bothered to put on her panties. As her eyes intercepted his, she didn't make any attempts to cover herself. At that moment, Mike was left wondering if she was offering an apology or perhaps she didn't care. Or worse, her innate instincts may have been forfeited for the likes of drink. Whatever the case may have been, the moment was interrupted by Peter's voice. She had left him upstairs to answer the door.

"Who is at the door, Crystal...? Just tell them we don't want any and get your ass back up here." The expression on Mike's face had shattered at the sound of Peter's voice.

"Just wait a fucking moment would you?" Crystal snapped. From upstairs, came no reply. The romance of their engagement was evident and summed up in the three brief sentences between them.

"I thought that I came here to visit a friend. I guess I was wrong. Whatever it was that turned you against me, I hope that you can live with it."

Through the mournful stare of sorrow-filled eyes he continued, "...I doubt that I will be able to." Mike turned and walked away.

"Wait, wait a minute," Crystal called out. "Answer just one thing for me, please. Did you steal from me?"

The horrified look on Mike's face should have been answer enough, but instead, Mike just stood in shock as she waited for his answer. The worst hurt that she could have ever inflicted upon him was as simple as her question. No doubt, somebody had filled her inebriated head with caustic lies. "I can't believe that you would even ask such a thing from me. You know me better than that, Crystal. Why on earth would I steal from you? Why would I ever allow our friendship to be sacrificed by such a deceit?" The hurt in his heart caused him to become angry with her.

"Just answer me, yes or no, Michael." The plea in her voice seemed to be delivered in the form of begging, and all that she had to go on in the search for the truth.

"No, of course not, Crystal," Mike looked at her with eyes filled with hurt. For the first time, he felt like she had betrayed him. What Mike didn't know, but suspected, was the fact that Peter was the one filling her head with lies. The day Mike moved out from the house, Peter proved his point by destroying almost all possibilities of salvaging the friendship between Mike and Crystal. He burned all photos of them together, even the one's he found in her wallet of them in photo booths and candid shots of them at different clubs. He also found the Polaroids of them together in bed. In addition to the insult, cash was removed from Crystal's wallet along with some jewelry from her wall safe. Peter discovered the combination to the safe while he was searching the house for incriminating evidence to devolve onto Mike while she was passed-out in her bed the day Mike packed and left. At that time, only Crystal, her dad and Mike knew the combination to the safe. Naturally, when she awoke, Peter placed the blame on Mike, as planned.

"We both know that I would never steal that which you would gladly give me for the asking. For you to even ask is the most hurtful thing you have ever done to me, second to your drinking." Mike stood beneath the eaves of her front porch. The red in his face and the swell of tears in his eyes began to show. "I can only hope that when you learn the truth, it doesn't hurt you as bad as you've hurt me today." As Mike turned to walk back to his van, Crystal had asked him to wait, but Mike didn't want to hear anymore. He just wanted to leave rather than allow her to see him crying. The lump in his throat and swell in his chest almost made it too hard for him to say what he did.

Crystal stepped back from the door to the antique Renaissance Revival cupboard-base étagère that stood against the wall in the entryway. A hidden and locked panel door, located in the upper cupboard that no one knew about was released by a small button located beneath the marble surface of the countertop. Crystal depressed the button and from behind the panel door, she retrieved the leather cloth that was made by Miranda.

She placed her drink on the countertop and proceeded out the door. Her legs were weak and barely responsive from lack of exercise and use. As she lumbered out the door, she heard the engine of the van start up.

"Wait!" She shouted out again in desperation. But as she stepped behind the van, she saw the backup lights illuminate with a bright glow. Mike put the van in reverse and proceeded to back down the driveway. After hearing a loud thud at the back of his van, Mike slammed on the brakes. The tires emitted a short, loud screech. Crystal appeared at the driver's window.

"Don't be in such a hurry, you could kill someone," Crystal had smacked the back of the van with her fist. "Look, Mike, I'm sorry for hurting you. I only have this to offer you." She handed him the leather. "You have no idea how important this is that you don't lose this. I know why you left it here and I also know the truth, but unfortunately, it doesn't matter anymore and we cannot see each other anymore either." Her face was vague with empty compassion, but Mike was able to read the signs. "You have to find the girl that made it. It's very important that you ask her why she gave it to you. I should have been honest with you from the beginning."

"Honest about what?" Mike accepted the leather

as Crystal handed it to him through the window.

"Look at the back of the leather, Michael," he turned it over. "That stain is her blood. She sealed an oath on the leather that you cannot ignore. I must not tell you anymore about it than I already have. You will have to find her and have her tell you why she did it," her eyes were filled with sorrow that she wasn't willing to admit as she bade him good luck. "I must go back inside now. Try not to run me over, okay?" As she stepped back from the van, this time, walking in front, she looked back at Mike somewhat ruefully.

Mike couldn't discern if the look was for him or more for her. Then, suddenly, and with a serene calm and a true breadth of understanding through the grin she offered one last time, Crystal removed her robe and held it at her side as she slowly ambled back toward the house. She allowed him to look upon her splendid nakedness through the transparent material of her nightgown. With the sun at her side, the effect was well rewarding. She then entered the house and closed the door behind her. As she stared blindly at the patterns of the parquet tiles, she fell against the door with all her weight and slid down to the floor upon her bent knees. Her face turned to crimson as her eyes released a gushing river of tears. She could hardly keep from making any sound, as she wanted to cry aloud. As Peter called out to her once more in his rude manner, Crystal answered with retort. She had decided that the idle life of squabbling with Peter and drowning herself in alcohol was far easier than working with the pressures of life.

Mike held tightly onto the leather as he drove down from the canyon hillside. He knew that he would never see Crystal again. The famous grin she offered him would, no doubt, be her last. It was a wonder that he was able to sustain any hope for life at all. Although, if anyone who knew him could describe him in one word, most would know him to be a survivor. Mike's tears came to fall mingling with the leather in his hand. The stain of dried blood and the moisture of his tears blended in his grip. Without understanding why, Mike drove to the park behind the hospital. He emerged from the van, with the leather in his hand and walked around the park. A strange and familiar feeling continually bombarded him as he walked from one end of the park to the other.

Dozens of different visions would come to focus and fade as though viewed through a Kaleidoscope. None of it was making any logical sense. His head whirring with confusion, Mike couldn't take anymore of the inundating visions. He retreated to his van and attempted to leave the park. The visions were strong. Aside from the time he was stabbed by the biker in the alley, never had they been so strong and cogent in his mind. As he drove down Hollywood Boulevard and onto a side street, he found himself alongside The Boys Market, a local grocery store. His stomach was growling from pain-filled hunger and his head pervaded with mixed and scrambled visions, Mike decided to go into the market and conduct another of his gorged shopping sprees. He was already cleaned-up and dressed appropriately. In the large parking lot he parked the van and stashed the leather beneath the seat. As he approached the entrance of the store, he got an eerie feeling deep in his gut, but he refused to listen to the intuitive beckoning. The pain of his hunger precluded any warnings of danger. He stepped through the automatic swinging glass door and proceeded to gather a basket. As according to his plan, he shopped throughout the store with no regard to the warning signs. He didn't even notice the in-house store detective following him from afar throughout the entire duration of his shopping trek. As he got to the register, he pulled the same line on the cashier. His belly was filled with BBQ chicken from beneath the heat-lamps, a quart of chocolate milk from the refrigerator and a half box of pink and white animal cookies from the crackers and snacks aisle, Mike left the store feeling revived, replenished and strong once again. As he approached his van, he pulled the keys out of his pocket and disarmed the alarm with his keypad remote. Just as the alarm chirped its signal of disarmament, he attempted to stick the key in the door. From around the front of the van, hidden well from view, the detective clasped Mike's wrist with a handcuff. As the bracelet tightened around his wrist, Mike could hear the distinct sound of the clicking mechanism locking to its tighter girth. As true to his foreseen vision, with all the perceived sounds, with all the familiar faces and all the unsavory horrors of being arrested.

Mike was taken to jail on charges of shoplifting and possession of a concealed weapon. He felt the discomfort of embarrassment, second to that, he felt humiliated and angry with himself. He was angry for ignoring his premonitions and angry for having done such a foolish thing and having been caught. His van was impounded, Lucy was presumed to have been taken to the animal shelter and he was taken to the same station where he had identified his brother. The same station where he envisioned himself incarcerated in the back of a squad car. Since the attack in the alley by the biker, Mike carried a switchblade on him at all times. He had no idea of the consequences that would unfurl with the charges of possession of a concealed weapon, even a simple six-inch switchblade. According to the arresting officer, who frisked him at the grocery store, a knife blade longer than three inches is considered to be a deadly weapon. To be in the possession of a concealed, deadly weapon is automatically considered by protocol to be a felony arrest. Had he not been in possession of the knife, and had he been arrested for only shoplifting charges, he probably would have been released after paying a small fine and booked on a misdemeanor infraction. But instead, he was considered an armed and dangerous felon, and after he was booked the District Attorney informed him of his twenty-five hundred dollar bail. After all the formalities of being arrested were concluded, Mike was strip-searched and then incarcerated in a small and dank seven-by-seven foot cell. Even the strip search was not nearly as embarrassing as having been arrested by a store security guard and then made to walk back into the store with his hands cuffed behind him to wait for the police to arrive.

After a short while of talking with the man in the cell next to his, Mike learned of the unsavory dregs behind the court system. One of which was the fact that the court system comes to a complete halt on the weekends. The only system in operation was that of the continual arrests and the overcrowding of prison cells curing the duration of the weekends. Since Mike was arrested on Friday, it would be three long days before he would even get the chance to plead his case before a judge in hopes to reduce his bail. According to the District Attorney that was appointed to Mike's case, first offenders almost always receive reduced bail. Aside from that bit of news, he had little to hope for, except that of the free meals and they weren't much to look forward to either. By Saturday, Mike was already sharing a cell with four other guys. By Sunday, there were six in his cell, only one toilet and two beds. Two of the guys never sobered up until Monday morning, just hours before appearing before the judge.

By Monday morning, Mike was more than willing to repent, but to his dismay things didn't work out as he had hoped. The judge was stern and obviously had a bad weekend. After reviewing thirteen cases before his, the judge frowned on the fact that

Mike didn't have any prospects for a job. Also, because of the fact that the computer found the records of his unfortunate episode with the shooting
and killing of the biker, Mike was left with nothing
more than precarious hopes for his release. Even
though Mike was not convicted of any crimes involving that incident, the judge found it reasonable
to consider Mike a menace and a risk to society; he
was to be dealt with accordingly. The judge raised
the bail to five thousand dollars or ninety days in
county jail, to be served immediately following his
departure from the courthouse that day. It was all
happening in a pattern worse than any of his ugliest
nightmares. Mike had nothing to do with the death
of the biker, other than himself having been victim-
ized. But according to the laws and beliefs of the
old and balding, irate judge, there was no possible
way of convincing him of his innocence. As the habitually insipid and sloven District Attorney, who
was supposed to have acted in defense for his client,
said nothing further, as the judge hammered the
gavel to the bench, Mike felt as though the walls of
the building had suddenly collapsed in on him. As
the bailiff guided him back to his holding cell, he
felt a strong bitter hatred accruing toward the court
system. I'm not a criminal damn it, he thought to
himself. I wasn't going to stab anyone with the
knife. Hell, I was the one that got stabbed before...and ended up in the hospital. Mike dropped
himself to the hard concrete floor of his cell and
buried his head in his hands as the iron-barred door

slammed behind him...I just wanted to eat...I just wanted a job. For Chris' sakes, why the hell is this happening to me? I don't deserve this.

First thing on Tuesday, Mike was to be transported to the county jail. When he was greeted by a tall and slender black girl the night before, Mike thought he was dreaming. He didn't understand all that was happening. The girl was pretty with a very refined manner. She spoke frankly. In her eyes, Mike could see every expression and intent. She introduced herself as Dorianne and explained that she had paid the bail and that he was to come with her for the arrangement of payments. On Friday, the day of his arrest, he used his only call to inform Billy of his incarceration. Mike told him that he was not to pay the bail because he had no idea how long it would take him to pay back the money. He figured that doing the time in jail would probably be easier than trying to raise the money. He had no idea that the time he would have to serve would end up being anything more than just one week. The only reason he had called was to ask to try to get the van out of impound. It meant far too much to him than to accept losing it through the police impound auction. Billy made every attempt at convincing him that subjecting himself to prison life wasn't the answer. Billy didn't mind paying the bail for his friend. And at the time, it would have been twenty-five hundred dollars less expensive. Billy probably would have done anything to take his place. But Mike wouldn't allow for any of it. His pride wouldn't allow for it. His ego would allow for it. And if it weren't for Billy's actions, Mike's ego probably would have suffered a great deal more than he realized. Prison life wasn't meant for pretty boys like himself. The holding tanks of local jails are nothing in comparison to the county and state prisons. The papers were already drawn up and ready. Dorianne merely made a phone call to the station, and by the time she arrived, Mike's papers were in order and only the bail needed to be paid. As he was released from his cell and guided to the front desk, he had never seen the cops behind that desk act so respectable and cordial. It was as though she were the president's wife. As he walked out the door of the station, his curiosities and assorted questions were relentless. It wasn't until he saw the white Ferrari outside the station that he remembered where he heard the name Dorianne.

"Now I know who you are." Mike said as he searched through the large manilla envenlope that contained his possessions. "That's Clyde's car. You're the Dorianne that Billy was talking about. You're with Clyde, right?"

"The car is mine. My husband Clyde has one similar."

Mike stopped dead in his tracks. "Hold on now. Am I to understand that the reason for your paying my bail was to get me to work for Clyde?"

Dorianne looked at him curiously. "Would you

rather go to prison?" She took a step closer and grabbed hold of his hand with both of hers. "Do I frighten you, Michael?"

"No, of course not."

"Do women frighten or intimidate you?"

"No, they do not."

"I can see through you, Mr. Michael Shane. I know what you are all about. And the qualities that you possess can improve your lifestyle one hundred fold. What is it that keeps you from going forth with us?"

"Well, for one, it's not legal."

She looked at him steady in the eyes. "And stealing food is? Look, you needn't be so pious with me. Come and give it a try, if you decide that you have no interest in continuing with us, you will be free to quit at any time. We are not going to obligate you to any binding contracts, I promise."

"What about the bail money?"

"After I set you up with your first client, if for any reason you are not contented to continue working with us, I will eat the loss. I am that certain that you would be making a big mistake if you don't try us out before you make any long-term decisions. I know you're not afraid of hard work. And most times, the work is very rewarding. You could ask your friend Billy if I'm wrong, and he doesn't have half of your qualities. You have nothing to lose. But if you don't at least try, you're going to be indebted to me by five grand," she shrugged her shoulder as a tacit gesture of simplicity. "By trying it just once, you could be debt free. How could you miss with such a proposition?"

There really wasn't much that he could say or do to relieve himself from the predicament. "When do I start?"

Dorianne smiled and raised his hand to her lips. She gently planted a tender kiss in the center of his palm. "We start tomorrow night."

"We?"

"You and I, of course. We don't send young virgins out in the world alone without formal training. Our clients wouldn't appreciate that." She could see the hesitation in him. "Now, don't get nervous on me. I will teach you everything that you need to know. Things that the clients will expect from you, and things you will be able to provide effectively, emphatically, passionately and willfully," she wrapped her arm around his waist and guided him down the concrete steps to the car waiting in the street below. "Come now, let's go get your van and Lucy."

"How did you know about Lucy?"

She just smiled in reply. It would seem that she had him exactly where she wanted him. He had no idea that the culmination of his being arrested was going to come to such ends. It was hard for him to judge what the outcome of his new employment would be. In fact, he couldn't evoke any vibration or vision from the future at all. It was all new territory now and there was little he could do to change things. Fate had its reasons, and Mike had to accept that as fact.

Chapter Eighteen

*M*ike's training in the art of carnal vocations
was indeed very different from anything he
had expected. After the confirmation from their
doctor that followed Mike's complete physical examination, he received his training from Dorianne,
who knew her business as an art of perfection. Her
understanding of her clients gave her the edge on
her training techniques.

In the two weeks' time that she personally
worked with him, Nicky had already been fired by
Clyde. As far as Clyde was concerned, the only reason he had hired him in the first place was because
there was one client that was particular about his
type. His self-assured, chauvinistic, pompous right-
eousness was the perfect repertoire for his client to
gain her confidence. Once she had her fill of him,
Clyde no longer had any further use for him.

In the eyes of both Clyde and Dorianne, any
successful business must be run methodically, per-

haps crudely and impetuously. Clyde had the responsibility of having to discern the needs and desires of each of his clients, perhaps even before they
themselves knew of their needs. He possessed a
great deal of pride in his abilities, and no one
doubted or had any reason to doubt his skills. He
was very young when he had first been introduced
into the world of carnal procurement. His mother
grew up in France during the war. Her family was
very poor and she was forced to leave the house at
the very young age of fourteen and fend for herself
on the pernicious streets of itinerant war-torn soldiers. In order to survive, she sagaciously learned
the needs of the soldiers. She soon became their security, therapy and provider of love. Late in the
night, or in the bright of day, she would provide for
as many as twenty men in any given twenty-four
hour period. Before the end of the war, she had
saved enough cash to travel to the States where she
resumed her business. After she gave birth to Clyde,
from a father he would never meet, she retired herself from the business, but continued to provide her
clientele with girls she would hire and train herself.
Her work became a refined art, similar to that of the
skillful and dexterous Geisha girls of Japan. As her
son grew older, he came to know the girls and soon
became involved in the business. From the paperwork of the accounting, to the handling of public relations, Clyde was already running the business
before he graduated from high school. After taking
and passing the high school proficiency exam in the

first quarter of his junior year, he went on to take business management and accounting courses in college. Since his mother spoke a minimal amount of English, he was basically destined to take over the management of his mother's business. Within a few short years, after his receiving his degree in business management, his mother was able to retire from the business, after he set up some long-term investments for her. He was given the business to continue with in the manner in which he had been trained by the girls, which were fastidiously trained by his mother.

At the age of twenty-one, he met Dorianne and the following year they were married. Their business together became legally legitimate when it was redefined as an escort service. Since there were a great many governmental and judicial officials on the list of clientele, there was even less risk of litigation from any possible opposition. Even their financial investments, which were implemented from the payment funds of their clientele, were sound legal endeavors. The education from his mother and college taught Clyde well.

Mike was seeing just how the art of carnal splendor could be made very profitable. The first evening that Mike was to be trained by Dorianne, Clyde was out on business. Many times, Clyde would answer to the first call of his new clientele, with this common practice, he would learn exactly how to satisfy his clients' needs. Once they were comfortable with the idea and pleasantries of the escort service, he would then wean them onto his other employees. That's where Mike's job came into the picture. Dorianne would then instinctively learn what was necessary through Clyde's instruction and implement the same instruction into her training of the other employees. Sometimes, there were clientele that would choose not to see anyone but Clyde. For this very reason, he had a great many on his list of personal business, one of which was a very wealthy widow, named Alexandria. She was the one that he was paying first visit to when Dorianne had Mike come to their home for the first night of training. Mike had never seen such an eloquent lady before. Her speech and instruction were artistic. Her elegance and grace was undeniable. That evening, she was dressed in a shear, white, skin-tight dress of Dior, with matching earrings. The tress of her hair was wrapped in a tight bun. All her features were more than pleasing to the cosmopolitan.

The first day of his training lasted a duration of nearly five hours. And all of it was spent talking of what was expected of him and talking of the metaphysical. She told him of Clyde's history and how he grew up on the streets of France. She explained to him why Clyde had personal interest in him. He knew that Mike had the finer qualities needed to advance in his line of work. His training with Dorianne was to take a great deal longer than the others because Mike was to take on more of the clientele than the others. She taught him of her and Clyde's philosophies and attitudes. She drilled a confidence into him that he never knew existed. As she continued to work with him, he learned a lot, but even more than what was expected. She taught him how to look deep within himself. It was as though she was the mentor of a crash course in psychology and she enabled him to understand all the basics with little need for fundamental practice. Everything she said to him in her attempt at teaching him how to understand himself, made perfect sense and helped him to learn how he would be able to apply his skills onto the clients, and on into life in general. For six more days, Dorianne counseled and instructed him in the similar likes involving manner, attitude, etiquette and skills of managing himself. She had explained that the skills of self-management are the most important, and yet, the most difficult to learn. Instinctively, people look at, listen to, and watch others conduct their lives in everyday activities. But very few people realize that they are also judging and classifying them as well. These judgments and classifications take place through brief encounters. Many people can read others without ever having to speak to them. People carry themselves in the manner in which they see themselves. Some days vary with mood, but in general, the rule will always infallibly apply.

Understanding the rules can enable anyone to convey one's self-image, one's message of stature, position and integrity. Learning to control one's self-image was also included in Dorianne's training. That's where the importance of self-confidence was projected and noted as the integral of effectiveness in the field of work that Mike was soon to venture into. Providing one is confident in himself, it is likely that others will sense the same and react accordingly. The many great leaders of the world would never have been able to reach their summits of success had they lacked the image of self-confidence. If one is adamantly sure of himself, others will feel equally sure in him as well. Everyday instinct plays a bigger role in life than most will ever realize. The format is relatively easy once learned and put into practice. Other learned tips and theories along with many other philosophies were shared with Mike in the term of his training. For a couple of days, Clyde worked with him as well. Mike often felt it was all as though he were cramming for school exams. And in a sense, he was, because soon, he was to take his learned trade out of the training class and to the homes of Clyde and Dorianne's clientele.

Their escort business was dealt with strict caution and pampered care. If Clyde sensed any kind of fault in Mike, he certainly would not allow him to venture forth with his vitally important clientele; many of which were to be regarded with the utmost discretion. Those that were not so in need of such coddling were taken care of by the other employees, such as Billy and formerly, Nicky. Some of the customers had very simple needs. Many only have required a date to accompany them at formal functions like banquets or award ceremonies. Some merely needed company to talk to or swim by the pool, or perhaps, simply someone to watch. There was quite a list of voyeuristic patrons who simply like to watch their escorts follow their explicit instructions. From having them do their laundry in the nude, to watching them do housecleaning while dressed in the requested attire, or just masturbate while standing on the coffee table that was centered in the middle of the family room. The escorts were trained, prepared and placed accordingly for the pleasures of the clients. For five years, one man would hire the same girl to do all his dictation in his office, while she sat at his desk completely nude, save that of her pen and pad. He would never touch her or fondle her. And in all seriousness, the work that she conducted was vital to his company. His business was a legitimate one and was conducted as such. Only the escort service knew of his preference in giving dictation. There were hundreds of different kinds of scenarios requested by the customers; each was handled with confidence, assurance, success and confidentiality. The second week of Mike's training dealt with much of the same, with the addition of some instructional physical training, most of which was pertinent to the women he would be escorting. Dorianne showed Mike how to deliver pleasures he never knew existed in a woman. Truly, her given expression of him as a virgin was quite clear by them. From the simplicity of giving a hot liniment body-rub, to the complexities of handling a frigid widow of twenty years, she worked with him over every detail. After fifteen days of training and another week of mock trials with Dorianne as the portrayed client, Mike was ready to greet his first customer.

Mike found himself already knowing and understanding his first customer. Even though he had been trained by the best, he still had a bit of trouble emanating complete confidence. The woman he was to entertain was a young, single mother by the name of Katherine, who on occasion, would turn to the escort service and their professionalism. Katherine was quite attractive and never had any trouble finding dates but as she explained to Mike, her preference was with the expertise of the escort service. She was tired of risk and chance and meeting men with too many personal problems. Too many times she would be terribly disappointed by dating and all that implies. She didn't like going out into the public in search for or in hopes of, finding the right date. In much of her experience, the men that she would find attractive and possibly date-worthy turned out to be either married or gay—sometimes worse. The escort service had taken away most of the risk. Chance was dealt with through videos of the employees that Clyde provided his clients. It was her choice to meet with Mike, so she basically knew what she was getting. Upon the first time together, there was nothing especially kinky about their date. For several hours, they just sat and talked. Her kids were out of town and she had planned to spend the entire day and that evening with him. He took her to dinner via one of many of Clyde's chauffeured limousines after they got to know each other and upon returning back to her home, they talked some more. According to Clyde's business profile records on Katherine she was noted as being lonely, cautious and extremely fastidious. From the list of her past dates with the men of the escort service, she didn't always choose to go to bed with them. Some were better for conversation and outings, while others were meant only for sexual tension releases. In her search for an escort of both qualities, Clyde was given a good report on Mike's performance and style as being in possession of both those qualities. And so followed more dates with Katherine and training for the next client. After escorting Katherine, Mike decided to stay with the business. And since Clyde was so pleased with his abilities, he gave Mike his first job's pay of five hundred dollars; fifty percent of the monies taken from the client are given to the employee. In all, the arrangements of pay and work scheduling were acceptable to Mike. And in good faith, Clyde confirmed his agreement of Mike's not having to pay back any of the bail money.

As Mike was soon to take on more clients, Clyde and Dorianne were able to produce bigger profits. To Mike's surprise the business was more lucrative than Billy had first boasted. With the money that Mike and Billy were making, they were able to buy out and take over the payments of a small business that was fighting bankruptcy in Hollywood. The fact that the business was on such a large parcel of land drew Mike's attention. The business that they bought out was a small, family operated, East Indian restaurant of cuisine and exotic herbal menu. The front portion of the building was like a grocery store, with the more private areas of the back being the restaurant. They even offered movie rentals of their native land.

Originally, the family was from Bangladesh. They moved to Sri Lanka and opened a similar business there. And when they finally made enough money, they moved to the States to avoid the civil unrest that was developing on the island. Actually, their little business in Hollywood would have been a much better success had it not been for the ignorant vandals and the destruction that was continually occurring and costing the owners big bucks in repairs. Most unfortunately for them, the establishment was a target of racial discrimination. They had almost completely lost their insurance coverage because of so many prior claims, and because the present deductible had escalated to a phenomenal amount, there really wasn't any alternative for them except to sell the business or just go bankrupt.

For what it was worth, Mike and Billy offered a substantial amount of cash to buyout his business and the land it was on. Mike worked out the financing through a local bank with Billy, Nicky and himself as co-owners. But prior to that, Mike and Nicky drew up the plans for his nightclub with the help of a print shop who specializes in blueprints. Once that was taken care of, they took the floor plans and business plans to be approved by the building and safety commissioner. According to their proposed sight of construction and the plans of operation, all was accepted and approved by the commissioner. Once the bank saw the temporary permits were already approved and signed, the loan went through without any trouble. Mike was lucky enough to have been given a lengthy employment record provided by Clyde and his escort business. As far as Billy and Nicky's employment record was concerned, the bank assumed and was assured that The Passion Seekers were still together and performing regularly. Once escrow closed and they gained possession of the property, a contractor was hired to demolish the old building in preparation for the new construction.

In their spare time, the three of them, like brothers, would help out as much as possible with every aspect of planning their new venture. Had it not been for the money saved and the continual income of royalties, most of the financing and sizable payments would have been impossible. Unfortunately, Mike had little to offer outside of his income from the escort service. But just as Billy had known and took confidence in all along, Mike came through on the business side of things, which suited Billy and Nicky just fine. Within three months time, the parcel was cleared and fenced off, just waiting to begin construction. It took an additional seven months to collect more money and find the proper and most suited contractor to commence construction of the nightclub according to Nicky's plans. In the meantime, Mike was working hard and steady with the escort business. He did a lot of growing up in just a few short months. Deep inside he felt as though he were offering a good service to those in need. And at the same time, he was gaining a therapy and education of his own. And though he thought of Crystal a lot and wanted desperately to see her, he knew there would be no sense in doing so.

He didn't mind working for the escort service, and many times, found it to be very rewarding. Some of his jobs were different and somewhat strange or uncomfortable, but in the long run, the advantages certainly outweighed any discomfort. It seemed to him at times that he was in a stage of constant training. He began to wonder if Dorianne wasn't just taking a personal interest in him.

There were times when she would have him in her house to conduct what was supposed to be the training for a new client, but culminated in nothing more than a heated session of love-making. As far as rewards go, Dorianne was in ample supply of those as well, especially for Mike. It was obvious that Clyde didn't seem to mind. To the contrary, in his line of work and state of mind, it was all a part of work, fun and family to him. And to be able to please his woman, in any form of gifts or offerings, was just part of life's pleasantries. And similar to some of the clients that preferred to work in couples or with menageatrois, Clyde too enjoyed the voyeuristic properties behind knowing his wife was happy, pleased and well taken care of. Dorianne's personal training for Mike of her own idiosyncrasies was quite extensive. There was no doubt that she enjoyed being with him, and equally so, he enjoyed much of her. Prior to the escort service, he had never made love to a black woman before. Not that the difference of race would ever matter to someone like him, but the blackness of her skin was somehow overwhelmingly exciting and was soon to develop into a near fetish with him. There were all races and colors involved in the escort service. All of which were just as exciting as the other, except for the edge his mentor had over him. In time, she taught him how to meditate through deep breathing exercises. He probably would never before have taken the time to learn such a practice or concern himself with such a thing, a thing that he believed was nothing more than nonsense, but there was something in the way that Dorianne introduced the technique to him that caught his attention.

As a project for college credits a few years back, Dorianne had traveled to India to perfect her skills in the practice of meditation. She studied with one of the renowned Yogis of the present time. She already knew of the many hidden mysteries of meditation and mind and body control, but didn't yet understand how to harness the energies or center her focus.

When her project was complete, she had learned a whole new understanding of herself and the undeniable differences between the Western and Eastern way of thinking. To the people of India, their beliefs go far beyond that of mere religion. To them, it is the way of life...and the lives to come. When she returned to the States was when she met Clyde. She claimed that meeting him was due to destiny. When he was able to take time from his time-consuming business, she taught him the lessons she learned from the East. And soon, the lessons were applied to their work as well. In life in general, "all is relevant", she would claim. And to learn the art of the breathing exercises and the centering of one's concentration was simply part of the integral of reaching beyond the plateau of beta levels.

When she first introduced some of the more simple methods to Mike while she was giving him a body massage, he was deeply intrigued. In his relaxed state of being, she proceeded to work with him closely. And she could see quick results coming of her teachings. Mike was a fast learning individual, but more so in this particular new interest. In a formal way and without realizing the ramifications, she was helping him to develop greater control over his psychic abilities. Within a week, she had him practicing breathing exercises to help relieve him of his back pains that he would suffer frequently as a result of the car accident. Mike urged her to continue teaching him. And when he wasn't working for the escort service, or with the contractors, Mike was making every effort to learn more about the Eastern ways through his mentor. And with each phase learned, he would practice and work his lessons often. There was a curious and driving insatiable urge to take in as much as he could, as fast as he could. For reasons that were not quite understood by him, he seemed to find the teachings somewhat familiar. It was as if he had already known of the techniques and their intended results, but somehow through a void in the passage of time had forgotten about them. Of course, as far as Mike knew, he never did study the Eastern ways prior to meeting Dorianne, but somehow the feeling of familiarity was very strong and continued to be a driving force of curiosities.

After a year of working steadily with the escort service, the nightclub was well into construction. Unfortunately, the expenses of the building and the payments on the land were accruing slightly faster than the income. And most of Billy and Nicky's savings were already consumed by the high costs of hidden expenses. Into the second month of construction Mike was forced into making another financial decision. Fortunately, the decision and plan that he was able to conceive turned out to be the most correct path of fortune. After working out the accounting figures with his partners, they agreed to share in the partnership to help defray the impact of costs and to speed up construction. Supervising over the construction of his idea became a full-time job for Nicky, and lucky for everyone, he wasn't sore about having been fired by Clyde, because as it turned out, Clyde and Dorianne became the new co-owners and chief investors of the club. Once they chipped in with their share of the dues, the process of things came together like synchronized clockwork.

Within six months from the time construction first began, the club was finally completed. It was a two-level building with a lavish view from the balcony above to the extravagant decor of one of the dance floors below. The establishment was capable of accommodating three live bands at any given time. The upper floor was set up for one band with two large beverage bars, and the lower floor was divided for two separate bands and their dance floors, which also had an assortment of beverage bars. They even had a banquet room for private parties. For those who seek entertainment, people, uninhibited expression and passion of sorts, nothing was left to chance. To amplify the state of excitement, there was an exceptionally elaborate sound system installed for each dance floor with perfected acoustics to match. With all the publicity and positive feedback that they were getting, it seemed apropos to name the club after their band, The Passion Seekers. Mike made sure that they had legal propriety over the name. The last thing they wanted from Peter Walbrook would have been any residuals of litigation.

Nicky, Mike and Billy had thought of everything, from the personalized formula of their liability insurance and the arrangement of acquiring a liquor license, down to the number of security bouncers needed to operate the place practically and safely. Several ads were placed in the paper just prior to the opening night for filling the needed jobs and bartenders, waitresses, inventory clerks, bands for hire and more. Once everything was in order, they held a grand opening of free admission that lasted six weeks. After word got out of the greatest success and exceptional entertainment of the new club in town, the escalating momentum of fortune came to be as real as life. Billy eventually terminated his services to the escort business to devote all of his time to the management of the club. Nicky looked to be in a permanent state of euphoria, especially with the harem of beauties that seemed to attach themselves to him like some sort of appendage. As the executive of public relations, Nicky was perfect for the job placement. Working with the public was, no doubt, his comfort zone.

Clyde and Dorianne continued on with their own business. And aside from their investments, they had little to do with the club. As agreed, they were merely silent partners. With the new establishment doing so well, Mike was proposed with many dilemmas. He didn't mind working with the escort service. Billy made his adamant claims that Mike was needed more to work at the club. But something was missing in a way that even he couldn't explain. Working at either place may have suited him fine had it not been for the vision that had developed into an incessant preoccupation. In a sense, it would seem that Dorianne had unknowingly opened Pandora's box. Once she had shown him how to relieve himself of his back pain through breathing exercises, he was determined to learn more. And for several emphatic months, Dorianne took pleasure in teaching him. In time, Mike became focused with his energies. He learned to control and harness his powers. And with every challenge that was met, Mike was learning at an accelerated rate. Now, Mike was able to call upon the vision of the lady in white. Somehow, he knew that she was to play in an important role in his future. It was through her, he learned the meaning of the leather. She told him of great stories and adventures that he later found to be of true sources. With her help, it was as though he had tapped into knowledge of endless boundaries. Though he continued to work for Clyde, Mike's development was taking him away from his friends. The yearning to understand the curiosities that were happening to him was far too strong now to ignore. There was a passion in his heart that guided him along relentlessly. And willingly, Mike would follow, intrigued, driven, and almost mesmerized.

Through the process of meditation, Mike was traveling to places, and seeing people he knew he had never seen before. And yet, each new face would spark a flash of uncanny familiarity. In their faces he could read their lives and feel their personality. These people of his visions were like family to him. And the more he learned of them, the more he understood about himself and the way he felt about a girl he knew very little about, other than the fact that he knew he needed to find her. Much of his concentration was centered around finding her, but the lady in white would continue to tell him that he wasn't ready yet; there was more to be learned and more insight to be gained. Of course, Mike being mule-headed and strong-willed, he continued to search for the girl of mystery.

Chapter Nineteen

The Reunion

After understanding the true meaning of the leather and learned of the Griffin, Mike felt determined to find the girl of his destiny. She was close and he knew it; he could feel her presence in his heart. And he could feel her resistance. As denoted by her resistance, it wasn't yet time for him to find her. So Mike continued on, to fight her resistance, to try to out-stealth her ploy. With the help of Dorianne, he continued to take lessons in hope to find his destiny. Mike was made to wait and continue learning. Between Billy needing his help at the club and Clyde devolving more of his own personal clients onto him, Mike was working an average of eighty tiring hours a week. Whenever he would get the chance to get a way and consolidate his thoughts through meditation, he would attempt to do so at the park behind the hospital. His focus of energy seemed to be at its best when he was at that park. He would pull into the parking lot and immediately feel the favorable change in his mind and body. In the darkness of his van, usually parked next to the same little red compact car that always seemed to be there, he would sit and concentrate on his lessons. While working his way through the levels of meditation, the forces of energy around him seemed to gather like magnets of steel. The feeling in his gut was warm and serene like true love itself. Three hours of meditation in his van was like a full night's rest to him. And within the restful state, he would find himself merging with the elements of a forgotten past. Nameless, friendly faces had become his allies. And in his trance, he would understand more, become more perceptive to his surroundings, and slowly ebb his way closer to his destiny. In the interest of this phenomenon, Mike was spiritually guided to learn more by going to the library to read about the science of these types of encounters.

Six months into the operation of the club, things were working out well for every one of the investors. Profits were high and the establishment was becoming more popular. Thanks to Mike's intuition and everyone's struggle to make it happen, Nicky's dream had come true without a single glitch. On occasion, Nicky, Billy, Paul, Tawney and a replacement singer would perform their songs at the club. Although, they sounded fantastic and made the crowds roar, Mike could only hear the absence of

Crystal. It saddened him to see that this was what had come of her; a simple and empty replacement, and done so without a thought or reservation. Without Crystal up on stage, it just wasn't the same to him, and subsequently, he chose not to watch their performances. He would give his excuses and offer his apologies for not being able to attend, but most could see through him.

It would seem that the loss of Crystal was more painful than first imagined. She was a personality impossible to be compared with, and a tough act to follow. The emptiness of his loss would, many times, attack him without warning, leaving him hollow, pained and in morbid despair. His escape from the effects drove him further from his friends and closer to his research. By this time, he had been working with Clyde's service for more than two years. His research through the library and the lessons taught by Dorianne had brought him to new horizons that even Dorianne could barely fathom. He had read a great many books written by an author by the name of J. Matthews and via this man, he learned of many new discoveries in the field of psychic phenomenon, healing, and of communications with the spirit world. There were many available books on similar subjects, but none were as direct and cogent as this author. His written words were expressed with a familiarity that urged Mike to continue on with his dutiful search for knowledge. What surprised him most was the age of these studies. According to the age of the original printed books, Matthews' studies were over a century old, and yet, most people of the present time neither think of nor even know about most of these studies. Dorianne, who had studied the Eastern science of meditation hadn't even the slightest interest of taking the science a step further into the abyss of anew. Perhaps it was this trait that made Mike so different from the rest.

The night before Mike's twenty-fourth birthday, he was with a client named Summer, who took a special interest in him, aside from the escort service. After having spent the evening with Mike at a company dinner party, she asked him to spend the night with her, which was nothing unusual for his line of work. But what he didn't know what the true reason for which she had invited him to stay. At the party, she watched and observed him, and soon became deeply intrigued by the vibes that she was receiving from him. Aside from herself, she had never met anyone with the ability to control and influence a projected thought through Psychokinetics. To Summer, his abilities were obvious, yet, impossible to detect by others who didn't understand. This unusual phenomenon was just another form of art that he had learned through his studies. She took heed to his unnatural art when he first called attention to himself at the party.

Prior to this particular dinner party, Mike had never met Summer before, and the arrangement was for him to meet her there. At the Knob Hill Hall there were over five hundred guests, some were with their spouses, some were alone, as she was, and some were gathered on the dance floor mingling with one another. But instead of having her paged, as anyone else would do in order to find her, or perhaps even ask around to locate her, Mike merely used his intuitive skills to locate her. Similar to the way that he learned through his practices, he emitted a beam of focused concentration to search out her presence. Without ever having met her, he located her within a sweeping glance. She was seated at a table while talking with a business associate. Her back was to the door from which Mike had entered. To verify her identity, he used his developed skills to call upon her attention from across the crowded room. With a simple stare of concentration and an added boost of energy, he would imagine a mental picture of a colored beam of light emitting from the center of his forehead. When the intended target is in sight, as Summer was, Mike emitted his colored probe-like beam to travel across the room and come into contact with her.

In common cases, once the contact is made, a person will suddenly get a feeling of interest. The feeling is similar to that of being stared at, and in reply, one might merely look back in inquiry. With some people, a greater amount of energy is needed in order to call their attention. In some cases, a very minute amount of energy can be too much, as Mike learned through an unfortunate experience, which

happened one day during the months that he was
first experimenting with the effects and possibilities
of this skill.

While at the club, Mike found himself a target.
He knew that he could send any kind of probe-like
sensation that he pleased. His target was an attractive, young Oriental girl with long black, straight
hair that reached to the back of her knees. From
across a crowded dance floor, he wanted to call her
attention. In doing so, he concentrated on sending
her a pleasantly colored beam of excitement with
passionate intentions. Not only did she respond immediately by turning around at once to find the origin of the beam, she excused herself from her
friends and walked the distance across the dance
floor to stop face to face with him. No sooner had
he smiled at her, the beautiful and seemingly very
proper Oriental girl slapped him across the left side
of his face with a bitter anger and then turned and
walked away.

Out of curiosity, he inquired to find out more
about her and what went wrong. He was informed
by one of her friends that she was very perceptive to
his probing message; many people have similar
abilities to his. What Mike didn't know at that time
was that she was deaf, and those who are, in fact
deaf, have a superior ability to receive such messages and almost a complete inability to block them
out. Obviously, he had insulted and offended her.
By slapping him, she had hoped he would soon
learn to control himself, or at least, learn to lessen

the extreme severity of his unfledged skill. In time, he understood what he had done, and practiced accordingly with moderate beams and with the variations of colors. From the Oriental girl, he learned some valuable lessons.

He discovered how to project his true feelings without fault or severity, just as Summer had recognized it to be. When Mike made contact with her at the party, she was pleasantly aroused by his mastery of many skills. It was only through her own acute perception that she could see his abilities. He wasn't one to boast and he was certainly trained likewise. The evening at the Knob Hill Hall went well and upon returning to her home, she unashamedly asked him where he learned such skills. In his formal and pragmatic, business-like way, he answered.

"I'm trained by the service that I was hired through. Why do you ask?"

"I wasn't referring to those skills. Those aren't the ones I'm concerned with. I'm curious to know where you learned to use those eyes of yours." She knew that she would first have to break through the barrier to put an end to his evasiveness.

"Excuse me?"

"Oh, come now, don't spurn me like I were some kind of ignorant fool. I know what you can do. Your vibes are very obvious to me and they're obviously effective too. Do you know what a medium is?"

"Why do you ask me this?"

"For Chris' sakes, Michael, drop your guard. Do

you always answer a question with a question?" Her eyes showed no anger.

"I'm sorry, it's just that no one yet has asked me of such interests before. Yes, I am very aware of what a medium is. Are you one?"

"Yes, and like yourself and different from most; I don't abuse it for financial gain or profit. I don't believe in that. I do, however, use my abilities to understand people, to protect myself and of course, to help others. I hate the negative publicity the psychics get. They're usually thought of as frauds. But if you think of it my way, I believe we're quite remarkable, actually. Think of it as a baseball player, a good batting average is what...three or four hundred?"

Mike nodded.

"Take that same average of thirty or forty percent and denote it toward the average of correct predictions. I could give you odds that there is few of us here on earth that wouldn't mind a prediction average as such. I certainly wouldn't mind dropping ten coins in a slot machine knowing that three or four will be a winner's jackpot. And for those who don't believe that a thirty or forty percent average of correct predictions is worthy of the case, then why are there so many baseball players and fans?"

Mike smiled in response. He felt she truly had a different way of thinking.

"Well enough about that, tonight, I'm going to help you. You know, I can feel the enigma of your facer. I can see it in your eyes," she said.

"How do you propose to help me?" Mike played

along with a faint show of doubt.

From out of her roll-top desk, she pulled out a Tarot deck that was wrapped in a silk cloth. "With these," she answered, sounding matter of fact.

"You're going to read my cards?" He sounded surprised. This was an absolute first.

"If you don't mind?"

"No, of course not. I didn't realize this sort of thing was still being done."...This ought to be real interesting. Everyone sustains a certain amount of doubt when it comes to the Gnostic, gypsy-type fortune-tellers. Mike certainly seemed to have some of his own.

She placed the Tarot cards on the table in front of him and asked that he shuffle the deck and concentrate on the questions he would want her to answer. As though querying her sanity, he did as she requested and followed the instructions as well. A moment later, she laid a number of them out on the table and had begun to recite their message. Within seconds, Mike was certain of the validity in her self-assured integrity. Of his past, she saw much of his pain and anguish. Of his present being, she had seen many favorable changes taking place all around him. And of the future that he was interested in, was confirmed by her reassurance. The inevitable destiny that pervaded his aura was prevalent and made clear to her. She was pleased to see such a positive and guarded force surrounding him and protecting him. Regardless of his past, Mike was indeed a very lucky person to have such loving guardians to protect him. He's an old soul with a young, caring heart. Though Summer could deeply appreciate the significance of the message that she was reading from his vibes, she was warned off from telling Mike more than he already knew about himself. She was, however, happy to make clear to Mike that the search for his destiny was near and certainly not being scrutinized in vain. In addition to that, she told him not to give up on one of his most prized ambitions, and that one day soon, he will have regaling stories to write about. The therapy that he needs is in the writing, when the time is right, the words will simply flow without falter.

"You're an interesting soul, Michael. But I'm sure you know much of that already. So, please tell me...I must know. Is it self-taught or have you had some sort of formal training with your abilities?"

"I suppose its been a little of both. I've been doing a lot of reading to better myself in understanding the phenomenon," Mike sat back in his seat and allowed his eyes to wander momentarily. "But I have to admit, most of what I have learned has been through some mysterious driven force that continually urges me forward. Whatever it is, it intrigues me and keeps me going. Perhaps, I will never find all of the answers, but I am going to have a great time searching for them. And how about yourself? How is it you came to learn of your talents?"

"The same as you, only I had my mother to help work with me. She too had some extraordinary talents." Indeed, Summer was very talented. It truly was inspiring to hear her confirm his aspirations. That evening they continued to talk late into the night about various subjects. It would seem that with every person that he would meet and talk with, he would gain just a little more insight on the trials of life.

When Mike left Summer's house, just before sun-up, he returned the company car to the yard and picked up his van. With the present feelings of spiritual inspiration and jubilation, he drove to the park. There were no other cars in the parking lot when he arrived. He climbed out of the driver's seat and made his way into the back and laid himself down in the bed. It was his birthday and Clyde had given him the day off. All he wanted to do was sleep. Hours later, Mike woke up to the sound of children's laughter. He tried to clear his head and wake himself up. He needed a shower and a shave, but refused to leave the park; today was his birthday and he wanted to spend it at the park without having to worry about his appearance. It was about a quarter to noon when he first emerged from the van. Standing between his van and the little, red economy car, he stretched and yawned. The parking lot was now full of cars and the park was full of children playing, lovers meeting and a workforce taking their lunch break. After taking a short walk around the park, he returned to his van. He reached into his pocket for his keys and in a fleeting moment of unexplained euphoria, he stopped and turned. He could feel a familiar presence, but couldn't locate its origin. He looked around and then sat on the bumper of the little red car, closed his eyes and just enjoyed the feeling. For several minutes he absorbed the sensation.

"Of all the cars in the parking lot you couldn't just on your own?"

He recognized her voice immediately. It was reckoned with the familiarity of the feeling he was experiencing. For a moment, he thought he was dreaming or experiencing a vivid clairvoyance.

"Hey fella, are you asleep or something?"

Mike slowly opened his eyes. The sensation was too good to allow it to vanish, should he open his eyes to fast. "It is you."

"Of course it's me," she said. "What were you expecting, Godzilla?"

"Expectation isn't really the word. It was more like...hoping or praying."

"For what?" she asked.

"For you...for more than four years, I've been searching for you, hoping to find you. You just disappeared from the face of the earth." He was almost sounding scornful.

"Well, you obviously didn't look too hard, Mikey. I have been working here since the last time we shared an encounter of injury."

"Here? You work here?" With a pensive look, he panned the park with the turn of his head.

"No, not here in the park, silly, there, at the hospital," she said, pointing to the building beyond the tall hedges.

KS. Michaels

"What is that place?"

"Kaiser, Kaiser hospital. I've been there for quite some time. Truly, if you were hoping and praying, as you say, why didn't you just call the hospital?"

"I did, Miranda. Believe me, I did," Mike intoned. "I called and left messages at every hospital that you told me of, and more. You have no idea how much it meant to me to find you. You could have told me that you were going to another hospital."

"I didn't know at the time. The transfer came with a promotion. So, I mean that much to you, do I?" She tried not to sound too flattered.

"Yes, you do. I went to visit you at the hospital and they told me you had been transferred away. I couldn't believe it! And for whatever reason, no one seemed to know where you were transferred. Believe me, Miranda, I was hurt." He looked at her sharply. "I thought there was something between us." He certainly wasn't being shy and wasted no time in telling her of his true feelings. It would seem that he wanted her to know exactly how he felt lest she disappear again without hearing his plead. "Is there...something between us or am I just dreaming?"

"Do you still have it?"

"Of course I still have it. And I now know what it means. Why would you give me such a sacred thing without telling me of its true meaning?"

"To prove to both of us that there truly was...something between us." She reached for his hand and held it in hers.

"Kind of risky, don't you think, Miranda?"

"It was worth it...you found me, didn't you?"

"I suppose, but I don't know how. What brings you to the park anyway?"

"It's my lunch break. I always sit in my car here at the park during my lunch hour and sometimes, out there in the field." She gestured toward the little red economy car that Mike had been sitting on, then towards the field.

"This is your car?"

"Yep."

"I spend more time here in this park than I do at my own apartment. I've seen your car here dozens of times but I never saw you. I can't believe it." Mike responded.

"Small world, hey Mikey?"

Mike nodded, "very small. So now that I found you, now what?"

"I suppose you can take me to lunch." Her eyes were filled with promise and warmth.

All Mike could think about was figuring a way to make sure that she wouldn't disappear from him again. He stepped closer to her and instinctively embraced her. "Don't do any more vanishing acts, please. I need to learn more about you." He whispered in her ear.

"According to the spirit world, we've never been apart," she said. "According to the spirit world, the journey is now officially completed."

Mike quickly unlocked and opened the door to the van, crawled inside and reached under the driver's seat. When he emerged from the van, he handed her the leather. "Please, take this and accept it as a token of a safe journey."

"I would be happy to, Mikey. We've come a long ways, haven't we?" Mike smiled in response. For the moment, he wanted to say nothing, just revel in the excitement of their reunion. After sharing a long, silent moment together, embraced in each other's arms, Mike suddenly knew where he wanted to take her for lunch. They climbed into the van and headed to the club. It was time for his buddies to meet the 'mystery girl' that he so often spoke of. As they were pulling out of the parking lot, they passed a long, black limousine that was waiting for Mike's parking spot. A strange feeling came over him as he passed the limo, but as he drove away, the sensation soon faded. The strange occurrence didn't seem to faze him much. At that park, there had been many such occurrences, none of which the lesser of an unusual encounter.

"It's not far from here. I'm going to take you to a very special place for lunch." After looking into the rearview mirror, Mike remembered just how grungy he looked. "Perhaps there I can grab a quick shower and a shave. Please, forgive me for looking so terrible. I spent the night in the van."

"Well, I'm glad you did. You look just fine to me, I mean, in comparison to the times I've seen you before," upon arriving at the club, Miranda questioned the place of his choice. "How is it, this place has shower facilities? You wouldn't, by chance be taking me to your home, would you? You know I'm not that type of girl." The banter in her voice made Mike feel comfortable with her.

"I should hope not. No, I'm not taking you to my home. I'm taking you to my place of work. There are some special people I want you to meet."

For the next two weeks, Mike and Miranda dated steadily. Mike wanted never to leave her side. Now that he finally found her, there was a growing bond between them.

Before Miranda learned of his employment with Clyde and the type of work that implies, Mike had already resigned, but not before he offered Clyde a gift of reciprocation for all that he had done for him. Clyde had spent thousands of dollars on private investigators that had been, for years, trying to locate his father. It was his own personal need to know more about himself. It wouldn't even have mattered if the man weren't successful; he just wanted to know who the man was and what he was about. Mike knew this day would eventually come and in preparation, he had already sought out Clyde's father. Through a garment that Mike had taken from Clyde's house, which originally belonged to his father, Mike was able to locate the man through the process of Psychometrics. His father was an American soldier, who had returned to France after the war, in search for Clyde's mother. He never found her and never learned of his son.

Billy couldn't have been happier to hear of the news. This meant that Mike would be working full-time with him at the club. Finding Miranda was like witnessing a miracle. Billy had his doubts that he would find her, but when he did, things changed all over in a chain reaction. Mike was back with his closest friends and they could see the revelation in his spirited ways. He was back to being an impromptu comic and someone that was fun to be with. Miranda was no less than a felicitous angel. After meeting her, Mike's friends were happy that he found her. Although they thought the circumstances were a bit odd, they were pleased with her just the same. Every moment spent together was like a constant source of familiarity. No doubt, everyone knew that they were intimates of a thousand lifetimes. She was everything he ever dreamed of and more. And he was the oath she promised to stand by through to the end of time. There was hidden mystery of knowledge that she kept close to her heart. Mike could feel it, but she wasn't yet willing to divulge the facts. When the time was right, he knew he would understand. Had it not been for Mike working at the club and Miranda working at the hospital, they probably would never have parted. While they were dating and getting to know each other better the visions of the lady in white had stopped visiting him. Although her features were different from Miranda's, Mike simply accepted the fact that the sudden discontinuance of her visits was due to the fact that he found her. At least, this is what he believed, until two weeks later.

Miranda had collected some vacation time and decided to spend a weekend with Mike. They stayed at the Ritz Carlton Hotel. The time they spent together there was very special and very spiritual. Mike had never been happier in his life and Miranda expressed the same. In such a short time, he learned a great deal about his mystery girl. Without any doubt, she was his destiny. The proof was even more evident the night after they first made love. When they woke the next morning, they had a vision together. Through the course of the vision, they found themselves at the park, in an area that they learned they both would frequently visit and sit at, in the grass, next to an old tree stump. But in the vision, something very different happens. From a shallow cavity in the ground, Mike had dug up an old cylinder shaped canister. When he attempted to open it, they both awoke. After thinking about it for a while, they both decided to leave the hotel and investigate.

They were barely able to keep their hands off of each other long enough to dress themselves. It was a wonder they were able to leave the hotel at all. They stepped into the elevator and suddenly found themselves at the designated ground floor with a dozen people waiting for them to stop kissing and exit, the embarrassment of the moment triggered Mike's humor into announcing to the onlookers that they had just met on the fifth floor and fell in love at first sight.

When they got to the park, there were very few people around. Mike parked close to the area that

they had seen through the vision. They got out of
the van, leaving the doors open so they could hear
the radio. They both immediately located the spot.
Prior to the time that they finally got together, the
two of them would almost always find themselves
at the same spot. Miranda had many times eaten her
lunch there. Mike had often meditated in that same
spot. It seemed to have some kind of significant importance, even before the vision they shared. Still,
Mike was amazed that they hadn't crossed each
other's path at least once before.

"Are we allowed to do this?" Miranda inquisi-
tively looked around.

"Probably not, but I can't see why we shouldn't
at least check it out. Besides, it's not like we would
be destroying anything."

"No, I suppose not." Still, Miranda continued to
keep a vigil while Mike took a two-and-three-
quarter inch pocketknife along and began to excavate the area. When they were certain of the correct
spot, he impaled his knife deeper into the sandy
soil. After about an eight-inch hole was dug, he
found a hard metallic object.

"Miranda, look." Mike was surprised to have
found it.

"Is that it?" She abandoned the vigil just long
enough to get a closer look.

"I suppose so. What else would be buried here
in the middle of nowhere?"

"Can you pull it up?"

"Not yet," Mike grunted as he made the attempt,

"in the vision it was quite long. I'm going to have to dig further down. It's really wedged in there." As the excitement and uncertainty escalated, Mike bustled with the soil, trying to clear away the surrounding weight that held the cylinder tightly in the ground. As he continued to dig, he recognized many similarities to the vision. It was as though the both of them were experiencing a simultaneous episode of déjà vu. The things they said, the way things looked; all seemed to be coming to reality and witnessed through something like a time-lapsed film. He had a hard time managing a firm grip on it because of its cylindrical shape. Once enough dirt was removed, it slowly began to show some movement. Deeper, he continued to excavate around it. By this time, both of them had a hand in scooping out the slow to recede soil. With one last hearty tug, Mike pulled at the canister. While rocking it from side to side to allow the sandy soil to sift back into the siphon of the cavity's void, the container was eventually freed from the ground. Looking exactly as it was to them in the vision, its girth was approximately eighteen inches; the length was at least two feet and it was heavy for it's size. For its age, the aluminum alloy construction was later found to be quite ingenious. The lid was kept sealed by a protruding waxen gasket. As Mike held the base, Miranda twisted at the top in the attempt at opening it. Once the gasket had broke, they heard the seal give way like a vacuum. It sounded something like the opening of a pickle jar. Not knowing what to expect, Mike slowly removed the lid. What he found inside was stunning to both of them. When Mike was in jail for the time he was arrested for possession of a concealed weapon, he had a vision of a young girl who was imprisoned like him; only she was imprisoned for witchcraft. When Mike had reached into the canister, he pulled out a dozen or so old, black-and-white photographs and one hand-drawn portrait of an enchanting young girl; the very same girl of his vision in jail. An eerie chill shot up the nape of his neck. The second picture that Mike revealed was a photo of a beautiful Indian woman in a white buckskin dress. The name etched below the image in the mat was "Ceenatanee." There was no doubt in his mind that she was the lady in white. To Miranda, the picture was obvious; she immediately recognized the image. The next photograph was of Jason Mathison. It took a few seconds, but Mike realized that the picture was identical to that of J. Matthews' at the back of one of his books. As he continued to study the photographs, Mike could feel the vibrations from the visions. Suddenly, the faceless many were given identities. He continued looking through the handful of pictures. After making his full inspection, he would hand each one to Miranda. When she first saw the image of Jason, a smile stretched across her lips. All her former dreams and visions had somehow come to rest in the mysterious canister. The two of them were so enthralled with their find, that they hadn't noticed the old woman with wire-rim glasses hanging from the end of her nose, as she stood by the van.

"Hello, good afternoon to you both." She greeted them with a kind smile.

Miranda jumped back with a sudden shirk, obviously startled by the old woman's sudden appearance.

"Oh, I'm sorry. Don't be frightened, honey. I didn't mean to surprise you so." She had a friendly manner. Mike could see that there was nothing intimidating about her.

"What could we do for you?" He asked, sensing a familiar vibration from her presence. As he looked beyond her, he saw the car in which she arrived. It was the same long, black limousine that he had seen waiting for his parking spot in the park, two weeks before. He recognized the Massachusetts state flag on the radio antenna.

"What you can do for me has already been done, just by your showing up here today. Actually, I'm here to greet you both...and give you this," in her hand was a large envelope. "Can I—"

"Of course." Mike waved her to come closer. With every step she took, he felt more comfortable by her presence. "How is it, I get the feeling that I know you?"

"Well, I'm not exactly sure as to why, but I'm not at all surprised," with her hand out, she introduced herself. "You don't have any idea how pleased I am to meet you both. I'm Rosemary, most everyone calls me 'Rose'."

"My name is Mike and this is Miranda." They both stood up, slapped off the dirt and shook her hand. "If you don't mind me asking, Rose, are you related to Jason Mathison, pseudonym, J. Matthews?"

"That's why I'm here. It was Jason's wish that someone of his progeny be here to give you this on this special day. I believe most of your questions should be answered by the contents of this envelope." She handed it to him.

"Do you know what's in this, Rose?" He already knew the answer by the warming smile on her lips.

"The envelope was sealed the day I was born. And about twenty years prior to that, my grandfather, Jason and my father traveled across the entire U.S. of A to get here. Yes, Mike I can say with certainty. I do know what is in the envelope," her eyes glowed as she stared in the direction of the capsule. "Just as well as I know what is in that time capsule. Grandpa wasn't certain as to how far along your abilities might have developed by this time, but somehow, he was most certain that you and your wife would find this. Although, he wasn't certain as to exactly what day you would be here."

"Then how did you know?" Mike asked, deeply intrigued by all that she had to say. And the sound of the word, wife didn't feel too terribly bad either.

"My father told me that I would know, just as Jason Mathison knew. I've been staying close for the past two weeks, waiting and watching for the two of you to arrive and find the capsule. For all my eighty-six years and longer, that package of memories has been waiting for you. Why don't you go ahead and open the envelope? There's a letter from Jason written to you."

He did as she requested. Inside, he found copies of the same pictures found in the capsule. "These are identical." He handed them to Miranda.

"As I stated, Jason wasn't sure how far along you would have developed. Or for that matter, how much you would believe."

"I believe it all, Rose. And I'm finally beginning to understand just who I really am," he briefly studied the picture of Jason and Ceenatanee. "I don't know why it took me until now to figure this out, but if I'm not mistaken, Jason was married to Ceenatanee. Who were also your grandparents?"

Rose smiled in response.

"And Jason knew that the three of us would be here together, at this given time, and that Miranda and I would find the capsule. So, am I crazy, or is the relation between Jason and myself, and the relation between Ceenatanee and Miranda more than just uncanny?"

Miranda slipped her hand into his and whispered into his ear, "Say 'hello' to your past, Mikey."

"You knew, didn't you? Both of you knew."

"Read the letter, Mike." Rose said, as she seemed to be getting impatient.

"Actually, it would mean more to me if you would read it to us, Rose." He handed her the letter, the nervous shake of his hand was slightly visible.

Rose accepted the letter and immediately began to read aloud. The letter was brief and to the point, just as Jason would have wanted to hear the news for himself. After she read it, the mystery was suddenly over. Deep inside, Mike knew the truth; there was no mistaking what he was presently feeling. Rose told him that there were a few more items in the capsule. One of which, he found right away as he knelt down and reached inside, it was heavy and brick-shaped. When his hand emerged from within, he let out a gasp. His eyes couldn't believe what he was seeing! He had never seen anything like it before. It truly was a brick all-right, a ten-pound brick of solid gold!

Rose began reading the closing paragraph of the letter. It explained that the gold was to be used toward the purchase of their home. Jason knew that the value of the gold bar wasn't going to be too great, but at least enough for a down payment on a home. Mike couldn't have thought of a better gift to give to someone, especially if that someone was going to be himself. The other two items in the time capsule were Jason and Ceenatanee's matching wedding bands. They were meant for Mike and Miranda to use as well. Mike just stood up and shook his head in whirring amazement.

"This is so unbelievable. To have found Miranda was the most special gift I could have ever asked for, but to discover that the dreams, visions and feelings inside, had more to answer for, is something no one would ever believe."

"That's where you're wrong." Rose's tone was resolute and assured, no doubt, by her own visions. "If you choose to, you can make them believe. After all, how often does love return through the portal of time?" As the three of them stood in a circle of silence, the song was announced from the stereo in the van with Crystal's voice passionately and melodically singing, 'When Love is Lost, You'll Always Have Me'.

Everything Rosemary said that afternoon was the unfurling of truth behind more mystery. She was an incredible old woman, born in Massachusetts and raised in South Dakota. She had traveled all over the world in her youth, and yet she claimed that nothing was as invigorating as finally meeting her grandfather and being reunited with her grandmother, who were better than sixty years younger than her. The three of them spent three wonderful days together before she had to get back home to her family. After she had left, Mike conceded that he had never met a more interesting woman. Three months after discovering themselves, Miranda and Mike were married with the rings provided by the past. The gold bar was sold for cash a year later, when the price of gold had gone up from four hundred dollars an ounce to six hundred, seventy-nine dollars an ounce. Mike had a hunch when the value would rise. One hundred, thousand dollars of it was used as a down payment on a house, as Jason had wished. Profits from the club paid off the balance seventeen months later.

Clyde found his father in Paris and brought him back to the States. When his father was reunited with his mother, the two fell in love again and were married within a month. As it turned out, neither one of them wanted to have parted when they did, nearly forty years prior, but a letter was lost just before he and his troops had pulled out, the silence between them was interpreted as a loss. Neither one had ever been married because no one else would have been the same. Clyde and Dorianne had retired five years earlier than expected, sold the business for a very healthy sum.

Nicky and Billy went on to make a fortune with the club and various investments with Mike and Miranda.

Crystal moved to Chicago with Peter and was never seen or heard from again.

Mike also dedicated his life to writing.

Printed in the United States
104229LV00003B/89/A